Someone was trying to kill them—but now dozens of people were caught in the crossfire...

Sofia and Adelina positioned themselves behind the altar. Every time he saw Sofia, he couldn't help but smile. Her playful side was out in full force. Her skin had a slight green tint to it. She'd teased her hair into a full rat's nest and added an unappealing wart to her cheek. Adelina went family-appropriate vixen. Sofia went comical.

"Happy Halloween! Is everyone having fun?" she asked.

The crowd clapped and cheered.

"Well, I suppose you are here to learn what witches truly do on Shadow Fest, or *La Festa dell' Ombra,* not what Hollywood and other organized groups tell you we do. Then I bet you hope to get a glimpse of the Headless Horseman!"

More loud applause echoed into the night.

"Most of you are aware from past years, but if it's your first time tonight, my sister and I are Strega. Italian witches. While we have many of the same beliefs as Wiccan witches and other pagans, ancient Italian witchcraft is, in itself, different."

While the sisters took turns explaining why the altar faced north and what each tool's use was, Armend gazed past the wooden split rail fence into the outlying meadow. For security reasons, the Headless Horseman would appear far away in the field. Two spotlights pointed at an angle to illuminate the area enough to create a menacing image as he rode through.

"There he is!" someone shouted.

In the distance, a figure came into view. Sofia stared at Armend with wide eyes and a troubled expression. It was too early. As the rider's pace picked up, his direction changed. The horse galloped straight toward them.

"Armend, something's wrong," Sofia hissed.

KUDOS for Solstice

A magical romantic suspense. – *Pepper O'Neal, award-winning author*

Solstice is fun and exciting. The plot has enough twists and turns to hold your interest and keep you turning pages from beginning to end. From people who don't like witches and want to run them out of town to avoiding mayhem and murder, Armend and Sophia race against time to save his life. I highly recommend it to anyone who wants an adventure while lounging on your couch. – *Taylor, reviewer*

In Solstice, Christiana created a world of magic and intrigue that keeps the reader turning pages, but she also opens up a window into a world where even people with special powers can feel like freaks. We all fanaticize about what it would be like to have special powers, at least I do, but we seldom stop to think how we would feel if the "normal" people shunned us because of those powers. I thought Christiana did an excellent job of presenting that point of view when Sophia's sister falls in love with a man that can't handle her witchy powers. I found it very thought-provoking and down-to-earth. All in all, Solstice is an excellent second effort for this new author. – *Regan, reviewer*

Time is running out for Armend Zogu. The 250-year-old family curse on his head will claim his life on his 30th birthday, the winter solstice.

Sofia Palmalosi might be just the Strega who can save him. A descendant of a long line of powerful Italian witches, her family's magic was a gift from the Goddess Diana.

Together Sofia and Armend embark on a journey from New York, to Sicily and the ancient ruins of Diana's temple, and back to New York, all the while fighting a battle of magic and wits with a psychopath who wants them both dead and the curse intact.

If the curse doesn't kill Armend, breaking it just might.

ACKNOWLEDGEMENTS

The act of writing is a solitary profession, but then many wonderful people travel the road of publication side by side with the author.

Heartfelt thanks to:

Black Opal Books, their editors, Karen, Faith and Lauri for all their hard work.

My dear friend, Cindy Hammock, whose beautiful artwork graces the cover of Solstice.

Jack, in the Black Opal Art Department for the awesome background and finishing touches on the cover.

Kathy Oliveri and Anne O'Brien for reading the drafts of Solstice for me, finding errors and telling me what worked and what did not.

Deborah Blake, author of *Everyday Witch, A-Z Spellbook* (and other books), and Raven Grimassi, author of *Italian Witchcraft: The Old Religion of Southern Europe*, for their insurmountable knowledge, help and generosity with their time.

Rayne Hall for her superb writing classes and expert critique of some of my scenes.

My husband, Bill and kids, Matt, AJ, and Ellie. I love you guys!

SOLSTICE

By

Debbie Christiana

A BLACK OPAL BOOKS PUBLICATION

Black Opal Books

BECAUSE SOME STORIES JUST HAVE TO BE TOLD

GENRE: PARANORMAL THRILLER/PARANORMAL ROMANCE/
ROMANTIC SUSPENSE

This is a work of fiction. Names, places, characters and incidents are either
the product of the author's imagination or are used fictitiously, and any resemblance to any actual persons, living or dead, businesses, organizations,
events or locales is entirely coincidental. All trademarks, service marks,
registered trademarks, and registered service marks are the property of their
respective owners and are used herein for identification purposes only. The
publisher does not have any control over or assume any responsibility for
author or third-party websites or their contents.

DEDICATION

For Tootie

June 19, 1931-May 22, 2012

Witchcraft, like any science or philosophical system, must be approached from a liberal point of view. When looked at objectively, we see that Witchcraft is just another theoretical body of knowledge. It is a process, not a person. Therefore, it is neutral, incapable of being either good or evil. Like all belief systems, Witchcraft is only as good or evil as the people using it. – *Lady Sabrina,* Secrets of Modern Witchcraft Revealed

PROLOGUE

Autumn Equinox – *Equinozio di Autumno*:

The guiding moonlight waned beneath the dense foliage. The dirt was cool on her feet and twigs cracked under each step. For generations, this worn and trodden path had guided worshippers to the sacred spot. Her long cloak rustled in the dried leaves. She clutched a covered basket to her chest.

In the distance fires glowed. A gentle breeze filled her ears with the soft hum of chanting. When she arrived at the hallowed clearing, the silver moon high in the sky, the others were waiting.

She kneeled before the venerable circle cast in stone. Jon, her most loyal member of their small coven, placed a spirit bowl filled with liquid in the center. With her fingertips, she dug four small holes, one in each direction of the Earth. Remnants of ash and smoke from past rituals rose into the air from deep in the dark ground. She set a white candle inside each cavity.

One strike of an elongated ceremonial match lit the four wicks. Another strike and the spirit bowl burst to life with a vibrant blue flame. Her arms stretched out in front of her, palms up, and Jon rested the athame blade in her hands. She caressed the serpent- shaped handle between her fingers, admiring the crystal eye of the creature sparkling back at her.

She rose and danced clockwise three times around the outside of the circle, with the athame pointed to the stars, and recited:

"Awaken, dear ancient ones from our past
"Help to keep my family's honor last."

She laid the athame in the circle, its moon-glinting blade facing north. Once again, Jon was at her side, offering three aged photos. One was of a woman, her aunt, and the second of an older man. Her eyes locked with those of the handsome young man in the third. She stroked his face tenderly with her thumb. He would be thirty years old in exactly three months. She leaned the photos, faded and yellow with the corners curled, against the flaming spirit bowl along with a lock of each person's hair.

She rolled the robe off her shoulders. The smooth velvet cloth slid down her back, crumpling into a pile on the ground. The crisp, September night air stung her bare skin. She uncovered the basket, reached in, and carefully lifted her familiar. Holding him firmly, she stepped into the circle.

The snake curled itself around her waist and slithered between her breasts. With a deep breath, she savored the serpent's every twist and turn along her skin. At the end of its journey, it coiled around her neck and rested its head on her shoulder. Its rattler dangled around her neck like a string of pearls.

The coven softly chanted:

"Hark! The dark of night
"And the moon so bright
"Hear us east and west
"Past the crow's nest
"Hear us south and north
"The witches' rune bring henceforth!"

The pulsation was soft at first, then steadier and louder. She closed her eyes and connected with the vibration of the chant and relentless sound of the snake's rattling.

The heat of power throbbed within her. Exhilaration and excitement surged in her blood. She rocked back and forth in a rhythmic beat as her energy and the serpent's convened. She opened her arms, raised them to the sky, and recited the invocation.

> "I beseech thee Mother Crone,
> "Enlighten to me the unknown.
> "Your knowledge and wisdom disperse,
> "To keep our enemy bound in our curse.
> "For the family to remain in our debt,
> "Please reveal their ominous threat."

She peered through the gray smoke swirling upward from the sacred bowl into the smoldering glow. The glimpse into the future revealed her family legacy in ruin. Her eyes watered and burning tears streamed down her face.

Her knees buckled with exhaustion. She collapsed onto the damp, soft grass.

CHAPTER 1

*Once in a lifetime you meet a person who takes your breath
away. Not because you want them to, but because
they are meant to. – author unknown*

Sofia paused on the marble steps outside her parent's art
gallery. The Manhattan street below bustled with New
York activity. People shouted, cabbies leaned on their
horns, and a siren wailed in the distance.

The warm October sun beat down on her, yet it couldn't
quell the chill that quivered down her spine. She stood still and
waited. From the corner of her eye, she caught a glimpse of
two casually dressed men. They appeared to be in a heated
conversation, but from behind their dark glasses, Sofia knew
they watched her every move.

Could she get to the front door of the gallery before they
made their move? She climbed a step and stopped. She rifled
through her purse and ascended another step. Three more to
go.

Powerful arms snaked under hers.

"Sofia Palmalosi?" a blond man with a southern drawl
asked.

She didn't answer.

"Please come with us," said the dark haired man.

Defiant, she crossed her right leg over her left and
dropped to the ground. "Ms. Palmalosi, don't do this," whispered an irritated voice. The man on her right tried to lift her
without drawing unwanted attention, but she remained seated
in her resistance.

"Don't make a scene. We're trying to help you."

Sofia closed her eyes and relaxed her body. With deep cleansing breaths, she cleared her head and summoned the *Lare,* the spirits of her ancestors. In her mind, she repeated the incantation.

Dear ancients ones, powerful and wise
Many times to you I've prayed
Please reach down from high in the sky
And offer to me your gentle aid.

The wind picked up and cool gusts blew against her face. Her eyes fluttered open. Bits of litter and leaves spun within the vigorous whirlwind that surrounded them. The men on each side of her fought to keep their balance against the unexpected squall. Their free hand flailed in the air as if they were swatting at a swarm of hornets. The *Lare* wouldn't hurt them. They were mischievous, not malicious. Sofia sat patiently as first one, then the other man, let go of her, needing both hands to break their fall as they tumbled to the ground.

From behind, another pair of firm hands gripped under her arms and raised her to her feet. This time her legs straightened and supported her. The wind had calmed. The *Lare* had vanished.

"What the hell are you doing?" a new voice demanded.

The arrival of another person wouldn't cause the *Lare* to disappear. Unless…

"What Mr. Palmalosi asked us to. Make sure his daughter arrived safely to his office."

"She's not a criminal." The third man steadied her on her feet. His warm breath was on the back of her neck. "Sofia, are you all right?"

She'd had enough. "Why is it—" She whipped around and was stopped short by dazzling, steel-blue eyes. She cleared her throat and continued. "You know my name, but I don't have a clue who any of you are?"

"I'll let your father explain." Mr. Steel Blue shooed the two men away. "I'll make sure Ms. Palmalosi gets to where she is going."

The taller of her two assailants spoke. "Ma'am, we'd like to apologize."

"You both work for my father?"

The stockier man nodded at Mr. Steel Blue. "Yes. All three of us do."

"My parents have never had security quite like you before."

They mumbled an apology or obscenity and left.

Sofia crossed her arms over her chest and looked to the last man standing for an explanation. Once more, spellbound by his eyes, she took a step back and caught her breath. She should be doing the bewitching, not him.

He stood a few inches taller than she did. His black hair was longer than most men chose to wear theirs these days. He sported a neatly trimmed beard.

He held the gallery door open for her. "Your parents are waiting for you."

Intrigued by the handsome man who caused the *Lare* to vanish, she went inside.

They walked in silence, past the empty reception desk and into the dimly lit and vacant main foyer. The building was quiet and deserted. Gone was the epic statue of the Roman Goddess Diana, standing bare-breasted, bow and arrow in one arm, her other hand resting on the neck of a strong buck.

Something was very wrong.

"I know the way to my parent's office," she said.

"I'll feel better when I see you go in," he said, staring straight ahead.

At the end of the hallway, they rounded the corner and approached two large oak doors.

Sofia inched ahead of him, turned the doorknob, and cracked the door open. Before she walked in, she peered over her shoulder, "Thank you—"

He was gone.

৫৩৫৩

Armend Zogu slipped into the small employee cafeteria. He opened the refrigerator, scratched his beard, and grabbed a drink. Glad to be alone, his thoughts went to Sofia.

He remembered the day he stumbled upon her visiting her parents. The moment he saw her, he fell harder than the young boxer he KO'd in the ring last month. Instead of intruding, he remained hidden. Since then, whenever she stopped by, he was content to stay in the background and watch her from a distance.

Several weeks ago, Silvio and Ersilia Palmalosi put him in charge of the Albanian photography exhibit. Albania was the homeland of his grandparents. Fluent in the language, he was excited at the prospect and delved into his research. As an added bonus, Silvio's Greek friend, Alexandros Gounaris, had agreed to lend his collection of lesser-known works of the famous Albanian Icon painter, Onufri.

Opening night arrived and Armend was prepared to answer any question put to him, but unprepared to come face to face with Sofia. She stopped at the display of black and white prints of the war-torn images of Kosovo.

"Why do we keep doing this to each other?" she asked. "We're supposed to be the most intelligent species on the planet, but after thousands of years we can't seem to learn that war and violence doesn't accomplish anything more than human misery."

With sweaty palms and butterflies raging a war in his stomach, he uttered his first words to the woman he'd obsessed about for months. "I think we know that, but ambition, greed, and the need for power often make us forget the toll it takes on innocent people. We *are* only human."

They spoke for a while longer until the man she was with, obviously bored with the conversation, urged to her move on. She shook his hand, thanked him, and followed her date into the crowd. He thought she stopped, her eyes searching back for him, but he was mistaken. She didn't recognize him today.

He, however, hadn't forgotten her. Hidden by a small circle of people who gathered around the photos, he had the luxury of a voyeur, admiring every salacious curve of her form–

fitting, strapless dress. The fullness of her breasts, the arch of her sleek back, and long, sexy legs revved his fantasies into overdrive. As she left his uninhibited view, the last thing seared on his brain was her sweet ass swaying from side to side.

He gulped his water and thought about his encounter with her today. He was glad she was safe but had to curb any further interaction with her. Sofia had no idea how he felt about her and he intended to keep it that way.

ℰↈℰↈ

"Sofia!" Silvio wrapped his arms around his daughter in a bear hug.

"What's wrong?" she asked. "Are you sick? Your face is pale and drawn."

"No, but we have something to tell you," he admitted.

Ersilia Palmalosi flew in the room and kissed her daughter on the cheek.

"Can you two please tell me what's going on?"

"Of course," Ersilia said. "Sit down."

Silvio paced around the room. "About a month ago, before the Albanian exhibit was to close, I received an unexpected phone call. The man spoke in a deep voice with a slight accent. His offer was straightforward, but repulsive." Silvio removed his glasses and rubbed his tired eyes. "He wanted a certain original landscape painting by Onufri. In return, he would provide me with a substantial amount of money, along with a meticulous reproduction he promised would fool even the most trained eye. I would then return the fraudulent painting to the owner. All I had to do was leave the alarm off, a side door unlocked, and have the security guards gone. When I arrived the next morning everything would seem as it was when I left the night before."

Sofia sat in disbelief. "You didn't—"

"Of course not," Ersilia said. "Your father loves and respects art too much to compromise his integrity for money or anything else."

"And I would never cheat Alexandros," Silvio added. "He has been a good friend for many years."

Sofia embraced her father. "I'm sorry to doubt you. I didn't think you would agree, but you looked so troubled, I thought maybe he threatened you in a way you couldn't refuse."

"Oh, he threatened me," he said stepping away from his daughter. "I told him I would never agree to his proposition and our conversation was over. He warned me I would regret my decision."

"Have you sent back the paintings yet?"

"No. We've shipped the photographs back, but Alexandros is traveling abroad. I promised I would keep the paintings locked up in our vault until he returned." Silvio pulled a manila envelope out of his desk drawer and handed it to her. "This came in the mail three days ago."

He watched his daughter read the daunting words, her expression changing from anger to surprisingly, a puzzled grin.

"What could you possibly find amusing in that letter?" Silvio asked exasperated at his daughter's capacity to find even a small redeeming quality in everyone and everything.

"This is his first time doing anything like this. I think he had no choice."

"Sofia, can you *feel* the man who sent this?" her mother asked.

"No. You know I have to touch the person in order to get inside them."

"Then how do you know?"

"I don't, but in the last paragraph he's practically apologizing for his actions. Expressing regret isn't intimidating. He also says he *needs* the painting, not *wants* the painting. It's two different things."

"Sofia, this time I think you're wrong. The morning after I received the letter, a massive amount of garbage was dumped outside of the Gallery. Yesterday the fire alarms went off every two hours. I have no idea how he'll harass us next, so we packed away the artwork and closed the gallery for two days. I was worried about you. That's why I asked security to escort you in."

"Have you called the police?"

"He was very clear that if we notified the police things would be worse for us. I've changed the locks, the code on the alarm and the vault, added more security cameras, and have twenty-four hour security guards."

"Yes, I had the pleasure of meeting two of them outside. And who's the new guy with the beard?"

"Oh, you've met Armend," Ersilia said excitedly. "He's not new. He's worked for us for close to eight months and I think he's available."

"Not again, Mom. Last time you played matchmaker it was a disaster, remember?"

"Did you like him?" Ersilia asked, ignoring her daughter's reprimand.

"I said five words to him and he was gone. When do the paintings ship?"

"Not for another two weeks."

"Do you know a witch who can see and feel a person from a material object they've touched? If you do, we can try to find the man ourselves, but it will be hard."

Ersilia gave her husband a cautious look. "We may know of someone."

"But their powers aren't near as strong as yours, Sofia," her father said.

"Then I think it's time to call the authorities."

Ersilia held her daughter's hand in hers. "There may be another way, if you're willing."

☙❧❦

"I think a couple days out of the city and in the country with me will do you good." Sofia put her parent's overnight bag in the trunk of her blue Prius. "I'll bring you back on Sunday."

"No need, dear," her mother said. "Armend can pick us up."

"Armend? Where's Patrick, your regular driver?"

"His wife, Maureen, had a minor operation. He has a few days off to be with her."

"Oh, I'll have to visit her." Sofia slammed the trunk shut. "What does Armend do for you exactly?"

"A little bit of everything. He's become an invaluable employee. Your mother and I are very fond of him." Silvio climbed in the back and let his wife sit in front. "I saw you talking to him at the Albanian exhibit. He was speaking about the Kosovo photos."

"That was Armend? He looked different." She remembered the man and their compelling conversation. He had a strange, almost captivating effect on her. She'd wanted to continue to talk to him, but her date had pressured her to leave. When she tried to find him later on, he wasn't at the photo exhibit. Where were his steel blue eyes that night?

"He's very handy to have around. If you need him for anything, let us know." Ersilia nudged her daughter's arm and winked.

"Mom, stop it. I can find my own date."

"Really? It's Friday afternoon and you're bringing your parents home for the weekend."

"My work keeps me busy. I'm very happy with my life." Sofia pulled out of the parking garage into a line of traffic. "Please drop it."

"I hope you're still not relying on the silly computer to find your soul mate," Ersilia said.

She glanced in the rearview mirror at her father. "Dad, please help me."

"Sorry, Sofia, this is a mother daughter conversation." He leaned back and closed his eyes.

"Thanks." She sighed. "No, no more online dating sites."

"Good. I don't like you going out with strangers. It's dangerous." Ersilia patted her daughter's leg. "Anyway, you don't need a matchmaking service. You have me."

જીજીજી

Armend arrived at nine o'clock sharp on Sunday morning and waited. His watch beeped, it was nine thirty. He couldn't imagine what was taking them so long. The Palmalosis were nothing if not punctual. He picked up the Daily News and looked at the headlines. He had moved on to the sports section when his phone went off.

"Good morning, Armend. Could you please come inside? There's been a change of plan. I'm sorry to have kept you waiting."

"Sure, Mrs. P. I'll be right there."

He opened the car door and stepped out. He had been hoping to pick up his employers without bumping into their daughter. Maybe she was a late sleeper.

No such luck. As he approached the front door, Sofia stood there with a warm smile and a hot cup of coffee.

"Good morning. Armend, right? Please come in." She handed him the steaming drink. "Black, just like you like it." He shot her a questioning glance. "My parents told me."

"Thanks." He took a sip.

"I wanted to thank you for your help the other day, but you disappeared."

"You're welcome." Her long dark hair, a streak of red on each side, was swept up on top of her head. Jeweled studs blazed a path up her ear and half-moon earrings dangled from each lobe. Her striking hazel eyes were bright and cheerful. He feared he was ogling too long when she went inside. He followed, enjoying the way she and her jeans moved across the room.

Silvio and Ersilia were sitting in the family room. "Armend, we've decided to stay and have an early dinner with friends, Ersilia informed him. "We hoped you could take Sofia to see Maureen and Patrick at the hospital then bring her back here."

Armend's expression remained neutral. As much as he would love to spend a day with her, he preferred to keep Sofia at a safe distance. Then no one would get hurt.

"Then can you wait here for us?" asked Silvio. "We shouldn't be late."

"Sure. Anything you need," Armend replied.

"More coffee?" Sofia asked and shuffled him into the kitchen. "I'm sorry. I'm perfectly capable of driving myself to the city. Sometimes my parents get carried away. If you have something else to do today, please go do it."

"No, I don't mind. I should pay Patrick and Maureen a visit, too."

"Great. I'll be ready in a minute."

෬෭෬෭

Armend opened the back door of the car. She stood with her hands on her hips and eyebrow cocked at him.

"I'm not sitting back there all by myself. I'll sit up here with you."

"It's pretty messy up front." The last thing he needed was to have her in such close proximity to him. "You'll be better off in the back."

"I'll get car sick in the back. If that happens, it'll be a worse mess than anything you have up front. Trust me." She opened the passenger door, scooped up the papers, food wrappers, and a thermos, and tossed them in the back seat. She got in and buckled her seatbelt. "Ready?"

What choice did he have? He slipped in behind the wheel and started the engine.

They drove in silence until Sofia asked, "So, you've been working for my parents for eight months?"

"Yes."

"Why haven't I met you before?"

"They keep me busy."

"You don't say much, do you?"

"I'm filling in for Patrick. Usually when I drive someone for your parents they sit in the back and we don't talk."

"I understand that, but I'm not a client. We're two people going to the hospital to visit friends, so relax." He nodded, kept silent, and let her do the talking. "I think we spoke at the Albanian exhibit about the war photos. I enjoyed our conversation."

"Thanks."

"I'm sorry I didn't recognize you the other day. You had sunglasses on the night of the exhibit."

"I had an eye infection. It was swollen and bloodshot. I thought it better not to have people see it."

"Oh! I need you to stop at that Italian pastry shop." She banged her fingers on the window. "Stop! It's there on the right. You missed it."

Armend whipped the car around the block back to the pastry shop, drove past it, and parked two blocks up. "You're going to have to walk. I'll wait here. This is why passengers sit in the back. It's distracting."

She gave him a smirk and got out. When she returned, she handed him a peace offering of a cappuccino and almond biscotti. "Patrick and Maureen are Irish to the bone, but they love a good cannoli. How's your biscotti?"

"It's one of my favorites. Thank you." He took a bite and her stare intensified. Uneasiness crept into the pit of his stomach. "Why are you looking at me like that?"

She didn't answer but watched him closely. He couldn't turn away. Finally, she said, "People lie, but their eyes don't."

❧❧❧

When they arrived at the hospital, Sofia didn't argue when he let her out of the car and said he'd be up in a minute.

"Sofia! What a nice surprise," exclaimed Maureen.

"I brought your favorite dessert." She hugged her friend. "Armend will be here in a minute, he's parking the car."

"Armend drove you?" Patrick smirked. "I see your mother is trying to play matchmaker again."

"What do you think of him, Sofia?" asked Maureen. "He's very popular with the ladies at the Gallery. Although sometimes I don't think he even notices them."

"I'm sure it's not his sparkling conversation that attracts them," Sofia replied, ignoring a small tug of something resembling jealousy over his many admirers.

"He's a little shy until you get to know him, but he's really quite charming and handsome."

"Should I be jealous?" Patrick teased.

"No, dear, you're the love of my life." Maureen gave his hand a playful slap. "But get out of my cannoli box."

The door opened and Armend burst in with a bouquet of flowers. "Top o' the morning to you my darlin'," he announced in the worst Irish brogue they ever heard.

Maureen giggled like a schoolgirl. He kissed her cheek and shook her husband's hand. So everyone at the gallery thought Armend was the greatest thing since man walked on the moon, except her. She didn't know he existed until two days ago.

"They're beautiful. Thank you, Armend."

"My pleasure. I hope you're feeling better."

After a half hour of small talk, Maureen yawned. Sofia took that as a sign it was time to leave. "We'll go and let you get some rest."

When they reached the door, Patrick asked Armend how the job was going.

"Pretty well, but I'm sure they'll be glad to have you back." He patted the older man's back. "I could use some advice. What should I do with a passenger who sits up front and talks your ear off the whole ride?"

Patrick winked at Sofia. "Lock her in the back seat and put the divider up."

✂✂✂

Sofia banged on the Plexiglas between them, but he ignored her. As a last resort, she pushed the intercom button. "I'm starting not to feel good back here."

"You're fine. I called your mother and you've never been car sick a day in your life."

She laughed. "Okay, you caught me. But I can talk as much from back here as I can in the front seat."

"I see that."

"Are we going the gallery?"

"Yes, I have a few things to do. Why don't you sit back and enjoy the ride?"

She turned off the intercom, took his advice, and stretched out in the back seat. On their drive uptown, she contemplated the good looking, but odd man in the driver's seat. His reserved personality only piqued her interest more. She was surprised Silvio let him keep a beard and slightly longer hair. Her father preferred his employees clean cut and shaven. She was glad her father allowed him the privilege. Armend was very sexy exactly the way he was. Sofia couldn't get a good read on what was going on inside him—yet. She would do that when the time was right.

When he pulled the limo into its spot in the garage, Sofia sat in the back and didn't move. He opened the back door and stuck his head in. "I thought you said this wasn't a job, and I should relax?"

"You're the one who wants to play by the rules," she said and stepped out.

"This could turn out to be a very long day, huh?"

"That's entirely up to you. Why don't you just—"

"I know, relax. What I have to do may take a while. Why don't you go shopping and meet me back here?"

Insulted, she said, "I won't jump to conclusions and assume you think because I'm a woman all I want to do is shop." An expression of doubt crossed his face. "You're right. It's going to be a long day. Let's go inside."

At the entrance of the gallery, Sofia recognized the added security guards. Over the weekend, her parents had decided to re-open the gallery on Tuesday. Crews of workers were replacing artwork and statues back to their rightful places. The mystery letter writer had been on his best behavior the last two days.

"Hello, Armend," said a burly looking man standing at the front door. The big man directed his attention to Sofia. "How are you, Ms. Palmalosi?"

"Good," she said and walked past him.

Behind the receptionist desk was a young, attractive woman. "Hi, Sofia, you may not remember me. I started working here a few weeks ago. I'm Gina."

"Hi, Gina, it's nice to see you again."

Gina focused on Armend. "Where have you been lately?"

"I was here."

"You haven't called me." Her fingers did a seductive dance around his shirt collar.

"I've been busy."

In classic damsel-in-distress style, she batted her eyes and pushed her eye-catching cleavage into him. "I'm nervous here by myself with all the strange things going on. I feel better now that you're here."

"There are plenty of people here." He moved away from her and down the hall. "You're more than safe."

"I'm off at three today," she called after him.

He didn't answer and kept walking. Sofia tagged along behind him into the elevator. They took the short ride up two floors in silence and strolled down a hallway to a door.

"Your parents let me stay in the small apartment above the gallery."

"I know. They've become quite fond of you."

"They've been good to me and I appreciate it."

Sofia entered a typical bachelor apartment. A stench resembling wet dog struck her right away. At her feet, an overflowing laundry basket waited to be rescued from its smelly contents.

"I have quarters if you need them for the machine," she offered.

"Today is laundry day, but I've been busy. I'll get to it tomorrow."

Embarrassed at her behavior, but unable to stop herself, she looked around for signs of Gin…um…a woman.

"Can I use your bathroom?" she asked.

For a reason she couldn't explain, she was glad to see the single toothbrush standing in its holder. Splattered around the sink was hardened toothpaste and remnants of beard trimmings. Wet towels littered the floor. She smiled. No indication a woman had recently been in this bathroom.

When she returned to the main room of his apartment, he was busy stuffing old food into a plastic bag.

"Are you and Gina serious?"

"Do you always pry into people's personal business?"

"It was just a question. I didn't think you would mind me asking."

"Are you serious with the tall, blond man you were with the night we talked at the gallery?"

"You remember the man I was with?"

"Vaguely."

"Do you remember what I was wearing?" she teased.

"No," he snapped. "Look, I have a lot of work to do."

"Sorry, I won't bother you." She kicked off her shoes, curled up in the corner of the couch, took out her iPhone, and made herself at home. In between emails, she would sneak a glance at the solitary man engrossed in a stack of art books at a small desk in the corner of his apartment. He wrote his notes long hand on a paper, ripped them off the pad, and stuck them in a certain page of the textbook. She found his traditional way of doing things endearing. After forty-five minutes of staring at the small screen of her phone, she got up and, without a word, left.

CHAPTER 2

*The worst way to miss someone is when they're right beside
you and yet you know you can't have them. –
Ray LaMontague, singer and songwriter*

Armend didn't ask where she was going. She'd be back.
He was her ride home. She kept her promise and
didn't bother him. She seemed happy and content
curled up with her work. She fit perfect in his small world and
he longed to have her in his life, but that was impossible. Due
to his circumstances, he was a self-imposed loner. He had become close with Ersilia and Silvio and would do anything for
them, which included not hurting their daughter.

When she didn't come right back, he reached into his
pocket and took out her earring. She hadn't realized she lost it
when she got out of the limo at the hospital. With the half-
moon shaped jewelry in his palm and his fingers wrapped
tightly around it, he closed his eyes and concentrated. His hand
grew warm with her energy. He could feel a small part of her,
but not nearly as much as he wanted. He wasn't strong enough.
Focusing on her as long as he was able, he shoved her earring
back in his pocket and laid his head on the desk. Sensing even
a small part of her had wiped him out and left him exhausted.

♡✷♡

Sofia tiptoed into his apartment, not wanting to disturb
him. Armend sat at his desk, sound asleep. His head was face
down in a book, his arms spread over his notes. She stood over
him and studied the mysterious, quiet man. Faint at first, a
white light began to illuminate from him. Within seconds, it

transformed into a powerful, brilliant blue. It startled and amazed her. Never before had she had the ability to see a person's aura. That was her sister's gift. She took a step back, but bathed in the good, generous energy radiating from him. Suddenly a muddy, murky-blue color surrounded him. His pain and sorrow gripped her heart. Struck with an overwhelming urge to touch him, she stroked his dark hair. With her soft caress, his positive aura returned and then flickered away. She ran her fingers down his arm and squeezed his strong hand. Her cheeks flushed as she imagined his hands on her.

When he didn't stir, she pressed his shoulder and murmured in his ear. "Armend, wake up. I have lunch."

Gradually he opened his eyes. "You're back," he said. "All this reading made me tired."

"Are you hungry or would you like to rest?"

"No, lunch would be great."

Sofia had carried the grocery bags to the kitchen when he called to her, "I'll make my own lunch. I'm used to being by myself."

"You've been working hard. Let me do it for you."

She handed him a plate filled with a club sandwich, chips, a pickle, and a glass of water. "Thanks," he said. "I'm not used to someone taking care of me. It's nice."

"You're welcome."

She sat next to him on the couch, her salad bowl on her lap, and asked about his family. He told her his parents and older brother were in Albania on family business. His replies were short and to the point, never answering her as to what the family business was and why he wasn't a part of it. Able to take a hint, she changed the subject. "What are you working on so studiously at your desk?"

"Your parents have a tortured artist exhibit starting in six weeks. The artists I'm researching painted their best work while suffering from a broken heart. Some of their lovers died while others were forbidden from having the love of their life."

"That's sad."

"Wouldn't it be nice if everyone was free to love who they wanted? The world might be a better place."

He started to get up when Sofia grabbed his hand. "Please. Sit here with me a little longer."

❧❧❧

Before Armend fully understood what had happened, he was back on the couch, Sofia's soft fingers entwined with his. She peered directly into his eyes. Even if he wanted to, he couldn't pull away from her stare. He was mesmerized as her eyes turned from their normal hazel to the most beautiful and incredible green he'd ever seen. He knew what she was doing and his only hope was that after his nap and much needed food, he would be strong enough to let her in only so far. He fought hard, but soon gave in to her.

After a few moments, Sofia closed her eyes. When she opened them, they were back to their normal hazel color, but full of tears.

"I know you and your parents are Strega." Armend hesitated. "They told me."

"Yes, I know. They trust you."

"Don't cry," he said.

She wrapped one arm around his neck and laid her other hand on his heart. "You have such a dark sadness inside you, it makes my heart ache. There is a fear of something, but I don't think even you know what you're afraid of. Why won't you let anyone close to you?"

The sensation of her touch had his heart racing. He should drag himself away, but he couldn't find the resolve to do so. "No one can help me. It's my destiny. And aren't we all afraid of the unknown?"

"I wish I could remove all the heaviness from your heart," she said.

It took every ounce of will power he had not to wrap his arms around her and tell her everything. Instead, he eased away from her.

"Most of my life I've been somewhat lost. I was in trouble when I was younger, always picking fights. I even spent a few months in jail. I tried getting my act together and took a few college courses while working odd jobs." He grabbed the glass of water off the table and gulped it down.

"Having family in Italy and Albania, old European architecture interested me. I took classes in architecture that eventually led me to art history. I've been at it for years. Sometimes I only take one class a year and I'm still far from getting my degree. Then I met your parents and they took a chance on me. Now I have a job I love and things are turning around for me." He placed his hands on Sofia's shoulders. "There's no need to worry. I'm fine."

"That's a nice story," she said. "But you just told me no one could help you and something is your destiny. And you're still scared of something."

He got up abruptly and walked to his desk. How the hell was he going to get out the mess he'd gotten himself into? "I meant only *I* could help myself, no one else, and yeah, I'm scared I'm going to screw up again. I don't want to let your parents down after all they've done for me."

Straightening up the papers on his desk and putting away his books, he wanted this conversation to end. "Everything I told you is true. I can finish this tomorrow. Let's get you home."

"Who's the lucky lady you're in love with, but insist on keeping it a secret?" Sofia asked.

Shit. "I don't know that I would consider her lucky." It pissed him off she'd gotten in that far. He was sure he stopped her, but he was no match for her. It was just his luck to be in love with a witch stronger than he was.

"That didn't answer my question."

"I've told you more about myself than I tell most people. You'll have to settle for that. I'm leaving. Are you coming or not?"

CHAPTER 3

When all the trees have been cut down,
When all the animals have been hunted,
When all the waters are polluted,
When all the air is unsafe to breath,
Only then will you discover you cannot eat money.
– Cree prophecy

S itting in traffic, heading north on the Westside Highway, Armend veered the conversation away from him and onto her to save himself from any further interrogation.

"So tell me about the Nature Preserve," he said. "You have a beautiful spot on the Hudson River."

"Thanks. It's a labor of love. Five years ago when my parents and I tried to buy the privately owned land, we found ourselves in a bidding war with a large construction company, backed up by not-so-nice people. They wanted to strip the land and build a development of upscale houses, complete with a scenic river view and easy train ride to Manhattan. I was twenty-two then and entitled to my trust fund. So I hired the best environmental lawyers my father knew and eventually we won."

"Environmental lawyers?"

"Yes. I knew I wanted to turn the land into some sort of conservation or learning center so I did some investigating. What the previous owners didn't realize was that Bog Turtles inhabit the land near the water and they are a protected species in the Hudson Valley."

"I'm impressed. It's not easy going up against big corporations."

"You like to research tortured artists and I like to research endangered species," she said with a shrug. "It helped our case that the Hudson River is an estuary."

Armend tried to remember what an estuary was. He thought it had something to do with salt and fresh water coming together, but he wasn't sure.

"We're in lower Westchester County, close to the mouth of the Hudson that meets with the ocean. The marine life calling that transitional part of the river home is very diverse. There are many ecological agencies, as well as the State of New York, trying to protect it and keep it clean."

"I'm glad your hard work paid off and you won your case. When my brother and I were small, my parents would take us hiking upstate along the river. It's a beautiful valley." Armend took the exit he needed off the highway. They didn't have much farther to go. "Was the house already there or did you build it?"

"No, it was there and I love it. It's small, quaint, and perfect for me."

"You're not the classic rich girl are you?"

"I don't know. If I'm not, it's because of my parents." Her phone went off. "Speak of the devil." Leaving him to his thoughts, Sofia spoke to her parents for the rest of the drive.

At the entrance to the Preserve, they came upon a small group of people holding signs. "Who are they? They weren't here this morning," Armend asked.

"They were probably at services. It is Sunday. They're a group from a local Pentecostal church. Ever since they discovered I was a witch they come and politely protest."

"Why don't you call the police?"

"Why? They've never threatened me. When they first started to come, I thought about screwing with them. I almost came out dressed in black with the traditional crone's hat and broom throwing magic dust around. Then I figured it would add fuel to the fire. So now when it's hot I bring them lemonade and cookies and in the winter I bring them hot chocolate."

He drove slowly past while Sofia smiled and waved at them. In return, they held their posters higher exclaiming only Jesus could save her.

"Can you pull over to that shed on the side of the road please?"

He did what she asked and stopped the car. She got out and went inside the small building. Exiting the shed with her arms full, she greeted the small crowd cheerfully. Armend rolled down the window and listened.

"Good evening, everyone. Here are a few umbrellas. I don't want you to get wet when it starts raining."

"It's a clear sky," someone mumbled.

"Believe me if I say it's going to rain, it will." She wagged her finger at them. "I would appreciate you putting them back in the shed when you leave. Have a good night."

Armend couldn't hide his amusement when she got back in the car. "That guy is right, the sky is clear. Are you thinking of conjuring up a storm tonight?"

"Of course not. I try not to mess with Mother Nature unless absolutely necessary." With a playful grin, she held up her iPhone, the weather map in full view. "The radar shows storm clouds headed toward the Hudson Valley from the west. They should be here soon."

∽∾∽

Hidden behind the dense bushes that outlined the property, she watched the car vanish down the driveway. To be on the safe side she buttoned her blouse up to her collar and removed the pentagram from around her neck.

She stepped out from behind shrubs. "Hello," she called out as she approached the group. "I was wondering if you could help me. My car got a flat about a half mile back." She waved her cell phone in the air. "Silly me, I forgot to charge my phone."

"Sure, Ma'am," a heavyset bald man said. "I have a jack in the back of the van."

"Do you work here? I'm lucky to find people out late on a Sunday afternoon."

"No, we're here to send a message."

She feigned interest in their posters.

"We're getting ready to leave. The resident witch says it's going to rain."

"Witch?" she asked.

"You didn't know?" an elderly woman replied.

"I've just moved here."

"Can you imagine our God-fearing town letting someone like that live here and own a business?"

"It's sad what the world is coming to," she sympathized. "I'm glad you told me."

"She just got home," another woman said. "And has a *man* with her. God knows what unnatural things they're doing in there. You know what they say about her kind."

"Disgusting." She covered her mouth with her hand as a proper lady would. "You know, there are better ways to get her to leave. You can circulate petitions or start a letter writing campaign. I'd be happy to help. That way I could meet more devout and morally upstanding people such as you."

They beamed with pride at her compliment and escorted her to the van. "I know our pastor would be interested in speaking with you. Why don't we take you to meet him?"

It was like taking candy from a baby. They were going to deliver her to his doorstep. "Thank you. That would be lovely."

CHAPTER 4

The blackest chapter in the history of Witchcraft lies
not in the malevolence of Witches, but in the
deliberate, gloating cruelty of their prosecutors. –
Theda Kenyon, author of Witches Still Live

Sofia put the leftover lasagna in the oven and was busy
chopping romaine and spinach for a salad when Armend
walked in.

"I'd offer to help, but I'm no good in the kitchen," he told
her.

"Do you have a room in the house you are good in?"

"Are you flirting with me?"

"Do you mind?"

"No man in his right mind would care if you flirted with
him."

"Good. Can you get the plates out of the cabinet over
there? The silverware is in the drawer to the left," she said
pointing. "The cheese and salad dressing are in the refrigerator. By the time you're done setting the table, dinner will be
ready."

Sofia went back to her greens when something brushed
against her ankles. She gazed down at her cat, standing between her feet, before it ran toward Armend and jumped in his
arms.

"Whoa. I see you come complete with a black cat. What's
his name?"

"That's Lautner."

"Lautner?"

"He's named after someone killed during Eastern European witch hunts."

He put the cat on the floor and reached for the plates. Lautner scratched the back of Armend's legs. He meowed quietly at first, but when ignored, the screeching began.

"Could I get a little help here?" he asked.

She laughed. "He likes you. You're going to have to pick him up. I'll get the plates."

Armend bent over and the cat leaped onto his chest and began to purr. "So tell me about my new friend's namesake. I'm assuming he was a witch."

"No, he was a priest," she said, setting the table. "The hysteria started when a woman took communion bread from her mouth and put it her prayer book. Apparently, that's a no-no. Later, they accused her of taking it so her cow would produce more milk. That's when the frenzy broke out. The Great Hunt lasted from 1636 to 1648. So many people, most of them innocent women, were killed, they lost count."

She placed the tray of hot lasagna in the center of the table. "First they were tortured in ways I can't even talk about. Sometimes they would decapitate them and then burn their bodies, but most of the time they were burned alive."

She poured them each a little wine. "Lautner was killed later on, in 1680. The Great Hunt had ended, but soon suspicions began to grow again. He was a local vicar who urged tolerance and calm. Because of that, they charged him with Witchcraft and burned him at the stake alongside a family. A family—with children." She couldn't stop the tears from streaming down her face. "What kind of deranged person ties a human being, much less a child, to a stake and sets them on fire? Then insists we're the evil ones." Armend squeezed her hand. "Anyway, I admired his bravery for standing up for what he believed in. Even with his life threatened, he wouldn't back down." She wiped her eyes with napkin from the table. "I'm sorry. I tend to wear my heart on my sleeve, down my arm, and everywhere else."

He undid his hand from hers. "Having a heart is a quality more people should have."

They sat in silence, Lautner contentedly curled on Armend's lap. Sofia cut the lasagna and put a piece on his plate.

30   Debbie Christiana

Pushing the food around with her fork, she pondered the man across from her. Her parents adored him, John and Maureen admired him, her cat loved him, the *Lare* trusted him, and…well, she wasn't sure what she felt. But there was something. Earlier at his apartment, his aura stirred something deep within her. Later, when she looked inside him, despite the fear and sadness, she saw a kind, gentle soul. Was it the pathetic romantic in her or was she falling in love with him? That was ridiculous. She'd just met him.

"Why don't you tell me what kept you so busy on your phone in my apartment?" he asked.

"This week we're hosting a program called *Folklore, Legends, and Myths from Around the World.* I'm very excited. I was confirming emails."

"What does that have to do with preserving Nature?"

"People are a significant part of Nature and remembering how our ancient ancestors saw the world helps preserve our human legacy."

"I know a few Albanian folktales. I can email them to you if you'd like."

"I have a group of fourth and fifth graders coming on Wednesday. Why don't you come and tell your tales yourself?"

"No, I don't think so."

"Why? You spoke very well at the gallery a couple weeks ago."

He chuckled. "Yeah, but talking to little kids, that's scary!"

Sofia kept pressing him until he admitted Wednesday was his day off. "Okay, what time should I be here?"

"You'll have to be here early. You can come Tuesday evening and spend the night," she said slyly.

"Would your parents approve of all this flirting?"

"They're not here are they?"

"I'll be here nine a.m. sharp."

છબછ

Armend followed Sofia into her family room, his furry friend at his feet. When she tried to pour him more wine, he stopped her. "One glass is good for me. I have to drive your parents back to the city."

She filled her glass and got comfortable in her leather loveseat. "The man I was with at the gallery is Daniel. He and I have been on and off for a couple of years. His job keeps him overseas quite a lot. If he's not seeing anyone, when he's in town, he calls me. If I'm available, we go out. Neither of us have any expectations. When he called a few weeks ago, I asked him to come to my parent's gallery."

"Do you sleep with him?" The question blurted out before he could stop himself.

"Do you always pry into people's personal business?" she asked.

He didn't answer; ashamed he'd even asked.

"Yes, sometimes," she said.

He flinched at her answer and in a daring move sat next to her. Leaning in close he whispered in her ear, "You were wearing a green strapless dress that fit you like a glove." With his two pointer fingers, he started on the side of her neck and traced the soft skin of her neckline. "You wore a pendant that hung down to about here." His fingers stopped above her cleavage. "It was red and matched the lovely streaks in your hair. You have a tattoo right here." Never taking his eyes off her, he reached down and touched the outside of her right ankle.

At that moment, he wanted to kiss her more than he wanted to breathe.

She brushed a strand of hair from his face and bent forward, her full lips inches from his. Coming to his senses, he put his hands on her shoulders and pushed her away.

She leaned back exasperated. "Staying faithful to your mystery woman? The one that doesn't even know you exist?"

"Sofia, I'm sorry. I shouldn't have said those things and touched you the way I did."

"No. You shouldn't have." She bolted up from the couch. "Tell my parents I went to bed." She flew out of the room leaving him alone. Lautner leapt onto his lap and scolded him with a swat of his paw and a deep meeooww.

"Yes, I know. You don't have to yell at me." He sank deep into the couch and closed his eyes.

What the hell was he thinking? He couldn't believe he'd done something so stupid. Tonight proved he couldn't be around her and stay in control. As much as he liked Silvio and Ersilia, he wondered if it was time for him to move on. There was no need for him to stay. It would all be over in December anyway.

CHAPTER 5

Legends die hard. They survive as truth rarely does. –
Helen Hayes, 1900 – 1993,
American stage and film actress

Armend sat at her kitchen table, coffee mug in hand and Lautner perched on his lap, when Sofia walked in. He mumbled a somber hello. "I wasn't sure if you still wanted me to come after my behavior the other night. I didn't want you to think I was a complete jackass."

"I hope you're here because you want to share your country's history with the kids, not to ease some guilt trip you're on."

"Sofia, please let me explain."

"Look." She interrupted him. "I'm an adult and have to take some responsibility. I like you, a lot, and I thought there was a spark between us, but I was wrong. I knew you were in love with someone else and I should have respected that." Sofia walked toward her back door. "Come on. Let me show you where you'll be speaking today."

He didn't move. "I never told you how much I enjoyed spending Sunday with you. You made me two delicious meals and we shared good conversation. You even revealed a little of your magic to me. You were more than nice to me and didn't treat me like your parent's employee, but like a friend. You're a beautiful woman. I'm a man and I noticed. I wanted to pay you a compliment, but didn't do it the best way I could have and I'm sorry."

Sofia laid her hand on his shoulder. "Thank you and don't be sorry. I wish you would tell this woman how you feel about her because you're wrong, she would be very lucky to have you." Her phone started to beep. "Oh, I'll be right back."

She closed the door behind her leaving Armend with his heart in his throat.

ോ

Armend inhaled the cool, crisp October air as they hiked the immediate perimeter of the Preserve. On their journey, they passed a large tipi with a small hut next to it. Set back in the woods behind the tipi was a small cabin. "This is where my friend, Bill Moonhawk, lives. He's a member of the Iroquois tribe native to the Hudson Valley. He's my most popular attraction," she joked. "He has a wonderful way with words and people come from all over to hear him speak about the Iroquois way of life, as well as the history of the Hudson Valley. He's also an expert on the ecosystem of the river. Each month on the night of the full moon, he leads a guided tour through the grounds. It's always sold out, even in the dead of winter."

They kept walking and she pointed out a small building off to the side. "That's our gift shop, run by my friend, Bridget. She's our resident Celtic witch and is the expert on neo-paganism.

"Where does she live?"

"She has a cabin here, but she's never there. She and Bill have been having quite the torrid love affair for at least three years now. They think we don't know, but we do."

"Affair? Is one of them married?"

"No, they're free to do what they want. We call it that because they keep it such a secret."

"Why?"

"I don't know. You tell me. Why do people keep secrets?" she asked matter-of-factly.

Not wanting to risk her getting inside him again, he climbed up a small hill. "Look, the school buses are arriving."

They made their way to the parking lot where the buses were pulling in. Sofia greeted everyone and pointed to a huge tent. "There's plenty of good things to eat and drink for breakfast. Go help yourselves."

A large blue van with a white dove on the doors raced into the parking lot, spitting small rocks up into the air as it slammed on its brakes. Sofia was busy talking and didn't see them. Eight men poured out the side of the van carrying a large banner. They formed a single line in the same spot they stood the other night next to the entrance sign that read *The Spirit of Nature – A Center of Learning and Conservation.* The tall man at one end unrolled the banner until it was open and their message displayed. A dark fury bubbled deep in Armend's core. The last thing he wanted was for Sofia to see it.

"Excuse me." With his hand, he positioned Sofia toward the tent and away from the parking lot. "That's a lot of kids down there. Are you sure you have enough food? Maybe you should go check."

She twisted around to face him. "I have done this a few times before. I know what I'm doing." Her face dropped as she caught sight of the row of men and their hateful sign.

"Sofia, I'm going to take care of this. I'll make them leave and they won't ever come back. You've let them harass you long enough."

"Mrs. Neil, will you please make sure the kids don't come back up here?"

"Of course, Ms. Palmalosi. I'm sorry—they are—" Mrs. Neil tripped on her words.

"Thank you. I'll take care of it. Armend, come with me."

"Sofia, please let me do it my way," he pleaded.

"I appreciate your concern, but no."

The next thing he knew he was stomping up the hill behind Sofia with a gallon of apple cider in one hand and cups in the other. She carried a box of donuts and they were heading toward the parking lot. She was too damn nice and naïve. He would address the men later, in a much different manner, without her knowing. He hadn't been confrontational in years, but seeing Sofia hurt awoke a part of his personality he thought was long gone.

When the group of protesters saw the couple approaching, the man holding the end of the banner stepped forward.

"Good morning, gentleman." Sofia stood face-to-face with the six-foot man. "I think you'll agree I have been more than patient with you." She offered each man a donut. "Attacking me is one thing, but I have children here today and they don't need to see adults behaving this way. This is a place of peace, not judgment. A place that teaches to value, respect, and preserve the earth and all its inhabitants."

"We don't want you teaching the children of this town anything," said the large man.

"Armend, the drinks please."

He refused and stood fuming in silence. He hoped they could tell by the look on his face that he was not of the same opinion as the compassionate woman he loved more than life. Sofia had now taken the cider from him and poured each of them a drink.

Preoccupied with their uninvited guests, he almost missed it. It was subtle. The air was different, no longer crisp and clean, but heavy. The top of the trees began to sway back and forth. The sun shone brightly on the tent full of children, but over the horizon, a large black cloud traveled in their direction. The weather change came in hearty gusts and the leaves twirled in circles. The only indication that Sofia was aware of the brewing storm was that she was now shouting at the men over the howling wind.

"Our religion is thousands of years older than yours. We had no notion of who your Satan was until you threw him in our laps. He doesn't seem a pleasant fellow and you can keep him. He has nothing to do with us."

Armend's eyes shot up at the dark cloud hovering over them. In the midst of the gale force winds, a lone black crow maneuvered expertly in the air. Down the hill, the kids ran around in the sunshine. Neither they nor the teachers seemed to notice the parking lot engulfed in its own private storm.

"If you want to stand here all day, be my guest, but you have to put the banner away. If you don't, I will call the police," Sofia bellowed. "Look at it this way, if you think I'm so wicked and in cahoots with your devil, you probably shouldn't get on my bad side, don't you agree?"

With that, there was an earsplitting crack of thunder. The men jumped and drinks spilled. A gust of wind swooped down and, one by one, they struggled to keep their footing. They thrashed and wrestled against their invisible attacker. Armend remained steady as the men tripped over each other and went down like a falling row of dominos.

The storm ended as quickly as it started.

"Hey, where'd she go?" The tall man asked as he stood and brushed himself off.

Sofia was gone. Armend made a three hundred and sixty degree turn and she had vanished.

"Let's get out of here!" A young man ran to the van and half the group followed him.

Armend approached the remaining few. "If I were you, I'd think long and hard before you decide to come back here. I'm not nearly as sympathetic and kindhearted as Ms. Palmalosi."

"You don't scare us," the tall man replied, his nerves clearly on edge.

"That's your first mistake." He started to walk away, but stopped. "And pick up your mess," he said pointing to the cups and food. "Ms. Palmalosi doesn't take well to littering on her property."

e/ɔe/ɔ

"Are you all right?" Armend asked Sofia who was waiting outside the building.

"Yes. I see they left. Did you threaten them?"

"No, I think you're disappearing act did the trick," he said. "Where did you go?

"I walked down the hill. I called on the *Folletto* for a little help."

"*Folletto*?"

"They're friendly, but playful, spirits Stregas have at our disposal. They live in the wind, hence the storm. While they kept you distracted, I walked away. You were victim to a little magic and a bit of illusion." Sofia raised a finger to her face. "I wish I could wiggle my nose and disappear, but I can't." She proceeded to move her nose back and forth. "See, still here," she said with a twinkle in her eye.

He laughed. "I think they were sufficiently spooked."

"Come on. The kids are waiting for you." As they walked down the hallway of the solar paneled building, she explained who else was speaking.

"In the first room Bill Moonhawk is telling Native American tales. The man who owns the business next to my parent's gallery is from Kenya. He's agreed to come and tell African stories. I have my dad's best friend telling Sicilian legends and you're in the last room."

Armend walked in. Staring back at him was a sea of eager looking faces and an indescribable fear hit him. This was a bad idea. He didn't know how to talk to kids.

"I wasn't sure if you were coming today so the room doesn't have much Albanian décor, Sofia told him. "I did buy a map and a flag."

"It's perfect." He let out a small moan. "I forgot. I left a block of Halva in your refrigerator. It's an Albanian dessert full of sugar, chocolate, and butter. I loved it when I was a kid."

"I'll get it for you," Sofia said.

"Where's Albanian?" a girl with braided pigtails sitting in the front asked.

"It's Albania." Sofia corrected her and pointed to map. "It's a country above Greece. It's only forty-five miles to Italy by boat crossing the Adriatic Sea."

"It looks small," said a little boy. "America is bigger."

"Yes, America is much bigger, but Albania is very interesting. This is my friend Armend and his family is from Albania. He's going to tell you some fun stories about his country and then he has a surprise for you."

"What's his name? Arnold?"

Armend got up and stood nervously next to Sofia. "Tough crowd," he said.

"Just be yourself. You'll do fine."

He faced his commanding audience. "Hi everyone, my name is Armend."

There were a few giggles in the back of the room. "Ladies, I haven't told my first joke yet, but I'm glad you think I'm going to be funny."

"They think you're cute," said another girl said rolling her eyes.

"Well, thank you."

"Is there vampires in Albania? We want to hear about vampires," another girl piped up.

"Vampires are stupid," said the boy next to her.

"You're stupid," she retorted.

Armend bit his lip and faced the side of the room so they wouldn't see his amusement.

"Okay, so vampires it is," he said. He got a resounding cheer from his audience. "I've never seen or met a vampire and neither has anyone I know. But many people swear they have." He inched his way through the rows of children. "In Albania, we call vampires *Lugat*. They are easy-going and much nicer than most you have read about. *Lugats* would never kill anyone. They're more annoying than deadly and wander around looking for a midnight snack. They don't have fangs either. Just normal teeth like you and I." He stepped forward with his right foot and dragged his left leg behind him hobbling through his captive listeners. "They aren't in a hurry and walk slow, like this. If they catch you, they may take a small bite out of your arm or leg. If they think you're yummy, they'll nibble on you and let you go." When they giggled, he was relieved. He didn't want to scare them and made his way back to the front of the room.

Sofia tiptoed behind him and whispered in his ear, "You're doing great. I'm going to get your dessert. I'll be back."

Much more comfortable with his young spectators, he continued with the legend of the *Lugat*.

తుసిం

Sofia finished saying good-bye and the last school bus pulled away. She was walking back when Armend appeared at her side.

"Thank you for coming today," she told him. "You were great. The kids loved you and your dessert."

"You're welcome. It was fun. I don't know why I was so nervous."

"Maybe I'll see you sometime at the gallery." She enjoyed his company and was touched when he'd tried to protect her, but she couldn't read anything into that. He was in love with someone else. "Take care," she said walked away.

"Sofia, wait."

"Good-bye, Armend." She stopped when she heard a vehicle pull into the parking lot.

The same van from earlier had parked and a man walked toward her shouting, "Excuse me. Sofia? Sofia Palmalosi?"

"Yes."

As the man got closer, Armend stood in front of Sofia. "I thought I was clear this morning about coming back here," he said.

Sofia stepped out from behind him. "Armend, please, he wasn't here this morning,"

"That's right. In fact, I came to apologize. My name is Aaron Nichols and I would like a few moments of your time." He offered his hand to her.

"She has nothing to say you," Armend said, taking a step toward the man.

"And who are you?" Aaron asked.

"Don't mind him," Sofia said shaking Aaron's hand. "It's nice to meet you. Unfortunately, right now isn't good for me, but if you come back tomorrow, I'd like to talk to you as well."

"Sure. Same time?"

"That should be fine."

"Thank you. See you then." He gave Armend a satisfied grin and strode back to the lot.

Sofia headed back to her house with Armend chasing after her. "Sofia!"

"You have to stop this. I can take care of myself. You know how I feel about you and you're making it harder for me. I'm not yours to protect. Your heart belongs to someone else. Please worry about her. I'm fine."

Before he could answer, his phone beeped alerting him he had a text. "It's your parents. They want me to bring you back to the city with me. They got another letter."

CHAPTER 6

Witchcraft…is a spiritual path. You walk it for nourishment of the soul, to commune with the life force of the universe, and to thereby better know your own life. – *Christopher Penczak, author of* The Inner Temple of Witchcraft

Armend leaned against the doorframe of the largest room in Silvio and Ersilia's New York apartment. The décor was tasteful. Classic artwork adorned the walls. His favorite piece was a sculpture of two lovers caught in a passionate embrace. Positioned near the fireplace, they seemed to come alive, the glow from the blaze reflecting the love in their eyes.

Silvio spoke first. "I've hired the best private detective in the New York area. He brushed the envelope and letter for fingerprints and did other testing. So we're all free to touch it."

"According to this, we're running out of time," Sofia said, folding the letter in half. "If you want me to use my power to help the witch *see* the person who wrote the letter, we'd better get going."

The moment of truth had arrived and Armend wondered how she would react. He remained as still and silent as the two bronze lovers across the room. Sofia spun like a top toward him. Their eyes locked. "I know you're a witch."

"You don't seem too surprised," he replied.

"It wasn't hard to figure out. Why didn't you tell me?"

"At the time I thought it was best if you didn't know."

"Why?"

He didn't answer her.

"Is your whole life one big secret?" There was an angry edge in her voice.

Silvio saved him from any further explanation. "Sofia, I'm sure he had his reasons for not telling you. We'll leave you two alone for a few minutes, but when we get back we have work to do." He put his arm around his wife's waist and led her out of the room.

"How did you know?" he asked.

Sofia sat near the fire and didn't respond right away. He couldn't blame her. He had royally screwed everything up these last few days where she was concerned. A small part of him wished he could go back to Friday morning on the gallery steps before they met. Things were easier then, but a bigger part of him wouldn't trade the time they spent together, even with his slip-ups. He loved her absolute kindness and ability to forgive his mistakes. He hoped she could do it one more time.

"At first, I didn't know for sure," she said staring into the fire. "The afternoon I looked inside you, I was blocked by something. I could have broken through. My parents are right you aren't that strong. But I respected your privacy and let it go."

"I appreciate that." He thanked the Gods his secret was safe.

"When the security guards grabbed me, I summoned the *Lare* for help. As soon as you showed up, they left. They wouldn't leave unless I was safe with you. This morning when the *Folletto* were blowing the men around, they didn't bother you. They only have influence on non-witches."

She was still distant, her back firmly planted toward him. Armend longed to slip his arms around her, bury his face in her neck, tell her he loved her, and how sorry he was. Knowing she had feelings for him made it almost unbearable not to touch her, but he resisted. "Sofia, please look at me."

She shifted her position, but refused to do as he asked. "I think Lautner is your familiar."

"He can't be. He's yours."

"No, he's my cat," she said, facing him. "I love him and he tolerates me, maybe even likes me when he wants to be fed or have his belly rubbed, but he's not my familiar. The familiar picks you, you don't pick them."

"I know. I've never had a familiar before."

Sofia rose and poked at the fire. "We'll have to discuss a time when I can give him to you."

"I couldn't take him from you," Armend protested. "I'll visit him."

"You have no reason to visit me and you two belong together. Now that's he's picked you, he won't be content with me. I don't mind as long as you promise to take good care of him."

This didn't set well with him. As hard as he tried not to, all he did was hurt her. Yet she was ready to give him her cat.

"Do you have a familiar?" he asked.

"Yes, a beautiful black crow named Solstice."

He remembered the lone crow maneuvering easily through the wind earlier. "Why did you name her Solstice?"

"She arrived at my window two years ago on the winter solstice."

"That's interesting," Armend said. "I was born on the winter solstice."

With the letter clutched in her hands, she disappeared down the hall. When she didn't return, Armend went to look for her. She was at the top of the staircase.

"Wait." He took two steps a time to catch her. When he got to the landing he asked her, "Can you forgive me?"

"I already have." She lifted his bearded chin so they were face to face. "There can't be any negative energy or this ritual won't work."

"Thank you. It means a lot to me."

She continued down the hallway to the last door on the left. They entered a small room. A leather chaise lounge sat against the north wall in front of a picture window. Half-melted candles waited to burn bright once again on tables of various sizes and shapes. Against the far wall was an antique mahogany armoire.

"What are we doing here?" he asked.

"You'll see." She pulled the large doors of the armoire toward her and to the side. "It's my parent's ritual altar."

Armend leaned toward the raised structure to get a better look. It was adorned with candles and other ceremonial tools. "What's does it all mean?"

"The altar changes seasonally. After the autumn equinox, we place a seashell to the left representing the Goddess and a pinecone to the right to represent the God you wish to call on. The four elements are also an important part." She picked up a match and struck it against a darkened piece of flint on the inside of the door. "Incense to the East for Air and a white candle to the South for fire." She lit each object and in an intimate gesture, held the glowing stick in front of Armend's face. He blew it out. She opened a drawer underneath the altar. Inside were twenty pouches. "We place sand to the North symbolizing earth." She sprinkled white sand she took from one of the sacks into a small dish and poured water from a small glass container into a chalice.

"Let me guess. Water to west," he said.

"Yes. The athame faces north and the spirit bowl is always in the center."

Ersilia appeared in the doorway with a large silver tray of food. "Armend please set this down on the chaise." Her father, right behind, carried a bottle of liquor. He held it up by the neck. "Afterward we get to eat and drink." He chuckled. "That's the best part. But for now, the spirit bowl gets her turn." He poured the yellow liquid in the bowl and put a match to it. A deep blue flame sputtered up and flickered.

At the sight of the food, figs, prosciutto, melon, and bread, Armend's stomach growled. They hadn't eaten since lunch. He licked his lips and agreed with Silvio.

Ersilia drew the curtains and the lit the candles. The ordinary sitting room had transformed into the sacred space of the Strega.

Armend observed all the preparations with wide eyes. He knew what was going on, but hadn't experienced it in many years. Sofia took a gold rope from the altar and positioned it in a circle. Using an old straw broom with a crooked handle, she swept the inside of the circle to purify and cleanse the area.

"You haven't seen this done before, have you?" she asked him.

"Not in a long time. I don't belong to a hereditary line of witches, like you. My grandmother was the first witch in the family. When we were kids we would participate in her rituals, but as a teenager, I lost interest. I haven't practiced in many years. I have one gift, but I've never had enough strength to do it well."

"You will tonight." She stepped inside the circle. "Please join me." Her parents dimmed the lights.

๏๏๏

She signaled her father and he handed Armend the envelope. Sofia spoke.

"I call upon the Goddess Diana,
"the earth, air, fire and water tonight
"to unite in our quest for a lost power to reignite.

"Armend, I want you to concentrate and be open and accepting of the energy I'm sending you." He nodded, followed her lead and sat in the circle. "When my eyes change," Sofia explained. "I want you to see the line of energy flowing from me to you. You must focus."

Sofia closed her eyes and held her hands in front of her face, six inches apart. Within the space between her hands she visualized an alluring white ball of light full of energy and heat. With deep breaths, she went far inside herself. This was her favorite part of the ritual, when the warmth surged through her. Her essence was able to generate enough intensity for her to leave her body, knowing her physical self would be waiting for its return. She straightened her arms toward Armend and envisioned firing a stream of power and strength to him as he clutched the envelope between his two hands.

๏๏๏

Silvio explained to Armend what he would experience during this ritual, but nothing could have prepared him for the intensity of Sofia. He was in awe as she traveled to a different place or dimension. Her body was there physically, but her true self was somewhere else.

When her eyes changed to a beautiful shade of sea green, he did as she asked and concentrated. He could sense her might and wanted to take her all in. The air in the room swirled around and his senses heightened. The soft sweeping noise of the long drapes swaying back and forth echoed like the wings of a bird flapping over his head. The strong scent of sulfur from the match strike lingered in the air and stung his nostrils. The heat from the spirit bowl scorched his skin. He was able to see a small speck of dust in the corner of the darkened room, fifteen feet away.

Sofia sat trance-like. It was up to him. With his finely tuned awareness, he cast his attention to the envelope in his hands. The rate of his breath increased and with each exhale, an image flashed in his mind. Frustrated with the speed that the picture show passed through his head, he slowed his breathing down.

When the visions appeared at a reasonable pace, he studied each one. The first image was a small cabin deep in the woods. Then an older gentleman with salt and pepper hair sitting outside. He could feel the desperation the man carried within him and a similar sadness crept into Armend's heart. When the man stood and went toward his house, he moved with a slight limp. An alarm went off inside Armend's brain and he willed himself to see the stranger's face. The man stopped, hesitated a moment, turned, and peered directly into Armend's eyes.

A sense of dread filled Armend. He needed to stop immediately. He hoped the expression on his face didn't give away his emotional revelation.

Not sure how to end the ritual, he threw the envelope on the ground between him and Sofia, hoping it would break the spell. She continued to sit still. Armend climbed to his feet, but stayed in the circle. "I've seen everything I can see."

Sofia lowered her arms and rose to face him. Her eyes were still a deep emerald green. Without touching him, she glided her arms over his whole body. He closed his eyes as her energy seeped out from him. While still aware of his surroundings, his senses lost their superhuman power, and he was once again regular Armend. His legs were heavy and weak and his body, without his consent, dropped to the floor.

One thing he'd learned from his grandmother was never to leave the circle until you thanked the goddess you had called on. Ersilia handed Sofia a small bunch of daisies and she expressed her gratitude to Diana. Her mother helped her to the floor next to Armend.

"Sofia, are you all right?" Armend asked.

She was pale and her breathing labored. "This particular ritual drains me of my strength. That's why we eat afterwards. How do you feel?"

"Better than you, I think. But I'm glad to be sitting down."

Ersilia poured them each a glass of the yellow liquid. "This is Liquore Strega. *Bevanda*. Drink."

He was curious about the foreign drink and sniffed its slightly-sweet aroma. He took a sip and let the semi-thick liquor settle on his tongue. He savored the bold combination of mint, fennel, and a taste he couldn't place. "That's good." He smacked his lips. "What makes it yellow?"

"Saffron." Sofia took her own sip and closed her eyes. As she swallowed, she let out a happy groan.

Silvio handed Sofia and Armend a plate of food and sat a warm bowl of olive oil between them. "*Mangia*. Eat. It'll make you strong again."

Armend dug into the small, but wonderful feast. The sweet and salty pairing of the melon and prosciutto, the bread, and the sting of heated garlic-flavored oil on his tongue warmed his weary soul.

When they were finished eating, Ersilia turned the lights up. Armend squinted as his eyes adjusted. Sofia continued to rest, but her parents ushered him to the corner of the room, eager to hear what he had to say.

Now came the hard part.

"Take your time, dear," Ersilia told him.

He decided to stay as close to the truth as he could and chose his words carefully. It would ease his conscience. "He's an older man, maybe sixty or so. He lives north of here. I think somewhere in the Catskill mountains."

"The postmark said it was mailed from Brooklyn," Silvio said.

"It's only an hour and a half north of New York. Not a bad trip, especially if you don't want to get caught," Armend replied.

"Go on."

"I saw a cabin. I can draw it if you like." The Catskill Mountains were home to thousands of cabins and he would depict one similar to what he had seen, but not exact. Ashamed, he looked away from the couple as he continued. "He's an honorable man, but there are circumstances beyond his or anyone's control, ruling his behavior right now. He doesn't want anyone hurt."

"Do you know his name?" asked Ersilia

Instead of answering Jorgji, he gave them the English translation, "George."

"What about a last name?"

Armend's jaw tightened as he told his first complete lie since the start of the conversation. "No, I'm sorry." He wanted to throw up.

"Why is he doing this?"

The four walls closed in on him. "I don't know. Even with Sofia's help, I wasn't able to see enough to help you as much as I wanted." He stood and took Ersilia's hands in his, squeezing them tight. Speaking from his heart he said, "I'm so sorry."

"Armend." Ersilia cupped his face. There was genuine affection in her eyes which tugged on his conscience without mercy. "Don't be sorry. You did a wonderful thing for us this evening. We know much more than we did. Thank you so much."

"That's right. It was your first time doing this. We know it's difficult and we appreciate it," Silvio patted him on the back. "Are you feeling okay? You don't look so good."

"I could use some fresh air if you don't mind."

e∕ɔe∕ɔ

Armend sat outside on the steps of the brownstone apartment. It was a clear night. Not many stars were visible, although the big city lights couldn't dim the brightness of the waxing moon. Almost full, it illuminated his surroundings in a comforting glow. He took a deep breath and noted how different the city air was compared to the country.

Sofia and her family. He groaned silently to himself. He had a hard time processing the fact that he knew the person responsible for their trouble and that he was partly to blame.

The door creak open and Sofia sat next to him. As gentle breeze blew by, he caught a whiff of the sandalwood incense she had burning inside the circle. "Feeling better?" she asked.

"A little."

"You did great in there. Especially for a virgin," she teased.

"Thanks, but I don't feel like I was much help."

"That's not true. If my dad could have, he would have his security on their way to the Catskills tonight. I'm sure he'll wait until the morning."

Damn. That didn't give him much time to figure out what to do.

Sofia rubbed her bare arms up and down to keep warm. He took off his jacket and put it around her, his hands resting on her shoulders.

"Thanks. That feels good," she said. They sat together, content in their silence. Armend had had a fleeting thought he might take a chance, tell her everything, and enjoy the time he would have with her. But after this evening's developments, it was out of the question. He was nothing but trouble for her and her parents. He had made up his mind. After tonight, he would stay out of her life. It would be hard, but it was for the best. He took his hands away.

"It's getting late. I should get you back home."

"I'll stay here tonight. I don't have to be back tomorrow until my meeting with Aaron."

"Sofia, I don't think—"

She put her open palm up to him. "Armend. We've already discussed this."

He relented. "Are you going to your parent's reception tomorrow night?"

"I haven't decided." Sofia stood. "Thanks again for your help. Don't forget to come back in and make a quick sketch of the cabin. Good night."

"It was nice having some of your magic tonight," he said. "Even though it's gone now, it was exhilarating."

She kneeled down and whispered in his ear, "It's not all gone. I left you a little." He started to say something, but she put her fingers at his lips. "Use it wisely or I'll pay you a visit. It won't be a social call." Using him as leverage, she rose to her feet and started to go inside. Before she shut the door she asked, "What's your last name?"

"You don't know?"

"No. One more thing you've never told me about yourself."

Tired of sitting, Armend stood as well. "Zogu."

"Thanks." She closed the door.

Armend stared at the decorative doorknocker with the name "Palmalosi" engraved on it. When he was sure she wasn't coming back out, he flew down the steps and sprinted to the corner of the block. He took out his cell phone and dialed. When the man with the slight limp answered, he shouted into the phone, "What the hell are you doing threatening people I care about?"

CHAPTER 7

You cannot shake hands with a clenched fist. –
Golda Meir 1898 – 1978, Israel Prime Minister

Aaron Nichols sat across the kitchen table from Sofia. She had been hospitable and polite. They went through the normal pleasantries and he apologized for his fellow congregants' rude behavior. He wasn't sure what to do next. He discreetly let his eyes roam around the room. As far as he could tell, it was a normal kitchen. There was nothing blatantly out of the ordinary except for the suspicious broom leaning in the corner and the crow standing on the windowsill watching the black cat on the counter give him the evil eye.

"You have a lovely home."

"Thank you. Would you like a cup of tea?"

"I don't want you to go to any trouble," he said.

She rummaged through different canisters of tea. "It's no trouble."

Aaron's fingers drummed the top of the table. His left leg bounced up and down. "Please, no thank you," he said, not sure what kind of tea she intended to serve him.

Sofia came back to the table holding a can. "What's wrong, Aaron? You don't want to try my famous witch's brew," she asked pulling out a familiar looking tea bag. "Lipton?"

He felt his cheeks turn five different shades of red.

"You can laugh. It *was* a joke. If you don't think I'm funny that's fine. I promise not to turn you into a toad or anything."

"I'm sorry. I came to apologize and I'm not behaving much better than they did."

"Oh no, you're very well-mannered compared to them."

"Can we start over?" he asked.

"Sure. I'm just a person, like you. Our only difference is we practice a different religion." In a lighthearted gesture, she hit her forehead with her palm, "Oh, and you're a man and I'm a woman."

Yes, she was most certainly a woman, a very attractive one at that. "You should take your act on the road," he said.

"If I left, what would your friends do with their day?"

"Point taken."

"I could show you around the Preserve."

"I'd like that."

☙☞☙

Sofia handed Aaron a bottle of water. They rested on a bench overlooking the Hudson River. Even on an overcast day, the view was remarkable. "Thanks," he said, opening it. "It's beautiful here."

"I'm very grateful I'm able to live and work at such a wonderful place. What do you do for a living?"

"Well," he said, with a chuckle. "My family will tell you I don't have a real job. It's hard for me to sit at a desk all day. I love photography and I love to sail. I have an old sailboat I'm fixing up. When I'm not snapping pictures or working on the boat, I freelance and create websites for people. I work mostly at night. That leaves my days for the two things I really want to do."

"Do you have someone special in your life?"

He took a drink and smirked. "Why do you have a love potion for me?"

"Of course, I do." She laughed. "But I wouldn't give it to you. We don't play with people's free will like that. You'll have to win the girl on your own."

"The man here yesterday, is he your boyfriend?"

Sofia turned her head away. "No."

"Oh," Aaron said. "He seemed protective of you."

"He works for my parents and feels the needs to look after me. He has someone special in his life."

"I'm sorry to hear that. I can tell you like him."

"It's that obvious?" She studied the man next to her. He was tall and thin with sand colored hair and light eyes. He wasn't her type, but was nice-looking in his own right. The crazy thing was that he was exactly her sister's type. Adelina, too, was restless, loved photography, sailing and was an expert swimmer. She drifted from job to job, uninterested in the positions her business degree offered. With her magical powers to aid her, Adelina was off on a new adventure with a group of ghost hunters.

The witch and the Pentecostal Christian—what a match that would make. *Ugh, I'm becoming my mother.* She put her head in her hand and giggled.

"What's so funny?" he asked.

"Nothing." She changed the subject. "I do have a proposition for you though. Next year, I'm hosting a summer camp for kids. I could use some pictures, a brochure, and my website updated. Are you interested?" He seemed excited at first, but after a moment, his face dropped. "Of course, I'd have to see your work," she added. "Do you have a portfolio?"

"Yes."

"What's wrong? Are you worried people may not approve of you doing a job for me?"

"Maybe...I don't know." He hung his head and pushed the dirt around with his foot. "If I was to work on your website, I'd have to know exactly what you believe."

She scratched her head. Where to begin? "I'm a *Strega*, born into a long line of Sicilian witches. My family has practiced *La Vecchia Religione,* the Old Religion, for thousands of years. The biggest difference between our religions is that we worship both Goddesses and Gods. Depending on the situation, most of the time, women have the strong spiritual power. We believe we are part of nature, not superior to it. We harm no one, unless it is to defend ourselves, and believe anything bad we do comes back to us three-fold. Because of that, we never strike first but will fight back with the intent to win. Due to our reverence for the Earth and nature, we are considered Pagans."

"Sounds like Karma," he said. "Can we walk while we talk?"

"Sure." They strolled down a well-manicured path that led to a small building.

Aaron hesitated. "What about the magic?"

"Ah," Sofia smiled. "That's what intrigues everyone the most." He wasn't ready for a demonstration, so she explained it the best she could. "Mother Earth is full of energy. Witches aren't jaded by the belief systems, cultures, and societies that tell us that it's wrong or evil to live in our true state as part of nature. We harness that energy and use it when needed.

"Every human has the ability to tap into that power. You could, too, if you wanted. It would take time. You would have to peel away the layers of ideology you've been taught and strip down to your true, authentic self, the way nature intended." He stared at her, his jaw open, as if she had three heads and six eyes. "Okay, that's enough for today."

As they reached the end of the path, there was a gathering of women at a large table. One woman called out, "Hello, Sofia."

Sofia waved back. "Enjoy your picnic." She turned to Aaron. "Look, the last stop on the tour is the gift shop, like any respectable tourist attraction."

He opened the door to the shop and Sofia walked in ahead of him. "Who are those ladies?"

"They're a local group of seniors who meet here once a month." A light bulb went off in her head. "I have another proposition for you."

"I haven't agreed to the first one yet."

"My new proposal is for your congregation. I'd like to invite them to celebrate their Sunday service here one morning. What better way to feel close to your God than to worship outside?"

"That may be too much to ask," he said.

"Why? They're here most of the time anyway. If it's easier, I won't be here."

"They don't hate you, Sofia."

"I know. However, they don't understand me and they fear what they don't understand. I would like that to change. I don't care if they do it in baby steps, as long as they are taking some steps."

"I—don't—know."

"You can't possibly be the only person at your church with an open mind. Why don't you approach certain people who you think may be willing and see what happens. You may be pleasantly surprised.

"People get married here. Other less mainstream religions have celebrated here. That's how we all learn about each other in a positive way."

"How much would you charge us?"

Sofia clicked her tongue. "No charge. The great outdoors belongs to everyone." She led him over to a small section of the gift shop. "Although a small donation to the Preservation of the Bog Turtles is always appreciated."

"I'm not sure I've met anyone exactly like you, Sofia."

"I'll take that as a compliment." The clock on the wall chimed five times. It was time to get ready for her parent's reception. "I am sorry, but I have to run." They moved toward the door.

"Thank you. I had an informative time," he said.

"I'm glad you came." She grabbed a card off the counter near the register. "Here's our business card with the website. I'll write down my cell and email. Call me next week and we'll pick a day to meet."

They shared a friendly handshake.

CHAPTER 8

Love is when you a shed a tear and still want him.
It's when he ignores you and you still love him.
It's when he loves another girl, but you still smile
and say, 'I'm happy for you,' when all
you really do is cry. – *Anonymous*

Armend watched Sofia emerge from the small group of people and walk toward the bar. She looked beautiful, but to him she was always beautiful. Their eyes had met once since she arrived. He didn't acknowledge her and turned away. It almost killed him, but it had to be done. Standing near a corner on the far side of the room, he wasn't worried about her seeing him. He was an expert at admiring her from afar.

She left carrying a glass of red wine in her hand. A handsome, well-dressed man intentionally stepped in front of her causing her to stop. He offered his hand and introduced himself. After a short conversation, the man put his hand on the small of her back and led her into another room. Pain pricked at Armend's as if someone wrapped him in barbed wire. It was an omen. Thanks to Sofia's magic, Armend knew that the man wasn't who he seemed.

❧❧❧

Sofia tried to listen to what Peter, who was trying to pick her up, was saying. He was nice, but he had one too many drinks in him. Not that it mattered. All she could think of was how Armend ignored her when she first walked into the gallery. She noticed a change in him last night after their talk on the stoop. He came back inside and drew a sketch of a cabin found in any wooded area in any state. Then he said good-bye and left. She wasn't sure he would be at her parent's reception tonight, but took the chance he might be.

As Peter explained in explicit detail the great importance of his job, Sofia felt the heat of Armend's body behind her.

"So I see you decided to come this evening?" he murmured in her ear.

"Excuse me, Peter." She faced Armend. "Oh, I didn't know you were here."

"I'm leaving in a few minutes," he answered. "I don't think we'll be seeing each other again."

"Armend, are you ready to go?" A lovely young woman appeared at his side and slipped her arm around him.

He took a step closer, boring his eyes into hers. "Good-bye, Sofia." He undid the woman's arm, took her hand in his, and walked away.

Sofia gulped hard at the finality of his words and squeezed her eyes shut pushing back her tears. He had taken her advice and told the object of his desire how he felt. The young woman seemed to take the news well.

"Sofia, are you all right?" Peter gave her back a slight rub. "Would you like to leave and get a drink?"

Spinning on her heels, she gave him a good hard stare. Against her better judgment and throwing caution to the wind, she said, "No, I'd like to have a few drinks if you don't mind."

෴

Sofia and Peter walked around the corner and down a few blocks. The first place they came upon was a seedy hole-in-the-wall bar. It reeked of smoke, stale beer, and piss. He gave her an uncertain glance, but she assured him this place would do fine. As they entered the dimly lit room, she was one of three women in the bar. The other patrons were all men, playing pool or standing around looking for a fight. To say she was overdressed was an understatement.

Tired of the voice in her head warning her to leave, she retaliated by telling the voice to screw off. The bleak, dismal atmosphere of the bar matched her mood and was a perfect place to drown her sorrows.

She could take care of herself. If anyone bothered her, she would use her eyes. In a matter of minutes, they'd be putty in her hands doing whatever she asked them to do. Sometimes she didn't even have to go that far. When her eyes changed, most people usually freaked out and ran for the hills.

Her makeshift date handed her a drink. He motioned her to a booth in a murky corner of the bar, slid in close to her, and gulped down his shot. Peter loosened his tie and put his arm around her. She removed his arm and slid away from him only to feel the wall up against her back.

"Sofia, don't be like this. I thought you liked me"

He leaned into her personal space and her annoyance grew.

"Peter, I'm sorry if I gave you the wrong impression. I—"

"No, you gave me the right impression," he said with a crooked smile. He stroked the side of her face. "Something's bothering you. Let me help you."

What she really wanted was to grab him by the balls and squeeze hard. But deep down she knew she would follow the witch's creed and not hurt him, especially when she had a defense that was harmless. "If I were you, I'd back off."

Ignoring her, Peter once again put his arm around her and pulled her close. He let his free hand drop to her thigh and caressed the inside of her leg. She allowed him the privilege. With her fingers, she moved his face toward hers. "Peter, would you look at me please."

ৎৡৎ

The young woman remained close enough to Armend to keep a cautious eye on him, but far enough not to be in his way.

"I'm sure I heard the lady tell you to back off."

"How about you mind your own fucking business," Peter fired back.

"How about you don't speak like that in front of a lady?"

"Yeah, what are you going to do about it?"

"I have it under control," Sofia said.

Armend grabbed the man by the top of his shoulders and yanked him out of the booth. "I'll show you what I'm going to do about it." He pinned the man's arms behind his back.

"Don't hurt him!" Sofia yelled.

When none of the other men even blinked at the brawl about to take place, the young woman felt she had to do something to stop him. "Armend! Please don't get into trouble. Not tonight, I need you," she pleaded.

He glanced at her then back at the woman named Sofia. Nevertheless, he dragged the man out of the bar and onto the street. The man, resisting his attacker, knocked over chairs and a table on his way out. A number of glasses crashed to floor, shattering. Before she went to make sure Armend didn't do something stupid, she hurried over to the woman in the booth and sat down.

"Sofia, right?"

"Yes."

"I'll be brief. Armend will be furious if he knows I'm speaking with you." With a sense of urgency, she spoke directly. "I don't know what's going to happen tonight," she said, lowering her gaze, "but whichever way it goes, Armend is going to need you."

"What are you talking about?" asked Sofia.

"Please listen to me. If you care about him come to his apartment tomorrow night around seven o'clock."

"He wants me to leave him alone."

"One more thing," she said. "It's important. Don't believe what you *think* you see and hear in the apartment. Things are not what they appear."

"Wait. I don't understand," Sofia said.

"I have to go. Please do what I say."

The woman ran outside, didn't see anyone, but heard faint voices in the distance. She darted down a dark, secluded alley and found the two men. Armend had the man by his collar pushed up against the building.

She ran up to him. "Stop it!"

Armend peered deep into the man's eyes. The man couldn't break away from his stare as his blue eyes turned an aqua color.

"What the hell?" the words trembled from his lips. "Are you some kind of freak?"

"Peter, this isn't the time to start name calling."

"How do you know my name?"

"That's not important. What is important is that you never bother Sofia again. Do you understand? If I even see you looking in her direction, it'll be the last fucking thing you do. Got it?"

"Yes," the man said. Beads of sweat formed on his brow. "Just stop looking at me with those creepy-ass eyes."

The woman saw that Peter was terrified. "Armend, that's enough."

He loosened his hold on the man and pushed him down the street.

"Can we go back to your apartment now? We don't have much time," she implored.

He checked his watch. "I have one more thing to do. I'll make it quick, I promise."

With no other choice, she conceded and followed him back toward the bar.

∽∾∽

Glad to be alone with her pity party, Sofia moved from the booth to the end of the bar. Most of the regulars were in the other room gathered around the pool table. There was one man and two women at the other end of the bar. With her drink half gone, she signaled the bartender she needed another.

In the mirror behind the bar, Sofia watched him approach. He stood behind her and waited. When she didn't speak he said, "Let's go."

"No. I'm going to finish my drink."

"Sofia, please. This is not a place for you to be by yourself."

"You proved to everyone you're a bully. I'm sure they'll leave me alone."

"You're welcome, but it's time to go now."

"I can take care of myself."

Glaring with defiance at each other in the grimy reflection of the mirror, neither one flinched. Armend reached in his pocket and threw some cash at the bartender. "Sorry about the broken glass. This should cover any other damage." The bartender grabbed the money and grunted his thanks.

Relieved he was leaving, Sofia was caught off guard when her stool spun around. His hands took hold of her waist and lifted her off the chair. When she landed on her feet, he grabbed her hand and dragged her out the door. The young woman was outside waiting for him, impatience branded on her face. "We have twenty minutes," she said.

"I know, I know. I'm sorry," he replied. "Let's start back to my apartment. When we get closer to the gallery, it'll be easier to hail a cab."

They stopped at the corner. When he let her hand go, Sofia almost walked away. How dare he impose himself on her evening? She could get her own damn cab.

Instead, she stood there fascinated with Armend's *Girlfriend of the Year*. She was more interested in the time than the fact her new boyfriend was helping another woman.

With Armend distracted hailing a cab, Sofia moved closer to the woman and attempted to capture her with her eyes.

"Oh, no you don't," she said waving her finger at her. "I know what you're trying to do. Please, just do what I asked and take care of him."

A cab screeched up to the curb. Armend opened the door. "Come on, Sofia. Get in."

Bone tired and wanting to be alone with her thoughts, she didn't put up a fight and climbed in the back seat of the car. Armend gave the driver her parent's address then threw a wad of cash on the front seat.

"Goodbye," he said and slammed the door. Sofia leaned back on the cold, leather seat as he put his arm around the woman and strolled to his apartment.

CHAPTER 9

Don't ever give up on something or someone that
you can't go for a full day without thinking about.
– *author unknown*

Sofia procrastinated in front of Armend's apartment door
holding a bag stuffed with cat food, litter, and a small
bed. Lautner was snug against her chest purring. It was a
few minutes past seven. It had taken her all day to decide
whether to do what the strange woman who had captured Armend's heart asked of her. In the end, she rationalized she
promised Armend his familiar and she liked to keep her prom-
ises.

Loud music blared from inside his apartment and he
didn't hear her knock. She looked at Lautner. "Now what?"

His response was a loud, "Meow."

"Okay, but if he's mad I'm blaming you." Sofia jiggled
the doorknob. When it didn't stop, she pushed opened the door
and walked in.

The spectacle she stumbled into tied her in a knot of
heartache.

Armend, his shirt off, was on his back on the couch. Gina,
clad in bra, panties and stiletto heels was on top of him, her
legs straddled at his sides. She was kissing him hard and he
was returning the favor. Between the music and their attention
focused on each other, neither of them noticed her standing
there.

Sofia closed her eyes and heard the woman's voice in her
head. *Things are not what they appear.* She opened her eyes
and took a closer look. This time she realized Armend wasn't
touching the half-naked woman. His arms weren't wrapped

around her in a passionate embrace. His wasn't fondling or caressing her. His right arm was up against the back of the couch, his left arm stretched out to the side with his hand clenched. Something dangled from his fist.

As Gina's hands inched to the top of his sweats, Sofia had enough. "Armend," she shouted over the music. "I need to talk to you."

He jumped at the sound of her voice. "Sofia?"

Gina whisked her head up. She wiped her auburn hair out of her face and glared at Sofia.

"Gina, can you give us a few minutes, please." Sofia struggled to get the words out.

"Armend doesn't want me to leave, do you, baby?" she purred stroking his chest.

"I think it might be best," he whispered. He sat up and, with a gentle nudge, got her off him.

"Why?" Gina snapped. "Because she's the boss's daughter?"

"I'm sorry," was all he said.

Her face flushed with fury and humiliation, she pulled her dress over her head and stood up. Lautner leapt out of Sofia's arms, screeching at Gina. He ran between her legs, almost tripping her. Catching her balance, she screamed, "Get that fur ball away from me."

Sofia scooped Lautner up in her arms. Taking the cat's lead, she snatched Gina's hand as she flew by and peered deep into the woman's eyes. She freaked out at the intense stare Sofia gave her and stepped back. "What kind of weird shit are you pulling on me? Let go of me right now." She ripped her hand away and slammed the door on her way out.

"What are doing here, Sofia?" Armend had his back to her, turning the music off.

"I brought you Lautner. I told you I would." She put the cat down and forced herself to concentrate on anything besides his broad shoulders and strong arms. Lautner ran toward him.

"Hi, buddy," he said, lifting his familiar into his arms. "Ouch, he's got sharp nails."

"It may help if you put a shirt on."

"Are you sure?"

"Yes, please put your shirt on."

"I mean about Lautner." He set the cat on a chair, grabbed his shirt, and pulled it over his head.

"Yes, he belongs with you." Her cheeks blazed with heat. "Thanks for asking Gina to leave. Lautner didn't like her. It'll help his transition if she isn't here." She removed two ceramic bowls from the bag. "I didn't get a good feeling about her. I think she's using you. I'll put his food and water in the kitchen."

"So what?" He plopped himself and his feline friend on the couch and shrugged. "I'm using her, too."

Determined to act nonchalant about Gina, Sofia got everything ready for his new roommate. "I'll put his cat litter in the bathroom, but you'll have to show him where it is."

"I'll do it later."

When she was through, she sat next to him. He looked like death worn over. The dark circles under his eyes were the size of quarters. His beautiful blue eyes were blood shot.

"Are you all right? What happened here last night?"

"I spent the night with Ardiana. Not that it's any of your business," he said looking down at his hands.

His words stung, but she remembered the woman's words one more time. "What's in your fist?"

"Nothing." He slid his palm into the large pocket of his sweat pants.

"Let me see it. It looks like my earring. I lost it the day we went to the hospital. If it's mine I want it back."

He opened his hand. "Take it. I have no use for it."

Sofia noticed the imprint the earring left in the palm of his hand. Reaching for her jewelry she asked, "Why were you clutching my earring? Were you trying to feel me somehow?"

"Why would I do that? I was more than happy to feel Gina, until you interrupted."

"I wanted to thank you for last night."

"I didn't do it for you. I did it for your parents. They love you very much and they've been good to me. They'd be devastated if anything happened to you." Armend jumped to his feet.

"I think you've accomplished everything you came for. Lautner and I are together, I'm fine, and you've expressed your gratitude for last night. You can leave now."

"You have quite a revolving door of women, don't you? Is that fair to your new girlfriend?"

"Everything is fair when a guy is just trying to get laid."

"Are you trying to shock me? It won't work. Remember, I saw your soul in its most vulnerable state. This isn't who you are. I don't know what game you're playing and I don't care. You've made it clear you want me out of your life. I'll oblige. You won't ever see me again." She grabbed her purse, marched to his door, and stopped. "One more thing. Don't mistreat my cat or misuse my magic. I'll know if you do, and I'll come after you. Everything I gave to you, I'll take away and leave you worse off than you were."

She turned the knob.

CHAPTER 10

Every man is afraid of something.
That's how you know he's in love with you;
when he is afraid of losing you.
– *author unknown*

Armend's stomach constricted with fear and regret. For her own good, he'd pushed her out of his life, but tonight he had gone too far. His behavior was unprovoked. At this moment, never seeing her again scared him more than anything that would happen to him in December. He called out to her. "Sofia—wait."

She paused with the door half open. From behind her, he raised his arms over her head and shut the door. He lingered with his body arched over hers. "I'm not all right. Please stay." He took a chance and slipped his arms around her waist. Her body stiffened and he held her tight. He pressed his forehead into the back of her head and inhaled her scent of lavender and sandalwood. "You're right. I didn't mean any of those things I said. I thought I could do it alone. I didn't let you in to protect you. But everything is crashing down around me. Sofia, I need you."

"I can't do this anymore. It's too many mixed signals. Let me go or tell me what's going on."

He spun her around. "I swear I'll tell you everything."

"You look terrible. What happened to you?"

"A lot," he said warily and led her to the couch. Sofia curled up in the corner. He sat as close to her as he dared. Lautner snuggled between them.

"I keep your earring with me so I can feel you whenever I need you."

"I don't understand."

Armend gently tilted her chin up. "Don't you see? You're the one I want, not Gina. It's been you since I first laid eyes on you eight months ago at the Gallery. We never spoke, but I feel like I've known you forever."

He waited for her reaction. She pulled her knees to her chest, wrapped her arms around them and considered what he said. "I'm the—"

"Yes, you're the woman I'm in love with."

"What about Ardiana?"

"I'll get to her later. I blocked you on purpose so you wouldn't find out. I don't blame you for being skeptical. I know every time we get close, I push you away." Armend offered his hands to her. "Go ahead, see for yourself. Even with your magic inside me, I'm beat. I haven't slept in thirty-six hours and don't have the strength to stop you."

Sofia interlocked her fingers with his and stared at him. He waited for her eyes to change color, but they remained their same haunting hazel color. Without warning, she softly brushed her lips against his. "I believe you. I don't need to see for myself." She squeezed his hands. "If we're going to be together, we have to trust each other."

Surprised by her swift, but sweet kiss, he wanted more. He released his grip from hers and ran his fingers through her long hair. "My sweet, Sofia, I do trust you. Sometimes I think you and your family are the only people I *can* trust."

She parted her lips in an alluring invitation. He drew her head close and kissed her. For months, he fantasized how it would feel to kiss her, to love her. She tasted as wonderful as he knew she would. She eagerly returned his kiss, rolling her tongue around his mouth, driving him crazy.

"Meeooww." Lautner, wedged between them, leapt off Armend's lap.

Armend let go of Sofia. There was so much more to say. "I'll tell you anything you want to know." He raised her hands to his lips and kissed them. "I'll warn you though. You're not going to like everything I have to say."

"Fair enough, just promise me you'll tell me the truth. No matter what."

He nodded his agreement.

"Why did you push me away and go to Gina?"

"I don't go to Gina. She comes to me. I slept with her once. It was the night after we spoke at the Albanian exhibit. I went to the pub across the street to drink you out of my heart. My feelings for you were growing stronger and I knew we couldn't be together. Out of nowhere, she was next to me and before I knew it, we were in the gallery parking garage, in the backseat of her car." Ashamed, he couldn't look at her. "It was all my anger, fear, and frustration coming to a head and I took it out on her. Now she thinks I have some unbridled passion for her, but I don't. I'm not proud of it, but I used her."

Curious about her reaction, he slowly raised his gaze to her. "Go on," she said.

"The same thing happened tonight. I'd brushed her off since the one night we were together, but when she knocked on the door, I let her in. I had nothing to lose. I tried to force you out of my life, but you're stubborn."

"Come here," she said.

Armend rested his head on her lap and nestled into her. She was a welcome refuge from his horrible nightmare.

"Why do you keep saying we can't be together?" she asked.

"We can. For a little while, but I'll be leaving in December."

"*That's* what's holding you back? Where are you going? Albania?"

"No, Sofia." He rolled on his back and stared up at her. Not bothering to wipe the tears from his eyes, he said, "I'm going to die."

CHAPTER 11

Being deeply loved by someone gives you strength,
while loving someone deeply gives you courage.
– *Lao Tzu, founder of Taoism, 600 BC – 531 BC*

Naples, Italy ~ 1760:

Ilir Zogu was the second-born son of Zamir and Dashurie
Zogu, Albanian immigrants who settled in Naples, Italy.
Italian high-society accepted them because of their flour-
ishing spice trade. Ilir's older brother, Basmir, recently be-
trothed, continued to climb in the ranks of the Italian Army.
Ilir yearned to fight for Italy, the only homeland he had
known, but his body was not healthy like Basmir's. Ilir was
broken. Born with a leg deformity, he walked with the help of
two wooden crutches.

With his parents travelling abroad and his brother in the
military, Ilir lived alone in the family manor with servants and
tutors. His legs nearly useless, he was educated in the arts.
Happier with a violin on his arm than an artist's brush in his
hand, he gladly took his instructions in music.

Despite his kindness and handsome face, no respectable
family would offer their daughter's dowry to a man who might
not be able to sire a healthy child.

To fill his lonely days, Ilir befriended a lovely servant girl
named Ambra, who saw past his limp to the man he was. They
would stroll through the gardens together. She was patient with
him and his slow pace, always encouraging him. One day he
overheard the cooks gossiping about Ambra and her family of
spell casters.

The next day, after his music lesson, he called for her.

"Ambra, I need your assistance in writing a love song that will send me my true love."

"Why me? Can't your music teacher help?"

"He's useless. I've tried many times to write the perfect song." He lifted his instrument into his hands. "Let me show you." A few bars of a melody tweaked out of his violin then he stopped. "This is as far as I can go. I need your help. Please, I know you have special...gifts at your disposal."

She flashed him a hesitant look.

"You can trust me, Ambra."

"Very well, but you must swear to never tell a soul."

"I swear."

"Let's go for our walk."

When they reached a clearing past the gardens, Ambra left and hiked into the woods. She returned with a hand full of plants and herbs. With a stick, she drew a large circle in the dirt. "You must lie in the ring."

Ilir leaned his crutches against a rock. With a determined hobble, he made his way to the middle of the circle. "I may need help to the ground."

"You're strong. You can do it."

His weak legs not providing the strength he needed, he lost his balance and stumbled to the ground.

She giggled. "Very graceful, my lord."

He brushed the dirt off himself and laughed. She was one of the few he allowed to see him at his most vulnerable. "I'm glad to provide the lovely maiden with her entertainment for the day."

Still chuckling, she said, "You must lie down." He leaned back onto the earth. "Are you comfortable?" she asked.

"Yes, of course." He smirked. "I'm always at ease and content on the cold, hard ground."

She positioned the plants and herbs in a precise design around his body and laid a dark, twisted root on his chest. "Hold this tight against your heart and close your eyes."

She shuffled around the circle, chanting. Some of her words were Italian and some were in a language he was unfamiliar with. When the spell was over, she knelt down beside him and told him to open his eyes. "My lord, you may stand now." She handed him his crutches.

She wasn't going to help him, but he didn't mind. When he was around her, he wanted to be self-reliant.

She picked up the plants and scattered them into the woods. With her foot, she erased the circle in the dirt. They journeyed back to the manor in silence.

❦❧❦

Ilir locked himself behind closed doors and worked end-lessly, day and night, until he created a perfect composition. He practiced until he hit every note flawlessly. One evening, with a crutch under one arm and his violin in the other, he lumbered outside to the garden. He sat on a sculptured stone bench amidst the various potted lemon trees. A faint citrus smell filled the air and he soaked up the quiet solitude.

He rested the violin on his collarbone, lifted his bow, and played his song. Finished, he laid his instrument on his lap and waited. Stillness. He took up his instrument once more and this time played louder. He waited patiently and swore there was a noise in the woods. He put his violin to his shoulder and began the melody again, this time with fervor. There was movement in the trees and he lowered his violin.

A beautiful woman materialized from behind the fig trees. "I prayed it would be you," he said as Ambra moved within reach of him.

"Your song is enchanting," she said. "It drew me to you. I couldn't stay away."

"Please, sit with me." He shifted to the left of the bench. "My song is what it is because of you."

"Oh, no, my lord. The song is yours alone. You needed no help from me. You did it yourself."

"But your spell—"

"I cast no spell on you. I picked weeds from the woods and walked around mumbling, nothing more. The love in your heart wrote your wonderful song."

Her words struck him. How she believed in him, when no one else did, was one of the many reasons he loved her. "My love is for you, Ambra."

"You are always kind to me and never treat me as a servant." Her beautiful brown eyes locked with his. "I am filled with love for you, as well."

Ilir cupped her face in his hand. Her skin was soft and supple. She looked beguiling in the moonlight. He gently put his lips to hers and wrapped his arms around her. Her mouth was warm and inviting. She broke away from his embrace and shifted her position, putting distance between them.

He didn't want to ask, but knew he had to. "Is it…my legs that worry you?"

"Never," she said with a warm smile. "I love you. All of you, just the way you are."

Relief swept over him. "Then what has you upset?"

"We are foolish to believe we can be together. You, an aristocrat and I, a servant…" She added with caution, "And a conjuror of spells."

"Not to worry. When my parents return from Spain in the coming months, I will explain I want to settle in Florence. There is no better city to live when the arts are your profession. They will agree to it, I'm sure." For the first time he shared a painful admission about his family. "I've been an embarrassment to them. They'll be happy when I'm gone."

"That's not true, my lord. They love you very much."

"They provide my basic needs and educate me because they are my parents. But love me unconditionally? No, I don't believe so."

"I'm sorry."

"They may not be able to give me love, but they have given me wealth. I will go ahead to Florence, establish myself, and send for you. No one will know who you are. We will be free to live as we wish. Have faith in me, Ambra."

She draped her arms around his neck and melted into his chest. "I do."

_❧◊❧_

Ilir longed to stand tall and strong and hold Ambra in his arms instead of relying on crutches or his back up against the wall for balance. He marveled at her grace and beauty as she lit candles around his bedroom. Many women had passed through his doors provided and paid for by his brother. Basmir's theory was there was nothing so bad in the world that the attention of a willing female couldn't fix. Women came and went with no feelings exchanged. Ambra was different. She was his love.

She took him by the hands and walked with him to his bed. With a light push, she moved his left leg alongside the bed and leaned his weight to that side. Putting her right leg firmly against his to steady him, she wrapped his arms around her waist and her arms around his neck.

"Are you a reader of minds?"

"Maybe," she said. An air of mystery surrounded her.

His lips came down on hers hard and she responded eagerly. She pulled away then unbuttoned his silk shirt. Rolling it off his shoulders, she traced the outline of his chest.

"I knew you possessed a strong form, my lord," she said.

"Ilir," he said. "I want you to call me by my name."

He was comfortable with his upper body. It seemed he did everything with his torso and arms and had the strength to prove it. What humbled him was his other half. After leaving her sweet kisses on his chest, she reached for the buckle of his breeches. He stopped her. "Please, Ambra. Let me."

"Ilir," she said, slowly, "it's me. You can be you're true self."

"I know. But this one time let me do it my way."

With a quick peck on his lips, she dashed to the other side of the bed, and with her back to him, waited.

He undressed with awkward movements and crawled into bed, pulling the blanket to his waist. He admired her long, dark curls and was anxious to have her and her locks all over him.

"Ambra," he whispered.

She undid her bodice then gracefully slipped off her petticoats. His eyes devoured her sleek back and every stunning curve. He licked his lips and took a deep breath. She sat on the bed, lifted the cover, and slipped between the sheets. She drew the blanket over her breasts and faced him.

He ran his fingers through her hair. Taking the back of her head, he pulled her toward him.

"Wait," she said. "There is something I must tell you."

He smiled at her. "It can't wait?"

"No." She touched the side of his face. "You are not the first man I have lain with."

"Did you love him?"

"No. I thought I did, but that was before I met you. Now I know what love is. You fill me with happiness every day." She reached up and put her lips to his. When she did, the sheet dropped exposing her exquisite round breasts. He tenderly caressed each of her nipples.

"Where is he now?"

"Last year he suffered from a fever and never recovered."

He replaced his fingers with his mouth and let his tongue roll around her breast. She moaned and drew his head closer to her. "Are you disappointed with me?" she asked breathlessly.

"No, I love you. You're so beautiful."

She kissed the top of his head and pushed him onto his back. She leaned over him, her long silky hair brushing along his chest. Her tongue teased his neck and worked its way down his chest. Her hand reached for the blanket. "May I?"

Ilir closed his eyes and shifted his head in the opposite direction. "Yes." He didn't want to witness her revulsion when she saw the deformity of his legs. She uncovered him and he felt the heat of her eyes on the thin, distorted part of his body. She didn't speak but her actions told him everything he needed to know.

First, she kissed the top of one thigh, and then slid her mouth between his legs. He reached for her. Following her wonderful rhythm, he massaged her shoulders. In an easy, unhurried manner, she found her way to the inside of his other thigh and kissed him. Working her way down, her lips moved along one leg then up the other. She sat up, bold in her nakedness, and stretched out next to him.

"I think you are the most handsome man I know, from your dark hair and beautiful brown eyes down to your toes."

Overcome with love, he lifted her on top of him with ease. Frantic with passion, they spun around his large bed, arms and legs entangled, their tongues rolling around each other's mouth. Ambra proved to be an uninhibited lover. The last time he landed on his back, she guided him inside her. Swallowed in her warmth and tightness, he couldn't help but groan aloud. He put his hands on her hips. She loved him with a fervent pace.

Increasing his grip on her, he rolled her onto her back. Now sideways on his bed, her head was almost off the edge. She arched her back and reached for one of the many pillows scattered on the bed. Slipping the cushion underneath her hips, it raised them to an angle that allowed him to immerse himself deeper into her. They both gasped. She put her arms around him and dug her fingers into his back. Writhing beneath him, her body shivered in a spasm of pleasure. "Ilir, my love."

With her still trembling under him, he moved inside her one last time. He nuzzled his face into her neck. "I love you," he moaned and surrendered to her.

Her breasts glistened with moisture in the candlelight, tempting him with each rise and fall of her breath. He followed their lure and gently nibbled on each one. The salt from her skin tickled his tongue.

"Ilir, you're wicked," she said slyly. "I haven't caught my breath yet. Are you insatiable?"

"Only for you, my love."

"You've left me happy, but in need of a rest." She burrowed herself into his side, resting her hand on his stomach.

They lay together with nothing covering them, still warm from their passion. Naked and exposed, for the first time he was not ashamed of his body. In fact, he was liberated and at the most peace he had ever been. He kissed the top of Ambra's head and thanked her.

She gazed up at him with sleepy eyes. "For what?"

"For saving me from the lonely and solitary life I was sure I was destined to have."

❧❧❧

For the next two months, they lived as lord of the manor and servant. They slipped off together on every available occasion. After making love, Ambra would massage his legs with a combination of witch's salt and oil. Sometimes she would place healing stones on his thighs. Ilir knew his defect had no cure, but each day his muscles became stronger.

One day in the garden, he told her his parents had returned.

"They've agreed to my request to live in Florence," he said filled with excitement. He wanted to kiss her, but restrained himself. It was the middle of the day and the gardener was busy nearby. Ambra smiled and asked him to meet her at their favorite spot in the woods.

She was waiting for him as he made his way up the path from the woods. With his legs' newfound strength, he was able to move quickly up behind her. Letting his crutches drop to the ground, he put his arms around her waist, and kissed her neck.

"We won't have to pretend much longer," he whispered in her ear.

"Yes, I'm so happy." She pressed her back into him and held his hands on her stomach. "I also have news. Your baby grows inside of me."

He twisted her around to face him. "A baby?" A smile broke out across his face.

"Yes," she said cheerfully.

He threw his arms around her and squeezed. "You've given me everything I never thought I'd have. I love you so much." With quick peck to her lips, he said, "We may have to change our strategy. How long until it's…visible you are with child?"

"Two or three months. I think it was the first night we were together," she grinned and rubbed the top of his leg.

"That may not be in your best interest," he warned in a playful tone as her hand moved to the inside of his leg.

"I'm sure it is," she said with a spark of desire in her eyes. She handed him his crutches and, as the sun lowered on a late June evening, lead him deep into the woods.

Hidden in a field of tall grass, safely away from anyone seeing them, she rested on top of him. His fingers stroked her back.

"I'll miss you when you're gone. It's only bearable because a part of you is inside me." She kissed him with a deep longing.

"I know, my love. It will be a hard separation, but I have a new plan. I'm leaving this week and I need you to meet me here before I go." Reluctantly he repositioned her to his side. "When I arrive in Florence, I'll be staying at the Palazzo Lombardi. I'll inquire about a home for us, explaining the urgency of the situation—my wife, who is with child—will be arriving shortly."

"I like how that sounds," she said and reached for his shirt on the ground. "But we are not married."

"When we meet, I will give you a wedding band, but do not put it on until I send for you to join me." She held his shirt open. "I'm hopeful we can marry in Florence, but this is all I can do right now. I'm sorry." He slipped his arms through the sleeves.

"I do not need a man whom I do not know to stand in front of us and announce that we love each other and will be together forever. I know it in my heart." She buttoned his shirt. "Your parents are entertaining for dinner and you'll be expected."

"I'd rather stay here with you." He stopped her fingers from their task and pulled her back on top of him. He kissed her and ran his hands over her wonderful body one last time before she dressed. When she responded to him, he wasn't sure how he was going to leave her next week.

∾∾

It was the day of Ambra's arrival in Florence and Ilir could barely contain his joy. He was thankful for her family, their freethinking ways, and the help they provided. He didn't fully understand their religion, if that was what you could call it. They lived by the philosophy that as long as no one was harmed, you could do what you pleased. They believed sex was a perfectly natural occurrence and to be enjoyed. When Ambra told them she was with child, they were not upset or ashamed. A new life was cause for celebration.

Neither Ambra nor her mother could read or write. Her father and brothers had minimal knowledge of putting their language on paper. Pietro, her oldest brother, was the most educated and the one he had notified when the time arose for Ambra to join him. He promised her family he would repay his debt of gratitude to them in any way they wished. They asked for nothing except for their daughter to be happy and have a good life. He would keep his promise.

He was outside waiting when the carriage arrived. He wanted to surprise her with how strong he had become. While they were apart, each night he would rub her ointment on his legs, then walk until his muscles ached.

She stepped out of the carriage, accepting the driver's assistance. Ilir's heart skipped a beat when he saw her. He missed her, worried about her, dreamt about her. She ran to him, but he stopped her. "Please, my love. Let me come to you."

He put his hand on the wall for the balance, and little by little, but with no crutches, walked down the three steps to greet her. She flew into his arms and nearly knocked him over. Once again, he caught himself on the wall.

"Oh, Ilir, I am so proud of you," she said, laughing through her tears. "I knew you could do it." She pressed herself against him, "I've missed you so much."

He could find no words to express his feelings. All he could do was kiss her.

"Ahem," said the older driver with a grin on his face. "Sir, if you are no longer in need of my services, I'll let you get reacquainted with your beautiful wife."

Startled, Ilir gazed at the man. "My apologies, Signore Garelli. *Grazie, Grazie*, for everything you have done today. I am very appreciative."

With Ambra's arm around his waist, they walked back up the steps and into her new home. She wandered from room to room with wide eyes. "It's gorgeous, Ilir."

"I've saved the best room for last." He opened the door and urged her in while he waited in the doorway. There was a large four-post bed against the wall, two big windows on one wall, and a fireplace in the corner.

"I love it and I love you. Please, walk to me. I have gifts for you."

He put one crutch down and hobbled to her. When he reached her, he took her hand, let the other crutch fall to the floor, and walked the rest of the way to the bed. They sat.

"You have done so much for me I wanted to do something for you. I saved my money and bought this for you. It's wasn't the grandest, but I hope you like it."

"Ambra, you've given my more than I ever imagined I would have." He opened the box. Inside was a man's gold belt buckle, engraved with a date: *April 11, 1760*. The night he first played his song and she came to him. "It's perfect. I'll wear it every day. I'll always remember the first time we were together."

"I have one more thing for you." She untied her boots and stood up. She undid the pin in the back of her head and let her hair fall over her shoulders. With complete ease and confidence, she began to undress. Within minutes, she was completely naked in front of him. His eyes moved over her whole body, from top to bottom. His heart pounded with desire as he ogled her more-than-usually well-endowed breasts, grateful for what his unborn child had already provided for him.

"Ilir, you certainly are a man, aren't you?"

"Guilty as charged, my love."

"Could you lower your gaze? Please."

Her stomach swelled with a small roundness. She held his hand tightly against her growing belly. "This is your baby. He has been moving inside me. I couldn't wait for you to feel him."

Ilir closed his eyes and waited. In a moment, he felt a tiny pulse against his hand, then a stronger one. He fought back his tears. "Him?"

"It's a boy. You will have a son," she said and pulled his head to her abdomen.

He wrapped his arms around her and kissed her belly. "I love you both." She eased him back on the bed and soon he was lost in the intoxicating haze of her love.

❧❧❧

The moment Ilir walked through the door he knew something was wrong. It was too quiet.

"Ambra!" She didn't answer. He didn't see her in the garden when he passed by. Even with her belly increasing in size, she tended to her plants and herbs faithfully. He began to move to the back of the house when he heard a noise. "Ambra! Where are you?"

"Ilir!" she screamed.

Fear gripped at him and he hurried as fast as he could. Damn to hell his legs and crutches. He was stronger and quicker than he had ever been, but still couldn't run to her. As he turned the corner, he caught a quick ripple of her petticoat and dress disappearing behind a door. Then, blinded by a scorching pain at the back of his head, everything went black.

❧❧❧

He gradually regained consciousness. His head throbbed and he rubbed his eyes to clear his blurry vision. Somehow, he was sitting on a sofa, his crutches at his side. He let out a soft groan. "Basmir?"

"Yes, Ilir, it's me."

"What happened? What are doing here?" He jolted upright as a memory flashed through his mind. "Where's Ambra?" Panic rose in his voice.

Basmir hung his head. "I'm sorry, Ilir. She's gone."

"Thank God you're here. You have to help me," he pleaded. "Someone took her. I heard her struggling when I—" He stopped and stared closely at his brother whom he loved and knew so well. Uneasiness crept into his stomach when Basmir shifted uncomfortably in his chair and wouldn't make eye contact. "But you're aware of that, aren't you?" His brother kept silent. "Aren't you?" Ilir shouted.

Basmir sat up straight and lifted his head high. "You weren't as discreet as you thought, little brother. Amusing yourself with the servant girl is one thing, but to keep house with her and claim the illegitimate child as your own, is unacceptable. We won't allow it."

Ilir forced himself to control the wrath vibrating through his body. He must stay calm if he wanted to find out what they had done with Ambra. Let Basmir think he was the same docile man he used to be. He wasn't. Ambra's love made his legs stronger and his love for her turned him into a man with a strong and determined will.

"It *is* my child and will not be illegitimate. He will have two parents who love him."

"In the eyes of God, he will be nothing more than a bastard, born out of wedlock."

"God chose to close His eyes while creating my legs. An honorable God would close His eyes once again and allow the happiness Ambra and my child will bring me." He rubbed the top of his legs. "I can't believe you would betray me like this."

"I'm sorry you see it that way. We did this for you, Ilir." Basmir stood. "We don't want you hurt anymore."

"We? I assume mother and father had a hand in this as well?" He stood without the aid of his crutches and watched amazement wash over his brother's face. "Yes, my legs are not the weak sticks they once were. Ambra has not hurt me. You have. She loves me."

Basmir shook his head and sighed in frustration. "I see she has used her magic on you in more ways than I thought, casting a spell on your heart as well as your legs. She is very dangerous. Be reasonable."

Ilir could take no more. His patience for this conversation was over. His jaw tightened and through clenched teeth he asked, "Where is she?"

"You will never find her."

He picked up his crutches, feigning their use. With rage burning inside him and having the element of surprise, he smashed the wooden props against the left side of Basmir's head. His brother made a noise that was a combination of shock and pain. He stumbled backwards, but did not fall, so Ilir wielded another solid blow to the side of his face. Basmir collapsed to the floor.

Before he could strike back in defense, Ilir slammed the crutches hard into his abdomen, then his ribs. Basmir struggled for his breath.

"I asked you a question. Where are they taking her?"

When he didn't answer, Ilir lifted his weapon over his head and bore it down with all his might, first on his brother's left, then right knee. "Answer me!" he demanded.

Basmir rolled on his side in agony. "I—don't know," he gasped. "Some place in—Switzerland. A convent." Through his pain, Basmir managed to give his brother a condescending smirk. "She will deliver the *bastard* there and it will be sent immediately to an orphanage."

He couldn't bear to think of Ambra alone and scared in an unfamiliar place, only to have their baby ripped away from her. Combined with Basmir's betrayal, his heart shattered into a thousand pieces. "Do you think that little of me? That no one could possibly love me or that I don't deserve to be happy and have a family?"

"Time will tell," Basmir said, wiping the blood from his mouth. "She was warned not to contact you again or she would be charged with sorcery. If she really loves you, she won't care about herself."

Ilir stared down at the man on the floor with disdain. Basmir's eye was beginning to swell shut and blood oozed from his mouth. Using the tip of his crutch, he sharply jabbed him in his already sore ribs. "Get out before I kill you."

எஷை

At Ilir's direction, the ambush was quick and efficient. Ambra's brothers and father, Basilio, had a sack over each of the victim's heads and whisked them into the carriage with ease. When they reached their destination, the brothers pulled the two men and one woman out of the coach and led them into the woods. There was a fire burning to the side.

"Where do you want them?" he asked.

"There." The woman pointed. "In the clearing."

The young men led them to the assigned spot and stood unyielding around their guests, preventing them from running off. Ilir ripped the bags off their heads. "Welcome, my loving family." He had a crutch under one arm and a bottle of whiskey in the other hand.

"Ilir? What is happening?" his mother pleaded, grasping her husband for protection. Her frightened expression and his father's confusion delighted him. "What is she doing?" His mother's eyes fixed on the woman drawing a circle in the dirt around them using the blade of a knife.

"I believe the correct terminology is *casting a circle*," he answered and took a swig of whiskey.

"He's taking his revenge on us," Basmir snapped, "for the servant girl."

"Ilir, you're drunk and have taken leave of your senses. Stop this right now!" demanded his father.

"I'm not drunk enough. I wish to be numb, yet my heart still aches for Ambra and my son."

"Ilir," his mother said. "We love you and want the best for you. How can you be sure it's your child? Her kind lay with many different men."

The woman, draped in a black, hooded cloak, finished her circle in front of Ilir's mother. She pressed the tip of the blade into the woman's heart. "Think what you will of my daughter and our ways. It matters no longer," she spat at them. "She was devoted to Ilir. The child was his." She lowered the knife to her side.

"This is Luigina. Ambra's mother." He put the bottle to his lips and gulped. "Luigina, meet my wonderfully compassionate family," he said with a sarcastic sting.

"Was?" Ilir's father asked.

His balance off, due to the alcohol whirling around his head, Ilir stumbled toward them on one crutch. Taking one more swig of his drink, he glared at them. "They're dead. Both of them!"

He wanted to cry, but had no more tears to give. Basmir started to talk, but his brother stopped him.

"Don't you dare speak to me," he hissed. "I made it to Milan in my search for her. The talk of the city was of a runaway carriage accident on its way to Switzerland. The tragedy was the death of a young woman, far along with a child. Something spooked the horses. The driver lost control and they tumbled down a ravine. Ambra was thrown from the coach. The driver and the other woman passenger survived.

"I wouldn't leave the city until I found the driver, to be sure of what I feared." Ilir closed his eyes. His hands fumbled inside his coat pocket. "When I explained to him I needed information about the accident, he asked me if I was Ilir Zogu of Florence. When I said yes, he told me Ambra was barely alive when he found her. He gave me this." He showed them a ragged, crumpled piece of paper. "I was teaching her to read and write. This is all I have left of her." He hobbled to a large rock and leaned against it. "She wanted to get a message to me. That she loved me and was sorry. She was writing to me before the accident. The driver promised her on his next trip to Florence he would inquire about my residence and deliver the letter.

"Ilir," his father said and acknowledged Ambra's family. "You have our sincere condolences. It was never our intention—"

"No one cares about your intentions," he spit in his father's face. "How dare you! Why couldn't you leave us alone? We were happy and I wasn't a bother to you."

"Ilir, please," his brother pleaded.

"Enough! Luigina, please carry out what we came here to do."

The older woman lit four black candles and placed them in the directions of earth. In the north she placed salt and to the west, water. The sky was clear with a crescent moon high above them. No breeze flowed past them. As Luigina began to speak, however, clouds floated over and covered the moon in darkness. The trees rocked back and forth, as a strong wind blew in from the east. Ilir's mother huddled closer to her husband. Basmir stood defiantly. Ilir remained with Ambra's brothers to show his alliance.

"I call on the ancient crones and the power of the universe,
"To assist me as I cast this curse.
"To help us grieve our loss and ease our sorrow
"That we may feel a better life tomorrow.
"The Zogu family will surely sow what they reap
"A soul from each generation will be ours to keep.
"For you see, one you cherish
"Will die and perish,
"On the birth of their third decade.
"Until the debt is repaid."

"Ilir. *No!*" sobbed his mother. "What have you done to us?"

"You have brought this upon yourselves," he said matter-of-factly.

"Why cause innocent people to suffer? Think of Basmir's children. Think of your own children," begged his father.

"My child is dead."

"How can we repay the debt?" asked Basmir.

"You can't," answered his brother.

"Then show some compassion," Basmir continued. "At least let there be a way for us to break the curse and save our children as well as our grandchildren and their descendants. They are blameless."

Ilir stared at his family for what seemed an eternity then limped toward Ambra's mother. Together they went to the edge of the woods.

"Where are you going?" yelled Basmir. "Come back."

He took a step toward the edge of the circle, when Luigina spun around. "Stay where you are!" she ordered. In one fleeting motion, she extended her arm at him. With a flick of her wrist, sparks flew from her fingertips and towering flames sprung up and danced around surrounding them.

"I'd do as she says," advised Ilir.

Basmir retreated.

When he and Luigina were through speaking, Ilir made his way to his carriage with the aid of his crutches. He rummaged through his belongings until he found what he was looking for. With a deep-seated sorrow, he returned to their small gathering. Stopping in front of the fire, he peered into the flames then at the violin in his hand. Unable to bear having the instrument at his shoulder to play, he tossed it into the fire. He continued walking until he reached his frightened family, still clustered together amid the soaring flames. "Very well," he said to them. "We've reached an agreement." He once again reached into his coat pocket, retrieved a piece of paper and unfolded it. "Here is the music to a serenade I wrote for Ambra. I will never play it or any other music ever again."

He tore it in two.

"I will keep one half and Ambra's family will have the other. If any member or descendant of our family can recover and join the two pieces again, the curse will be broken. I'm confident it will be an impossible task to complete, but we'll give you the opportunity you've asked for." He handed Luigina the two pieces of paper.

She kneeled and placed them carefully on the ground an inch away from each other. Dipping her fingers into a pouch attached to her cloak, she positioned four, round, polished stones on all sides of the music. Holding her hands over the paper, she spoke.

"This spell may be only be broken

"Not by any ordinary words spoken.
"But with a certain deed
"Of this, you must succeed.
"The torn song Ilir composed
"Must be joined together and exposed
"Both families must agree, no one opposed
"Only then shall the curse be closed."

Luigina gathered her stones one at a time, in silence, and retrieved their half of the sheet music. Her husband took her arm and helped her to her feet. Their sons followed them into the woods, never looking back or speaking to the three in the circle or Ilir.

Ilir stepped before the barrier of fire between him and his family. "You won't ever see or hear from me again. If you try to contact me to persuade me for my half of the music, I will not respond. When the flames die down you may leave the circle."

He reached for his half of the music, put his crutches under his arms and staggered away.

ↄkøↄ

Ilir kept his promise and never had contact with his parents. But they did see him again, one time, ten years later.

He traveled to Albania and enrolled as a student at the school of painting created by the Christian Icon painter, Onufri. He tried his hand at painting, but found no satisfaction in his work. It wasn't long before he was a broken, bitter, lonely man. One of the teachers took pity on him and let him stay in a small room in the back of the painting school. At night when everyone was gone, Ilir would wash the student's brushes, prepare the canvases for the next day, and mix the colors of the paint to earn his keep. He would return to his room each night, a bottle of wine his only companion.

He returned to Naples only once.

Well past midnight, with the light from a lantern to guide him, he ventured into the garden of his family's manor. He laid one crutch down on the same stone bench he had sat on many years ago to play his song for his beloved. Using the other crutch and the help of a cane, he ended up in the field where he and Ambra would lie together. He fell to the ground and curled up in a ball. For the first time in many years, he let his memories of Ambra flood his mind. He thought of their happiness, how her body molded with his when they loved each other, and afterward when she laid in his arms, their plans to have many children. He let a smile come to his lips and closed his eyes.

That's how his parents found him. Dead in the field of tall grass.

It was October 13, 1770. Ilir's thirtieth birthday.

CHAPTER 12

*A man reserves his true and deepest love not for
the species of woman in whose company he finds
himself electrified and enkindled, but for that
one in whose company he may feel tenderly drowsy.*
– George Jean Nathan, 1882 – 1958,
American drama critic

I won't let you die."

Armend's stunning admission and tragic tale of the family curse stung Sofia's heart.

"I have no doubt if anyone could save me it would be you," he said holding her in his arms. "But I'm the chosen one for my generation and there's nothing you or anyone can do."

"Why are you so sure it's you?" She forced herself to sit up and face him. "I don't want anyone to die, but you must have cousins." She hesitated then added, "Siblings?"

"The last few years have been hell for my family. My cousins, brother, and I were all born within six years of each other. There are five of us. My father had two sons and my aunt had one boy and one girl. I have an uncle that doesn't have children because of the curse." Sadness washed across his face. "There was another aunt who was dealt the unlucky hand. She died, leaving behind a baby girl."

He didn't say anything more and Sofia didn't push him. He promised her he would tell her everything. She would let him do it when he was ready.

"Everyone else has passed their thirtieth birthday. My brother is thirty-two, married with two kids. My one cousin and I are the youngest and the last to turn thirty this year."

"When is…his…birthday?" she asked carefully.

"Her. My cousin, Ardiana, was thirty yesterday."

Sofia's jaw dropped. "The woman you were with last night?"

"Yes. I spent the night with her, but not like you thought. We sat up all night waiting. Her mother was my aunt who died. She was incredibly brave. She was scared to death and we both knew what it meant if she survived the night. Since we were the last two, we promised each other we wouldn't let the other one die alone.

"I always knew it was going to be me. I thought I had come to terms with it and didn't have any serious relationships because of it. Then I fell in love with you.

"I was so glad it wasn't Ardiana," he continued. "She has a fiancé who loves her very much."

"Last night your cousin asked me to come here," Sofia said. "She wasn't sure what was going to happen, but either way you would need me."

Armend raised his head. "She and I were born a couple months apart and are very close. She was the only one I ever told about you. She stayed with me all day to make sure I was okay. Finally, when her fiancé came, I made her leave. That's when Gina showed up."

"It was as if she knew Gina would be here. She told me not to believe anything I saw here."

"Ardiana and I were the only ones born with some magical powers. She has always had an intuition or a *knowing* of some sort. Like me, it's never been that strong, but when something is important, she comes through."

"You're lucky to have each other." Sofia decided he'd had enough for one night. "Come on. You need to get some sleep."

"Wait," he stopped her. "There's more."

"Tell me tomorrow. You're exhausted."

"No. Please sit down." He agonized over what he was about to say. "It's my uncle," he said.

"What?"

"It's my uncle sending the letters to your parents." He let out a deep sigh. "It's every generation's responsibility to try to break the curse. My uncle swears he has proof our half of the song is hidden in Onufri's painting. When he discovered the painting was here in New York he didn't know what to do. He couldn't walk into the gallery and say he needed a piece of valuable artwork to break a curse. Everyone would think he was crazy. Unfortunately, he took a different route. It was a coincidence that I happened to work at the very gallery the painting was being shown."

A sudden realization hit her as he spoke.

"Sofia, before you say anything, let me finish. He was desperate. I've talked to him and—"

She threw her arms around his neck and kissed him. "That's wonderful!"

"Did you hear what I said?"

"Yes, I heard you. There are no coincidences in this world. It's a universal sign that you're right where you're supposed to be and I can break the curse. I had a sense from the beginning the man writing the letter was harmless."

"You're not angry at me or my uncle?"

"Why would I be mad? He thinks half the sheet music is in the painting—and we have the painting. We're ahead. We have two months to find the other half. It'll be easy. We just have to use our heads." She winked at him. "And some magic."

"Easy? I think you've lost your mind."

"I'm sure it's been unbearable living with this hanging over your head. I'm sorry for everything you've gone through these last few months, but you have to stay positive." She pulled him to his feet. "You need to sleep. Everything will be better tomorrow."

"Wait," he said.

"What?" she moaned. "Is there more skeletons in that family closet of yours?"

"No." He drew her to him and folded his arms around her. "I knew you were different the moment I saw you. You're an amazing woman. I didn't think it was possible, but I love you more right now than I did when you walked in here tonight."

He bent down and let his lips melt into hers. Gently at first, but as his hunger for her grew, his kisses left her breathless. Every nerve in Sofia's body was on fire.

"It's not fair to kiss me like that when you're so tired."

"I'm not that tired," he said, a sly curl to his lips.

"Oh no, I want you well rested and at the top of your game."

"Then I better get some sleep."

She led him to the small bedroom. His bed was up against the wall. Beams from the moon shown through the small window and illuminated the room with a shimmering glow. Not bothering to turn on a light, she opened his closet door. Taking a long-sleeved shirt off a hanger, she put her back to him. She pulled her blouse over her head, taking her time. Glancing seductively behind her at him, she undid her bra, dropped it with her top, and slipped his shirt on. Knowing he was watching her every move, she swayed her hips back and forth and shimmied out of her jeans.

"Sofia. Really? Talk about not being fair, you're making me crazy."

She fastened the last button on the shirt, stood on her tiptoes, and kissed him. "Good." She crawled into his bed, close to the wall, and patted the empty spot next to her. "Come on, time to get some rest."

He left his sweats on but took off his shirt and threw it on the pile of her clothes. Sofia gulped hard. No, *this* wasn't fair. She thought of something unpleasant—doing her taxes—as he and his perfect, long, lean torso climbed into bed. He lay on his back. A single line of dark hair ran from his belly button to the top of his sweats. She wanted nothing more than to trace the tempting trail to whatever treasure awaited her at the end, but that would have to wait. Tonight he needed something different from her, a warm and loving place to rest his tired body and spirit.

She held her breath as he put his arms around her, not wanting to make a silly girl noise at his touch.

"Will you be here when I wake up?"

She let out her breath, savoring his warm body next to hers. "Do you want me to be?"

"I want you here every night and every morning."

"Then that's where I'll be."

"I love you with all my heart and soul, Sofia," he said and closed his eyes and drifted off.

She gazed down at the troubled, vulnerable man asleep in her arms and her heart swelled with a love she had never felt before. She kissed the top of his head. "I love you, too."

CHAPTER 13

There is no surprise more magical than the surprise of being loved. – George Morgan, 1894 – 1958, English playwright and novelist

Still groggy, Armend reached for Sofia. While his hands fumbled around in the emptiness of the space next to him, he opened his eyes. The sheets were cold. She had been gone awhile. He rolled on his back, stared at the ceiling, and came to grips with Sofia leaving. He couldn't blame her. He loved her optimism, but she had finally come to her senses. He was in no way a glass-half-full situation. He was definitely a half-empty glass, if not bone-dry.

This was his burden to bear alone and what he done for a good part of his life. She was young, beautiful, and had her whole life ahead of her. The last thing she needed was his cursed and recently criminal family weighing her down.

He heard a strange noise coming from the corner of the room and looked over. Lautner was staring at him. "What?"

The cat leaned backwards, with its front paws stretched forward, digging at something. Armend sat up in bed and realized he was playing with Sofia's clothes from last night. "She's still here! She wouldn't leave wearing just my shirt."

He hopped out of bed, lifted the cat to his chest, and scratched behind his ears. "Thanks, buddy." They walked to the doorway. "Hey, do you smell that?"

He and his feline friend snuck around the corner, following the sweet aroma of fresh-brewed coffee, and peeked into the kitchen. Sofia was beating eggs in a bowl and didn't see him. She and her long, perfect legs looked very sexy in his shirt.

He couldn't help but smile. Despite his mistakes, secrets, and two-hundred-fifty-year-old hex on his head, she loved him. He tiptoed back and took the fastest shower he had ever taken.

ಲಿಲಿ

Sofia felt his arms around her waist. "Good morning, *dashuria ime*." His lips found their way to her neck. His beard tickled and his damp hair teased her skin. He smelled good. She turned around and was struck once more by his steel-blue eyes. This morning they were clear and glistening at her with a desire that made her whole body quiver. She put her arms around his neck. "What does that mean?"

"It means *my love* in Albanian."

"It's beautiful."

"You're beautiful," he said, moving his hands down her back. "With you next to me, I had the best night's sleep I've had in a long time. I consider myself very well rested." He kissed her and murmured in her ear, "Will you come back to bed with me?"

Her answer was a long, hard, and deep kiss. He picked her up and she wrapped her legs around his waist. He carried her the short way from the kitchen to the bedroom. As soon as her feet hit the floor, she lifted his shirt over his head. Sliding her hands over his remarkable chest she asked, "What do you do to stay in such good shape?"

"I do a little boxing at the neighborhood gym."

Sofia stroked a small bruise on his right side and gently kissed it. "Is this from boxing?"

"Yes, I have a sparring partner, Jimmy, and sometimes he gets a good shot in." He slid his arms around her. "I don't want to talk about Jimmy right now."

He kissed her one more time and they tumbled onto the bed. She landed on top of him, put one leg to each side of him, and sat up. He touched her cheek and let his fingers leisurely stroll down her neck until he reached the top of her shirt. He undid the first button. Sofia's heart raced with excitement at the anticipation of loving this man who affected her on so many levels. Since the day she'd delved inside him and gotten a rare glimpse into his aura, he'd had a peculiar hold on her.

Then Dave Matthews began to sing.

∽∽∽∽

"It's your parents."

"It's certainly been awhile since they unwittingly interrupted me during an intimate moment," she teased. "You better answer it."

He reached over to the small table and grabbed his phone. "Hello."

His attempt to have an intelligible conversation with Silvio was pointless. Sofia nibbled at his neck and crisscrossed her tongue back and forth over his throat and top of his chest. He didn't even hear the question he blurted a response to. "I'm sorry—Silvio—I—um—overslept." He squirmed beneath her. "Could you—hold on a minute?" he said catching his breath.

He put the phone under the pillow to muffle their conversation. "Sofia," he whispered. "Please don't do this when I'm on the phone with your dad. It's too weird."

"I'm sorry," she said with a mischievous grin. "I'll behave."

He put the phone to his ear. She placed her head on his stomach, her tongue dancing around his belly button. Her warm mouth was at the top of his sweats and traveling south.

Not able to take much more, he gasped, "I'll be right there, Silvio. Let me finish my…breakfast." He hung up and the phone dropped to the floor.

He ran his fingers through her hair. "Oh, Sofia," he murmured happy to let her do whatever she wanted for as long as she wanted.

Her head perked up. "Well, you've done it now."

"What?"

"You said you'd be right there," she said undoing her legs from around him.

"What are you doing?"

"If you're not there in five minutes, he'll be banging on your door." She got off the bed.

"You're leaving?"

"Yes, and you're coming with me." She offered him a sympathetic look. "I'm sorry. You're too damn cute and sexy and hard to resist. We better get going."

She left him in need of another shower. A cold one.

ↄ⁄ↄↄ⁄ↄ

They walked into the elevator together. "You owe it to Gina to tell her you won't be in need of her company anymore."

"Really, why is that?" he said matter-of-factly.

Sofia giggled and ran her hand up the inside of his leg. "Don't be mad at me."

"Troublemaker," he stopped her before she caused him any more problems. "I can't be mad at you."

The elevator chimed as it reached the main floor and the doors opened. Standing there was Silvio.

"Oh, I was just coming up to see you." Sofia gave Armend an 'I told you so' look. "Sofia? What are you doing here?"

She hugged her father. "Let's go to your office."

The three of them walked into the large, airy office. Silvio had small replicas of famous artwork hanging on three walls. The fourth was lined with books, on all topics of art, and photos of his family. The first thing that always caught Sofia's eye was a picture she had drawn for her father when she was seven years old. He had framed it and put it front and center on his desk.

They no sooner sat down, when Ersilia walked in. "Good morning, Sofia. What a nice surprise. I didn't know you were coming this morning."

"We have news," she announced. "Armend and I are together now."

He took hold of Sofia's hand. "I love your daughter very much."

"Of course you do, dear," Ersilia said. "We've watched you torture yourself for months. Always staring at her from a distance and hanging on her every word, but you would never speak to her."

"So we decided to do something about it," Silvio said. "We asked you to pick us up at Sofia's then made plans so you would have to spend the day together. We had a feeling something might spark between you two."

"We?"

Silvio laughed. "Ersilia gets all the credit. She loves to play matchmaker."

"We couldn't be happier," Ersilia said.

"You may change your mind after you hear what I have to say," Amend said. "I made this appointment with you the other day because there are a few things I need to talk to you about." With hesitation in his voice, he retold the tale of his family, their curse, and his ill-fated lot in life.

"Oh, you poor thing," exclaimed Ersilia. "Of course, we'll do whatever we can to help you. You're fortunate to have Sofia on your side. If anyone can help you, it's her."

"I know how lucky I am to have Sofia in my life," he said.

"Armend, there's more, isn't there?" Her father removed his glasses and folded his hands in front of him. "You said your ancestor, Ilir, gave up music and went to Albania to study at Onufri's school. I own a gallery and you work here. I have a famous Onufri painting locked in my vault and a person who wants the painting is threatening me. Who is it?"

"It's my uncle," he said in a low voice. "I'm sorry. I didn't know until Sofia gave me the power to see who sent the letter. I've talked to him and he doesn't mean any harm. He's adamant that one-half of the sheet music is hidden somewhere in the painting. I'm going to the Catskills today to talk to him. I'll make everything right, I promise." Armend propped his hands on Silvio's desk and bent close to him. "He's just trying to save my life."

Ersilia walked behind Armend's chair. He sat back down and she rested his hands on his shoulders in a show of support.

Sofia waited for her father's reaction. He was a fair and honest man and had never let her down before.

"I see," he said leaning back in his chair. "You three are in solidarity."

"Yes, we are," his wife, answered. "I know how fond you are of Armend. He hasn't betrayed us and has been honest and up front about his uncle."

"Sofia," her father asked. "Do you love him?"

"With my heart and soul," she said. "It will be easier to break the curse with the help of the painting and with your blessing, but I can do it without it—and I will."

Silvio studied the three of them. "Very well," he said. "Armend, I understand your uncle's motivation and I can even sympathize a little, but I can't and won't condone his actions. The painting is scheduled to go back to Albania later this week. You talk to your uncle today. If you bring me back credible proof the sheet music is in the painting, I'll see what I can do to stop it from shipping."

"Thank you, sir." Armend offered his hand. "I don't know what to say."

Silvio shook his hand. "Don't thank me yet. I need proof."

CHAPTER 14

"Sex is hardly ever just about sex." –
Shirley MacLaine, American actress

At sixty-five and widowed for a year, Pastor Hayward Marshall prided himself with his physical fitness and distinguished good looks. A full, thick head of salt and pepper hair, he swam laps three times a week and filled the other days at the gym. His only day of rest was Sunday.

After forty years of faithful service to God and being a loyal and devoted husband to his wife, God rewarded him with the succulent creature next to him to help him with a certain problem he was having. Who was he to refuse God's gift?

Slumbering on her side with her back to him, he yearned to touch her once more. With one finger, he traced her curvaceous outline beginning at her shoulder. He continued down the slope of her waist and up the incline of her hip.

"You're awake?" she purred and drowsily rolled over. "I can't imagine what made you so tired. It wasn't little ole me, was it?"

To say he was shocked when this young woman walked in his office with a proposition was an understatement. Aware he was a silent partner in the group of developers who lost the environmental court case to Sofia Palmalosi, she, too, had a bone to pick with the conjurer of spells. How she had come to have this information, she wouldn't say. That intrigued him. God certainly did work in mysterious ways.

Her proposal was honest and to the point. She, too, would like Sofia's amusement park for tree huggers run out of town. Her words were strong. Words his wife would never have used. She was edgy and dangerous. That excited him. She assured him no one would be hurt, just frightened enough to re-think their position. That suited him. Fear was a wonderful tool to get people to do what you wanted. The only thing she need-ed to bring her plan to fruition was money. They finished their conversation over dinner and sealed the deal later at her apart-ment.

Just thinking about losing to the Palmalosi witch made him see red. He was certain they would win and had the archi-tectural drawings to prove it. With one bang of the judge's gavel, his plans were shattered. Instead of a mega church, school, and religious center, bog turtles and other creatures lived happy and safe on prime real estate. It was ludicrous. Worse, it provided the enchantress the perfect ruse for what really went on there—devil worship.

"No, my dear, it wasn't you," he lied. "Although you pro-vided me with a vigorous workout, I'm afraid I didn't sleep well last night." Another lie. He'd slept like a baby as she had exhausted him the day before as well.

He reached for her. She swayed toward him, her lips open, inviting and pressing hard against his. She positioned herself so her lovely breasts dared him to caress and kiss them. He obliged.

"You're a wonderful mystery," he said between nibbles. "But it may be advantageous if you told me why you dislike Ms. Palmalosi so much."

She lifted his chin, leaned down, and kissed him. Before he knew it, he was on his back. "You needn't worry yourself about that," she said, her head between his legs.

She had quite a flair for this particular art of lovemaking and whenever he questioned her reasons for revenge, she im-mediately entertained him with her talent. He didn't really care about her motivations, but he made sure he asked about them, often.

What he did care about was that she did what he wanted, in his bed and out. Then everything would be just fine.

❧❧❧

Men, she thought to herself as she casually flicked her tongue down his stomach, were all the same. Weak and pitiful. They considered themselves strong, smart, and in control. But with a flutter of an eyelash, a glance at some cleverly presented cleavage, or a brief swing of the hips, they were putty in most women's hands. He had been one of her easiest conquests. Considering his disdain for woman who practiced magic, his reaction when he discovered who he had been sleeping and conspiring with was a wickedly delicious bonus.

Because he was a man with cash, he assumed he was in charge. She let him believe it, but she was the brains behind this business arrangement. *Let's face it, I have him right where I want him—by the balls.*

What he didn't know was that Sofia was the consolation prize. She couldn't wait to bring that arrogant bitch down a peg or two, but her main objective was Armend. Another easily led male. Just thinking about what she was going to do to them made her giddy with pleasure.

She heard him moan, "Oh, God," and praise her gifted tongue and mouth. He wasn't the worst lay she ever had since she instructed him there was more than one way to have sex. His wife probably died of pure and utter boredom.

He tugged her hair and groaned louder. Good, she would be through here soon. She actually had something important to do today.

As long as he did what she asked and kept the cash flowing, everything would be fine.

CHAPTER 15

*Our most basic instinct is not for survival but for family.
Most of us would give our own life for the survival of a
family member, yet we lead our daily life too often as if
we take our family for granted. – Paul Pearshall*

Armend parked Sofia's Prius in front of his uncle's cabin. The car may be eco-friendly but in no way was it six-foot man friendly. He fit in the car like his size-twelve feet fit in a size-eleven shoe.

This isn't how he'd wanted to spend his day. He longed to be back at his apartment with the door locked, cell phone off, and Sofia all to himself. If life demanded, they might emerge sometime late Sunday evening, unless he could persuade her to stay until Monday. Instead, they were in the Catskills until tomorrow.

"Your uncle knows I was coming with you?" she asked as she opened the car door.

"Yes. I told him we're together now." Armend opened his door, wishing he had some grease to allow his knees to slide out from under the steering wheel with ease. He twisted his upper torso, hooked his hands on the roof of the car and eased himself out with a groan. "He also knows you're a witch and the daughter of the gallery owners he was threatening."

"What did he say?"

He walked around to her side of the car. "That you being here should make for an interesting conversation," he said with a smirk.

"What about Lautner?"

"He's happy to have him here. Apparently, he has a mouse problem." He opened the back door to Lautner's low-pitched chirp. The feline wasn't happy enclosed in his carrier and had told them so for entire ride. "I know how you feel, buddy." He sat the carrier on the ground. "Not much shakes my uncle. He's seen a lot in his lifetime." He bent down to undo the latch. "Can I let him out?"

"Sure. He won't wander far from you." The cat leapt out and rubbed himself against Armend's legs, purring his relief at being free.

As they walked toward the front porch, they gazed at the woods surrounding the cabin. It was late fall and most of the trees were barren, although the mountains were a lush green with hemlock and evergreen trees. There was a slight chill in the air. "It's beautiful here," she said. "I haven't been in a couple years and forgot how close I feel to nature here."

The front door burst open and a man emerged. Even with all the turmoil he had caused the last two weeks, Armend was glad to see him. George was a robust man with a larger than life personality. He lumbered down the steps toward them.

"Armend! It's wonderful to have you here." His arms enveloped him in a loving, but strong embrace.

"*Xha Jorgji.*" He undid himself from his uncle. "This is Sofia, *dashuria ime.*" He reached for her hand. "Sofia, this is *Xha Jorgji*, my uncle George."

Sofia extended her hand. "It's nice to—"

"Sofia! Welcome. Please, call me George. You're even lovelier than Armend described," he said beaming. "I understand you have been *his love* for many months. I'm glad he mustered up the guts to tell you how he felt."

"I'm—"

"I know. Certain events have transpired in the last few weeks, causing some tension between our families. I would like to apologize and hope we can put all that in the past. I know Armend is important to both of us and we'll do whatever we have to keep him safe. Won't we?" He opened his arms wide. "May I?"

Sofia giggled and waited a moment to speak. "Of course," she said and walked into his bear hug. "It's nice to meet you,

George. Yes, I love him very much and would do anything for him."

"Good." He put his left arm around his nephew and his right around Sofia. "Then we better get started." They walked into the cabin together with Lautner following close behind.

☙☙☙

The inside of the cabin wasn't what Sofia expected. Cheerful and decorated with a feminine influence, it was tidy and spotless. Armend could have used a few housekeeping tips from his uncle. This was not the typical home of a life-long bachelor. Fresh flowers sat in a vase on the kitchen table. Pastel colored eyelet curtains hung at the windows.

As the two men talked, the family resemblance struck her. Armend was six foot, but his uncle had an inch or two on him. George, whose hair had been as jet-black as his nephew's at one time, now had sprinkles of gray. He was clean-shaven and although Armend's beard covered his face, their features were similar. They shared the same dazzling blue eyes.

"What makes you so sure the music is hidden in Onufri's painting?" she asked. "My father would like solid proof if you expect him to try and keep the piece of artwork at the gallery."

"A wise man, indeed," replied George. "Come with me."

When they followed him into a small room off the kitchen, Sofia noticed his limp. Against the wall in front of the windows was a large table covered with boxes, mountains of papers, stacks of book, and a magnifying glass.

"This is years of information accumulated by our ancestors and present day family in our quest to break the curse." They stepped closer to the table. George opened one of the boxes. "Most of the items in these cartons are notes. Immediately after the curse was placed, Basmir travelled to Florence and talked with anyone who had any contact with Ambra and Ilir." He slid a much smaller container across the table. "This one has the few facts gathered about Ambra's family. From what we can tell, they stayed in Italy, but left Naples, moving from city to city." When he removed the lid, the box contained a solitary book. "It may not look like much, but twenty years ago it led me to something wonderful."

"Twenty years ago! Why didn't you tell me?" Armend's body tensed and Sofia could sense his irritation, but she stayed out of it. It was between the two men.

"You were ten. We didn't know you were the chosen one at the time and there was more work to be done. And—if we're being honest—you tend to fly off the handle."

"No, I don't. What about the rest of this stuff? It directly relates to my life or lack thereof." Armend's voice rose. "I've felt so helpless, like there was nothing I could do, when I could have been combing through all this. My parents left for Albania without even telling me so I couldn't come along. What's the hell's wrong with all of you? Do you think I enjoy waiting around every day to die?" He threw his arms up in frustration and stomped toward the door.

"Armend," George said.

"What?" he snapped.

"Are you through?"

"No. I'm pissed and I think I have the right to be."

"Good, because if that pissed you off, what's behind this locked door will really upset you. I don't want you to calm down just to get all riled up again. It's not good for your blood pressure." The older man winked at Sofia.

Armend glared him. "I'm glad you think this is a joke."

"You know better than that." George took a key out of his pocket and inserted it into a padlock. "I wouldn't have spent most of my adult life working on the curse if I didn't take it seriously."

"George, why don't you get whatever else you'd like to show us out of hiding?" Sofia suggested. "We'll be right back."

She led Armend to the kitchen and he fell into a wooden chair near the table. She came up behind him, kissed the top of his head, and massaged his shoulders. "Take a deep breath." Moving her arms down his chest, she placed her hands on his heart. He leaned back against her and relaxed. "You need to let go of all the negative energy you've been carrying around," she told him. "It's not healthy and clouds your judgment with anger."

"What are doing to me? I feel all tingling and your hands...they're warm, no, they're hot."

"Is it bothering you?"

"No. It feels good."

"Then close your eyes and unwind." Sofia rubbed her hands over his chest and back to his shoulders. She caressed his neck and kneaded his ears between her fingers. Finally, she rested her hands on the top of his head. "Feel better?"

"Wow. I do. Not only better, but lighter somehow." He reached behind him and pulled her onto his lap. "What did you do?"

She circled his neck with her arms. "I took away all your harmful energy."

"And put it where?"

"Don't worry about it. Eventually it will get dispersed throughout the universe."

"It doesn't hurt you in any way, does it?"

"No."

He drew her into him. The effect he had on her was instant and sent all her senses overflowing with pleasure. It wasn't the new-relationship-inspired release of hormones. She had been through *that* plenty of times. When his blue eyes gazed into hers, he saw deep into her soul. When he touched her, his hand caressed her spirit.

The room started to spin. Even though his kisses left her delightfully dizzy, this was different. It would only get worse. She eased herself way from him.

"I was thinking we could finish up everything with my uncle this evening." There was a hint of desire in his eyes as he spoke. "Drive back to the city, have enough food delivered to last till Monday, stay in bed, and forget about my damn curse."

Sofia steadied herself by putting her hands on his shoulders. She forced a smile and, with one hand, playfully tugged at the beard on his chin. "You're incredibly sexy and so is your offer, but George would be disappointed if we left early. I think you should go back in there and see what secret he has behind door number two. Take Lautner with you. He can help you figure out what is important and what's not. Where is he anyway?"

Armend's eyes shot to the corner of the kitchen. Lautner was about to torture a frightened mouse he had trapped.

"Lautner! You know better than that." Sofia climbed off Armend's lap, took a step, and grabbed the counter for balance.

"Sofia, are you all right?"

"Yes. My legs fell asleep." She bent down and picked the mouse up in her hands. "Let me put him outside. I'll be right back."

"He's just being a cat," he said.

Feeling nauseous, she flew out the back door.

The rush of fresh air in her face gave her a brief respite from the queasiness. She dropped the mouse and it scurried underneath the cabin. She staggered into the woods hoping Armend was with George and not looking out the window at her. She didn't want him to see her like this; it would only upset him.

When she was deep into the woods, she knelt behind an old oak tree. The dark energy she had absorbed from Armend was battering her insides. Her body ached to get rid of it. On her hands and knees, her body convulsed. The black mucus rose up the back of her throat. It wasn't until it spewed out from her mouth on the cool autumn ground, that she felt better.

CHAPTER 16

Recognize that the other person is you.
– *Buddhist proverb*

"What do you think, buddy?" Armend asked as Lautner slinked up and down the table, using his nose to rifle through all the papers.

The cat's green eyes sparkled and he jumped in the box containing the book about Ambra's family. He popped his head up, rested it on the edge of the box, and purred.

"Smart cat," said George. "How's the mouse hunt coming?" He rubbed between the cat's ears. "He's right. That's an important part of the puzzle." He limped toward the door he had previously unlocked. "But I think you should see this first."

When George swung the door open, instead of a closet, it revealed a small storage area. Ducking his head, he leaned in and disappeared.

"Can I help you?" ask Armend.

"No, I know exactly where it is." In the midst of shuffling boxes, a distinct "ouch" echoed out into the room.

"Are you okay?"

"Yes. I always forget I can't stand up in here."

Armend waited patiently, wondering what was taking Sofia so long to return. Thanks to her, he was calm and, for now, possessed a brighter outlook on his situation. Although, it might be only temporary, he appreciated it. The thought of his time with Sofia ending in two months burned at his core. On top of that, the time they did have together had to be spent trying to save his neck. He wished he could sweep her away to some exotic place to play and have fun. Unfortunately, that wasn't in the cards for them.

When a loud clamoring noise resonated from inside the small quarter of the room, his attention returned to his uncle.

"That woman! I love her to death, but wish she wouldn't move my things around," he grumbled.

"What woman?"

He slowly backed out of the tight fitting space. "Gisella."

"Who's Gisella?" asked Sofia.

"There you are." Armend said. "Where have you been?"

"You forgot Lautner's things in the car. Are you even going to remember to feed him?" she joked. "After playing with a mouse and cat litter, I thought I should wash up."

"Now that everyone's here I can show you the piece de resistance." George brushed specks of dust off his sleeves and handed Armend a book.

"What's this?" The minute the book touched his palm a shiver ran up his spine. He pulled a chair out from the table and sat.

"It's Ilir's journal."

Armend stared down at the old, tattered, leather-bound book. It fell open with ease and the musty smell of its age floated through his nostrils. The pages were yellowed and stiff.

"Be careful," warned his uncle. "The pages are fragile. We've already lost parts of some of the entries."

"Ilir, who reaches from the grave to inflict death and sorrow on his family for two hundred and fifty years." He handed it back to his uncle. "I want no help from him. I'll beat him and his damn curse on my own."

"It wasn't only Ilir. Basmir, their parents, and Ambra's family all had a hand in it. There is plenty of blame to go around. It was a long time ago and right now you have to set aside your feelings. The best way to defeat him is to let him save your life," his uncle pleaded. "It's in this journal he writes of hiding the sheet music in the Onufri painting."

"No." He continued to hold the journal out to his uncle. When he wouldn't take it, Armend let it drop to the floor with a loud thump.

"Armend." Sofia kneeled beside him. "What if you could get inside Ilir's head? You have the power to know how he felt, right or wrong. You don't have to sympathize with him, but maybe it will help you understand the reason for his actions."

"You mean…"

"Yes. You have the strength to glimpse into the past and get the answers you need."

His beautiful Sofia, the voice of reason, always trying to find the good in even the most despicable people. "What if I hate him even more afterward?

"What if you don't?" she asked.

Knowing he couldn't refuse her or win this argument, he relented. Sofia left the room and returned with a plain brown pouch with frayed edges and a few small rips that had been sewn. "What's that?"

"It's my Nanta Bag, an ancient pouch of the Strega. This belonged to my great-great grandmother. It has everything I need for witchcraft on the go." She laughed. "We don't need to cast a circle, it's not a spell, but we should cleanse any negative energy from the room."

"Can I help?" asked George.

She handed him a sage stick. "Can you light this for me? It will purify the area."

Armend watched as Sofia dimmed the lights and lit a few candles. She walked around the room carrying the sage. "All you have to do is concentrate like you did with your uncle's letter." She kissed him for good luck and stood next to George in the corner of the room.

He picked the book up off the floor and held it tightly between his hands. Lautner lay at his feet.

He began to focus his attention on Ilir's diary. His eyes started to flutter. Once again, his senses heightened. The scent from the sage burned his throat and his eyes watered. Lautner's purring boomed like a lion's roar. He pushed all that from his mind and soon the pictures began flashing in his head. Slowing them down to a reasonable pace, he was able to see two people in a garden.

"I see Ambra and Ilir walking. She's a stunning young women and he loves her very much." He spoke in a low whisper, his own voice deafening. "He feels inadequate except when he's with her. She tells him how strong he is and that he can do anything he puts his mind to." He paused. "I can see his legs. They are…unpleasant.

"They are making plans. Both of them are thrilled with the baby growing inside Ambra." Armend swallowed and moved the images forward to their life in Milan. "When he hears Ambra struggling he is overcome with panic and fear. He tries, but he can't get to her fast enough. He can't protect her as a man should protect a woman. She's gone and it's his fault. He has failed her and his child."

Armend wiped the perspiration from his brow and moved the book around in his sweaty hands to get a better grip. "Betrayed by one family and his other family taken away, a dangerous fury grew inside him." Armend clenched the journal until his knuckles turned white. "By the time he makes it to Milan it's too late. All he has to remember her by is a small note. He will never hold his son. He is inconsolable, his grief and guilt, all consuming. He will never forgive himself or his family."

Armend sat back in the chair and closed his eyes. He began to breathe heavily. George made his concerns known to Sofia. She assured his uncle Armend was fine. They spoke briefly. Armend let the diary fall to his lap and clasped his hands to his ears. He wanted them to stop screeching. Sweat trickled down his face. He lifted the book from his lap and continued.

"The family is huddled together in a ring of fire. Ilir is drunk and filled with a cold, deep hatred. The curse has been placed. He'd hoped vengeance would bring him relief. It hadn't. He feels nothing, but emptiness and hopelessness.

"He is talking with Luigina. She tells him Basmir will be the first to die." Armend's shoulders slumped and his head drooped forward. He was silent for a few moments. "At Luigina's words, Ilir is motionless, the cruel consequence of his actions hitting him hard. He is sick to his stomach." Armend slowly straightened up. "She does not want to provide a way to break the curse. Ilir offers her a deal. He agrees to die in Basmir's place on his thirtieth birthday if she will allow a remedy to the curse. She accepts, with the condition that the solution must be difficult, if not nearly impossible. Ilir nods his agreement. She puts her hands on his head and mutters something in his ear. The pact is sealed."

Armend had had enough. He could have continued on, to see what Ilir did next, but he was exhausted. "No more." He shoved the book off his knees and it landed at his feet.

"Wait! One more thing, please," George pleaded. "I didn't realize you had become more experienced with your talent. This is wonderful." Using Armend's chair for balance, he picked up the journal and put it on his nephew's lap. "Go to the end of his entries. The day he left for Italy, he wrote about the painting and the music. Can you see the landscape he's referring to? If you can, we have our proof."

"I'll try," he said warily. "I'm tired."

"I know you can do it."

Armend laid his palm on the back cover of the book and started to see an impression. The picture was cloudy as if he were looking through a fogged-up window. He deliberately used all the energy he had left to bring it into to focus. "I see the painting. It's a field of tall grass with trees in the background. It looks like the special place he and Ambra would go to be together. It triggers unwanted emotions inside him. He— he—it's fading. I'm sorry I can't see anymore."

He made his mind go blank, pushing away the scenes from the past. His eyes began to flutter and the noises in the room returned to a manageable volume.

Sofia sat in a chair across from him, their knees touching. "How do you feel?"

"Like I could sleep for hours."

"I'll get you a drink and some food." She pushed her chair away from him.

"Wait." He grabbed her hand. "You were right. I'm glad I did it. I could feel his desperation. It's how I would feel if you were taken from me. I wish he wouldn't have acted on such impulse, but I understand his anguish."

"We tend to make bad decisions when we are badly hurt. We'll do whatever we think will help ease the pain at the time, not thinking about any future outcomes," she said.

"He regretted it immediately and tried to make amends by sacrificing himself to let his brother live. I would have never known that if I hadn't looked back."

"We can never truly understand another person until we can see and feel things the way they do. You're lucky you have that ability."

Armend felt George's big bear arm around him. "She's right. You gave our most despised ancestor a little humanity. A part of him we were never able to see before. I know it will help us through this. I'm very proud of you."

"Thanks." He had a sudden pang of guilt for snapping at his uncle earlier. "After I eat, I need to change my shirt and wash up."

"Good," said George. "When you get back, we're off to the hospital."

"The hospital? What for?" asked Armend.

"So you can meet Gisella, of course."

CHAPTER 17

When you forgive, you in no way change the past,
but you sure do change the future. – *Bernard Meltze,
1916 – 1998, American radio host*

Armend splashed cold water on his face, rinsed his neck
and upper body, his skin sticky from sweat. He was
refreshed, had a full stomach, and was in a better
mood. He unzipped his duffel bag and on top was the shirt Sofia wore to bed last night. His mind wandered to how inviting
she looked, how good it was to have her in his small bed, and
their brief time together this morning. It awakened his desire
for her and he went back to the hall, picked up her overnight
bag, and put it in his room. It was a modest cabin with little
privacy, but he wanted her lying next to him, even just to
sleep. Since it was a cool October afternoon, he slipped on a
brown Henley and went in search Sofia and George.

Their voices echoed from the front porch. He walked
through the living room and listened through the screen door.

"I think if you show my father Ilir's account of his last
day in Albania before returning to Naples," Sofia said. "He'll
do whatever he can to help. He has firsthand knowledge of
Armend's ability to see into the past, so he'll be totally on
board. I'm sure of it."

"Sofia, I'm so glad Armend has you. He's always been a
loner, but the last few years it's been worse. He would never
let anyone close to him. You changed that. I know you two
will be happy. I see the way he looks at you."

"He's touched me in a way no else ever has. I'll be by his
side for as long as he'll have me."

Armend stood rigid. Was it possible they were close to breaking the curse? Did he dare hope to escape his fate? A fate so many others were unable to avoid. Should he allow himself to dream of a long, normal, life with Sofia? She was in his soul and belonged with him forever. But how long was his forever? Two months?

No. He wouldn't let himself to go there just yet.

The screen door squeaked open and he stepped onto the porch. He plopped down in a red Adirondack chair next to Sofia. "I'd like to join in your enthusiasm, but you're forgetting one important thing. We need both pieces to break the curse."

❧❦❧

Gisella sat propped up in her hospital bed in the darkened room. The blinds, drawn tightly, blocked her enjoyment of the late day sunshine. She held a cheap plastic pair of sunglasses in her hand. George had driven her to the emergency room yesterday morning. Since she was dehydrated, they hooked her up to an IV immediately. She had battled diarrhea and vomiting for a day and a half. Dismayed at her slow recovery, she thought she would be better by today. Instead, a new symptom plagued her, Mydriasis. Her pupils stayed fully dilated. The least bit of bright light blinded her. The doctors ruled out a minor stroke and trauma as the cause. They asked her about recreational drugs. As a young woman in the seventies, she took pleasure in the occasional joint, as did most people of her generation, but that was long ago. A specialist would visit her tomorrow.

"Can I bring you some Jell-O?" asked the nurse. "My shift ends in a few minutes."

"No. My friend George will be here soon. He'll get me something if I want it. Enjoy your evening."

The nurse refilled her water pitcher. "Why don't you put your sunglasses on? I have to open the door to the bright hallway. I don't want it to bother your eyes. Good night."

Gisella slipped the glasses on and burrowed deep into the pillows. She closed her eyes, ignored her nausea, and thought about her soon-to-arrive visitors. George, the love of her life, loved his nephew like a son. Two years ago, when Armend and Ardiana were the last two who hadn't turned thirty, everyone, including Armend, assumed he was the doomed family member. Ardiana's mother had been the victim of her generation and never had two members of the immediate family been chosen. Did the curse have a shred of decency? No, a curse was malevolent and couldn't be trusted. Since then, Armend crawled further into his lonely shell and his disgust for Ilir and Ambra's family increased.

What would his reaction be when they met for the first time today? When he learned Ambra's brother(s) was her great, great, grandfather?

ಌಌಌ

Armend didn't like hospitals. Being a visitor and not a patient made it tolerable, barely. The smell, the atmosphere, and the sterility of the surroundings made him uncomfortable.

He didn't have a clue why his uncle was so secretive about Gisella. All he'd told them on the ride here was that they met twenty years ago when she was thirty-five and he was forty. But Armend would soon find out as they were outside her door.

Lying in the dimly lit room was a woman with short, dark hair, wearing large sunglasses. He couldn't tell much about the rest of her features, the glasses hid most of her face. George shut the door behind them, walked to the side of the bed, and kissed her. She put her arms around his neck and returned his affection.

"Your eyes haven't gotten better?" he asked softly.

"No, I'm afraid not." She glanced at Armend and Sofia with her hand held out. "Hello. You must be Armend and Sofia. How nice to meet you both."

Armend shifted closer to the bed, his hand extended. She removed her sunglasses and he jumped back. Her eyes were eerily wide open. In place of her irises were large circles, black as the night. "Are you...all right?" he asked.

"Yes. My pupils are fully dilated," she smiled. "I feel like an owl."

"Armend, Sofia, this is my love. Gisella—" Armend's hand was in hers as George finished the introduction. "—Rossi."

Armend's arm swung away from her like a pendulum. With narrow eyes, he shot his uncle a fierce look.

"Armend, what's wrong?" asked Sofia.

He didn't answer and directed his attention at the Rossi woman. "What the hell do you want with us? Are you here to make sure I'm six foot under in December, where I belong? I bet you can't wait to dig the goddamn hole."

"Armend! Apologize right now," George growled, and with two large strides he was face to face with his nephew, fists clenched at his sides.

"Can't you see what's going on here?" Armend's voice rose with anger. "She's only with you to get our half of the music. Then the curse will never be broken."

"Sofia," George called out. "Take him outside and calm him down. He has it all wrong."

"No. I would like him to stay," Gisella announced calmly.

Armend's head spun. How many more times was the uncle he loved going to screw him? He sought out Sofia, the only one he could count on. She had seen all of him, the good and the broken, and loved him despite it all.

While Sofia gently massaged his shoulders, she whispered in his ear. "You know I love you and am always on your side. They've been together for twenty years. I think you need to hear them out."

"Please sit down here with me," Gisella said. "Sofia, can you drag that chair over for Armend."

He stared at the thin, tired looking woman. "I'm sorry," he mumbled, his head down. "I shouldn't have accused you of anything. I know my uncle cares deeply for you."

"Don't worry," Gisella assured him. "I know you're upset and frightened. No one wants to die young." She shuffled the pillows behind her. "We have a lot to tell you, but first I had hoped you'd try to forgive my ancestors for the harm they've caused your family. It may be hard to do, but it will help."

Armend's jaw tightened and apprehension travelled up his spine. Sofia stroked his hair. He hesitated. "Yes." His tongue struggled to get the words out against his dry mouth. "I forgive you." He let out a loud sigh. "My family wasn't innocent. Ilir initiated the curse." As soon as he spoke the words, a heaviness, that clung to him for far too long, was gone.

"Gisella is right," Sofia said. "If the cursed person offers an act of kindness or forgiveness to the person, or in this case the family, who cast the spell, it weakens its power."

"How do you weaken a death spell?" he asked solemnly. "Will I be comatose for the rest of my life instead of dead?"

George slapped his nephew on the back. "Twice in one day. I'm so proud of you.

Armend looked up at his uncle. "I need to know what the hell is going on."

CHAPTER 18

Hatred is a very underestimated emotion. –
*Jim Morrison, lead singer and lyricist
of The Doors, 1943 – 1971*

She held a Styrofoam container in one hand and plastic utensils in the other. She peered through the small window of the hospital room door and watched the four of them intently. At first it appeared they were arguing, the mood tense, but now they seemed relaxed. Gathered around the bed, they were talking, even smiling. Wasn't it mature of them to work out their differences?

Yes, so much so she wanted to puke. She squeezed her left hand tight around the plastic knife.

How dare that old fool, George, bring his nephew to the hospital? The men of that family were pricks and continued to treat her family's women like whores. Take what they want and discard them like garbage. It began with Ilir, that weak, useless cripple, right up to George and his treatment of her mother. She would never forgive him for having her committed. As soon as he got her out of the way, he went after her aunt.

Her eyes scanned toward the corner of the room at Armend. She knew how *that* was going to end, with him dead. That, she would make sure of.

Her hand pulsed harder around the knife, the plastic teeth grating against her skin.

None of this would be happening if the old witch would just die. She should have been dead yesterday. Let her fight the poison churning through her body all she wanted. She couldn't win.

In her fury, she clutched hard at the knife one last time. Blood trickled down her wrist and a drop splashed on the sparkling white hospital floor. She stomped on it and smeared it across the floor like a dead bug. She wiped the blood from her hand on her dark blouse and turned to leave.

It was time to up the ante.

CHAPTER 19

We can never judge the lives of others,
because each person knows only their own pain
and renunciation. – *Paul Coelho, Brazilian novelist*

Armend watched his uncle pace back and forth across the room. Finally, he stopped near Gisella and began his incredible tale. "Armend, when you were about ten, your father and I went back to the old country, to see the peasant relatives living in Albania. We had written on and off through the years and finally arranged a visit.

"They had trunks full of family possessions collected through the years. The younger generation didn't care about any heirlooms. The curse didn't affect them, just the direct descendants of Basmir. They let us rummage through the trunks. We found a notebook dated from the early nineteen hundreds. It was the only information we had about what happened to the Rossi family. Come to find out, they came to New York with the influx of immigrants in nineteen eighteen, moved to New Jersey, and opened a bakery." The older man shifted his weight from his throbbing leg to the other.

"Is your leg bothering you?" Armend got up from his chair and offered it to his uncle. "Sit down. Is that the book back at the cabin?"

"Yes." George moaned in relief, as he tried to get comfortable in an old hospital chair. "Thanks, that's much better. Anyway, I decided to look them up and see if it was *the* Rossi family. It was. Long story short, I started dating Celia Rossi. She was attractive, divorced with one daughter, and a couple years younger than I was. I admit my intentions were not honorable. I thought if we married, I would be able to get their half of the music. That's why I got angry when you accused Gisella. I was the one doing the using, not her.

"Celia was not an easy woman to have a relationship with. She was difficult, erratic, and possessed a coldness I couldn't break through. I didn't love her, I didn't really like her, but I was willing to do what I had to do to get the music.

"I was in the bakery one evening waiting for Celia to get off work, when a woman walked in, looked at me with a smile that lit up the room, and hurried into the back."

George laughed when Armend and Sofia's glance turned to Gisella. "Yes, Gisella is Celia's sister. I hadn't met her yet. She was working the next shift. From the second I laid eyes on her, I knew she was the one. After the introductions, I learned she was married and my heart sank. Nevertheless, I couldn't stay away from her. Over the next few weeks, I would sit in the bakery and we would talk. Finally, one night I mustered up enough courage to ask her out, and she agreed."

"But you were married and you were engaged," Armend said pointing to each of them.

George shrugged. "I loved her. It was out of our control."

"And I loved him." Gisella leaned over and patted his hand. "I truly believe people come into your life when you need them.

"Our family has seen a lot of tragedy due to this horrible curse," Gisella explained. "My niece and I are the only direct descendants left. Many of the women in our family have trouble conceiving or experience multiple miscarriages. I was never able to have children. I often wonder if it's the universe's way of punishing us for the curse, by wiping out the responsible family." She fumbled with the sunglasses on her lap. "But the worst thing is the line of madness that plagues the women. Sadly, my sister was a victim. My father and I had her committed when she could no longer take care of her daughter. I offered to take her in, but she went to live with her father. Every day I thank the Gods my niece and I were spared from mental illness."

"How can you be so sure?" Armend asked sharply.

Sofia jabbed him with her elbow and mumbled something in his ear.

"Armend, behave," warned George. He turned to Gisella with an admiring gaze. "She's wonderfully crazy, but not insane."

Gisella continued. "Yes, I was married, but when I couldn't have children, he didn't hide his infidelity. I was devastated and depressed at the news and George helped me through it while my husband slept around. He wasn't being faithful so I decided to be with George. When his girlfriend became pregnant, we divorced."

"Even though I knew she might leave me, I couldn't lie to her," George explained. "I told her who I was and the reason I was engaged to her sister. I asked her to forgive me. That's when she told me the toll the curse has taken on her family and she wanted it broken as well. She's been with me ever since, reading through old journals, and looking for clues to where our half of the music is."

"You've kept this secret from the family all these years?" Armend asked.

"Your parents know. They've even met Gisella. The time wasn't right for anyone else to know until now." George pushed up from his stiff chair and limped over to Armend. "Now that we know where Ilir hid his piece of the music, we're home free."

"Do you know where your family's half is?" Armend was terrified of the answer, but couldn't stop the question from pouring out of his mouth.

"George, will you help me up?" Gisella asked.

She moved slowly, weakened by her mysterious illness, but stood tall in front of Armend. Her fingers lightly touched the side of his face. "I've waited for a long time to be able to say this." Her wide, dark eyes sparkled. "I have the other half. I always have. It's in a safe deposit box. And I'm thrilled to be able to give—"

Armend swept her up in his arms, held her tight, and twirled her around. Her laughter filled the room, until she told him she was dizzy and lightheaded. He gently put her down and kissed her cheek. "I don't know how to thank you. You've—you've saved my life. How do I repay that?" He hugged her again. "I'm sorry for the things I said earlier."

"I know. You forgave us before you knew I had what you needed. That was important. The curse won't have such a hold on you now. We still have time before the pieces will be reunited, but you'll be in control." She reached her hand out. "George, I don't feel good. I need to lie down."

After helping his uncle get her in back in bed, he squeezed her hand one more time. "Thank you."

"You can thank me by living your life to fullest." She nodded toward the back of the room. "I wish you a long and wonderful life full of love."

Sofia. He turned. She leaned against the wall, hands stuffed in her jean pockets with one leg crossed over the other. A solitary tear ran down her cheek.

He didn't remember making his way across the room, but his body was firm against hers. One arm wrapped around the perfect curve of her back, the other hand cupped her face. His thumb lightly wiped away her teardrop. He rested his forehead on hers and closed his eyes. His mouth full of words, he didn't speak. Instead, he let his kiss tell her how he felt. They shared a tender caress at first, but soon the fire in his heart roused his need, and his lips pressed down hard on hers. Her body rose to meet his, her fingers tugged through his hair-

"Um—Armend."

He raised his arm behind him, waved his pointer finger in the air, signaling *just a minute* to his uncle. He lifted his head. "I have you and my life back. I don't need another thing."

She gave his beard a gentle tug. "I love you."

"George. Why don't the three of you go get a cup of coffee? I'm sure they have a lot of questions," Gisella asked. "I'm tired."

"I don't want to leave you alone."

"I'll stay with her," Sofia said. "You two go and we can have some girl talk."

❧❧❧

Sofia noticed Gisella's pallor wasn't good, her skin ashen and pasty. "That was a wonderful thing you did," she said. "You saved a life and made a family very happy."

"I never understood why someone hadn't tried to stop it sooner." Beads of sweat formed on the woman's brow.

"Do you feel okay?"

"I think I'm going to be sick again." She gasped and grabbed the railings on the bed.

Sofia quickly handed her a plastic container and supported her. After Gisella spent an agonizing five minutes of throwing up, Sofia guided her to the bathroom, giving her privacy to wash up.

"Thank you. I'm sorry you have to see me this way." Gisella politely declined Sofia's assistance back to bed. "I'm so frustrated. I'm never sick and like being self-sufficient. I can't image what sort of bug I managed to get."

"Do you want me to call the nurse?"

"No. What are they going to do?"

Should I offer? Sofia chose her words carefully. "Do you still practice the craft?" She opened her purse.

"A little. Is that a Nanta Bag? I haven't seen one of those in years." Gisella gave Sofia a curious stare. "Are you offering what I think you are?"

"Yes, but I need your permission."

"A healing spell?"

Sofia nodded.

"Yes. I would like that. The people here certainly can't figure out what's wrong."

Sofia gazed up at the ceiling. "I suppose if I light a candle the sprinklers will go off."

"I'm sure the hospital will understand," Gisella teased. "When we explain what we were doing."

Sofia felt an immediate kinship with the woman. She admired her stamina, determination, and sense of humor and wanted to help her. She rummaged through her bag and pulled out two large vials and one small one. "Can you sit up?" She sprinkled a dab of lavender oil in her palms and massaged the women's temples, forehead, and neck. Gisella closed her eyes and took in the soothing aroma. "Since the problem seems to be in your stomach," Sofia continued, "I'll use dried lemon balm and mint." She placed the herbs on the woman's belly and covered them with her hands.

"When I'm through speaking, I'll keep my hands pressed on your body for a little while. Then we'll be done." Sofia put her hands on top of the Gisella's. "I want you to envision yourself surrounded in a healing blue light." She summoned the Goddess of Healing.

"Goddess Angitia
Grant Gisella healing
"Of body, mind heart and spirit
"Send your healing energy
"To mend what is broken
"Center what has become unbalanced
"And soothe what is painful
"So mote it be."

CHAPTER 20

All things are poison, for there is nothing without
poisonous qualities. It is only the dose which makes
a thing poison." – *Paracelsus, 1493 – 1541,*
Swiss physician and alchemist

She ducked behind a corner as two nurses left her aunt's
room. They stopped a few feet from her and finished
their conversation. The back of her head hit the wall in
disbelief. They might have all the time in the world for chit-chat, but she did not. People were always in her way prevent-ing her from doing the things she needed to do.

"Isn't Ms. Rossi's recovery amazing?" said one nurse. "It
must have been the last IV of antibiotics. The doctor ordered a
stronger dose."

The second agreed. "Even her eyes are almost back to
normal. I bet she goes home the day after tomorrow." They
strolled away, their voices fading down the hall.

With her teeth clenched, she stood unyielding against the
wall. Recovery? They must be mistaken. It wasn't possible.
She was meticulous and didn't make mistakes.

Two days ago, she surprised her aunt with tea and home-made bread topped with a special honey spread. Honey made
from the California Buckeye, a beautiful, flowering plant hon-eybees couldn't resist.

Unfortunately, the California Buckeye is poisonous to
humans and honeybees. Most apiarists don't allow their bees
to indulge in the fatal shrub, but Mr. Bakos was an enterprising
soul and realized the benefit of letting the bees make their
deadly honey, then die. He swore on his *golyos* the honey was
discreet, potent, and would solve her problem. When she got

hold of his no good Hungarian balls, he'd be swearing *and* screaming.

Her left eye twitched as she forced herself to manage the white-hot anger searing through her veins. This was not the time to lose control. She regained her composure and remembered the thermos. The solution was in her hands.

⳾⳾⳾

Sofia, delightfully buzzed, heard George pop the third bottle of champagne. Curled up in Armend's lap, his arms around her, she couldn't remember being happier. While his lips traced her neck, she slipped her hand under his shirt and stroked the warm skin of his firm stomach.

"How about we ditch this party and celebrate in private," he murmured.

"I have one more toast," George announced entering the room. He poured them each a little of the bubbly and handed everyone a glass. "Here's to Sofia." He raised his glass in the air. "Thanks to your healing touch, Gisella is much better. She was even able to keep a little food down." He leaned over and kissed her cheek. "I just spoke with her and she's very grateful. We can't thank you enough."

"I was glad to help." Sofia's glass clinked against the others, and she took a sip. "Gisella is a strong woman. Her own energy played a part in her healing." She put her glass down and rubbed her eyes. "George, the dinner and champagne were wonderful. I'm warm and fuzzy...and itchy." She scratched one arm and the back of her neck. "I think I'll call it a night." She draped her arms around Armend's neck and murmured in his ear. "Finish your champagne, but don't be long." Her tongue flicked around the sensitive area behind his earlobe. A deep moan rose from Armend's throat. "Good night, you two."

As soon as the bedroom door clicked shut, she yanked the sweater over her head. The cool air of the room hit her skin, providing a brief respite from the uncomfortable stinging. She looked at her arms, then down at her chest and stomach. She ran into the bathroom, picked up a hand mirror, swept the hair off her neck and checked her back in the larger mirror. "Oh, no," she muttered. Peeling her jeans off as fast as she could, she sat on the toilet seat and watched large red welts appear on her legs. She opened her arms and turned her palms toward the ceiling. The marks on her arms were now festering blisters.

Her body shook and goose bumps popped up between the swelling wounds. She gripped the small sink and stood. Her bloodshot eyes caught their own reflection in the mirror. It all made sense now. She had to tell Armend and George.

She pushed the bathroom door open, ran to the bed, and rummaged through her overnight bag for something loose to throw on. She saw Armend's shirt and slipped it on, careful not to disturb the blisters on her arms. With trembling fingers, she managed to fasten the top three buttons then decided under the circumstances, she was sufficiently covered.

Through runny and inflamed eyes, she navigated down the dim hallway the best she could and reached the doorway of the small living room. The men had their backs to her and didn't see her clinging to the wooden doorframe, her shirt stained with red spots and a mixture of blood and pus seeping down her leg from the open sores.

"Gisella," she gasped, "isn't sick. She's being poisoned."

҂ѻ҂ѻ

Patience being one of her attributes, she waited in the cold, concrete stairwell on the hospital's fourth floor. It was eight-ten. Visiting hours were over and evening rounds would begin with her aunt's room. Eight-thirty. She inched the heavy door open a crack and peered to the left at the nurse's station. Quiet. Eight-forty-five. Another guarded look out the door revealed the nurses huddled around the desk busy with coffee and conversation, paying no attention to any activity down the corridor. She tiptoed into the hallway, careful to close the door quietly behind her, and made it unnoticed to the entrance of her aunt's room. The door partially open, muffled voices resonated from the television.

"Hello, Aunt Gisella."

"Hi, dear, what a nice surprise! Aren't visiting hours over?"

"I explained to the nurses I drove for over an hour to get here and they took pity on me." She dragged a chair to the side of the bed, its legs squealing like nails on a chalkboard against the floor. "They told me you're feeling much better." She sat.

"Yes. I am. I had quite a day today." Gisella pointed the remote at the television and the screen went dark. "You've never met George's nephew, Armend, have you, dear?" She shook her head. "He came to visit today with George and brought his girlfriend, Sofia. A lovely woman and a powerful Strega."

"That's interesting."

"We shared a healing ritual and within the hour I was feeling much better. Isn't it wonderful?"

"Wonderful." She agreed through clenched teeth. "I'll make sure to thank her." She held up the thermos. "I've been getting back to the craft myself these past few months."

"I'm glad to hear that, dear. Your mother would be happy."

"I went through her herbal recipes. I made you a special soup I thought would help you." Her shoulders drooped in disappointment. "I guess you won't need it now."

"That was sweet of you. I just ate dinner, but would be glad to keep it until tomorrow."

"I worked hard on it. Could you have one small cup?" She gave her aunt the same pout she did when she was a child.

Gisella gave in. "Of course, I could manage one cup."

The steaming liquid fell into the cup like a small waterfall. She moved to the top of the bed near Gisella's head and handed her the cup and a spoon. "Be careful it's hot." She watched her sip the broth like a hunter watches his prey anticipating the kill.

"This is delicious," Gisella said finishing the last bit. "What's in it?"

"Oh a little of this and a little of that, but the main ingredient is Lily of the Valley."

Gisella's head bolted up, her eyes wide with confusion. "But Lily of the Valley is—"

"Poisonous. Yes, I know." She fluffed her aunt's pillows. "Don't worry. It'll be quick. I don't want you to suffer. I'm not cold-hearted."

Gisella's hand flew toward the call button. Faster than the old woman in bed, she flicked the small remote off the pillow and onto the floor before her aunt could catch it. "There's no need to bother outsiders with family matters."

"Why?" Gisella demanded and tried to get out bed. "What have I done except take care of you when your mother couldn't?"

"Now, now, it will be easier if you relax." Shoving her back into bed, Gisella's face was bright red and sweat dripped and formed on her brow. "Hot flashes are first, then cold sweats, followed by some vomiting." With a napkin, she wiped her aunt's face. "Your pupils will dilate too, but you're a pro at that."

Gisella slapped her niece's hand away. "Don't touch me." She gasped and doubled over in pain. "Tell me why."

"You've become a problem. A highly irritating one. George brainwashed you and now you're a Zogu family sympathizer. As long as I'm alive, the curse will never be broken. They deserve everything they get."

"It's too late." Gisella managed a defiant laugh. "I've already told Armend he could have our half of the music." She took a few breaths, licked her dry lips and continued. "He knows it's in the safe deposit box."

"I'm a signer on the box."

"You don't have—" Gisella threw up a combination of Jell-O, toast, and liquid into her lap. Vomit running out her nose and dripping from her mouth, she lashed out at her niece. "A key. Only George and I have one."

"That's where you wrong, Auntie dear." A small key dangled from her hand. "When I came to visit a few days ago, I took it. You're very predictable. You've kept important things in the same box under your bed for years."

Before her aunt could react to her news, she threw up again. Pain knotted her face and she thrashed back against the bed. It wouldn't be long now.

"You only have yourself and the *wonderful* Sofia to blame. If you had let the honey do its job, this wouldn't be happening."

Gisella glared at her with hate in her eyes, but struggled to speak.

"Don't exert yourself, it will make it worse." She picked up her thermos and threw some napkins on her aunt's lap. "Yes, my first attempt failed, but not this time."

"Please."

"Don't beg. It's unbecoming. Have some dignity."

"It's not for me." Her upper body fell back on the bed. "Promise—me you won't hurt—" she croaked out her final word. "—George."

That stopped her in her tracks. She thought about her aunt's request. It wouldn't be to her advantage to have dead bodies piling up. It wasn't as if she *wanted* to kill anyone. Circumstances were out of her control. "Oh, all right. I promise."

The older woman writhed one last time in pain. A slight gurgle left her lips.

When the coast was clear, the niece walked down the hallway and into the elevator.

❧❧❧

Armend raced down the hallway with Sofia trembling in his arms, his uncle lumbering close behind. One side of her unbuttoned shirt fell open exposing the raw spots on the smooth skin of her stomach. The lesions on her legs and feet were bleeding. She gazed up at him with wide, reddened eyes. Light pink tears ran down her face, a combination of teardrops and blood. "Baby, what's happening to you?" The desperation in his voice scared him. Her eyes blinked then closed. A terror he never experienced seized his chest. "Sofia!" He kicked open the bedroom door.

"Hurry, get her on the bed," George shouted. "I'll call 9-1-1."

Armend laid her down and caressed her face, she opened her eyes, and a wave of relief washed over him.

"George," she said warily. "Please don't call 9-1-1. They won't understand and won't believe me if I told them."

"Baby, we have to call. You need help."

"Armend. No! Please, trust me."

Her pleading eyes melted his heart. "Maybe the 9-1-1 operators won't believe you, but I will. If you want me to trust you, you have to tell me what's happening to you and why. Are you in pain?"

"No, but I'm so–c–c–cold," her voice squeaked through chattering teeth. Armend pulled her shivering body close to him and covered her with a blanket. "George, go to the hospital and tell the doctors Gisella is being poisoned."

"What?"

She pulled the blanket around her neck and inched closer to Armend. "I have special curative powers. During a healing ritual, I'm able to take a person's illness or bad energy from their body into mine, but I have to expel it. It usually happens quickly, so when I felt fine all evening after my time with Gisella, I thought it was a weakened virus of some sort and my body absorbed it." She pushed the cover off her and showed her legs. "As you can see, there was a great deal of poison in her system. Someone did this to her."

George stood perfectly still, a bewildered expression on his face. "Who would want to hurt her? And she's better. I talked to her on the phone."

"Uncle George, go. Hurry, I'll take care of Sofia, you take care of Gisella."

The older man gave Sofia a quick peck on the cheek and squeezed his nephew's shoulder. He ran out the door without saying a word. Armend swore there was a tear in his eye.

⁊⁊⁊

Armend shifted his weight in order to get both arms around Sofia in an attempt to keep her warm, but she continued to shake next to him. He slipped his arm from around her and got out of bed. He took off his shirt, unbuckled his jeans, and let them drop to the floor. He stood in only boxer briefs when he heard, "Nice ass."

Her head was half-buried in the pillow with one eye visible watching him. "Even with poison oozing out of you, you're checking me out?"

"I'm sick, not dead."

"You really are going to be okay, aren't you?" She nodded. He slipped between the sheets and reached for her. "Let's get your shirt off."

"Excuse me?"

"For body heat. Skin to skin contact helps the warming process."

"No." She crossed her arms over her chest."

"What?"

She rolled onto her back and shuddered. "I don't want to be covered in red, gross sores the first time you see me."

"This is no time for vanity."

"I'm not being vain. It's a girl thing. You ask any woman in my situation and they'll agree."

"I don't think there are too many women in your shoes, lying in bed, freezing and sick because of a healing spell that I could ask."

"No." She replied firmly holding her ground.

"You'll always be beautiful to me. I love you."

She rolled her eyes. "No."

"You're being ridiculous."

Women! He got out of bed, walked across the room, and flicked the light switch off. Complete and utter darkness fell over the room. His eyes strained to adjust to the sudden blackness. Certain the bed was to the right, he stretched his arms out in front of him, took a step, and then another. Confident he was in the clear, he picked up his pace and rammed his toe into the foot of the bed.

He stumbled, lost his balance and caught himself on the corner of the box spring. "Shit!"

"Are you all right?"

"Yes, but it hurts like hell." Using the edge of the bed to guide him, he made his way along the mattress until he reached the pillows. "Okay," he sighed, "I have my back to you and its pitch dark in here. Take off your shirt." When he didn't hear any movement from the bed, his tone hardened. "Sofia, take off your shirt or I'll do it for you."

"Fine," she muttered. After a minute of rustling noises she said, "Okay."

Like déjà vu, he crept back into bed and reached for her. This time she willingly flowed to him, pressing her trembling body next to his, her hard, erect nipples against his chest. He ran his fingers down the smooth curve of her back, careful not to irritate her sores, then over her rump. He didn't need his eyes to see her splendor. His hands showed him everything. While he fought his growing desire, she draped her leg around his hip and melted into him. "Umm," he squirmed. "Sofia, maybe this wasn't a good idea aft—"

"No, please." Her breath tickled his neck. "Your warmth feels so good."

When she shook with an uncontrollable quiver, he made himself remember the real reason they were practically naked in each other's arms. She was there for him last night and she needed him tonight.

He concentrated on his throbbing toe and rolled onto his back. "What else can I do?"

"Nothing. You being next to me is all I need. People don't realize how powerful and healing the touch of love is."

She tucked herself into his left side, filling in the spot next to his heart, the spot that had been empty for as long as he could remember. He'd assumed he never found anyone he wanted to spend more than a few weeks with because, at some point, the fate of his curse would rear its ugly head. Now, he knew different. He had been waiting for Sofia, his other half.

இ௸௸

Armend awoke with a start to a loud banging. It was still pitch black in the room and, for a minute, he was uncertain where he was.

"Armend," the knocking was harder. "Please, I need to talk to you."

Without disturbing Sofia, he got up and opened the door. The brightness from the outer room basked his uncle in an aura of light. He had to squint to see him.

"How's Sofia?" he asked.

"She's much better and sleeping. What happened at the hospital? How's Gisella?"

Armend never heard such a groan of anguish come from a human being. George collapsed into him and he tried to catch the big man as best he could.

"Armend," George sobbed. "She's dead!"

CHAPTER 21

Death ends a life, not a relationship. –
Robert Benchley, 1889 – 1945,
American humorist, writer

George sat in silence and watched Sofia sleep. He promised Armend he would take care of her while he was gone. Doing so gave him purpose as his once happy world crumbled around him.

She stirred and reached across the bed. "Armend," she whispered.

"He went to the city to get your parents. He thought they would want to be with you." She rolled toward him, rubbed her eyes, and smiled through her sleepiness. "How are you feeling this morning?" he asked.

"I feel like I've been beat up." She lifted her arms from beneath the covers. Most of the sores had scabbed over. Some had turned to bruises. "It looks like it, too."

He rose and handed her a pink, silk bathrobe. "You can put this on. I made coffee. Are you hungry?" He kept the conversation going to avoid the inevitable question. He couldn't bear to say the words *she's dead* again. "I can make eggs, pancakes, whatever you like."

"Thank you." She took the robe from him. "What did the doctors say when you told them about Gisella?"

"Get dressed. Then we'll talk." Instead of leaving, he stood with his back to her and waited. He didn't want to be alone, even for a few minutes.

"My parents are coming here? Don't worry. My father's bark is worse than his bite. He was angry. No, he was majorly pissed at you, but I'll make him understand."

"I have no problem taking responsibility for my actions. Your father is the least of my worries."

There was a light tap on his shoulder. "Okay, I'm decent." He didn't move. "George?" Her fingers squeezed his arm. He closed his eyes and she spun him to face her. "What's wrong? How's Gisella this morning?"

His bottom lip trembled and even though he tried like hell to fight the tears from coming, they won. "George, is she worse?"

"No, Sofia. She's—she's—" He mouth couldn't form the word.

"*No!*" Sofia cupped her mouth in shock. "Oh, George." She wrapped her arms around his waist. "I'm so sorry. I hoped I had gotten all the poison out of her system."

"This isn't your fault. You did more than anyone should be asked to do." He squeezed her tight. "What am I going to do without her? For twenty years she's been at my side through good and bad."

"Let's sit down." Sofia released him and sat on the edge of the bed. He fell into the chair across from her. "I don't believe anyone truly leaves us." She put her hand on his chest. "You'll always have her love in your heart. No one can take that from you. And your memories, they are yours to cherish and keep forever." She took his hands in hers. "The best part of her is all around. Whenever we go somewhere or touch something, we leave a piece of us behind in the form of energy. Armend was able to see into Ilir's book through his life force lingering on the pages of his journal, even two hundred and fifty years later. When you need her, go to one of her favorites places in the house or outside and open yourself to her. You'll feel her. She may even surprise you on occasion when you aren't reaching out to her because she needs you. Those are the special visits."

Touched by her words, he kissed the top of her head. "Thank you, Sofia. Armend is blessed to have you and we are fortunate to include you in our family."

"You're welcome."

George got up, limped to the window, and gazed out at the dreary day ahead of him. Rain pelted the glass with a loud tap. "I was driving when the hospital called and asked me to come right away. They said when the nurses did their rounds Gisella was fine. She had eaten and was watching TV. The next time they went in, they found her." He shifted back toward Sofia and rested his hands on the back of the chair. "It was sudden. She never called for the nurses."

"Did you mention the poison?"

"No. I didn't know how to explain my suspicions. 'I have a sick witch at home from the poison she removed from Gisella during a healing ritual.' They'd lock me up."

"I understand. Will they do an autopsy?"

"I think so. But unlike television, it'll take weeks to get the results, not days."

"No one else came to see her after we left?"

"No. She would have told me on the phone. Visiting hours were over. Why?"

Sofia tucked her leg under the covers and nervously played with the fringe on the edge of the blanket. "Even if I didn't get all the poison from her, what was left wasn't enough to…you know."

"So you think it was something else?"

"No. I don't know. Let's wait for the autopsy. I don't think we should talk about this anymore."

George agreed and changed the subject. To keep his mind off his devastating loss he would focus on his family. "I thought as a gesture of goodwill, I'd give your father the Rossi's half of the music. Hopefully between that, Ilir's journal, and Armend, he'll agree to let us dismantle the painting and find the other half of the sonata."

"That's a wonderful idea. He's very fond of Armend and, although he may be upset with you, he'll do whatever he can for him."

"Gisella would want me to keep working to free Armend. We've worked very hard for a long time to get this far. I can't lose him as well."

"She'd be very proud of you."

"As soon as your parents get here, I'll go get it out of the safe deposit box."

"Go now." She yawned and sunk back into the pillows. "I'm exhausted and I want to go back asleep."

"I promised Armend I'd stay with you."

"Go. What could possibly happen?"

CHAPTER 22

Fear is the enemy of logic. – Frank Sinatra,
1915 – 1998, American singer, actor

Something crashed against the door with a thud, followed by a high pitch screech. Sofia bolted up from bed and jerked the door open. At her feet was Lautner, soaking wet and laying on his side. Short screams came from deep in his belly.

"Lautner! Are you all right?" She lifted him in her arms and peered down the dark hallway. Through the dimness, she caught a quick streak of movement. At the sight of the docile cat in her arms, anger took over, leaving her common sense far behind. "Hey, come back here." She hit the switch on the wall and a dome light on the ceiling came to life. With Lautner secure against her chest, she went toward the kitchen. The cool tile on the bottom of her feet sent a chill up her spine. She listened for any noise, but the pounding rain on the roof made it impossible to hear.

She entered the living room. The cabin, set deep in the woods, didn't get much light on a sunny day. Today with the bad weather, the small room was downright gloomy. Sofia turned each lamp on by hand until the room resembled daylight. "Hello," she called out not expecting an answer.

Snap. Click. Her head whipped around. The deadbolt locked. "George?" She walked to the door, tried to unlock it, but it wouldn't budge. A twinge of fear snuck in replacing her initial anger. Sofia headed back to the kitchen to grab a knife. After two steps, an invisible force slammed her hard against the wall. She cried out in pain, the lesions on her back still tender, slid down the wall, and landed on the floor like a rag doll.

Magic. It was a woman. Male magic had a different vibration to it. She didn't know whom she was up against, but she knew what. Under normal conditions, this witch would be no match for her, but her ordeal last night had left her in a weakened state. She pulled her knees to her chest and hugged the cat close to her. He was hurt and not her familiar, but she needed him. *Lautner, please help me call on the Lare. It's our only chance.* He purred against her chest. She took deep breaths and began the incantation to summon her ancestors. All of the sudden, the television turned on, the volume loud and voices blaring at her.

Pop! One by one, the bulbs in the lamps exploded. As each light went out, the room grew dimmer and dimmer. The glare from the television drew unwelcome shadows on the wall. Sofia lost her concentration. Exhausted and drained, she squeezed her eyes shut and pushed her hands over her ears.

The lamp on the table smashed against the wall next to her. She jumped. A barrage of knickknacks and small pictures came at her. She ducked to avoid them as best she could, but shards of glass sliced at her skin. She had never been this vulnerable, this exposed.

"What do you want?" she screamed. "Stop it!"

Something sharp swiped her face. Lautner meowed at her frantically and slapped her cheek with his paw.

Sofia stared into his green oval eyes and his message came through. This wasn't like her. How dare she let some second-rate witch unhinge her with unimaginative parlor tricks? Wallowing in a pool of fear wouldn't win this fight. She wasn't defenseless. Her wand and phone were in the bedroom. "Thanks, sweetie. Let's go."

With a renewed sense of purpose, Sofia jumped to her feet and rushed down the hall. The dome light above crackled, shattered, and dropped to the ground. She covered her head and hurried into the bedroom.

Carefully placing Lautner on the bed, she ran to the corner of the room to her purse. It was gone. She threw the closet doors open and rifled through clothes, shoes, and boxes of junk. On her hands and knees, she searched under the bed. She tossed the sheets and blankets in the air, shaking them out.

Slam. Snap. Click. Sofia's shoulders drooped and she moaned in despair. It would do no good to bang on the door or try to get out.

She crept back into bed next to Lautner and stroked his wet fur. "I'm sorry. I fell into her trap. I took the bait and came back here to get my wand. Of course, it's gone."

Lautner struggled to stand on the bed, his back leg not doing its part to hold his weight. "Sweetie, your leg is hurt." Sofia massaged his hindquarter. "She wants us cornered in here for a reason. Whatever it is, I have my head on straight now and won't fall apart. We'll have to wait and see what she has in store for us. I'll be ready this time."

Lautner's back arched and his fur bristled. His long tail twitched.

"What is it?"

He growled then hissed at the floor.

Sofia leaned over to see what had Lautner's attention. She squealed and scurried back to the top of the bed. *Shit! Could this day get any worse?*

She believed all creatures of nature deserved to live on earth and be respected—except for snakes. When she was twelve, she hiked in the woods, recited a kind, but firm incantation asking for a truce between her and the slimy reptiles. Waving her wand around, she'd promised not to hurt them, but thought it best if they stayed out of each other's way. They agreed and she hasn't seen a snake since—until now.

It wiggled and twisted from under the dresser forming a perfect S as is came toward them. With rapid shakes of its tail, it stared at her. The rattling noise grated on her nerves. She pulled the blanket around her neck. Lautner inched closer to her while the snake slithered up the wooden post of the bed.

When its head peeked over the top, Sofia did what she had to do to pull herself together. Her eyes locked with Lautner's. They were still as statues.

Without warning, Lautner leapt off the bed. The snake lunged at him. Sofia hurled the heavy blanket on top of the scaly creature. Quickly, she rolled the blanket into a ball and threw it on the floor. "Yuck!" Yanking the large bottom drawer out of the dresser, she dumped the contents on the floor, and placed it over the soft confinement. Remembering the suitcase in the closet, she grabbed it, opened it, and placed in on top of the drawer. She filled it with books from the nightstand and zipped it shut.

Satisfied her cold-blooded attacker couldn't escape from its homemade prison, she picked up Lautner. "We make a good team, you and I." He rubbed his head alongside her neck. "It's been quite a morning. I could use a cup of coffee. I hope someone gets home soon."

Click.

The door unlocked.

ত১৩৩

It was dread, not fear that weighed Sofia down. Was it a sign of an inexperienced witch, her magic only able to last for a short while, or did another assault lurk down the hall?

There was one only way to find out.

Her hand, clammy with anticipation, had trouble gripping the handle. Another try and the knob twisted to the right and the door rasped toward her. The dome light lay in pieces on the floor in the middle of the murky corridor. She took a cautionary first step and waited. Nothing. Halfway down the hall she stopped and opened her arms. With her palms facing upward, she could sense any recent enchantments, good or bad, that might be near.

The house remained quiet.

In the living room, the television was off. The front door opened with ease. Her assailant's magic had worn off. "Amateur," she called out to the empty room. "Next time we meet, there'll be a different outcome. Mark my words." This wasn't a random attack. It was personal. Another encounter was inevitable.

Careful where she stepped, Sofia tiptoed into the kitchen without cutting her feet on the abundance of broken glass, twisted frames, and cracked ceramic. Cleaning this mess up would be a daunting task, but right now, she needed food.

As she put the breakfast dishes in the sink, a car pulled into the driveway.

ⲉⲋⲉⲋ

Sofia waited on the porch. She pulled the bathrobe's collar around her neck and tightened the silk belt to protect again the damp, cool downpour of rain.

Silvio and Ersilia dashed toward her, one umbrella between them. Her father's arm wrapped around her mother's waist, displaying an intimacy still alive and well after close to thirty years of marriage. They threw their arms around her and the three of them stood like football players in a huddle. "Sofia, are you all right?"

"Yes, Mom, just a little tired."

"We're so glad Armend decided to come get us."

Armend hurried toward the porch, his feet splashing in the pooled rain, his jacket over his head. When he reached the top step, he rung out his jacket and hung it on an Adirondack chair. "Hey, baby. You're up. How are you feeling?"

"Better, but I missed you."

"Let's get inside out of the rain," Silvio said.

She blocked the door.

"Sofia? What are you doing?"

She bit her bottom lip. "Promise me you won't freak out when you go inside."

"Why would we freak out?"

"There was an incident this morning."

"An incident? What kind of incident?"

"Are you hurt?"

"Where's George?" Armend demanded. "I asked him to stay with you."

"This is what I mean!" Sofia threw her hands in the air. "Calm down. I'm fine, but Lautner's leg is bothering him."

"As long as you're not hurt, what could be so bad?" Her mother reached for the doorknob. Sofia hesitated but moved aside. Armend took her hand and they went inside.

Their reaction was predictable. Silvio's face dropped and her mother made a squeaky noise. Armend, in his need to protect her, let his temper get the best of him. "What the hell happened, Sofia?"

"I'm not sure."

"Not sure? Who did this? It looks like a war zone."

"This isn't so bad," Sofia quipped. "There's a snake rolled up in blanket inside a drawer with a suitcase of books on top of it in the bedroom."

Armend appeared to be trying to control his anger, without much success. "You weren't supposed to be alone."

"Don't you dare blame George. He didn't want to leave, but I made him. In twenty-four hours, he's lost Gisella and now his house has been ransacked. He doesn't need any more grief from any of you." She gave both Armend and her father a warning glance.

Before they could answer her, the door burst open.

CHAPTER 23

No one ever won a chess game by betting on each move.
Sometimes you have to move backward to get a step forward.
– *Amar Gopal Bose, American billionaire, entrepreneur*

Georgie almost rammed into the four people standing at his front door. He could tell his nephew with his arms crossed over his chest wasn't happy with him for leaving Sofia alone. The man next to him, Silvio, he assumed, was pissed at him for a number of reasons. The woman, Ersilia, was like Switzerland, lovely, but neutral. He could care less how they felt about him right now. There were much bigger problems to deal with.

He longed for Gisella to be at his side, to help him fight the coming battles. She always knew what to do when he got himself into a jam, which was often. But she was gone and he was on his own.

Sofia approached him. "George, I'd like you to meet my parents, Silvio and Ersilia."

He could hear Gisella in his ear. *Be generous and forthright and you can't go wrong.* George offered his hand. "I'm truly sorry for my dishonorable behavior. I'm a man with the unfortunate habit of acting then realizing there's a consequence."

Silvio's hand remained at his side while Ersilia's elbow rammed into her husband's waist. "This is not the time or the place," she muttered out of the corner of her mouth.

"Armend told us about Gisella. I'm sorry." Silvio extended his arm. "I'm not without compassion and although I may be able to understand your motivation, I cannot condone your actions."

"Thank you. I understand," replied George.

"We're so sorry for your loss, George," Ersilia lightly embraced him. "We're practically family and will do whatever you need including cleaning up this mess."

"Thank you, Ersilia. I see where Sofia gets her beauty and kindness. Um, what mess?" The four of them moved aside and George got his first glimpse of the shambles that lay before him. He hobbled to the side of the room, fragments of glass and pottery crunched under his steps. With the help of the chair arm for balance, his bad leg stiff, he bent down on one knee and picked up the pictures of him and Gisella. He brushed off the bits of glass and stared at them. With her tucked safely in his jacket pocket, he asked. "What happened?"

"If you had stayed with Sofia like I asked, you'd know what happened," Armend snapped.

Sofia came to his defense. Her parents had questions of their own and soon everyone was talking over everyone else, until the shrill of a whistle filled the room.

Sofia stood with her fingers in her mouth and blew her alarm again until everyone was quiet. "Listen up," she said. "I'll try my best to explain what went on here, but first things first. Someone needs to get that *snake* out of the bedroom. Now!"

They followed her down the hall in single file. "Snake?" George asked as he trudged behind.

ℰↄℰↄ

Armend walked deep into the woods and kept his promise not to hurt the reptile. He undid the bundle and watched the rattler slither under a pile of wet, dead leaves. Lost in his thoughts, the rain now a gentle mist, he took his time getting back to the cabin. The irony of the situation wasn't lost on him. Whenever a man in his family fell in love with a witch, things turned out badly, especially for the woman, Ambra, then Gisella, now Sofia. He would leave and never have contact with her before he would let her be hurt again.

Near the front porch, he spotted Sofia's pocketbook on the ground and took it inside. She sat on the couch, Lautner on her lap, complaining that she was more than able to help as Silvio and George put the scraps from the broken furnishings into two large garbage bags. Ersilia followed them around with the vacuum.

"Hey, look what I found outside." He sat the purse next to her.

She ripped it open like a kid unwrapping a present and dumped the contents out. Her smashed cell phone didn't seem to bother her. It was when she picked up three small pieces of broken wood that she put her hand to her mouth and cried, "Oh, no."

"Oh, Sofia, I'm so sorry. That was a delightful wand," Ersilia sympathized.

"You have a wand?" Armend asked. She raised her eyebrows at him implying it was a silly question. "Okay, sorry." He closed her palm around the broken wand and held her hand. "I think it's time you told us what went on here this morning."

ထာထာ

George and the others listened to Sofia as she retold her ordeal that morning.

"It was as if she knew I was tired and weak and she would have the advantage," explained Sofia. "Ugh, and the snake!" She rubbed her hands up and down her arms and shuddered. "Her magic wasn't very powerful and under normal circumstances, I would have won easily. Instead, I let her get to me."

"Who would want to attack you?" Armend said.

During the course of Sofia's tale, George's mind reeled with thoughts of Gisella. Her sudden death didn't make sense and neither did the strange attack on Sofia. Seeds of doubt scrambled the thoughts in his mind. At the mention of the snake, a horrible realization hit him like a brick. He stood and bolted across the room. Half way there, his bad leg gave out. Armend, the closest, steadied him before he went down hard. "Let go. I'm fine," he snapped. "I'll be right back."

Clutching the side of the bed, he was struggling to his knees when Armend walked in. "What are you doing?"

"Please, just crawl under there and get the box. It's important."

Armend bent down easily and handed him what he wanted.

"Thank you." George grabbed it from his nephew, lifted the top, and rummaged through the papers. He reached for the phone on the side of the bed and scrolled down until he found the number he wanted. When the message started, he slammed the phone down, pushed Armend aside, and strode back into the other room.

"Sofia, I'm so sorry. If I had only known, I would have stayed with you." He leaned against the couch for support, the open box in his hands.

"George, what's wrong?" Sofia asked.

"Everything."

"Enough!" Silvio's voice thundered from the other side of the room. "We've been more than patient under the circumstances." He walked toward George as he spoke. "Since her arrival, Sofia has been poisoned, terrorized, and attacked. 'I'm sorry' isn't going to cut it."

Silvio was right. Sofia had been nothing but kind to him and Gisella and, in return, she had been put through hell. It was his fault.

"George." It was Ersilia's turn. "I know you're upset, but you have to understand our concerns."

"I know who did this," he said.

∽∾∽

George sat in Gisella's favorite chair, his legs splayed open, with an elbow resting on each knee. He leaned over a small glass jar. He took a spoonful of the contents, hesitated a moment, then savored the sweetness against his tongue. He directed his question to Silvio and Ersilia. "What do you know about Gisella?"

"Armend told us everything on the ride here. She was a descendant of Ambra's and has their half of the music," Ersilia answered.

George dug his spoon into the bottom of the jar and took another small scoop. He wavered a few seconds, but soon the thick, syrupy treat rolled around his mouth. He could feel their questioning stares on him. "I assure you I haven't lost my mind." He clicked his tongue.

"I went to the bank this morning so I could give you the Rossi half of the music as a token of good will." The next three words were going to be some of the hardest Armend would ever hear. "It was gone." He watched his nephew's body slump, his head resting in his hands. Sofia put her arm around him. "Armend, I'm sorry," George continued. "But it's a temporary setback. I'll find it. I promise.

"The condition to break the curse is for both families to be in agreement. The only Rossi relative who opposed was Reggie, Gisella's niece." This time he scraped the sides of the jar clean. The last bit on his spoon, he waited to put it in his mouth. "She doesn't like me much, for reasons I won't go into now, but mostly due to my last name. She's always been difficult, like her mother, and the streak of madness that runs through the family did not bypass her, as much as Gisella would have liked to believe it did."

He held the spoon in front of him. "The three of us are signers on the safe deposit box. Only Gisella and I had keys. I keep mine on me. Gisella kept hers in this box underneath our bed. The family box carved with a pentagram and two rattlesnakes on the side."

He slowly lifted the spoon to his mouth. "Reggie dabbled in witchcraft on and off for years. Her magic was never as strong as she wanted. The key is gone and Reggie knew her aunt's habits well. I just tried to call and her phone number is no longer in use. This was the last thing Gisella ate before she got sick. It was a gift from her niece, who seemed to have a sudden change of heart concerning the curse."

"George, no!" yelled Sofia.

"What the hell are you doing?" Armend slapped the spoon out of his hand, but it was too late. "Are you crazy?"

With a final flick of his tongue, the last bit of honey melted in his warm mouth.

CHAPTER 24

Could a greater miracle take place than for us to look through each other's eyes for an instant? – Henry David Thoreau, 1817 – 1862, American author, poet

Armend gawked at his uncle in disbelief while Sofia and Ersilia huddled around him. "Silvio," Ersilia said. "Go to the car and get my bag. I have some herbs that may help him when he starts to get sick."

"Will he be okay?" Armend asked.

"He's a big man, much bigger than Gisella," Sofia said. "I don't know what the poison is. Hopefully the ratio of his size to what he ate will cause symptoms similar to a mild case of food poisoning."

"I'll be fine." George piped up. "It's the only way to prove my suspicions. If it will help find out who did this to my Gisella, I don't care how sick I get."

Armend admired his uncle's resilience and courage to take the untraditional route to get things done. George, as well as his parents, had spent years of their time and energy on this damned curse. It was time he took the reins. The curse wanted him and he wouldn't go without a fight.

The first thing was to find Reggie, get the Rossi half of the music back, and haul her ass off to the police. He would like a few words with her before that, but he would play by the rules not to upset Sofia. But he needed evidence. The honey might prove who it was to George, but the authorities would need much more than that. He flopped down on the couch. Something hard and sharp stung him on the butt and leg. He shifted. Lying next to him were the three broken pieces of Sofia's wand. He picked them up and let them roll between his palms.

Reaching over, he tapped Sofia's back. "Hey, babe, do you think she broke your wand with her bare hands or with magic?"

She glanced at her wand with a dismal expression. He was sorry to remind her, but it was important.

"The pieces look splintered and cracked," she said. "If she used magic, it would be a clean cut. I think she broke my phone and wand the old-fashioned way. Why?"

The pieces of wood began to warm between his hands. "I could see and feel her through the wand, right?"

"Yes, but I'm sure George has a picture of her."

"No, I want to get a sense of what she's like. That way when we meet we'll know what I'm up against."

"Good idea," George said.

"Don't you mean what *we're* up against?" Sofia asked.

"What's a good idea?" Silvio asked handing his wife her satchel.

"*Meow!*" Lautner was standing on all fours, his tail jerking high in the air.

"I think his leg is better," Sofia said. "Let him help you."

"I'm going to get a sense of just who our enemy is," Armend answered Silvio. "Come on, buddy." He lifted his familiar to his lap and circled him with his arms. Clasping the wood tightly between his hands, he concentrated. His eyes fluttered and he became highly sensitive to his immediate surroundings. There had to be a nice way to tell Ersilia her flowery perfume was overwhelming in normal conditions, but almost unbearable when he was in his finely tuned state. In the small room with everyone crowded around, he had a sense of claustrophobia. "Can everyone take a few steps back, please?"

When the wand was almost to point of burning his skin, he hung his head and gave in. An outline of a woman began to form. He had to slow down her actions.

"I can only see her from a distance. She's running through the woods, Sofia's purse in her arms. She's smashing the phone against a rock. Now she's holding the wand in her hands." Armend jolted back against his seat. "She's—she's—cold—devoid of any feelings of remorse or shame, with no conscious. A predator. She's breaking the wand. Anger is her driving force." He focused on her image, forcing his mind to zoom in on her face like a magnifying glass. Her hair and body shape were clearer. Just a little closer and he would see her.

"Holy shit!" He flung the broken pieces into the air and sat up straight. After a few deep laboring breathes he was back to his usual self, but he sat trembling.

Sofia stroked her fingers through his hair, damp from sweat. "What is it?"

"George, is Reggie short for something?"

"Yes. Regina."

Armend looked directly at Silvio and Ersilia. "It's Gina."

෬৲෬৲

Sofia watched the air leave her father's body like a balloon deflating after being stuck with a pin.

"Are you sure?" Silvio's voice cracked. "I can't believe she's capable of this."

"Yes, I'm sure," Armend said.

"Why don't you call and see if she made it to work today?" suggested Sofia.

"You look like you could use some air." Ersilia coaxed her husband out on the porch with her. "Come with me and we'll see what's going on at the gallery." He followed his wife outside.

Unlike the others, Sofia had no emotional ties to this woman. George was devastated, her parents were shocked, and however brief and meaningless their physical relationship was, Gina did work and spend time with Armend.

The only sentiment Sofia had toward Gina was anger. She would do whatever she had to do in order to protect her loved ones from this deranged person.

"We need a plan," Sofia said.

"More important, we have to be careful. I've always believed she's a borderline psychopath," George said. "She knows I'll figure out it's her as soon I discovered the key is gone and her phone doesn't work. She doesn't care."

"We still have the advantage. We know that Reggie and Gina are one and same." Armend stretched his arm toward Sofia then let it drop to his side. "I'm sorry you got dragged into this. I knew in my gut I should have stayed away from her, but she got me when I was weak, trying to drink you away."

He still didn't touch her. This was not the time for him to pull away from her. They were in this together. "This isn't your fault." She stepped toward him and he backed away. "This woman, whatever her name is, will do what she wants, when she wants, whether you are with her or not." Gina's obsession with him scared Sofia more than she wanted to admit. She had the power to save him and refused, but wanted him in her bed. She was playing a sick and twisted game. "Don't shut me out. You need me."

"Yes, I need you alive. This is why I chose to keep you at a distance."

"Gina called in sick today," Ersilia said as they came back in.

Armend turned his back to her. "I'm sorry," he said. "Do you two think you can act normal around her? I need you to be our eyes and ears in New York. I'll stay here. Sofia needs rest and we have to see what happens with George. In a day or two, I'll send George to Albania with my parents and Sofia can stay with you. Everyone will be safe."

"No!" George and Sofia yelled in unison.

Armend ignored them. "Silvio, you believe me when I told you that I saw Ilir put the music in the framed Onufri painting, right? I'll give you his journal as added proof. If we flaunt the fact we have the other half of the music, we can lure her out. I imagine the one thing she wants even more than me dead is both halves of the music."

Sofia lent George a hand when she saw him struggle to his feet.

"Damn leg," he muttered. "Armend, I've worked too long and hard not to see this to the end. You will not ship me off like a useless old man." He limped toward his nephew. "I'm not going anywhere. I have to pick up Gisella's ashes and take care of her final wishes. Besides, I know Reggie better than any of you."

Sofia held her tongue as Armend paced around the room. "George, I appreciate everything you've done, but I don't want anyone else to get hurt. This is my responsibility and mine alone. Sofia, after we leave here, I'll be on my own. You won't see or hear from me until after the solstice. Don't try to call me, I won't answer. Don't come see me, I won't be there. End of discussion."

Her father let out a loud snort.

Her mother chuckled. "Armend, you poor dear."

☙☙☙

Armend and Sofia stood in silence.

"George, let's leave them alone," Ersilia suggested.

"Why don't you show me Ilir's journal," Silvio said.

"I have everything in the other room."

After they left, Sofia picked up the largest piece of her broken wand and twirled it between her fingers like a small baton.

"Have a seat." With a flick of her wrist, Armend's feet yanked out from underneath him and he plopped into the soft back chair.

He attempted to get up but couldn't move his arms or legs. "Sofia, what the hell?"

"That was simple magic with a broken wand. What are you going to do when Gina does something like this or worse?"

He would show her what he'd do. "This is my battle, Sofia, not yours. Lautner. Come on, buddy." The cat jumped on his lap. He paid special attention to the energy coming from his familiar and knew his eyes were changing. He concentrated on the remaining pieces of the wand spread out on the floor. The smaller one of the two slowly rolled toward him.

Sofia laughed, leaned over, picked it up, and tossed it at him. "This'll be quicker. Let's see what you got, blue eyes." It landed on his lap.

Showing her sassy side, was she? If he wasn't so pissed off at her right now, he might find it amusing. He still couldn't move and refused to let her win without a fight. In his mind, he pleaded with the wand to break the spell on his legs. His muscles constricted and he pushed with all his might. His foot moved an inch.

A sharp poke stabbed his heart. "You're dead!" She removed her two fingers from his chest and pressed her face inches from his. Her eyes were a deep emerald green. "Now you listen to me. It's two o'clock in the afternoon and I've already had a shitty day. Your grand announcement that you're leaving me, to go off and combat a psychopathic witch, was the proverbial last straw. I understand you want to take her on, but when two people love each other, they fight for each other, together. We'll get you a wand. I'll teach you to tap into your magic abilities and one day you'll be a strong witch. But in the time we have, you won't be powerful enough to go against her alone. So until you're ready, let me help you."

Her lips parted and reached for his. He whipped his head to the side. He wanted nothing more than to have her by his side while he conquered the curse, but he couldn't chance her getting hurt or worse. If he let her kiss him, he would soon forget why he wanted this temporary separation, and he couldn't let that happen.

"Be that way," she said. "I know the male ego doesn't like it when a woman gets in its way. But I still love you more than anything and always will."

She walked away, stopped, and peered over her shoulder. "You can get up now."

❧❧❧

Sofia picked up the plates from dinner and put them in the dishwasher. Before Silvio and Ersilia left for New York, they brought dinner for the two of them. Not feeling well, George went to bed with herb tea Ersilia made and plenty of water to keep him from dehydrating.

After a strained dinner conversation, Sofia knew she had to do something to get Armend to see her side of things and to soothe his bruised feelings for her getting the better of him. The first thing she'd do was apologize. She would then make him believe it was his idea to let her help him. She would play on his overwhelming necessity to protect her at all costs, which most of the time was charming, but today was particularly annoying. She'd have to convince him he could protect her better if they were together. *Men!*

"I'm sorry if I went too far before." She sat down at the table and gave him her most sorrowful expression. "In a battle of wits or fists, I'd bet on you every time, but this is a different kind of fight, and I wanted to make sure you understood that. And on a selfish note, I don't want to be dumped."

His body relaxed and the tension dropped from his shoulders. "Baby, I could never leave you. It's a temporary situation for two months to keep you safe."

"I understand. It was a personal attack this morning and I wouldn't be surprised if she tried again. I'm her enemy. I caused her humiliation the other night in your apartment and now we're together. In her mind, I've taken you away from her."

"It was a brief time together, once, in the back seat of her car. I did ignore her afterward. Hell has no fury as a woman scorned," he said with a smirk.

"That may be true." She beckoned him closer, gesturing with her pointer finger. "Let me tell you a secret about the female psyche. Even if the man did the betraying, more often than not, we'll go after the woman. She's our direct competition. After all, if she hadn't tempted our man, he wouldn't have strayed. She'll blame me, not you. Between that and the fact she's nuts, she'll come after me again. I'm sure of it." She settled back in her chair. "I'll make sure my father's two security guards, Abbott and Costello, are always with me. I have my magic, but I do need a new wand, that will take a few days." She brushed him off with a wave of her hand. "I'll be more than safe. Don't worry."

He tightened his lips and his eyes narrowed. He was wavering. "I know what you're doing."

She didn't flinch. "Is it working?"

"Maybe."

"Everything I said is true." She rose and provocatively positioned herself on his lap. He kept his hands at his sides. "And I know what you're doing." She wrapped his right arm around her waist, held it there, and snuggled into his chest. "But this is straight from my heart. You were there last night, holding, healing, and loving me all with one embrace. Look how much better I am today because of you." She took a chance, lifted her hand off his, and put it around his neck. Not only did he keep his around her, he pulled her closer. "Let me be there for you. We're good together–strong, united, and impossible to beat."

With his free hand, he lifted her chin. "If anything happened to you I'd never forgive myself."

"Nothing is going to happen to either one of us. Trust me. Besides my magic, I have a secret weapon." With a smile, she added. "Literally."

CHAPTER 25

A religion without a Goddess is halfway to atheism. –
Dion Fortune, 1890 – 1946, British occultist and novelist

S ofia steeped the spearmint leaves in boiling water, then added cloves, turkey rhubarb, and cinnamon. She'd been mixing this remedy and many others since she was a child learning at her mother's side. Herbal cures were Ersilia's specialty and someday Sofia would pass on the magical and ancient ways of the Strega to her own daughter.

Armend stuck his head in the kitchen. "George is awake."

"I've got more tea for him. It's important he keeps drinking it."

She checked on George, refreshed his pot of her family's brew, and walked down the hall to their room. Weariness settled deep in her bones. She slid into bed and welcomed the clean, crisp sheets she'd put on earlier. But with Armend stretched out long next to her, his head propped up on arm, her pulse quickened.

"Everything I do, whether you like it or not, is with your best interest at heart," he said.

"The best thing for me, for both of us, is to be together, through good times and rough times."

He slipped one arm underneath her, wrapped the other around her, and lifted her toward him, as if she were light as a feather. In one sweep, his mouth crashed down on hers. Although Sofia had been kissed passionately by many a man, nothing compared to this. He kissed her slow and deep, with his whole being, until she was delirious.

When he released her and rolled on his back, she reached for him, wanting more.

"I think you should get some sleep," he said. "You've been through a lot. You need to rest."

"This is most time I've spent in a man's bed without being—" She put the back of her palm to her forehead. "—ravished," she joked, doing her best southern belle imitation.

"Thanks. I don't want to think of other men ravishing you."

"Jealous?"

"No, you're very ravishable." He kissed her nose. "But from now on I'm the only one doing the ravishing. Got it?"

"Got it, sir." She gave him a mock salute and nuzzled him. "I don't think I can't sleep right now. I'm over tired."

"Then tell me about your secret weapon."

It shouldn't surprise her he was interested. It was her fault for bringing it up earlier. Damn her loose tongue. She needed to stall him to think things over. "Did I see a couple of beers in your uncle's refrigerator? I could use one."

"I don't think beer and poison make a good combination."

"The poison is long gone from my system. It'll help me unwind."

"I'll be right back."

If she revealed her family's legacy to Armend, he would be the first non-spouse, otherwise known as an outsider, who would know their secret. Stregas were permitted to tell and initiate their spouse or partner in the ancient mysteries of their ways, but no one else. Her mother hadn't told her father until Sofia was born.

But she believed in her heart Armend would be at her side forever. He told her his family secrets and she expected him to let her fight side by side against Gina. It was only fair she do the same.

She was the chosen one of her generation to be sanctioned with the power over a certain weapon. Ersilia had been on her butt about going to the temple and charging the weapon. Traditionally, the ceremony was performed as a teenager. At twenty-seven, she was a reluctant recipient of the family heirloom. In fact, it scared her. She was content with her dominant magic and gifts and preferred to use her head and reason to get things done.

That was before she met the man who was an intricate part of her. Their bodies hadn't united and yet it didn't matter. They were connected and unified on a higher level. When they came together physically, it would be that much stronger.

Her mother was right. It was time.

"Here you go." He twisted the cap off, handed her a bottle and slid next to her.

She tipped the neck of the bottle against his. "Congratulations. You're the first non-family member who'll learn the history of how we became a very powerful family of Stregas."

"Are you not supposed to tell me?" He gulped his beer. "I don't need another curse on my head."

"No," she laughed. "It's a Strega's choice."

"Sounds like a poker game."

"I can bet you'll be surprised." She sipped her beer and got comfortable. It was the first time she would chronicle the events to someone and she was a little apprehensive. "Our family received our magical power and knowledge directly from the Goddess Diana. Diana was Goddess of many things including women, childbirth, the moon, and the hunt."

"The statue in the gallery shows her with a bow and arrow and her hand on a buck."

"Yes. She is also the Goddess of witches, or wise women, as the Romans referred to them. Diana turned to Vulcan, the God of fire and blacksmith, for her weapons. Even though he created weapons for Gods and mortals, he was more of a lover than a fighter. His forge was located inside the foot of Mt. Etna."

"The volcano?"

"What better place for a blacksmith's furnace?"

"I guess. Go on."

"What story would be complete without a lovely young maiden?" Sofia and her beer got out of bed for a welcome stretch. "Her name was Messalina and she lived in a small village at the foot of Mt. Etna. One afternoon Vulcan spotted Messalina bathing in a stream and was smitten. Vulcan was an intimidating God, clad in boots with leather bands crisscrossed around his bare chest. He carried a large hammer wherever he went. At the sight of him, Messalina cowered in fear.

"He crept off, not wanting to scare her, but returned the next day and found her sitting near the stream. She scrambled to her feet and started to run. Knowing her name, he called to her, assuring her he meant no harm. He presented her with a statue of a woman, explaining the memory of her beauty inspired him to craft the gift for her.

"From that day forth, she waited each day at the stream for him. He would come to her, black with dirt and sweat from his work. They would bathe together in the stream and spend the rest of the day and night together.

"It wasn't long before Diana came to check the progress of her weapons. There were rumors Vulcan was playing around with a young mortal and she worried it would affect his work. Vulcan defended his relationship and the happiness of being with Messalina showed through his work. When he offered the recent dagger he had forged for her, Diana was impressed with the quality of his workmanship and insisted on meeting the young woman.

Upon seeing the girl, she appreciated her modesty, loyalty, and gentle nature. Each time she came to see Vulcan she made sure to spend time with Messalina and they soon became friends.

"One afternoon, Vulcan never showed at the stream. His young lover was worried but didn't know what to do. She couldn't go Mt. Etna. The Cyclops lived there and assisted Vulcan in his work."

"The Cyclops?" Armend said with a mouthful of doubt.

"Yes. Ancient Sicilians believed it was the furnace of Vulcan and the Cyclops overheating that caused the eruptions."

Armend almost spit out the slug of beer he had just taken. She threw a pillow at him.

"Don't be disrespectful. I didn't laugh at your silly Lugat story. Who ever heard of a vampire with no fangs who moves at a snail's pace?"

"Okay, okay." He held his hands up in surrender. "I'm sorry. And it's not silly, just different."

"Anyway," she continued. "A week passed and Messalina hadn't seen or heard from Vulcan. Diana found her sobbing and inconsolable and decided to tell her the truth. Vulcan tricked her with the statue. He enlisted the help of the Goddess Venus to enchant the statue and make Messalina fall in love with him. He didn't love her and, in fact, had grown tired of her.

"Messalina was brokenhearted and Diana wanted to help her young friend. Being a Goddess, the only power she could pass to a mortal was instruction in the ways of magic and the power of the earth. They spent two days and nights together in the woods. When they emerged, Messalina was a strong and wise woman, bestowed with powerful magic. Confident she would use her new knowledge sensibly and fairly, Diana rewarded her with a gift of her own, the Diana Dagger. It was a beautifully-crafted blade with a pure gold crescent shaped hilt. A solitary moonstone decorated it."

Sofia got back in bed. "I suppose you can guess Messalina was our ancestor."

"You own an ancient, solid gold dagger?"

"Yes. I have it at home. I'll show it to you. My father had one of his art friends appraise it. They confirmed it's at least three thousand years old."

"And worth a lot of money."

"Yes, but that's not important to us. Its worth lies in its power. It gives us the opportunity to call on Diana in dire circumstances. Diana is one of the more kind and caring Goddesses, but she has a ferocious dark side if angered. The frightening thing is that when you call on the magic of the Dagger, you get the good and bad of Diana. I'll have to be strong enough to control her dark side."

"I've felt your might. You can do it. I'm sure of it."

"You're more confident that I am."

He put his arm around her and she snuggled next to him. "Gina's magic isn't that strong, remember? If you're not comfortable opening the door to the Dagger, then don't. We don't need it. Together we're unbeatable. You said so yourself."

Sofia didn't want to talk about it anymore and feigned a yawn.

"You must be exhausted. Let's get some sleep." He kissed her good night. "Thanks for the family's history lesson. I love you."

"I love you, too. We have a busy day tomorrow. We're going to get you your first wand."

CHAPTER 26

The universe is full of magical things patiently
waiting for our wits to grow sharper. –
Eden Phillpotts, 1862 – 1960,
English author and poet

Lautner dashed through Armend's legs and crouched between a blanket of golden dried leaves, his ears back and his body swaying from side to side. Without warning, he pounced at some unsuspecting creature crawling beneath the fallen foliage.

"He seems to be enjoying himself," Armend said. They'd hiked a mile into the woods behind his uncle's cabin. The scent of pine and moist vegetation hung in the air. With the sun buried behind the clouds and the thick forest covering, it was a damp, dismal day.

"He's used to running around the nature preserve," Sofia said. "More important, he's going to help you chose your wand."

"I don't know, Sofia. I never pictured myself as one of those crazy people who talked to plants."

"They aren't crazy." She nudged his arm. "Oh, look, red mulberry trees. Fruit bearing trees are ideal for wands."

Armend lagged behind as she hurried into a less dense area of the woods to a cluster of trees reaching heights of between thirty to forty feet. It was late October. Most were bare, but one or two bigger trees retained custody of a few bright yellow leaves sprinkled through the lower branches.

"We never take a live branch from a tree without asking permission first. You don't have to speak aloud. Place your hands on its trunk and ask with kindness and sincerity for a piece of her and why. You'll know if she agrees or not."

Armend awkwardly positioned his hands on the rough, brown bark. He hoped the guys back at the gym back in New York never found out he was attempting to telepathically talk to a tree. When nothing happened, he shook his head at her. They moved from tree to tree with no success. He was sure he was doing something wrong, probably because his heart wasn't it in.

He leaned with his hands firmly against the last tree. Lautner decided his shin would make a good scratching post. "What, buddy?" The cat leapt away and Armend chased him. When he caught up with him, the animal circled around a tree set away from the others.

He stood ten feet back from the tree. With no visible wind, the crown of the tree swayed back and forth, as if motioning to him.

"Go ahead," urged Sofia. "She's calling to you. Don't be shy."

He moved toward the tree and glanced up. It was smaller than the other trees, no more than seventeen feet high. He placed his hand on its slim trunk, bowed his head, and once again explained what he needed.

The effect this time was different. He immediately became aware of the life force of the tree. The source came from the earth, pulsing through its roots as human blood runs through our veins. It spoke to him and a bond he didn't understand was forged.

A loner like Armend, she grew by itself, away from the rest of her kind. She wasn't as mighty as the other mulberry trees and his magic wasn't as potent as Sofia's, but someday they would both be strong. She was willing to give him a piece of her, to help him, as long as he treated her gift will care and respect.

The experience stirred his soul and he thanked her. Not sure what to do next, he rested his back on its trunk and slid down until he hit the hard ground below. "Wow. I can't believe that just happened. The tree is…alive."

"Of course."

"No. I mean *really* alive!"

Sofia laughed at him. "Yes. I know. Dig a small hole next to you."

He dug his fingers deep in the dark, rich soil. Two beetles, not happy at being disturbed scattered away.

"After you cut your wand we'll leave an offering."

He stood, brushed himself off and followed her around the tree.

"A wand is usually the length between your elbow and middle finger. When you see a branch you like, you'll know it."

He lightly stroked a few long, thin branches. Then he came upon a thick, crooked branch filled with knots. He wrapped his hand around the thickest part of the branch, and his thumb rested on a large bump in the wood. It felt good in his grip. "This is the one."

"It's beautiful," Sofia said and tapped him on the shoulder.

He turned to see her pointing an ominous looking weapon at him. The crescent shape blade rested on a decorative white handle. "Where did you get that?"

"My jacket pocket. Gina didn't get to all my tools."

"Tool?"

"It's my *Boline*. It's a ritual knife." She handed it to him. "It's very sharp. Be careful. Take the branch in one, quick, clean slice." He took the knife and severed the limb from the giving tree. Sofia reached into her jean pocket and removed a small vial. He exchanged the blade for the glass bottle. "Pour the honey in the hole you dug as a thank you and cover it up."

"What about your wand?" he asked while she threw birdseed around the base of the tree. "What's that for?"

"You never take from nature without giving back to nature. That was a sturdy bough. Birds and squirrels may have used it to rest or eat on. It's just a small gesture to them as well." She wiped her hands on her jeans. "I have a special fig tree back at the reserve that all my wands come from."

"Now what do I do?"

"You can strip the bark from it, make it smooth, carve and decorate it if you'd like."

"Nah, I'd like to keep it in the natural state she gave it to me in."

"She'll appreciate that. The next step happens tomorrow night during the full moon." She gave the inside of his leg a seductive fondle. "Then we'll celebrate."

✑✑✑

George was sitting up in bed when they entered in his room, "Where have you two been?"

"We went for a walk in the woods," Sofia said. "Are you feeling better?"

"Yes. I think the worst is over." He took a sip of tea. "The brew really helped." He sat the teacup on the nightstand. "Silvio called. Reg...er...Gina is at work today."

"We shouldn't expect a visit from her then," Armend said.

"He also called a couple who are experts at art restoration. He explained what he needed and they can be in New York tomorrow to start dismantling the frame."

"Good. It's already October twenty-fourth. We have less than two months to get both sheets of music together. It'll be interesting to see if Gina reveals her true self to me when she finds out I have our family's half."

"We? I take it you're letting Sofia and I help you?"

"I've learned I'm much better when the people I love are around me."

"Glad you came to your senses." George swung his legs over the edge of the bed and sat up. "One more thing, Gisella's ashes are ready. I told them I wasn't up to getting them and asked if my nephew could pick them up. You just need to bring identification."

"Sure, whatever you need."

"I want to save my energy for later." He stood up with the help of the bedpost. "Sofia, I know Gisella would be pleased if you presided over her soul passing. I don't know the ritual and it's what she would want."

Before he knew it, Sofia had her arms around him, squeezing him tight. "I would be honored. Where does she want her ashes released?"

"There's stream behind the cabin. It was our favorite place to go."

⊱⊰⊱⊰

George stood with Armend to his left and Sofia to his right. The rapidly moving water, gurgling and bubbling past, calmed him like the sound of a familiar friend. In his hands, he held a small silver box that Gisella had bought in an Albanian antique shop for just this occasion.

He had kept his emotions in check until they arrived at this particular location. Their secluded place where they walked and talked, hand in hand, for hours. His mind wandered back to their younger days when they would make love on a blanket under the sun, then the moon, whenever and wherever the mood hit them. Her spontaneity was just one of the many things he loved about her. She was the only woman he ever met who was uninhibited and with enough guts to keep up with his recklessness.

Sofia began. "We've come to this beautiful and special spot today to honor Gisella, whose soul has begun its passage into the next realm. We send you on your travels with our love and friendship. May you find joy as you reunite with the cherished souls who journeyed before you. May the great Goddess greet you and prepare you for your rebirth. We will miss you but shall not grieve for you. For we all will meet, remember, and love each other again in another life."

She took a step back and urged George forward. "Speak from your heart," she told him. "Then if you're comfortable with it, you may end with the words we went over."

"Gisella, I will always treasure the time we had together and the love we shared. I'm not a man of many words when it comes to matters of the heart, but you know you were my life."

He opened the box away from him. "I would never want my love or sorrow at your departure to tie your spirit to this earth. If you wish to see or talk with me, do so as you see fit. I know our love will last forever.

"George, place the open box at your feet," she said.

"Let me." Armend took the box from his uncle and sat it on the ground.

Sofia held her hands open in front of her, palms to the sky. Her body began to rock back and forth. With her eyes open and a deep hum emitting from inside her, she seemed to go into some sort of trance. "Dear elements of wind and water, in your wisdom, release the physical aspect of Gisella to Mother Earth, where she will find happiness and contentment."

A graceful waft of autumn air elevated the ashes from the box and spun them gently around George. He watched in awe as Gisella gave him one last soft embrace. Some of her remains floated down like confetti on top of the water near a tree stump. He supported himself against Armend. "She would sit on that stump and dangle her feet in the cool water." As the ripples of small waves carried her downstream, tears fell down George's cheek.

Others landed under a large oak tree, leaving the base covered with a light dusting. "We used to picnic under that tree," he sobbed.

Armend wrapped his arm around his uncle's shoulder. "She'll be happy here and whenever you come to this spot, you'll feel her."

Sofia remained perfectly still for a few moments then spoke. "Be well, Gisella, our beloved sister. We will remember you on the next *Tregunda, La Festa dell' Ombra,* October thirty-first, when we honor the Great Lady as she descends to the underworld to understand the mystery of death."

"Blessed be," the three said in unison.

CHAPTER 27

If you can't get rid of the family skeleton,
you might as well make him dance. – *Anonymous*

Armend entered the sparsely populated lobby of the gallery. It was Wednesday, not usually a busy day, but he recognized small clusters of college art students examining certain paintings and taking notes.

He stood to the left of the reception desk and watched Gina's every move. He had given Ersilia and Silvio the difficult task of behaving normal around her, and they hadn't let him down. Now it was his turn and he couldn't do it. Sick to his stomach, he felt his body quivering with a loathing like no other. A woman was dead, his uncle devastated, and the one thing that could save him was in her possession. But it was her attack on Sofia that made his body burn like a volcano about to erupt.

His fists and teeth clenched. His body, no longer trembling was stiff as a board. He spun on his heels and marched out the door. He needed a date with a punching bag, who in his mind, would look remarkably like Gina.

❧❦❧

Ersilia rested her arms on the desk close to where Gina sat. "I have a favor to ask," she said.

Gina continued her work and never glanced in her direction. "Sure, Mrs. Palmalosi."

She bent near the young woman's ear. "This is a delicate matter and I know if anyone can be discreet, it's you, dear."

Her head perked up. "What's going on?"

For the first time, Ersilia truly stared into the depth of the woman's eyes. What returned her gaze were cold, hollow, mahogany circles. She looked away but kept her resolve to plant a seed of interest in the witch's head.

"It seems one of our paintings may hold an important clue to a two-hundred-and-fifty-year-old puzzle. Intriguing, don't you think?" She paced behind Gina, finally stopping on the other side of her. "We'll issue a press release if it comes to fruition, but until then we don't want to draw any attention to ourselves. What if it turns out to be nothing, how terribly embarrassing would that be?" Ersilia fanned herself for added dramatic effect. "Anyway, when Clarence and Gertrude Wilton arrive please escort them to the Restoration Room. Silvio and I will greet them there. It will be less conspicuous."

Gina swiveled her chair toward Ersilia. "Is it a treasure map of some sort?"

"No, I believe it's something musical."

Gina cocked her head and pushed her chair away from the desk. "Do you mean a lost sonnet from a famous composer?"

"It's nothing personal, dear, but I don't want to give out too many details." Ersilia walked away, but spoke over her shoulder. "Thanks for your help."

She hurried back to her office and let out a sigh of relief. Just speaking to the woman made her skin crawl. You didn't attack her daughter, wreak havoc in the lives of people she cared for, and get away with it. When the time was right, she would have her moment with Gina.

ತ◌ಌ

After a vigorous workout, Armend stood in the lobby once more, out of sight from Gina. His anger now manageable, he forced his feet to take him in her direction. He'd been distant toward her since the regrettable drunken night in the backseat of her car, so to spark up a conversation would be out of character. He wasn't worried. She never let him pass without stopping him to flirt.

"Hi, Armend." She sat up straight and pushed her shoulders back. "Where have you been the last few days?"

Right on cue. He didn't have to act somber. His heavy heart was real. "I was upstate in the Catskill Mountains. There was a death in my family. My uncle's friend of twenty years died suddenly."

"I'm sorry to hear that." A look of genuine sorrow crossed her face. "Was she sick?"

"How do you know it was a woman?"

Cool, composed, and confident, she rose and walked out from behind her desk. He stepped back not wanting to be any nearer to her than he already was. "Family doesn't gather for a relative's loss of a buddy, but at the loss of a lover."

"Sadly, she had no family at the disbursement of her ashes."

"I'm sure her family wanted to be there. Maybe there were circumstances that prevented it." She went to her chair, ran her hands down the back of her skirt to smooth it, and sat. "You shouldn't judge people until you know their side of the story."

She was unflappable and it unnerved him.

"I guess you're right."

"I'd ask you if there was something I could do for you." She twirled a strand of hair around her pointer finger and ran her tongue over her top lip. "But rumor has it you and Sofia are a couple.

"Not true. I told you, I'm a free agent. I don't commit to any one team for a long period of time." A family appeared at the desk. "Go help them. I have an important meeting in the Restoration Room with Silvio, Ersilia, and some other people. I don't want to be late."

Her head jerked to one side with a startled expression before she collected herself.

Got her. He had chiseled a small crack in the ice queen.

એએએ

Sofia entered the gallery through the service door in the back of the building. She moseyed down the softly lit corridor and stopped behind a pedestal holding a replica bust of Caesar. Peering to the left of the Emperor, she had a rear view of Gina at her desk, talking on the phone.

She checked her watch. Right on time. Alexandros, her father's friend and owner of the Onufri painting, should be demanding to speak with Silvio.

Gina appeared to put the caller on hold and walked down the hall. Sofia swiftly mingled into a small group of people, pulled out her new phone, and texted Armend. *She's on her way.*

Sofia slinked to edge of the corner, close enough to hear, but out of sight. Gina tapped on the door. "Excuse me, Mr. Palmalosi, I'm sorry to interrupt, but Mr. Gouraris says it's urgent he speak to you about the painting. He's on hold on line one."

"Thank you, Gina. I'll take it my office."

Sofia heard her father's footsteps approaching. As he went past, he glanced in her direction and nodded. After a minute, she followed him partially down the hall and sat on a bench, camouflaged by a large, full palm tree. Her view was somewhat obstructed, but she could make out Silvio, who had left the door half-open and Gina, who had sauntered to her desk and then circled back to the meeting room.

Sofia sent another text. *She's outside the door. Make it convincing.*

Sofia wasn't privy to the conversation, but Armend knew in order to lure Gina out, he must reveal that the painting held his family's half of the music. She leaned back, parted two palm branches between her fingers, and watched Gina's reaction.

⌇⌇⌇

Gina pressed her back up long against the cool wall and tilted her ear to the open door. It couldn't be true, merely a coincidence. Armend was a part-time art researcher so he would naturally be interested in an age-old puzzle and many a treasure had been hidden in artwork through the ages. But she wouldn't rest until she knew for sure.

"Show Gertrude and Clarence the journal," Ersilia said.

"My ancestor, Ilir, wrote a specific passage in his journal his last day in Albania before he travelled back to Italy."

Gina listened as the sound of pages turning evoked a response from the restorers. "Be careful with that," the man, Clarence, said. "The book itself is of great value."

"Ilir worked at Onufri's school as a mere handy man. He polished the newly added frames."

Gina's fingers tightened around the pen in her right hand.

"That makes perfect sense," Gertrude said. "In Onufri's time, artwork was not framed. That came to be in the eighteenth century."

"This particular landscape piece reminded him of the field where he and Ambra would lay together," Armend continued. "He tried to leave a clue to the family in the journal, but either they never saw it or didn't understand it. Here take a look."

"Yes, I agree. It's a precise description of the painting in question, even down to the colors in the horizon," Clarence agreed.

Gina's arm swung back and forth like a pendulum, the pen jabbing into her thigh.

"Besides the fact it's a family heirloom, it seems to have a greater importance to you," Gertrude said.

"Let's just say there has been bad blood between our family and Ambra's for centuries. If we can connect the two pieces of music, we thought it would act as a symbolic gesture of goodwill."

The pen thrust into Gina's leg as her arm swayed harder and faster, back and forth. *No, no, no!*

"Do you know the whereabouts of the other half?"

"We had it, but it was recently taken from us."

Blood trickled down her leg. *How dare he tell outsiders their business?*

"It seems both families would like to end the animosity, except for one member on Ambra's side," Ersilia added.

"We think she stole the music from my uncle, the rightful owner. We're confident we'll get it back."

They continued the conversation, but Gina had heard enough. They might think they were clever enough to outsmart her, but they shouldn't underestimate her. She'd always be a step ahead. When this was over, the curse would claim Armend, and she would have both pieces of music.

This was that backstabber George's fault. But she wouldn't break her promise to her aunt and hurt him. Someone else would have to take the fall for him and she had the perfect person in mind.

CHAPTER 28

If we are to have magical bodies, we must have magical minds. – Dr. Wayne Dyer, American author and lecturer

It was disturbing to watch." Sofia pushed hanger after hanger from right to left, looking for just the right size for Armend. "She kept gouging herself until I'm sure there was blood. Then she walked away into the ladies room as if nothing happened."

"I'm not surprised," Armend said. "She's not stable. Her reaction tells us we struck a chord and got her attention. I'd be lying if I said I wasn't a little nervous about her next move. We'll have to stay alert." He strolled into her walk-in closet. "Um, should I question why you have a closet full of men's robes?"

"No. Here try this one." She handed him a black, hooded robe. "When I belonged to a coven, I always had extras. Now I prefer being a solitary witch, practicing alone or with my family."

He slipped his arms through the sleeves and she pulled it closed across his chest. "Perfect fit." She rested her hands on his chest and he cupped her face in his hands. Their lips collided with a scorching passion that had ignited the day they met. Pulling her arms over her head, he held her firmly against the closet door. She yielded and thoughts of him inside her, loving her, filled her body and mind with undeniable pleasure.

"Armend, later, please. The moon." The words left her mouth, but she paid them no attention and pulled him into her, kissing him harder. "It's full tonight. We have to stop." She shoved him away with a strength she didn't know she had. He stood still. His chest rose and fell with each pant. His steel eyes burned into her with a desire that nearly caused her to say, "What the hell, there's another full moon next month," push him down on the bed, rip his clothes off, and climb on top of him. Instead, she moved further away from him. "I'm sorry, but the moon has to be a certain degree in the sky. That happens soon. I need my new wand charged tonight in case she attacks."

"I know." Armend sat down on the edge of the bed. "Just give me a minute."

"We'll have all night after the ritual."

He gave her a devilish grin. "I'll have you back up here and out of your robe before you can say 'blessed be.'"

"I'm counting on it." Not trusting herself, she kept her distance from him. "Now go in the other room so I don't have any more distractions, take off your clothes, and put your robe on. I'll meet you downstairs in five minutes."

"What?" He groaned. "Is that necessary?"

"No." She grinned. "But it's more fun."

❧❧❧

At the edge of the meadow, the night sky was clear and welcoming. The moon hung low, pale as a ghost. The October chill embraced them, but they were warm in their robes. Armend laced his fingers with Sofia's as they stood mesmerized by the glistening moonbeams on the Hudson River below.

"*Gumusservi*," Sofia said, "is a Turkish word for moonlight on water."

"It's beautiful."

She faced him and took his other hand in hers. "Armend, you have to concentrate and believe fully in what you are saying tonight. If you don't, it won't work."

"I know," he said, trying to focus despite the fact she was completely naked underneath her robe. "I believe. I remember the life force of the tree. It's not something you soon forget."

"Good." Letting go of his hands, she backed away from him. She splayed her arms to the side forming the letter T. "Solstice, come!"

They waited in silence, the song of the cicadas the only noise. Armend looked to the sky for the bird that was Sofia's familiar, but only saw the twinkling stars. A low cawing came from the distance. In a quick graceful swoop, the crow perched on her right arm.

"Isn't she gorgeous?"

Armend thought she looked like a regular crow. It was dark and the bird's feathers were black so it was hard to tell. "Yes. Can I pet her?"

"I wouldn't just yet. She doesn't know you." She reached in her pocket and fed her friend a cracker. "Soon you two will be friends. Solstice and Lautner have gotten over their natural rivalry." She placed her hand over his. "Now take your wand and face east." Solstice flew off her arm and landed at her feet.

"My Lady, Mistress of Night and of Magick,
"You who rule the star-filled heavens
"Bless and empower this wand.
"We sanction this wand to the element of air
"And charge Armend with its care
"On this special enchanted night
"Fill his wand with magical delights."

She removed her hand and motioned to him. He clasped the wand between his palms. It was warm to his touch and his hands began to tingle. A sense of empowerment and pleasure fell over him as the wand's energy vibrated up his arms and throughout his body. It had accepted and connected with him. The expression on his face must have given away his exhilaration. Sofia gave him a proud smile and blew a kiss in his direction. He spoke the words she taught him:

"I pledge to use this tool in its natural way
"The laws of the universe I will obey
"Never used for harm or to offend
"Unless called to protect and defend.
"Blessed be."

He lowered the wand. Sofia was at his side. "Congratulation, you're the owner of a powerful wand. It's a gift from the universe and must be respected. I'll teach you how to use it. It's a slow process and you have to be patient."

The whole experience left him speechless. He carefully placed the wand in a leather sheath she had given him earlier. Now, it was her turn.

Sofia faced the moon and held up her wand. It was small and delicate and gave the appearance of fragility. He knew she would pass to it her strength and might and a potent partnership would be formed. A partnership one would be wise not to anger.

At ease in this environment, she danced around the field, her arms open and accepting of everything the earth and cosmos had to offer. She was graceful and elegant. He could watch her all night. Solstice soared high above her in circles.

"Blessed be." The words spoken, she ran to him. Her cheeks were a light pink color and her wide eyes sparkled with joy. She threw her arms around him. "I'm so happy to share this wonderful night with you."

"Me, too," he said and stroked her flushed face. "I love you."

"I love you, too."

"Are you ready to go back?"

The crow flew over their heads and into the night.

"More than ready."

He took her hand. After a few steps she stopped. "Wait."

"What's wrong?"

"I'm not sure." She faced south against the wind and raised her hands and head to the sky. "There's negative energy pulsing in the air."

"Gina?"

She shuddered. "I don't know."

Armend put his arm around her. "Let's go."

CHAPTER 29

We loved with a love that was more than love.
– Edgar Allan Poe, 1809 – 1849,
American author and poet

Sofia dimmed the lights and lit candles around her bedroom. She let the calming scent of lavender and vanilla relax her. She slipped into her sexiest stiletto heels and waited for Armend. Still uneasy about the troublesome force outside, she stood in front of an arched window and peered into the darkness.

Armend walked up behind her. His hands rested on her shoulders and he kissed the back of her head. "Still worried?"

"A little." With a quick flip of her wrist the silk rope holding her robe together was undone and hanging at her side. "I could use a diversion."

A low guttural groan escaped him. Her robe fell provocatively off her shoulders, exposing the sloping curves of her breasts. Never taking her eyes off their shimmering reflection in the window, she reveled in the darts of pleasure that stung at her as he hungrily feasted on her neck, like a creature of the night feeding off his prey. His arms enveloped her waist and released her remaining grip of the robe. He coaxed the dark garment down her arms, past her waist, until it crumpled in a pile on the floor around her feet. She stepped over the robe, making sure he saw her black pumps, and kicked it to the corner.

"Mmm." He raised his head and stared at her in the blackened glass, his gaze transfixed with desire.

Shameless in her nakedness, she lifted her arms behind her. Taking his time, he let his palms graze over her breasts.

He fondled and caressed them, circling her erect nipples with his thumb, eventually giving them a gentle squeeze between his forefinger and thumb. "*Dashuria ime*, you'flike an exquisite piece of artwork."

If that was true, then he was the artist—his hand, the brush that brought her to life with every tantalizing stroke.

His fingers seductively roamed down her sides while he nibbled on her shoulder. Then he rested his head next to hers. Together they gazed at their mirror image as his hands strayed to her stomach, playing with the turquoise jewelry that dangled from her belly button.

"Sexy," he whispered, his breath hot on her throat.

He moved lower, tracing the outline of her thigh. She widened her stance and he firmly clutched between her legs. His fingers lingered, magically dancing inside her.

Watching him love her and seeing her body react was sensual and erotic. It heightened her arousal to a breaking point. Ripples of pleasure flowed through her. She shoved her pelvis toward him and gasped with delight.

"Turn around." His voice was husky and demanding.

ॐॐॐ

Like a poised dancer, she spun to face him. "You're a little over dressed, don't you think?" Armend yanked off his robe and tossed it on the bed. Her hazel eyes, darkened by her large pupils, scanned his entire body with lustful abandon. She curled her lips in a wicked smile.

"You're a bad girl."

"I'll take that as a compliment."

He wrapped her arms around his neck and she stepped closer to him. He swept her dark hair to one side. Now he was the lone voyeur. The reflection of her sleek back, illuminated by the flickering flames of the candles, was for his eyes only.

As if he wasn't already hard as rock, she parted her legs, arched her back, and stuck her bottom out. She had the sweetest ass, ever, and now it was in his solid grip. He drew her into him as his heart slammed into his chest. His palms desperately reached down to the back of her thighs and lifted her. She wound her legs around his waist. He pinned her against the wall. Their bodies locked together—perfectly.

He'd fantasized about this moment since he first laid his eyes on her. He never thought it possible, but she was in his arms, her eyes full of love and desire. After tonight, things would change. He wouldn't be able to stay away from her, even for her own safety. They already shared a deep connection, but after their bodies joined, a bond would form. A bond, for him, that was forever.

She parted her full lips, "Ar—"

He stopped her with a hard, deep kiss, his tongue rolling around her warm mouth. Her fingers tangled with his hair and she pulled his head back, responding with such passion, it sent chills down his spine.

"The—bed," she said breathlessly.

He didn't make it to the bed but toppled into a cushioned straight back chair set in the corner. She straddled him, her legs forming a sexy ninety-degree angle high up on her heels. His head bent toward her. Having had his hands on her, he hungered for her taste. His mouth rolled over her breasts, kissing and sucking. His tongue slid along the crease underneath them. Her soft skin was salty and moist.

She straightened her long legs and stood over him, making him crazy. "Please Sofia," he gasped, "sit down." With her left hand on his shoulder, and holding him in her right, she lowered herself guiding him inside her.

☙❧❧

Never before had she wanted to surrender herself completely to another man. As he sunk fully inside her, she wanted him to consume her, possess, and own her.

With his eyes closed and his hands gripping her hips, he controlled the rigorous pace at which she moved, causing her to ache with pleasure.

The veins of his neck bulged and his muscles tightened. "Baby, you feel amazing."

The heat of their passion left her speechless. Their bodies came together like a wonderful chaotic storm. Euphoria riddled through her body. He held her tight, thrusting himself inside her one final time. His back arched in spasms and she pressed herself against him, both of them drowning in a sea of ecstasy.

☙☙☙

They clung to each other. Sofia cradled her head in the crook of Armend's neck. Her hand, pressed against his warm, damp chest, caught his heartbeat. A heavenly haze of sex, passion, and love embraced them and she wished this moment would never end. Sexual tension and a desperate desire for each other made their coupling ardent and frenzied, but at the core was pure love.

He lifted her chin and kissed her tenderly on the lips. "Come on." With a reluctant sigh, she got off his lap only to have him scoop her up in his arms. He carried her to the bed, laid her down on the soft down comforter, and covered her with his discarded robe. "Sorry, we didn't make it here earlier."

"That chair will always be special to me."

As he stretched out next to her, she closed her eyes to force back tears, but they escaped from her anyway.

"Sofia?"

"Heart on my sleeve, remember?" She inched close to him and they naturally entwined their arms and legs. "I've never been this close to someone, this loved before. I don't want—"

"Shh." He put his finger to her lips. "I knew when I first saw you that you were my *pergjithomone nje.*" He kissed her stream of tears away.

"Is that a good thing?"

"Yes." He laughed. "My Albanian grandmother believed every person had a *pergjithomone nje*, a forever one. Any attractive person could make your heart beat fast, your breath quicken, and be the object of physical desire. When you met your forever one, it was different. Your heart would stop cold as if pierced by a sharp object."

"You won't be able to breathe and have to catch your breath," Sofia countered.

"While you desire their body—"

"You want to know their spirit and mind as well."

"Yes. That's your forever one." He raised an eyebrow to her. "How did you know?"

"It's exactly what happened to me the first time I saw you on the steps of the gallery.

He rolled on his back and pulled her on top of him with ease. "I guess we're stuck with each other forever." He ran his fingers through her hair. "I just hope my forever is longer than December."

She pushed herself off him and sat up in a huff. "I hate it when you talk like that. We've been through this. Nothing is going to happen to you. I'll make sure of it."

"Hey." He rubbed her back. "I know with you by my side we can beat this thing."

At his mere touch, she melted. His strength and willpower were admirable. Even with a dark cloud looming over his head, he was able to love and protect her. He laid there, a handsome temptation. His entire, beautiful being had been created to be united with her being in this life. She thought it would be a good idea if they did what nature intended and came together again, and soon. Her mouth trickled down the length of his lean torso. "There's so much we didn't get to do."

"We can fix that," he groaned as she wantonly teased him with her tongue.

"We'll take our time."

"Just promise me," he gulped, "you'll leave the shoes on."

"I promise." Her head fell onto him as she took him in her mouth.

CHAPTER 30

I put a capital N on nature and call it my church. – *Frank Lloyd Wright, 1867 – 1959, American architect*

L autner jumped on Armend's head, waking him. "Hey buddy, hungry?"

Sofia lay sprawled across him, her face down in the pillow, snoring. Remnants of the previous night's celebration littered the room. Two empty bottles of champagne lay on their side on the floor. Lautner leaned over sniffing at the half-eaten platter of leftover chocolate covered strawberries teetering on the nightstand.

He shook her softly. "Sof, you need to wake up. It's eight o'clock Sunday morning."

He had been here four days and couldn't be happier. Every day he had left early and gone to the city. He had snuck up to his apartment and then made his appearance in the lobby, making sure Gina saw him arrive from upstairs. This morning, however, he was ecstatic. He had to remember to call George.

"I thought someone declared Sunday a day of rest," she groaned a protest. "I have a headache."

"Not for us." He gave backside a love pat. "I have to get to the gallery and you drank too much champagne."

"It was a special occasion." She sat up, stretched her arms over her head, and yawned. Her breasts rose in an enticing display. He gave them each a quick nibble, wishing he had time to give them the full attention they deserved.

"What a nice way to be woken up." She took his face in her hands. "This is one of the best days of my life. To think, we have your half of the music, safe and sound in my father's personal safe."

"I know, baby, and I have you to thank. If you hadn't given me some of your magic, I wouldn't have seen Ilir hide the music."

"You've always had the power. I just gave you a small prod."

"I better get going. I want to thank Clarence and Gertrude. I appreciate their willingness to put on this show today, even though they found the music yesterday. I have to set everything up before Gina gets there." He pushed the blanket to the side. "I wish you could be there with me."

"I'll be there in spirit. It's better this way. The longer we keep Gina in the dark about our relationship, the better."

He leaned over and kissed her. "Finally, we're getting close to breaking the curse and freeing my family."

᙮

The cold liquid from Sofia's second glass of water swirled around her cottonmouth, having a soothing effect. She chased that with aspirin and ate oatmeal topped with fruit for breakfast. She washed her face and threw her hair up in a quick bun with a clip. The clock struck nine. Aaron and his small group of congregants would be here soon. She slipped her sunglasses on and stepped outside into the bright sunshine of the tepid Indian summer, October morning.

"Morning, Sofia," Aaron yelled from across the field.

She picked up her sluggish pace and met him half way. "Hi, there. You certainly have a beautiful morning for your worship."

"I wish more people were coming. Only ten signed up."

"You may be surprised. Humans are curious by nature. More may show up to say they've been to the witch's lair."

"And lived to tell about it," he added with a shy grin.

"Good one." She laughed. "We put this tent up yesterday. I have two large coffee pots and I ordered donuts. I hope that's okay."

"It's very generous, thank you."

A man and woman approached carrying a large wooden object. Aaron introduced them. "Juan and Maria, this is Sofia, our host."

"Good morning," they replied in obvious discomfort about being there.

"What a beautiful carved cross," exclaimed Sofia. She put her hand out to touch it. They pulled back. "Last year my father had a display of different religious symbols from around the world at his gallery. The workmanship is top notch. Is it old?" She stepped closer and again, they moved away from her.

So this was how it was going to be. She could take the high road—or she could play with them a bit. "You know, witches are fine with crosses. It's vampires that don't like them. Although the vampires I know aren't bothered by them either," she said with a chuckle.

Not a smile between them. She rolled her eyes behind the safety of her sunglasses and laid her hand the top of the cross. "Ouch!" She jumped back and gave them her most shocked face. She poked Aaron and giggled. "Just kidding."

Aaron shot her a pleading glance, although she saw a glimmer of amusement in his eyes. Fine, she'd let them win. Her pounding head wasn't up to much more. "I'm sorry. It wasn't my intention to offend you. Enjoy your service and the wonderful morning nature has provided."

As she walked away, Aaron caught up with her. "Sorry about that. They are two of our more conservative members. I thought if I could convince them to come, others would follow. Everyone else is much more open-minded and friendly."

She tried to ease his worries. "Aaron, I'm just glad they're here. It's a first step to a better understanding. I'm sure in the end most of us will be friends." She ushered him back to the tent. "Look more people are coming. I'll see you later."

∾∾

Aaron was unfolding chairs and setting them in rows of five. He would set up for twenty on the small chance Sofia was right.

"Need some help?" a female voice asked.

Aaron looked up to find a woman before him, steam rising from a cup of gourmet coffee in her hand. "Sure," he said.

Soft brown curls fell to her shoulders framing her attractive face. Her eyes matched the color of her hair and were bright and cheerful. She wore a V-neck sweater, exposing a long, swan-like neck. However, it was directly below her neckline his eyes came to a stop. He didn't mean to stare, but couldn't look away.

"That's some nice equipment you have there." The words came out before he could stop them.

"Why, thank you. Would you like a better look?" Her free hand slid past her breast and grabbed the Nikon D700 camera that hung from a black strap. She put her coffee down on a chair and pulled the camera strap over her head. "Here." She handed it to him.

"It's a beauty. I have a Canon EOD 7D." They passed the next few minutes discussing shutter speed and lag, interchangeable lenses, and the advantages of manual verses automatic focus. She was knowledgeable and he was impressed.

"Where are my manners? Hi, I'm Aaron." He offered his hand. "Are you a new member of the church?"

"Hi. I'm Adelina. No, I'm here for a visit."

"I have to finish setting up. If you're still around after the service—" He hesitated. There was a simplicity about her he liked and he wanted to talk with her again. "Maybe we could meet under the tent for coffee."

"I'd like that."

"Adelina!" Sofia and the woman threw their arms around each other, squealing in joy. "I'm so happy to see you. I have so much to tell you."

"Tomorrow is Halloween. I wouldn't miss celebrating with my family."

"Aaron, I see you've met my sister."

His heart sank. Being Sofia's sister and celebrating Halloween as an important family holiday meant she too was a witch. "Yes. I was admiring her camera. I have to run."

"Bye, Aaron," Adelina said. "I'll see you later for coffee."

He didn't answer her and disappeared into the small crowd of parishioners.

ⅇⅉⅇⅉ

Aaron welcomed and thanked everyone for coming, then turned the service over to the Deacon. Adelina strolled around snapping photos. Standing tall, her posture was strong and confident. Graceful and limber, she bent, swayed, and kneeled to get just the right shot. She was a rude distraction with her fitted jeans, heeled boots, and sweater that clung to her every curve. He shifted his position away from her and listened intently to Paul's Letter to the Ephesians.

When the service was over, he was surprised. More people than he expected had shown up and everyone agreed how refreshing it was to be outside for their worship. Sofia circulated among the small crowd, shaking hands and thanking them for coming. She was gracious and charming and although most the congregants seemed to respond to her, there were a few holdouts.

Out of the corner of his eye, he saw Adelina waiting for him with two cups of coffee. He didn't want to stand her up, but there was no use in pursuing this any further. She was a nice woman and he wished her well, but there was no future for them.

Then a man he recognized began to speak to her. They didn't call him Larry, the Ladies Man, for nothing. He supposed the least he could do was rescue her from his stale come-ons.

"Hi there," she said as he approached. "Larry, it was nice talking to you, but I have to show Aaron something." The two men acknowledged each other as Larry walked away. "I have some great pictures of you during your introduction. You're very photogenic." Her voice had a husky edge to it. Was she flirting with him?

"That's great. I'm sorry, but I forgot I already told someone else I'd meet them after church. Can you give them to Sofia?"

"Sure." Disappointment clouded her voice. "I understand."

"Thanks." He darted to other side of the tent when Sofia stepped in his path. She stood unyielding with her arms crossed and a stern look on her face. "You're perfect for each other," she said. "I knew it the day I met you. Beside photography, she loves the water and could teach you a thing or two about sailing."

He faced the river and admired the sailboats drifting smoothly along, the wind at their rear. He wished he were on the water. Floating aimlessly with no worries and definitely not having this conversation. "No, it won't work."

"You haven't even tried.

"You know why."

"Witch, bitch, snitch. They're all labels we give to each other. Unfortunately, we let society, politics, and religions tell us who we are. We're all human beings first, human beings that want the same thing: to be happy and to be loved."

"We're too different."

"Then be a man about it and tell her the real reason."

She was right. This wasn't like him. Adelina rattled something inside him. Something that hadn't been *rattled* since his heart was broken. He was ashamed at his behavior and turned to go back.

But she was gone.

CHAPTER 31

Revenge is a small circle. – *Edward Counsel,*
1849 – 1939, Tasmanian author

Gina stepped into the elevator and pushed the button to the third floor. Armend would be in his apartment by now.

He was going to a lot of trouble to keep up this charade, but she would play along. She was well aware he spent his nights with Sofia.

She despised his cowardly lies. They had shared something special and still would if that bitch Sofia minded her own business and didn't ruin everything. His betrayal was two-fold. She loathed the idea he told total strangers their family history *and* turned to them for help.

After he gets his prize today, he'll call George and they'll have a touching family moment. Do they think the other piece of music will magically float into their hands? It won't. What he didn't realize is that while he was enjoying his time between the sheets with Sofia, she stayed focused on being ahead of the game.

George was a minor obstacle, but there was no reason for him to come to Manhattan. Armend wouldn't dare remove the music from the safety of its hiding place to show him.

He would do his part from the Catskills and try to track down the disobedient niece who didn't do anything wrong except take what was rightly hers.

She'd pay close attention today. Silvio and Ersilia trusted her. Armend and George had no clue that she and Reggie were one and the same.

Finding and obtaining their part of the music would be a walk in the park. They would soon pay for their disloyalty.

The elevator doors glided open. She sauntered down the hall to Armend's apartment.

CHAPTER 32

We are bound by the secrets we share. –
*Zoe Heller, English journalist and novelis*t

Aaron paced back and forth on Sofia's front porch, a check for one hundred and twelve dollars made out to the Bog Turtle fund tucked in his pocket. He thought about mailing it, but when Adelina went inside with Sofia, he decided to use it as an excuse to see her.

It was unseasonably warm for the end of October and the front door was open. The only thing separating him from the thing he needed to do was the screen door. Muffled voices traveled from the back of the house and his attempt at knocking was drowned out by women's laughter. He opened the door and went inside.

He wasn't intentionally being quiet, but the lush area rugs silenced his footsteps. They didn't hear him approach the kitchen. He heard his name and stopped to listen.

"Aaron's a great guy," Sofia said.

"You're reading too much into it, Sofia. We just met. I mean he's very attractive and, wow, he had a great aura, pure and honest. He asked me to meet him for coffee under the tent. Isn't that charming?"

He had a great what? Very attractive? He knew he wasn't handsome, not in the rugged, hot way women liked. Instead, he was always referred to as the cute, responsible, nice guy. This was his first "very attractive."

"He may come around."

"I'm used to it," Adelina sighed. "You meet someone and are hopeful, but I know it's hard to bring a witch home for Sunday dinner."

"Armend's back," Sofia said and the back door squealed.

There were rustling noises and a brief *pwah* sound. Were they kissing? Their relationship had apparently changed since last week.

"My sister tells me you've already met."

"Adelina, nice to see you," Armend said. "We met in August at the gallery before she went off on her ghost hunting adventure."

Ghost hunting! Aaron shook his head in disbelief. He had made amends with Sofia. Members of the church had met and spoke with her. He was hopeful they would stop protesting her. He was done here and should leave, but it was as if his feet were stuck in concrete. He didn't move.

"So how did it go?" Sofia asked. Chairs scrapped along the floor. "I told Adelina everything. I hope you don't mind."

"Nah, I don't mind. The nightmare is almost over. It was so cool to hold my destiny in my hands," Armend explained. "Even though they would only let me hold it for a minute and I had to wear white gloves. It was old and fragile and we wanted to put it back where it was safe. The only thing that would have made it better is if you and George were there."

"I'll be there when we get to merge the two pieces together. What about Gina?"

"Sof, I think you need to cancel the festivities tonight."

"Why?"

"Gina was different today. It was eerie. She knocked on my apartment door and told me your parents wanted to talk to me. She didn't flirt with me or use sexual innuendos like usual. She barely gave me the time of day."

"Are you complaining?"

"No. It might be flattering if she wasn't a psycho," he laughed. "Afterwards we called her in to the office on the false pretense that Gertrude and Clarence needed two witness signatures on a legal document. She and I signed it. We were subtle with the clues. We would refer to it as 'the old music,' but never mentioned anything about its importance to me. She watched us put a fake envelope into your father's safe in his office. That's where she thinks it is."

"It sounds like the plan worked. Why would I cancel to-night?"

"She came up to me as I was leaving. She said she thought you and I made a good pair and hoped we worked it out. That it would make Ersilia and Silvio happy if we were together. It was weird. The look in her eyes—it creeped me out. I think she may be watching us."

"It's an annual event I have each year the night before Halloween. If I call it off, it will disappoint a lot people, especially the kids. Then Gina wins. I won't do it."

"What if she sabotages the event somehow? You already said you think she'll attack you again."

Attack. Aaron had heard enough and, with more bravado than he felt, walked into the kitchen. "I'm sorry to interrupt, but Sofia, if you're in trouble, we need to call the police."

Armend came at him, grabbed his arm, and pulled him in the other room. "I'll make sure nothing happens to Sofia. This isn't your business." He wasn't surprised by Armend's reaction. He remembered his defensive behavior the day in the parking lot.

The two men stood at the same height. Armend was broader and probably had more experience in the brawling department, but Aaron could hold his own if need be. He yanked himself loose from Armend's grip. "Then do the right thing."

"I don't need you to tell me—"

"Armend," yelled Sofia. "Aaron's my friend. I hate when you get like this. Let's go." She marched him back in the kitchen.

Aaron felt he had caused enough trouble and headed toward the front door. "Don't go." He stopped mid gait. How could he face Adelina now? He'd just made a fool of himself. He relented, turned, and admired her slender figure resting against the doorframe. The sweater, jeans, and boots she wore were just as distracting as they were earlier. The sun gleaming through the window sparkled in her eyes.

"I'm sorry about before," he said.

"It's okay."

"It's not what you think."

"Yes it is. I'm—"

"Used to it. Yeah, I heard."

"Are you a professional eavesdropper?"

"I'm not so attractive anymore, huh?" *Did he just say that?*

"On the contrary, I find you quite attractive. Your aura is still pretty fine, too." She flashed him the kindest most genuine smile he'd ever seen and for a moment, it stole his breath. "Take a seat. If I know Sofia, she'll want to talk to you."

He sat on the couch in the hopes she would sit next to him. Nothing could come of it, but he didn't see any reason why he shouldn't enjoy her company for a few minutes.

Armend appeared, like a dog with its tail between its legs, hand extended. "Sorry. Sofia is fond of you and we should try to be friends."

"Sure." They gripped each other in a firm handshake.

"That wasn't so hard, was it?" Sofia asked. "Aaron, how much did you hear?"

"Oh, he heard everything," Adelina said a sly smirk on her face.

"Well, then, when you listen in on other people's secrets you become a part of them."

"I heard bits and pieces." He rose to his feet. "I have to go. Your secret is safe with me."

Sofia pushed him down on his butt. "Oh no, you don't. We have something we need the two of you to do for us. Consider it an adventure."

"Me—" He touched his chest with his fingers, gulped, and pointed to Sofia's sister. "—and her?"

Adelina and her sweet fragrance of vanilla and orange plopped next to him. "An adventure! Count me in," she said, rubbing her hands together like a cartoon character. "What do you want us to do?"

"What you two like to do most," Sofia said. "Take pictures."

"It's perfect," Armend said. "Neither of you know Gina. She started working at the gallery after Adelina left. We'd like You to keep an eye on her."

"I'm not spying on anyone," Aaron argued.

"You will if you want to keep Sofia safe."

"I don't even understand what's going on."

"We'll explain everything," Armend slapped him on the back. "Now that we're pals, what's your preference, beer or wine?"

"Beer." He was curious about the threat to Sofia and worried it would extend to Adelina now that she was here. He would hear them out, decline their offer of espionage, and call the police.

CHAPTER 33

And above all, watch with glittering eyes the whole world
around you because the greatest secrets are
always hidden in the most unlikely places.
Those who don't believe in magic will never find it.
– Roald Dahl, 1919 – 1990, British children's author

Aaron scraped the beer label with his thumbnail. He longed for one more gulp of beer to help him grasp everything they had told him. A modern day wacko witch, ancient witches, numerous dead people through the years, one person recently murdered, and now they were close to breaking the curse that started all this, *and* they wanted his help. They were just as crazy as the woman who was after them. He did have a twinge of remorse for the tragedy Armend's family had gone through, but Armend was young, strong, and healthy. To think he was going to drop dead in two months due to a curse was ridiculous.

"So will you help us?" Sofia asked.

"This is way beyond what normal people can deal with," Aaron said. "You need to call the authorities, explain to them Gina murdered her aunt, and now she's stalking you. You said your father is having the jar tested for poison. There's your proof."

"That won't prove anything except the honey was what killed her. It'll be her word against ours. We don't have proof she's the one who gave it to Gisella." Sofia took the empty bottle from him. "Anyway, we're not normal people, remember?"

"I've never seen you do anything out of the ordinary."

She whipped around and challenged him. "Do you doubt my magical abilities?"

"Sofia, don't," Adelina cautioned.

"No—I—" he stammered.

"Shh!" Sofia placed the long neck of the beer bottle on the top of his head like a Queen about to Knight one of her faithful. He'd spent enough time with her to know it wasn't in her nature to hurt someone. Still, he held his breath and braced himself for whatever was about to happen.

She tapped him three times and spoke.

"Aaron wishes for his eyes to behold
"So nothing from him will I withhold,
"To hear the witches cackle and wail
"As the mysteries of magick they unveil
"Join us he must in the circle we cast around
"Magic, Magic will abound!"

Adelina squeezed his arm. "Translation, stay for the Halloween party tonight and you'll see plenty of magic." The two women burst into laughter.

"Come on, Adelina. I need help getting ready."

Armend loomed over him. "You can breathe now." Aaron let out a sigh. "I could use your help tonight," Armend continued. "If there was another set of eyes watching for something suspicious, I'd feel better. After that, you can leave and never look back."

❧❧❧

Aaron trudged through the grassy field with his arms full of candy. The property oozed eerie Halloween ambiance. Cauldrons bubbled over with purple, orange, and red mist, courtesy of dry ice and battery operated lights that he and Armend had spent the afternoon setting up. Jack-o-lanterns hung securely within the branches of the trees, their ominous eyes peering down on the innocent visitors as they passed by.

Excitement pounded his chest and he thought back to his childhood. His family loved Halloween until he was ten and his father died suddenly. At twelve, his mother remarried.

They joined a new church and from that day on Halloween ceased to exist for him and his sister. His church friends wouldn't understand his being here tonight, but Halloween was tomorrow, so he convinced himself he wasn't celebrating All Hallows Eve.

He arrived at the barn where the *spookateers,* the teenagers who worked at the Preserve during the summer and volunteered at Halloween, would distribute the treats to the kids. They had done a great job at transforming it into a haunted house for the evening. He tossed the candy in an old wheelbarrow and left.

ℓ∕ɔℓ∕ɔ

This year's turnout was one of the best and Sofia was thrilled. Bridget was busy in the gift shop. Armend and Bill Nighthawk were helping kids bob for apples and pick a souvenir from the witch's bag. She had already explained the working altar of the Strega and true meaning of Halloween or Shadow Fest once this evening. She and Adelina would do it one more time, later. Right now, she and her sister were whittling down the long line of patrons interested in holding a genuine wand and having their picture taken with a bona fide witch. On Halloween, people came to see the witch and she didn't disappoint.

Aaron did his job and snapped pictures of them with kids and families—when he was able to take his eyes off Adelina. Her sister, adorned in a long, purple cape tied at the neck but otherwise open, looked hot in her tasteful yet tight black dress, fishnet stockings, and knee high boots. Her hair was in an updo, her eyes accented with more make-up than she usually wore, and her lips were ruby red.

"That's the last one," Sofia said. "Come on, you two, it's almost eight o'clock and time for our last altar presentation and special guest."

"Special guest?" Aaron asked.

"Yes. Sleepy Hollow is two miles up the road. For some strange reason," Sofia said, winking, "the Headless Horseman shows up every year and is the hit of the party."

ɛ∕ɔɛ∕ɔ

Armend stood in the front of the crowd, Aaron at his side, camera to his eye, which acted as a ruse while he scanned the area for anything out of the ordinary. Although he readily admitted everything about this evening was strange to him.

Sofia and Adelina positioned themselves behind the altar. Every time he saw Sofia, he couldn't help but smile. Her playful side was out in full force. Her skin had a slight green tint to it. She teased her hair into a full rat's nest and added an unappealing wart to her cheek. Adelina went family-appropriate vixen. Sofia went comical.

"Happy Halloween! Is everyone having fun?" she asked.

The crowd clapped and cheered.

"Well, I suppose you are here to learn what witches truly do on Shadow Fest, or *La Festa dell' Ombra,* not what Hollywood and other organized groups tell you we do. Then I bet you hope to get a glimpse of the Headless Horseman!"

More loud applause echoed into the night.

"Most of you are aware from past years, but if it's your first time tonight, my sister and I are Strega. Italian witches. While we have many of the same beliefs as Wiccan witches and other pagans, ancient Italian witchcraft is, in itself, different."

While the sisters took turns explaining why the altar faced north and what each tool's use was, Armend gazed past the wooden split rail fence into the outlying meadow. For security reasons, the Headless Horseman would appear far away in the field. Two spotlights pointed at an angle to illuminate the area enough to create a menacing image as he rode through.

"There he is!" Someone shouted.

In the distance, a figure came into view. Sofia stared at Armend with wide eyes and a troubled expression. It was too early. As the rider's pace picked up, his direction changed. The horse galloped straight toward them.

"Armend, something's wrong," Sofia hissed. "He's supposed to stay far away so no one gets hurt. Help me get everyone back."

"For your own safety we all need to go back toward the barn." Armend kept his voice relaxed, but firm. "We think the horse has been spooked. Stay calm." With the help of Adelina and Aaron, and amid growing panic and cries of fear, they managed to get everyone out of harm's way in an orderly fashion.

From the corner of his eye, Armend saw Bill Nighthawk jump the fence and run toward the runaway horse. "Will he be okay?"

"Yes," Sofia said. "He knows what he's doing. If anyone can calm a spooked horse, it's him."

Bill moved in smooth flowing motions. His elongated shadow seemed to dance an Indian ritual as the massive, speeding stallion headed right for him. As they approached, it was apparent the rider had lost control and consciousness. He lay limp to one side of the horse.

The older man crouched over slightly, almost in a boxer's stance. When the horse got closer, he began to jog. As it caught up, he ran faster and, in an amazing feat, pulled himself up on the beast's back. He grabbed the reins and the stallion's head shot up as far as it would go. He started to buck, snort, and stampede toward the fence. Bill sidestepped over the horse and, with one foot in the stirrup, rode him out in circles, all the while speaking to him softly. After what Armend assumed was a combination of Bill's tranquil voice and pure exhaustion, the horse trotted to the fence.

The headless rider fell off like dead weight onto the ground with a thump. "Make sure the kid is okay," Bill said. "The horse doesn't need any more anxiety." He dismounted and led the animal off in the other direction.

eↄeↄ

Adelina kneeled down next the fallen horseman to get a read on his aura. Armend and Aaron pulled off his costume, an apparatus that allowed him to be headless while peering out the see-through material at chest level. Lying before them was a young man with blood running down his face. Sofia felt his neck. "His pulse is strong, but he got a hard blow to the head. How's his aura?"

"His red life force is good, but dull because of his injury." Adelina held her open palms over his chest. "I think he'll be fine."

The danger from the horse gone, the crowd began to gather near the fence.

"This is the best Halloween show I've ever been to," a voice shouted. Everyone agreed.

"They think it's part of the show," Adelina said. "If it keeps them composed, let them think it."

Sofia whispered to Armend, "Go where they can't hear you and call nine-one-one."

"Look! Out in the field," a woman cried out.

"Adelina." Aaron tapped her on the shoulder. "Who are they?"

Five boding figures marched toward them. Clad in hooded robes, three held lanterns and two carried torches aglow with fire. With the waning moon dangling behind them, it was a scene out of medieval times. "Is this what Armend worried about?" she asked her sister.

"I'm afraid so," Sofia answered.

Adelina's heart raced. She hadn't been this pumped since she stood up to Amelia, the ghost of a Madam, who tried to chase them out of her brothel in Omaha last month. "Are you packing?"

"Please, Adelina, not everything is a movie. Yes, I have my wand."

As they got closer, their muffled chant became clear, "*Sofia e il diavolo.*"

"What are they saying?" Aaron asked

"That Sofia is the devil."

Twenty feet back they stopped, but their mantra continued. The individual in the middle, wearing a deep maroon cloak came forward. She couldn't see the person's face hidden deep in the hood, but the slink of her stride was feminine.

Sofia leaned against the fence. "I know what you want and you'll never have it."

The woman smashed the lantern onto the grass in front of her. It exploded into the air like a firework. Colored flames and sparks ignited and spewed in all directions. A cloud of smoke settled upon them. When it cleared, the five were gone. The crowed *oohed* and *ahhed*.

"More cheap parlor tricks. Let's see how they stack up against some real magic." She was up and over the fence, her flowing robe rippled behind her.

The crowd cheered her on. "Go get 'em, Sofia."

"Right behind you, Sis."

"Adelina, wait!" Aaron screamed. "Where—what are you doing? You can't go after them by yourselves. I'm coming with you."

"You wanted to see some magic." *This will knock your socks off.* She grabbed his hand and dragged him toward the woods to the left. Sirens howled in the night. When the audience discovered it wasn't an act, she wondered if they would still be on their side.

༄༅༄

What the hell was he doing? Everything Aaron had been taught about witches and witchcraft had been put to the test and failed miserably. He was fond of Sofia and, yes, he liked Adelina and didn't want them hurt. If what he was doing was wrong, then God would have to figure out a way to forgive him.

She squeezed his hand. Did that mean she was glad he was with her? Whatever the reason he liked it. What he didn't like was the woods. There was no way he was going into the dark abyss without some light. He undid his hand from hers and rotated the spotlight so it shown into the dense woods.

"Good idea," she said.

He was at home on the water, day or night. He was a strong swimmer and the sound of the water's gentle lapping was like music to his ears. In the woods, birds squawked and branches creaked. It wasn't relaxing. It was downright creepy. He interlocked his fingers back with hers. "Let's go."

They stayed out of the direct path of the light and to the side of it. Their shadows followed like a faithful friend, but it was a chance they would have to take.

Adelina slowed down their pace. Feet shuffled in the dried leaves, and voices rose ahead, one of which was Sofia's. They ducked behind a distorted tree trunk.

He blinked his eyes into focus. A cloaked adversary was running toward her. Sofia aimed her wand at his feet. "*Sradi plantor*!" her voice echoed through the trees. The tip of her wand flickered like a sparkler on the fourth of July. The ground shook as the tree's roots ripped up from the soil, wound around the man's ankles, and yanked him to the ground. He struggled against the binding as smaller roots wrapped around his chest.

Sofia peered down at him. "I wish you no harm. Where is she?"

He spat at her.

"*Stringere*." The vine squeezed tight against him and he winced. "But I will fight back."

Aaron floundered for words. "Did…I just…Did that just happen?"

There was no time for an explanation. His photographer's eye saw the flash. They had let their guard down. The wand snuck out from the robe's sleeve. The end glowed bright red. "No!" he shouted and rushed toward her. His hands on her shoulders, he shoved her down hard, falling on top of her.

"Argh!" he grimaced as his arm shattered in pain, taking the hit meant for Adelina. Fear, pain, and adrenalin made it hard to catch his breath. "Are you all right?" he gasped into her ear and slid off her.

She rolled to her side. "Yes, but you're hurt." A loud hissing noise, followed by a stream of electric energy, flew over them and slapped the tree next to them. "That was the bravest and nicest thing anyone has ever done for me. Thank you." Her cool palms cupped his face and then her warm lips were on his. It was a quick, but tender kiss. For a moment, his arm didn't throb and he didn't care that he was in the middle of a war of the witches. "Stay here and keep flat. She can't see you. I'll be right back." Adelina crawled on her belly, darting magical jolts, to safety behind a large rock.

"Hey, get back here." With a massive twinge of pain, he flipped on his stomach. His right arm worthless, he dragged himself, using his left arm, close to where she was kneeling on the ground.

She stood up behind the boulder. "Over here!" She waved her hands at cloaked figure.

Did she have a death wish? Maybe she had never been struck with whatever comes out of a wand, but he could assure her it hurt like hell. He couldn't move fast enough to stop her.

The attacker lunged forward, wand pointed directly at Adelina's chest. A small silver disc appeared in her hand. She tapped it three times with her wand. As the silver sparks poured at her, she held the disc in the air and said, *"Grabatto proteggere."* Instead of landing on her heart, the streak of lightening turned direction and went straight to the disc, like iron to a magnet. Her body flinched at the impact.

With two hands, Adelina held it in front of her, unyieldingly reflecting the magic back to the hooded woman. She dropped her wand. Her body arched in agony and slammed against a tall hemlock tree. Sofia stepped out from behind and put her hands on the trunk. *"Lirum Larum."* The lower branches came alive and wrapped around her torso securely.

She crouched over the hooded figure, but Aaron couldn't make out her words. Once again, he heard her say *"Stringere,"* and then a woman grunted. She hadn't answered her question.

ⱭⱭⱭ

The woman captured by the tree thrashed her legs in an attempt to kick her wand close enough to grab it with her feet.

"Sorry, it's mine now." Sofia picked it up and walked away. The deeper they went in the woods, the darker it became, although a small amount of light was better than none. She made a three hundred and sixty degree circle and scanned the forest. It was too quiet and had been too easy a fight so far. Gina had something else up her sleeve. Sofia was sure.

She spotted Adelina and Aaron and hurried toward them. She had seen him protect her sister and was grateful, but didn't think there was much time before the next attack. They were sitting ducks and she wanted Aaron out of there. It would do nothing but hinder their fight if she and Adelina had to worry about him.

"How's the arm?" she asked.

Adelina pressed the silver disc against the hole in his arm.

"It feels better. What's that horrible smell?" Aaron asked.

"I'm afraid it's you," Sofia said.

"When you get hit by this kind of magic," Adelina said, continuing to work, "it's a combination burn and gash into the flesh." He looked like he was going to be sick. "The disc's energy only lasts for so long. There's probably not much left, but there should be enough to help your arm a little."

"Can you make it back to the house?" Sofia asked. "Tell Armend I'm fine and the best thing you two can do for me is to make sure all my guests are safe."

"Do you think he's going to listen to me? Plus, I don't want to leave you two alone."

"We can handle it," Adelina assured him.

"I need you to do this for me," Sofia said as she and her sister helped him to his feet. Giving him no choice, they nudged him to the right. "Stay straight, there's a path. You'll be back in the field in a few minutes. Hurry!"

When he was gone, Sofia took her sister's hand. "Are you sure you want to do this? Gina's not rational. She may turn up with a gun and start shooting. I have no idea."

"If she was going to shoot you, she would have done it already." Adelina laughed. "Come on."

They groped in the shadows between the oak and hemlock trees, careful not to make noise where they stepped.

"Ladies," a voice whispered doing its best Vincent Price impression. The hair on Sofia's neck bristled.

They spun around. The tallest, lankiest man Sofia had even seen was in front of her. Donned in his dark robe, his hands were folded in front him in an almost docile appearance. Gina remained far to the rear of him, her identity concealed, happy to let her cohort do the talking.

"This has all been a misunderstanding," the man continued. "It seems you have something My Lady wants." His body swayed in the direction of Gina.

Sofia half listened to him. It was obvious what they wanted. She wasn't going to give it to them so he could talk all he wanted. What bothered her was there was still one more of them. Would he show up on the other side and surround them?

"You seem to be a reasonable woman. This could all end peacefully, which I'm sure you would prefer. It's up to you."

Going for her passive side, were they? They'd be surprised.

"Well as Mark Twain once said, 'Everyone is a moon and has a dark side they never show to anyone.'" She tightened her grip around the hilt of her wand.

"You're declining our offer."

She bent her knees slightly. "Yes."

"I'm sorry to hear that."

He pounced.

CHAPTER 34

You may have to fight a battle more than once to win it. –
Margaret Thatcher, 1925 – 2013, British Prime Minister

"This is exactly what they *don't* want us to do," complained Aaron.

Armend had spent too much time with his new pal today. They were on the edge of the woods and arguing wasn't getting them any closer to Sofia and Adelina.

"I asked Bridget and Bill to help with the crowd while I looked for Sofia. Are you going to show me where they are or not?"

"I didn't want to leave them alone either. But this is way out of our league. You didn't see what went on in there."

"All the more reason to get going."

"Those two are very capable. I wouldn't believe it if I hadn't seen it with my own eyes. They know what they're doing. We would be defenseless."

Armend didn't want to play this card, but had no choice. He undid his jacket, reached inside, and flaunted his new wand. *So there.*

"You're a Strega something or other?"

"Stregone is the male term."

"You are?"

"Not...exactly."

Aaron threw his arms up in aggravation and paced around.

"But I'm learning." He tucked his wand safely back in his pocket and zipped his jacket. "I'm going in with or without you. It will take me longer to find them without you."

Aaron rubbed his temples. "I've already been zapped once. It can't be worse than that. Magic isn't fatal, is it?"

"I have no idea."

They headed into the lion's den.

ↄ∕ↄↄ∕ↄ

He dove forward.

"*Tripudio.*" A hand on each end of her wand, she sprung high in the air to escape the assault. She wasn't the target. At the last minute, his wand veered off toward her sister. Sofia landed hard, losing her balance. "Adelina!"

Her sister, quick on her feet, dropped to the ground and rolled left. Her weapon aimed high she yelled, "*Kesk Ma'sik.*"

With a vicious sneer, he countered back at her, "*Mazak Hala.*" Bolts of electric energy flew from both theirs wands and converged in the air as the two of them engaged in a battle of wills and magic.

"Go," Adelina gasped. "Find her. I can handle him." Sofia looked in Gina's direction. She was gone. Her sister, winded from the strenuous fight, swung her arms as if she was hitting a baseball and zapped him with a hard jolt. Stunned, he wobbled, giving her sister a minute to wedge between a rock and two conjoined trees for cover and a breather.

Their attacker, still dazed, allowed Sofia a momentary advantage. "*Virga perversum,*" she said.

His hand holding the wand automatically faced toward him. "No!" he yelled. He fought with his other hand against the attack, but it was no use, his own wand betrayed him and pointed at his head.

"*Obdormio.*" He slumped to the ground. Sofia leaned over him. "My battle isn't with you. Where is she?"

He struggled against the sleep that was overcoming him. In defiance, he whipped his head to the side.

"Sweet dreams." She took his wand and left him sprawled on the ground.

She was confident her sister could fend off whatever he threw at her. After all, they grew up fighting against each other during magic lessons, but it would leave her exhausted. Sofia wasn't going to leave her alone. They hurried into the dark forest after Gina.

☙☙☙

Armend stared down at the man shackled to the ground by the tree's roots. His stout body flailed in every direction, trying to break loose. Dirt smeared his face. Dead leaves and grass tangled within the strands of his long hair. "Sofia did this?"

"Yes. If I didn't see it with my own eyes, I wouldn't believe it."

A faint whimper came from farther down the ominous path. They came upon what appeared to be a scared young girl, maybe eighteen or nineteen, constrained by the lower branches of a hemlock. He ignored her. Her tears and puppy dog eyes didn't sway him. She should have never challenged Sofia. As they moved past, the girl's mouth twisted into a snarl as low chirping sounds left her lips.

"What's she doing?" Aaron asked.

"I'm not sure. It may be a signal of some sort. Let's keep moving."

Aaron pointed into the murky night. "I left them down here a ways."

Dampness settled in and Armend watched a wispy layer of fog slither around his feet. His throat tightened as worry and fear strangled his thoughts. Sofia had thrown herself in harm's way to protect him. He had to find her and get her out of there.

With a hard tug on his sleeve, he was face down in the dirt and wet leaves. He spit out the muck from his mouth while Aaron, lectured him. "You're not paying attention and I don't want to get zapped again!" Armend rubbed his eyes and got accustomed to the darkness. They were on the ground behind a dilapidated stonewall. "Keep down. Didn't you see the movement in the shadows to the left? Someone's coming."

No. He hadn't seen anything. He had been distracted.

"Look." Aaron helped Armend sit up with his back against the wall. "I know you're worried. I was in love once. But if you don't keep your head on straight, you won't be any help to her."

Aaron knelt beside him with a bloodied sleeve, his own face encrusted with mud and sweat from his earlier run in with a bout of magic. He hadn't really known the three of them before today and here he was deep in the trenches with them. Armend couldn't have been more wrong about him. "You're right. Sorry."

He brushed himself off and took in his surroundings. There was nothing but dark forest. What had he expected? Through a good size hole in the wall where a rock had once sat, Armend peered out to the other side. Their visitor was leaning over the bulky man constrained by the roots. "He's over there."

"Shoot your wand at him."

"It's not a gun." Armend unzipped his coat. Even as his cold fingers fumbled for his wand, he wasn't entirely sure what he was going to do with it. Remembering how Sofia flicked her wrist at his uncle's cabin, he flipped his palm with a hard shove through the break in the wall. Nothing.

"They all say something strange."

"Yes, I know." It was combination of Italian and Latin. Armend's Italian was okay, he knew no Latin. He decided to call the wand by its Italian name. "*Bacchetta!*" He thrust his fist through the hole. The wand didn't cooperate.

"Try Hocus Pocus," Aaron said and shrugged.

"I'm not trying to pull a rabbit out of my hat!" Armend snapped and jerked his arm back. He hit the wall and loose rocks tumbled forward onto the dirt. A sizzling sound filled the air and sparks of magic flew over their heads.

"He knows we're here."

They couldn't stand. The wall wasn't high enough to hide them. Armend stretched his body out and started to tumble over the rough terrain. Aaron followed his lead letting out a small groan each time his arm hit the ground. They reached the other end of the wall and stopped.

"I thought you said you were learning," Aaron panted, lying flat on his back. His breath rose from his mouth, reminding Armend of smoke signals.

"Wand lessons aren't going so well." *Zap. Hiss.* Blasts of magic came at them faster and faster, rebounding off rocks and tree trunks. A shower of sparks rained down on them. Armend spotted a few large dead tree limbs. "I think we're going to have to fight our friend, Igor, the old-fashioned, mortal way," he said.

"Great."

The thuds of their attacker's footsteps drew closer. Armend dragged one large branch over to Aaron.

"I can't hit him hard with my arm like this." With the defeated demeanor of the unlucky one who pulled the short straw Aaron said, "I'll distract him. You whack him."

A loud crackle thundered next to them and they both jumped. A small fire smoldered on top of a rotted tree stump and curls of smoke floated in the air.

Armend didn't like the idea, but Aaron was right. It was the only way. "Okay."

"Make sure you hit him hard and don't miss! I don't want to end up like that tree stump."

"Don't worry. I've been in more than a few fights," Armend assured him.

"Why am I not surprised?" Aaron rummaged through his coat pocket and showed Armend a silver disc.

"What's that?"

Aaron shrugged. "It was Adelina's."

He crawled on his hands and knees back to the hole in the wall. He flung the disc into the trees. It hit a number of branches causing them to rustle. Igor twisted toward the noise and fired his wand. Armend snuck closer, his wooden weapon in hand, and hid behind a tree. He motioned to Aaron to keep going so that the man's back was to him. It would be dangerous. The stone wall would no longer conceal him. Any movement he made would put him in the direct line of fire. He would need to maneuver between the trees to dodge any attack. Aaron nodded.

With both hands clutching the log, Armend put one foot in front of the other and crouched slightly. He was ready.

Aaron tossed a rock in the opposite direction of their adversary to thwart his attention. He sprinted past the hooded man, close enough to be visible, but hidden partially by the woods. His arms covered his head to ward off any attacks of magic.

"*Diffindo*," the man roared and flashes of electric energy pelted toward Aaron like a machine gun.

Armend rushed up behind Igor, his arms raised in the air. Before the man could fire another barrage from his wand, he smashed the log down square on his back and head. Igor bobbed back and forth. Armend wielded another hard blow and his victim collapsed to the ground.

Armend had to hurry. Igor wouldn't be out long. With the edge of his boot, he shoved him onto his back, undid the rope from his robe and let him fall back on his stomach.

Armend twisted the man's arms behind him. "Aaron!" Are you all right?"

"Yeah, I'm here." A battle weary Aaron appeared from the woods. The bottom of his left pant leg was gone. "A jolt nicked my leg. My jeans took the brunt of it. I'm okay."

"Hold his arms together while I tie him up."

"Let me do it. I'll use a sailor's knot."

Armend was impressed how secure the binding was. They each grabbed a leg and dragged him behind a big boulder. Relieved they had subdued yet another member of Gina's group, they felt their odds were better. Armend looked over at his worn out partner. It was a somewhat strained alliance but he owed him a debt of gratitude. "Thanks for your help."

"Sure. I'm glad you knocked him out fast."

Their awkward male bonding moment over, they noticed a bright light exploding over the treetops in the distance. Under different circumstances, it could be mistaken for lightening, but they knew what it really was.

"There they are." They ran into the blackness.

eɔeɔ

Sofia and her sister treaded softly through the deepest part of the woods. It was getting harder to see the farther they went. She wondered if they were being lured into a trap. As far as she was concerned, there was one more of Gina's cronies on the loose. They had to be alert.

"Ouch," yelped Adelina as she tripped on over an exposed root. "Sis, how about some light?"

Sofia stopped in her tracks. "It has to be a small one. We don't want to draw attention to ourselves." She remembered the three wands she had collected. They were no use to them. A wand only worked in the hands of its owner. Sofia clasped the wands in her hand and Adelina's wand was ready to light them.

"Allow me," a voice croaked from above. "*Accendere*!"

The sticks in her palm erupted into flames. Sofia stared at her sister's expression. Her pretty face aglow from the fire, she suddenly winked. A free spirit, Adelina took every situation in life with a grain of salt. She was glad they were together.

"If it isn't Saint Sofia," Gina continued in a disguised voice. "The witch who puts her enemies to sleep, or ties them up, careful not to hurt them. It doesn't seem like the workings of a capable and powerful Strega."

Sofia sometimes wished she were more like Armend. Instead, she was a slow burner. Her body tensed and her teeth clenched. A week was more than enough of the murderous Gina and her bullshit.

"Uh oh," Adelina muttered. "So–fi–a."

"Stay close," Sofia whispered. "But look for the one left of her group."

She turned to face her opponent. Gina stood high up on a rock, a condescending queen peering down at her subjects.

"You have no idea what I'm capable of." Sofia's arm rotated in a full circle. When her wand came down in front, it pointed directly at Gina's stone throne. With a simple "*Secretum secrevi*," her pedestal of stone split in two, down the middle. Gina stumbled and dropped into the jagged gap in the middle of the rocks. She landed in an uncompromising position with her limbs splayed awkwardly. Sofia softly said,

"*Constrictum,*" and the two stones tightened in against her. Amid the woman's grunts, groans, and the scraping sound of the rocks closing in on her, she fought to free her wand. Sofia let her struggle. It would only wear her down. With one last jerk, Gina freed her hand and pushed her wand along the ground.

Sofia's foot came down hard on her arm. "Sorry." Her other foot kicked the weapon free and watched it roll away. "Had enough, *Gina*?" She whipped the hood off her head. The rocks stopped creeping and creaking. "No more games. Give me what I want. It's not yours."

"Never, my family is the rightful owner." Gina grimaced as she struggled between the compromising rocks.

"Do you think your aunt would want you to have it after what you did to her? You can't win. I won't let you."

"Sofia!" Adelina screamed running from the woods. "She has another wand."

It was too late. Gina wiggled her other arm free and shouted, "*Difendere contro l'attacco.*"

A scorching pain punched Sofia in the chest. Her body folded forward and she flew through the air. She landed face down, the wind knocked out of her. She thought she heard Adelina yell, "*Oppungo,*" and Gina shriek, but her head was spinning. She raised her face a few inches off the ground.

"Sis, are—"

"Little sister should shut up. *Silenzioso voce.*" Gina commanded, waving her wand at Adelina.

Without words to instruct her wand, a witch was helpless. Sofia quickly put her hand to her throat and squeaked out, "*Defense nos,*" to protect herself against the spell. As she pushed up to her hands and knees she saw Gina had escaped from her confinement.

"Adelina, get out of here," she tried to shout.

"No need to protect her. I'll do it," Gina mocked. "*La gabbia di fuoco.*"

A blazing cage of fire enclosed her sister. Adelina jumped only to move forward from the heat at her back.

Sofia was on her feet. "Let her go. Your issue is with me." Adelina paced around in a small circle, her arms crossed at her chest, more pissed off than scared. "You're not going to want to deal with her when she gets out."

"She won't be getting out and neither will you," Gina said and came at her.

Sofia marched straight ahead. She was tired, but Gina was weakening.

Sofia's shoulder thrashed as a zap stung at her. She kept going. Her leg gave out as her opponent's attack nipped the inside of her thigh. She forged ahead.

"Too nice to fight back?" Gina berated.

When she was closer, Sofia made an X in the air with her wand. "*Magus exhibeo.*" A firestorm of magic bombarded her adversary.

"Oh my God, Adelina!" a male voice yelled.

Sofia turned. Adelina motioned for Aaron to go back. Gina shot and landed a direct hit. Sofia stumbled to the ground.

Armend was at her side with his arm underneath her back. "I'm okay," she told him. "What are you doing here?" He helped her sit up then approached the crazed Gina, whose back was propped against a tree for support. She was spent. "I'm the one you want dead," he said. "Leave them out of it."

"Well, isn't this heartwarming?" she panted. "But I can't do that." She wiped the hair from her face. With two hands clenched to her wand, a look of pure hatred on her face, she murmured, *"La gabbia—"*

"Watch out!" Sofia attempted to stop her. Armend would have taken the brunt of the strike. He leapt out of the way but it was too late.

"—di fuoco, tris."

Immediately, columns of fire burst up from the ground engulfing each of them in their own prison of fire. Oppressive heat radiated from flames and filled her lungs with every breath.

Adelina was furious and stomped around even harder in her tight area. She signaled to Aaron to sit down and stay calm. Then she gave Gina the finger. Surprisingly, Aaron appeared unruffled. He seemed amused at her gesture, took off his jacket, and plopped down on his butt.

Gina was on the ground, her head rotated back, and her eyes closed. This spell had taken the last bit of strength she had. Good. But Sofia would have to choose her next incantation with care. She, too, was becoming fatigued and they needed Gina alive and unharmed if they wanted the other half of the music.

She and Armend were close enough to talk.

"What do you want me to do?" Beads of sweat rolled down his face. His jacket lay at his feet and he loosened the top of his shirt.

"I'm going to need everyone's help later. I have this one." She pointed her wand downward and twirled it in small circles in front of her.

"On this eve of Halloween
"Mother Crone I beseech you to intervene
"Gina's thoughts help me distort
"Her malicious magic we'll thwart
"With her mind a blur
"Her evil spells we can deter
"For a time her head we'll confuse
"And this battle for sure she'll lose."

Gina jacked herself up on her elbows. "What are you doing?" On shaky feet, she loomed toward Sofia, who continued to twirl her wand quicker and quicker. "It won't work!"

"*Conturbo Aegresco.*" She aimed her wand straight through the pillars of fire. Gina grabbed her head and massaged her temples. She stumbled side to side dazed and confused. "My spells *always* work. *Perversum.*

"Argghh!" she screamed and fell backward, a small bush breaking her fall. She dropped to the ground and curled up in the fetal position. "Jo–Jon!"

There was a noise in the woods and a hulk of a man appeared, dressed in black from head to toe. He rushed down, scooped her up easily into his arms, and they were gone.

"Who the hell was that?"

"The last of her thugs, I guess. Adelina and I took care of three of them. Gina and he make five."

"Aaron and I got one. There must have been six." Armend's lips were dry and cracked. Sofia's hair stuck to the back of her neck and her throat was parched. The heat was getting to all of them. She had to get them out of there.

'Sis, it's hotter than a Vulcan's balls in here.'

Sofia twisted toward her sister. She couldn't speak but she could send her thoughts. Even in a dire situation, Adelina could always make her smile.

'I know. I'm working on it.'

Armend tried to put his arm through the small space between the horizontal rows of fire and touch her, but jerked his hand back when his palm hit the scorching blaze. "Baby, you look exhausted. I want to help." His voice was hoarse and dry. "Why can't I run through the bars fast and roll around in the dirt. Then I'll help each one of you out. We may get minor burns but we can't stay like this."

"Magical fire is different. I doubt you can break through."

With the tip of his boot, he kicked at one of the columns in front of him. He foot stopped hard as if he hit a metal pipe. He mumbled some obscenities.

"I think I can fix this, but I need everyone's help." The three of them feebly moved their head in agreement. "I'm going to try and make it rain. A spell to ask Mother Earth and the Element of Water to do something they're not scheduled to do takes a lot of energy, which I don't have right now. I have no authority over nature and it doesn't cooperate if it's not in the best interest of the planet. But under the circumstances, at the risk of the whole forest catching on fire, I hope they'll grant my request." Sofia faced east and mentally prepared herself. "Please, everyone, concentrate and send your life force to the universe."

"I don't know how," Aaron said.

"Pray, Aaron. Pray—like you've never prayed before—for rain."

Sofia bowed her head, opened her palms to the sky, and began to picture a downpour.

"Dearest Mother Earth and beautiful Element of Water
"I, Sofia, descendant of Messalina, student of Diana,
"Your humble daughter,
"Faithfully ask with care and respect
"For us, flora and fauna to protect
"Against the threat of fire with the gift of rain
"To pour down on your earthly terrain.
"Blessed be."

She waited. You didn't rush Mother Earth and you only asked once. In the distance, there was a low growl of thunder followed by a flash in the night. Sofia was hopeful, but kept her focus. A droplet fell on her head. Then another and another. She recited *imber ymber* three times. Mother Earth had granted her permission to ask for a pelting rain. The sky opened up and it poured.

A loud hissing sound filled the air as the rain cascaded down on their personal infernos. The flames wrestled against the storm, but were soon defeated and reduced to plumes of smoke. Sofia savored the coolness of the rain hitting her as the heat left her body.

"Baby, you did it!" Armend threw his arms around her and kissed her. Rain dripped from the tip of his nose and down his face. She ached from the hits Gina got in. Her shoulder and leg throbbed. She deteriorated into a pile of fatigue and crumbled into him. He felt good so she held him tight.

"I got you, baby. You need to rest." He squeezed her tighter. The rain subsided to a light drizzle.

Aaron and Adelina ran toward them, splashing through the puddles that had instantly formed, even though the rain had subsided. "Are you two okay?"

"Yes and no," said Aaron. "What's the matter with Sofia?"

"She's exhausted. What's wrong?"

"Adelina can't speak."

Sofia couldn't help herself and started giggling. It was her overtiredness causing the reaction, but the thought of her sister at loss for words was too much to resist.

She pulled away from Armend. "I'm sorry. I'll fix it."

"Are you up to it?" he asked.

"Yes." Sofia held up her wand. "Adelina, put your hand around mine and focus on your voice." She held the tip of the wand to her throat. "*Dictum verbum.*"

Adelina gasped. She took another breath, hunched over, and let out a horrific barking cough. Aaron put his hand on her back to steady her. She slowly straightened. "Thanks." She spoke but it came out a whisper.

"You're welcome. Thank you everyone. The rain would not have come if it wasn't for you sending your beautiful life essence to help me. Let's go home."

Armend draped his arm over her shoulder and they started the slow trek back to the house. "What do you think Gina will do next?"

"I don't know. It's not over. I'm sure we'll be hearing from her." Sofia leaned her head on Armend's chest. "She can't show up at work. Her cover is blown. It's a whole new game now."

"What did you do to her," Adelina asked as she and Aaron strolled behind them.

"I confused her magic. Just her magic, don't worry. Her head is already screwed up enough. Any spell or conjuring she tries will not get the result she wants."

"So she can't attack us?"

"She can, but not with magic. It's temporary, maybe ten days."

They continued to hike through the wet woods in silence. Sofia shivered. It wasn't long ago that they were so hot they could have passed out. Now in their damp clothes in the cool October night, it was cold.

They stumbled upon a hooded figure, water pooled around him, asleep on the ground. Even the driving rain didn't wake him. They paused for a moment and kept going. They reached the edge of the woods where Gina's other accomplices were bound by the trees.

"There's another one behind the rock over there," Armend said pointing in the distance. "What should we do with them?"

In her heart, Sofia knew she couldn't leave them in the woods. They, too, were wet and trembling from the cold.

"Relashio." Sofia waved her wand over the two of them. With a loud creaking noise, the mighty tree's roots, branches, and vines loosened and slid off them like snakes slithering away. They sat staring at her. "Go. Get out of here and don't come back. I won't be so nice next time."

They scrambled to their feet and took off down the path. She maneuvered herself over the fallen logs to the boulder. The last man struggled against the ropes constraining him. "Untie him."

"I'll undo it." Aaron knelt down to the side of the man and released the rope.

"You, too. Get out of here and don't ever come back or you'll regret it." Like the others, he didn't argue and took off. Sofia climbed up on the rock and faced the woods. "I can't forget sleeping beauty back there. *Rilasciare dal sonno.*" She twirled around and saw the flickering blue and red lights in the outlying field. *Oh, crap.* She had forgotten about the police. Armend offered his hand and she let him help her down off her perch.

She spoke with authority to Aaron showing him a side of her he had not seen before. "All things pertaining to witchcraft are handled among ourselves. It's one rule that is never to be broken. Even Gina will abide by it. That's why I let them all go. There is no need to involve the police in something they can't begin to grasp or understand."

Aaron swallowed hard, but didn't argue.

Sofia sighed. "Before we go any further let's get our story straight."

CHAPTER 35

Magic is dangerous, but love is more dangerous still.
— *Cassandra Clare, American author*

Adelina stepped into the kitchen through the back door Aaron held open for her. Like the rest of them, he was tired, battered, soaking wet, and chilled to the bone. Still, he behaved like a gentleman. He would have to stop treating her so kindly. She was already swooning over his chivalry.

He plopped down on a chair and rested his head in folded arms on the table. He looked like an elementary school boy at naptime. She sat next to him.

"How are feeling? That was a lot for you to take in out there." Her voice was still raspy.

He groggily lifted his head. "Like I was in an episode of *The Twilight Zone.*"

"Come with me." She led him upstairs to the guest bathroom. "Wait here." When she returned she held up two hangers. "You can have this slinky pink number," she said showing him a short women's bathrobe. "Or this." She handed him a large black hooded robe. "But either way, get out of those wet things. Take a hot shower if you'd like. Then come downstairs and I'll look at your arm." Not giving him the chance to argue, she left and closed the door behind her.

Back in the kitchen, she went through Sofia's pantry until she found what she was looking for, pure beeswax, comfrey oil, witch hazel, and tea-tree oil. As she whisked the ingredients together, she peered out the window onto the front porch. The police were still questioning Armend and Sofia. She and Aaron had gotten off easy with the interrogation. But Sofia was the owner and the police had questions about the recent protesters.

Aaron silently appeared in the doorway. He had chosen the black robe and his arms were full of his wet clothes.

"The washer is in the mud room." She pointed to a small room off the kitchen. Within a few minutes, the sound of the washer chugging echoed and Aaron was back at the table. He had been through and seen things that most people never do. His mind was probably reeling with confusion.

"Can I see your arm, please?"

He slid the cloak over his shoulder and took out his arm. There was a large gash caked over with dried blood. Other than that, he had a nicely toned and muscular arm. "Are you a swimmer?" With a gentle hand, she cleaned out his sore.

"Yes." He jerked when she hit a tender spot.

"I can tell." She sat a small bowl on the table. "This is a homemade salve that's been in my family for generations. Your arm will look and feel much better tomorrow."

"You just made it? For me?"

"Of course. You got hurt protecting me. It's the least I can do." She dipped her fingers in the thick mixture and, with care, rubbed it into his wound. "I know this has been hard on you. We appreciate you sticking to the story we agreed on in the woods."

"Sofia could have easily blamed it on the protesters from my church, but she didn't. I'm already in this deep. I wouldn't throw you under the bus now."

"She may rearrange some of the events, but she would never accuse someone of something they didn't do." She wrapped a gauze bandage around his arm. "Is that too tight?"

"No." His gaze met hers and for a fleeting moment glistened with tenderness and a hint of desire. Her heart fluttered. Then, as if he suddenly remembered she was a witch, he looked away. "You held your own tonight. I was impressed."

"Thanks, but I'm no Sofia." She taped the bandage and eased his arm back into his sleeve. "I couldn't have made the trees uproot or have the rain pour down. That's her gift."

"Well, I'd have you on my team anytime. You were great."

Before she could answer, Sofia and Armend walked in.

∞∞∞

Armend had his arm around Sofia's waist. It had been a long day and night and they were dog-tired. He was surprised to see Aaron wearing a Stregone robe, but a lot about Sofia's friend shocked him this evening.

"Aaron, I don't know how to thank you for tonight. I'm sure it wasn't easy for you," Sofia kissed him on the cheek. "I'm eternally grateful."

He answered her, but Armend didn't pay attention. A text came in from an unknown number. He moved to the far side of the kitchen to read it. *This is between you and me. Dump the know-it-all bitch and maybe she won't get hurt.*

"Who's texting you at this hour?" Sofia asked.

"Oh, it's just George." He hoped the combination of terror and anger seizing his gut didn't show on his face. He typed a reply. *I'll meet you once. I'll have everything I want by the end.*

"Sofia, do you think Gina is getting stronger?" Adelina asked. "That fire spell takes power."

"I learned a lot about her tonight," Sofia explained. "She's clever and came with a strategy. She had an extra weapon and someone waiting in the wings to help if she needed it. On the other hand, she would have been smart to silence me, not you. In the heat of the moment, she acts on raw emotion. Her group did most of the fighting until the end. I think her strength is limited to a small amount of time and a one or two lavish spells."

Armend's phone went off.

I'll be in touch. Leave the slut alone or you'll be sorry.

He leaned against the sink and swallowed the bile rising up the back of his throat. If Gina touched a hair on Sofia's head, he'd kill her. It was that simple.

"Aaron, I want you to spend the night here," Sofia said. "Look at you. You're exhausted. I have three bedrooms. You can have the spare. I won't take no for an answer."

"Good idea," Adelina chimed in. "Then I can put the salve on your arm again in the morning. Here, Sis, I made some for you, too. Didn't Gina get you in a couple of spots?"

"Thanks."

Armend felt Sofia's hand on his back. "What's wrong?" she asked.

"Nothing." He put on his best face. "I'm just tired."

"Adelina, will you show Aaron to his room?" Sofia took Armend's hand. "Come on. We're going to take a nice hot bath, then hit the sack."

That sounded like heaven to him, but he had to take care of one thing. "You go on up. I'll be right there. I have to call George and explain what happened."

He watched the three of them trudge with fatigue up the stairs. When they were out of sight, he pressed his uncle's contact number. After three rings, he answered.

"George, I'm going to need your help."

ℰ✺ℭ

Aaron caught a quick glimpse of his reflection as he passed the mirrored dresser. Minus the robe, he liked what he saw. All his life, he had stayed on the straight and narrow, following the rules, even if he didn't agree with them, in order to not ruffle any feathers. Tonight was different. He went off course and did something unexpected, spontaneous, and out of the ordinary. It felt good and—did he dare admit?—exciting. Would his newfound chutzpah remain? He wasn't so sure.

Adelina told him this was their parents' room when they came to visit. It was a small, earth-colored room with a full size bed, dresser, and cushioned chair. A vase of fresh flowers and a few drawings on the wall were the only decorations. The bed was his main concern. His body longed for sleep. He stripped off his robe and heard a loud clunk. On the floor was Adelina's silver disc. He'd spotted it as they were leaving the woods and picked it up. He thought about giving back to her, but for some strange reason he wanted to keep it. Maybe it was his good luck charm. Whatever the reason, he slipped naked between the sheets, slipped the disc under his pillow, and closed his eyes.

ᴄ◌ᴄ◌

"Aaron. Aaron. Wake up."

Someone was shaking him and he didn't want to be disturbed. He was having a wonderful dream and didn't want it to end. "Adelina," he muttered into the pillow.

"Yes. It's me. It's eleven o'clock in the morning. You're sleeping your life away," she said, giving him one last shove.

His eyes flew open, but didn't see her. In a panic filled moment, he flipped over and his legs tangled in the sheets. She was standing on the side of the bed, fully clothed. A moment ago, she was in a much different state of dress with her long legs wrapped around his waist and her tongue in his mouth.

"Were you having a dream?"

He yanked the blanket up over him. "What?"

"It must have been some dream to get you so discombobulated."

"You—you have no idea," he stammered under his breath. It was awkward with the vivid images of her in his head, but he wasn't ready to let them go yet.

"Here, have some coffee." She sat a cup down on the nightstand. "How's your arm this morning?"

"I don't know. I haven't had a chance to think about it."

She positioned her lovely self on the edge of the bed close to him. He reached for his coffee and eased away from her familiar, yet enticing, scent of vanilla and citrus. Her face crinkled in a frown. "We've had a setback. Gina has seen us. It'll be hard to follow her now."

Thank God for that. The last thing he needed was to sneak around behind some psychopath.

"So we're just going to have to be extra careful," she said with a gleam in her eyes.

He almost choked on his coffee. "Are you crazy?"

"No, Gina is, and my parents won't be able to keep an eye on her at the gallery anymore. Someone has to watch her."

"No. It's too dangerous. What if she sees us and throws us in a cage full of…spiders!"

"What's wrong with spiders?" She crossed her left leg over her right. "Her magic is screwed up, remember? She won't use it."

She had an answer for everything, didn't she?

"She's just a regular nutcase for now," she added.

That made him feel *much* better. "There has to be another way," he said.

She leaned toward him as if about to tell him a secret. Her soft curls swayed directly at him. "I have the Canon EF 17 Zoom lens," she purred in a sultry voice then licked her pink lips.

"Wide range?"

Her sly camera accessory seduction was entertaining and amusing.

"Yep." Her pointer finger playfully ran down the blanket against the length of his leg. "I haven't even taken it out of the box yet. I could use a little help…" She didn't finish her sentence. Instead, they both burst into laughter. "I'm sorry," she said through the last of her giggles.

"Don't be." To say he hadn't met anyone exactly like her before was an understatement. "You're funny."

"I'm going to New York today to spend the day with my parents." She slapped her hands on the top of her thighs and stood up. "I'll call you when I get back and we can plan our next move. It won't be until tomorrow."

"I'm not spying on anyone, especially the Wicked Witch of the West."

"Yes, you are," she said with confidence. "You have a sense of adventure inside you, I know it. Stop smothering it. Let it out to breathe and see the light of day once in a while" Her arms made an invisible circle in the air. "You might enjoy it."

"Why can't Sofia and Armend do it?"

Her body slumped as she spoke. "They had a huge fight this morning. Armend stormed out of here and went back to his apartment. Sofia is pissed off, but I think he'll be back. He really loves her." She moved toward the door and paused at the chair in the corner. "Here's your clothes, all washed and dried. Don't leave until I see your arm." Then she was gone.

He relaxed back against the pillows and enjoyed the rest of his coffee. He couldn't believe Armend would leave Sofia alone with Gina lurking around. Although she could take care of herself. She proved that last night. Adelina was right, Armend would be back. His short fuse got the best of him, that's all.

Well, it wasn't his concern. Aaron had his own problems to deal with.

He was falling for a witch.

CHAPTER 36

I believe in getting into hot water.
It keeps you clean. – *G. K. Chesteron,
1874 – 1936, English writer*

George sat across the table from Ersilia and Silvio in a cramped greasy spoon diner halfway between New York City and the Catskill Mountains. It was noisy. The dull hum of conversation filled the room, plates clanked together, and the persistent dinging of the bell reminded the waitress her orders were ready. It was the perfect place for the talk they were about to have.

They were apprehensive. Ersilia tore her napkin into tiny pieces and Silvio had been stirring his coffee for five minutes. It was understandable. They were upstanding citizens with a thriving business in Manhattan. If it were even suspected they had dealings with certain people, it could ruin them.

"Armend assured us if anyone could help us and quickly, it would be you," Ersilia whispered as her eyes roamed around making sure no one was listening.

"We know firsthand you seem to have a somewhat *unconventional* way to get things done," Silvio said.

"My way isn't for everyone." He motioned to the overworked waitress to fill his coffee cup. "I'd be lying if I didn't say I have landed in some trouble occasionally, but Gisella was always there to help me out."

"Are you aware of what happened at the Preserve a few nights ago?" Silvio asked, finally laying his spoon down on the side of his cup.

"Yes. I'm afraid Reggie is going down the same path as her mother. Her madness will continue to make her more and more dangerous, especially if she feels she has nothing to lose."

"Are you ready to order?" The gum-snapping woman asked while she filled George's cup with something closer to mud than coffee.

"Can we have a few more minutes, please?" George asked politely. The woman spun on her heels and took off in a huff. "How's Sofia, under the circumstances?"

"She's fine and can take care of herself," Ersilia said.

Armend and Sofia hadn't spoken in days and he didn't know where Armend was. He prayed it was a temporary situation, but one never knew for sure. "I'm sure Armend is doing what he thinks is best for her." George took a gulp of coffee, slammed the cup down on the table, and pushed it away. "God, that's awful. Anyway, tell me exactly what you need."

"We need two fake passports and a private round trip flight to Sicily. I can pay cash. I don't want paper a trail." Silvio said. "We don't want Gina to follow."

"I understand."

"We also need security to look the other way," Ersilia said. "A parcel will be on the flight that wouldn't normally pass the scrutiny of airport security."

"Give me two days. I don't want your money."

"Discretion is of the utmost importance."

"Of course." He would do whatever he could for them. Because of his hasty and careless behavior earlier this month, their business had been compromised, he had lost his half of the music, and Sofia had been attacked. That was a lot to account for. "If something unforeseen were to happen, it will fall on me. Your names will never come up," George assured them.

"We appreciate this." Silvio offered his hand across the table. "I want you to know we harbor no ill will toward you. The slate is clean."

"There is one more thing," Ersilia interrupted. "How did you come to know these certain individuals?"

George rested back in his chair and massaged his throbbing thigh. Only a few people knew the answer to that question, his brother, Gisella, and Armend. On the other hand, he knew he could trust them

"Vietnam, nineteen-sixty-nine." That simple sentence captured their undivided attention. "I was twenty one, deep in battle within a jungle-cloaked mountain area near the Laos border." He closed his eyes. "I pushed most of those horrible memories from my mind a long time ago. Besides the enemy, the conditions were unfathomable. Extreme heat, poisonous insects, disease, and limited water."

"George, I'm sorry. I should have never asked," Ersilia said.

He opened his eyes and stared past the two of them into the crowd of dining patrons. "Me and the new kid, Tony, were dodging through the dense foliage, weapons in hand. We were close to our unit. One minute he was next to me, the next he was on the jungle floor, screaming in agony. Snipers. I dropped to the ground next to him for cover. He'd been shot twice." His gaze returned to his breakfast companions, and he tried to forget how the blood pouring out of Tony's chest, mixed with sweat and dirt, turned his shirt to a dreadful brown color. "He grabbed my collar, yelling 'Georgie, Georgie.' He was terrified. I had no control over whether he would live or die, but I could control *where* he died if his clock had run out. It wasn't going to be alone, covered with leeches, on foreign soil in a god-forsaken land. The least I could do was get him back to the unit where there might be a medic and people he knew.

"I threw him over my shoulders in a fireman's hold and headed in the direction I hoped was the right one. We hadn't gotten far when there was an explosion. Long shards of bamboo pierced our bodies everywhere. The pain was excruciating. I tripped over my own feet and tumbled to the ground. Rounds of high caliber rifles riddled the air all around us. There was no way out. I didn't think I could take much more when I heard Tony's voice. 'Georgie,' he said. 'Leave.' He didn't finish his sentence. I called his name, but he didn't answer. There was no way I was going to leave him there.

"I figured it was the end of us if we stayed. If we were going to die, we should die trying to survive. I don't know what happened, adrenaline they tell me, but I was on my feet, Tony still around my neck, and I ran for my life. Luckily, we were closer than I thought. About six hundred yards away I collapsed, but I was near enough to our unit that they saw us. The last thing I remember was lying in the dirt shaking uncontrollably."

"Is that what happened to your leg?" Silvio asked.

"Yes. The doctor explained that inside the human thigh there's something called the neurovascular bundle, made up of main arteries, veins, and nerves. A large splinter of bamboo tore my bundle to shreds."

"I'm so sorry, George," Ersilia said sympathetically.

"Hey. I'm alive. I can live with a limp and sore leg. Anyway, when I woke up in the hospital I didn't see Tony. I asked everyone, but no one knew what happened to him. They sent me home to the Bronx and I got a job driving a delivery truck. One day, like out of a Hollywood movie, two thugs came up behind me and threw me in the backseat of a black sedan. Next thing I know I'm sitting in front of Giuseppe Caldarone."

Silvio was flabbergasted. "The head of the New York Caldarone crime family?"

"The one and only. I was scared shitless—excuse me, Ersilia."

She brushed him off with a swat of her hand. "I'd say the same thing, maybe worse, if I were in your shoes," she replied.

"I couldn't imagine what they wanted with me. Then Tony walked through the door." Silvio and Ersilia's mouths dropped open. "I had a similar reaction. Apparently, Tony D'Aroni, as we knew him, was Don Caldrone's oldest son."

"So they are now in your debt," Ersilia said. "We're Sicilian. Mafioso or not, we have a strong sense of honor when it comes to family."

"We speak once a year, on the day I pulled him out of the jungle. For forty-three years, he's asked if I needed anything. I've always said no. Until—" He owed them the whole truth. "—this year. I told him I needed a forged painting, a large sum of money, and maybe a little persuasion. But I was adamant no one be hurt. He was happy to be able to repay me after all these years. When I found out Armend worked for you and the whole thing fell apart, I gave the artwork and the money back."

"So that explains the garbage being dumped."

"And cleaned up. I made sure that was part of the deal."

"Yes," Silvio grumbled.

"Are you ever hesitant to deal with them?" Ersilia asked.

"I've never taken advantage. I've been honest with them and returned everything. The only thing I need is to save Armend's life. So your request will be no problem.

The gum-snapping waitress returned. "If you're not going to order, you'll have to pay for the coffee. We need the table. See the line of people over there." She tilted her head toward the door. "What'll it be?"

George was happy for the interruption. He'd said all he was going to on the subject. What he didn't tell them was that as soon as they had the Rossi half of the music, he was going to call Tony with one last request—to stop Reggie once and for all. "Let's eat."

CHAPTER 37

How ridiculous and how strange to be
surprised at anything which happens in life. –
Marcus Aurelius, 121 – 180 AD, Roman emperor

Adelina sat in the driver's seat. Aaron slept in the seat next to her, his New York Mets baseball cap pulled down over his eyes. It was ten o'clock in the morning. They were in White Plains, New York, waiting at the end of the block up from the old two-story house that had become Gina's new digs since Halloween.

He stretched his arms, took off his baseball cap, and scratched his head. For the love of Diana, he was adorable, with his ruffled hair and sleepy eyes. She could still picture him asleep the other morning, his broad shoulders and swimmer's arms rising up down with his breath. There was no use dwelling on it. He would never see her as anything but a witch.

"Here she comes," Adelina said.

He sat up straight and looked out the tinted windows of the Jeep Wrangler. They watched as Gina got in a yellow Volkswagen Bug and drove away in the opposite direction of their parked car.

"Damn it," she murmured under her breath. She put the jeep in reverse, backed up a little, jammed it into first, and pulled a U-turn in the middle of the narrow residential street. She let two cars go between her and the bug, threw it in gear, hit the gas, and stayed a safe distance behind.

"I'm glad you decided to tag along," she said and followed Gina on to Interstate 684.

"I didn't have a choice. With Armend gone, we have to watch out for Sofia," he yawned. "Where are they going?"

From the highway, she exited onto a two-lane road and let a school bus go ahead of her. "Connecticut, I guess." A large billboard hung over the road welcoming them to the Constitution State.

They stayed safely hidden behind the yellow bus. Aaron peered to the side. "They're turning right at the light."

When they reached the intersection, a sign reading, "Connecticut Landing—Cabins for Rent," pointed to the right. She made the turn and drove slowly down the rut-filled dirt road. The Volkswagen was far ahead of her.

"It's a dead end," Aaron said pointing to the notice asking people to turn around in the small parking lot. She pulled in and parked.

"Let's go the rest of the way on foot." She put her hair in a ponytail, tucked it under a large brimmed straw hat, and slipped on sunglasses. "How do I look?"

"Like a tourist."

She grabbed her backpack from the back seat and opened the door. "Perfect. Let's go."

മാരമാ

Aaron jumped out of the Wrangler. He stopped to admire it. Reckless and very cool, it was his dream car. Like him, the ten-year-old Honda he drove was reliable and practical. "I meant to tell you that I like your wheels."

Adelina was half way up the entrance to the cabins. He jogged after her, the chilly November morning air filling his lungs. He came up behind her and lingered for a minute. The sway of her hips was an unnecessary diversion right now, so he sped up next to her. "So, what are we going to do?"

"I don't know," she said. "We'll see when we get there."

"You don't have a plan?"

"No. You know the expression, the best laid plans..."

She loved to walk down a path of the unknown and take him along with her. He didn't mind. The familiar exhilaration from the other night was back and he was suddenly wide-awake.

They came upon a second, larger parking lot. Next to it was a small lodge that said "Office" on the door. Gina waited outside. Her back was to them. SUV's filled the lot, but when she noticed the sound of their footsteps on the stone drive, they hurried to duck down behind a small compact car. Aaron stretched out on his belly and peered underneath the car. A pair of black high heels walked toward them. "She's coming!" he whispered loudly.

Adelina's hand patted the side of her large hat and, like the magician she was, pulled out her wand. He hadn't noticed it. It blended in with the straw. She crawled down next to him and pointed her weapon under the car.

He snatched her hand. "What are doing? She'll see the magic."

"Shh." She aimed. "It's hard to walk in heels on gravel. I hope she doesn't *fall!*" With a flick of her wrist and power in her last word, Gina's ankle bent sideways.

"Ug. Ow."

A man's brown leather loafers were there to rescue her. He spoke in a muffled voice.

"No sparks, funny words, or anything?" Aaron asked somewhat confused.

"Nah. These are small, easy spells that don't take much energy. English works."

"Look, they're leaving."

"How about one last stumble for the road?"

"I thought you weren't supposed to hurt anyone unless defending yourself?"

"Hurt her? She trapped us in a freakin' cage of fire."

"You're right. Let her have it."

She turned her attention back to the duo walking away. With another twist of her hand she recited, "One step, two steps, careful not to *slip*. Three steps, four steps, watch you don't *trip*." Gina went down hard, but her companion steadied her on her feet. After a few minutes, they continued on their way.

"They're gone." Aaron sat up with his back against the car. "Now what?"

Adelina snuck her ahead around the side of the vehicle. "It looks like they reserved the end cabin at the bottom of the path. Very secluded. That's good for us." He started to get to his feet, but she reached her arm across his chest, stopping him. "Not yet." She lowered her arm, "Let's walk around the back. We can figure out the best place to watch them."

Without arguing, he got up and followed her into the woods. He didn't remember ever spending this much time surrounded by trees. It was evident witches preferred to go deep into the forest to work their magic.

It was a typical early November day, cloudy, damp with a cool breeze. Most of the big oak and maple trees were bare. It wasn't a great time of the year for camouflage.

Adelina abruptly stopped. The cabin was set back in the distance. He watched as her head shot from side to side looking for some inspiration. Then her interest focused in on an object. He hoped it wasn't what he thought it was.

With her eyebrows raised and mischief in her eyes, she motioned to her left. "What do you think?"

"No. Absolutely not." He waved his hands in front of him and took a step back.

"I told you I have a zoom lens. It's perfect. They'll never see us."

"I'm not climbing a tree to become a peeping Tom. You're the free spirit here, not me."

She put her hands on her hips. "You don't hold a regular job because you don't like the hours. You do your websites in your spare time so that you can spend your day doing what you want—refurbishing an old boat. That sounds like a free spirit to me. Yours is just a bit more reserved than mine." She grabbed his hand. "We can fix that." She dragged him to a huge oak tree. Its trunk was massive and thick, sturdy limbs stretched in every direction. "You have to climb up first and help me. I wouldn't have worn these fancy boots if I knew we'd be scaling a big tree."

He gazed up at the daunting tree, then back at Adelina. She had taken off her hat and let her hair down. Her sweet curls blew gently in the breeze. Jeez, he was screwed. What was it about her that made him do things he wouldn't normally do? He knew exactly what it was, and he wasn't in the mood to have his heart broken again so soon.

"We'll have to go a little at a time if you want help. I'll get to the first branch, hoist you up, and then we'll keep going."

She wrapped her arms through the straps of the backpack. "Good. Thanks."

He secured his foothold and climbed up. Bracing himself, he offered his hand and lifted her up. They repeated the move two more times. "There's a good solid branch right over there facing the cabin. Ready?" He grabbed her hand and pulled. She lost her footing and slid downward. He took hold of her other arm and stopped her from falling. "Don't worry. I have you."

"I know you do. I'm not worried."

Those few simple words tugged at his heart. She regained traction against the tree trunk and, holding on to him, made her way to the tight spot next to him between the limbs. Their bodies pressed together and, for a moment, he forgot the reason they were there, until she leaned on him for balance and sat down.

"Unzip my backpack and get my camera and lens out."

He straddled the large limb, sat behind her, and removed the expensive equipment. "May I?" he asked.

"Sure."

He got her up the tree. Now he would get her camera ready and in focus and let her do the rest of the dirty work. That left him an innocent bystander.

It wasn't an easy target. They were far away, other bare tree boughs criss-crossed in front of them, and the one window they had access to had horizontal blinds. Luckily, they were open enough to get a view between the slats.

"I hope it's not the bathroom window," Adelina said.

"Just give me a minute." With his expertise, he managed to zoom in and focus. "Nope. The bedroom."

"We may have to wait until later for some activity there."

"How long are you planning to stay here?" He started to lower the camera when something moved.

Gina untied the belt of her coat and threw it on a nearby chair. She stood seductively in her bra and panties, with her long legs, slim waist, and full breasts spilling out of her push up bra.

"Wow," he muttered, His next thought was of what she was capable of and her momentary sexual allure disappeared.

"I'm guessing, from your comment, they are in there and she's looking pretty sexy."

"Maybe at first glance." He gave her a quick laugh. "But being a deranged killer doesn't turn me on."

The object of her desire faced her and she began to undress him. He knew he should look away, but there was something familiar about the older man. The angle was off. He needed them to shift to the left.

"What are they doing? Enjoying a little morning delight?"

He didn't answer her, but concentrated on his task. Gina lured him onto the bed, fluffed up the pillows, and he reclined back. Aaron thought he could get a good look at his face, but Gina glided on top of him. It was the man's turn to undress her, while his hands and mouth enjoyed what she was offering. Gina rolled to her side and he got the picture he needed.

He suddenly felt sick to his stomach. "Oh—my—God." He zoomed in the last increment the camera would allow. He continued to watch the sex show, not because he was getting off, but because the shock left him frozen. "Oh, God."

"No fair you get watch all the fun." Adelina grabbed the camera from him and raised it to her eye. "Oh my," she said rotating her head to one side. "She's flexible, that's for sure. That is one happy man."

"It's not a joke. Put the camera down. We're done."

"What's the matter?" She rubbed his arm. "You're trembling."

"I want to leave. I'll help you down."

"Not until you tell me what's gotten you so upset."

He didn't think he could speak the words. His whole world had changed in a single second. He put his face in his hands and rubbed his eyes. Nothing could rid him of the image of the man thrusting himself into the woman who just the other night would have been happy to see him dead.

His hands dropped to his lap. "I know that man in there." He licked his dry lips. "He's the pastor of my church."

℘℘℘

Before she even thought twice about what she was doing, Adelina swept him up in her arms. At first, he was rigid as a board, but he slowly relaxed against her. This must be devastating for him. Her religion viewed things differently. Everyone was responsible for their own actions. As long as you harmed none, emotionally or physically, you could do as you wished. She knew, however, that Christianity held their leaders to a high standard and this wasn't acceptable behavior. "I'm sorry."

When he didn't respond, she removed her arms from around him. "Why don't you go out for a while?" She slipped the pack off her shoulders, unhooked the small pouch in the front, and dangled the keys in front of him. "I'll stay here and watch them. Take all the time you need. You don't even have to come back. I'll walk out to the road and you can pick me up."

"I don't want to leave you alone."

"You're sweet," she said, "but right now, take care of yourself."

"Thanks." He stared at her with kind and appreciative eyes. "You're a good friend."

Friend. She supposed it was better than, "You're a good witch."

He maneuvered himself to the ground and glanced up at her. "Are you sure?"

"Yes. Go." He caught the keys she dropped down to him and started on his way. "Wait. What's his name?" Having seen him in such an intimate state, the least she could do was put a name to his…er…face.

"Pastor Hayward Marshall."

Adelina returned the camera to her eye. The peep show was over and the mood had drastically shifted. Gina and the pastor appeared to be having an intense argument. Adelina wondered if he knew whom he was dealing with. Either way, Hayward Marshall probably shouldn't cross her.

ↄ∂ↄↄ

Hayward sprang up and out of bed. "You knocked him out?"

His reaction was unexpected. "I didn't. Someone else did." He had been out of town and she was excited to tell him about the commotion they caused at Sofia's Halloween festivities. Just minutes ago, he was eager to see her. Now his attitude changed and she didn't appreciate it. "He had to have a few stitches. They kept him overnight. He's fine."

"You promised no one would be hurt. Do you know how dangerous it was to have a horse run amuck with its rider unconscious? There were children there. It was irresponsible and foolish." He slipped his pants on and stood by the window.

Not bothering to cover herself up, she stood next to him. "You're overreacting."

"The rider was just a kid himself."

"Life is tough. The sooner he learns that the better." In a deliberate snub, he put his back to her. She grabbed his shoulder and spun him around. "Don't turn your back to me!"

He slapped her hand away like an annoying insect. "It may be time to end our arrangement. It's not working. Sofia and her preserve are as popular as ever and even some members of my congregation like her."

"That's that twit Aaron's fault, not mine," she said. If he only knew that Aaron was fighting side by side with a pact of witches. One more wonderful morsel of information she couldn't wait to tell him—when the time was right.

"Your stunt didn't help. People will flock there out of curiosity." He threw his hands up in disgust and walked away.

Her body quivered with fury. The disheveled bed and her bra and panties strewn between the sheets from their sexual escapades only fueled her wrath. How dare he use her body to pleasure himself and then discard her? If he wanted their arrangement over, she would to be happy to oblige. Although, he might not be fond of the way she terminated relationships.

She methodically put on the few clothes she arrived with, while a plan formed in her head. Pulling the belt of her coat tight around her waist, she stopped in front of a mirror and rehearsed sorrowful expressions. With her most remorseful pout plastered on her face, she picked up the rest of his clothes from the floor and went to find him.

He was drinking a glass of water in the small kitchen. "I'm sorry," she said, a demure pout on her face. "You're right. What I did was stupid." She handed him his shirt. "From now on, I won't do anything without asking you first." She approached him and began to fasten the buttons of his shirt. He let her. "I'd like to make it up to you."

"What do you have in mind?"

"I think we need a little time apart. You stay here, go for a walk, and clear your head. I'll go to town and get food. We'll have an early dinner and talk this whole thing out."

"I am tired," he admitted, his demeanor more agreeable than before. "The flight got in early this morning."

"You rest. I'll take care of everything."

"Don't be long. Everyone thinks I'm arriving home this evening."

"Sure."

Outside she punched her bank account number into her phone. He had made the deposit on time. Sadly, this would be his last payment. She would use it wisely. Thanks to him, she hadn't touched her nest egg. She had enough money and plenty of aliases to use until she dealt with Armend one final time and disappeared for good.

CHAPTER 38

In revenge, and in love, woman is more barbaric than man is.
– Fredrich Nietzsche, 1844 – 1900, German philosopher

Adelina remained hidden in the tree as Gina whizzed past in a yellow blur that was her car. She peered through her lens at the cabin in hopes of seeing Hayward. A wave of relief hit her when he stepped onto the front porch and headed into the woods. Unable to follow Gina and, stuck in her perch, she decided to make the best of it. By the time the pastor came back from his walk, she had snapped some beautiful scenic pictures.

He went inside. When he didn't come back out, she took a quick look. He was sprawled out on the bed in what she hoped was nothing more serious than a nap.

Deciding it was safe to come down, she inched her way gradually to the ground. She didn't need Aaron's help to get down or even up there in the first place. Men liked to feel needed, especially by women. On the selfish side, it was nice to have his hand in hers and his arms around her waist.

On the trek back to the small parking lot, her Jeep rumbled down the driveway. She was glad he was back and hoped he had the heat on. Instead of warming up as the day wore on, it had gotten considerably colder. The wind chill went right through her and her jacket had stopped being warm an hour ago.

She opened the door and a waft of hot air hit her. She jumped in and blew warm breath on her cold hands. Aaron looked better. The color had come back to his face. "How are you feeling?"

"Okay, I guess," he shrugged. "You're cold. I'm sorry if I was gone too long." He hesitated before he asked his next question. "Anything else happen here?"

"Gina left, but your friend stayed. Drive up to the main lot. They can't see us in here with the tinted windows. Maybe she'll come back or he'll leave."

Aaron slowly pulled into a spot and parked. "Let's sit in the back and watch from the rear window. I brought you something." He climbed in the back and extended his open hand to her. Not one to miss an opportunity to touch the kindest man she had come across in a long time, she slipped her palm in his.

Adelina sat with her legs crossed underneath her. He shook open an old blanket crumbled in a pile on the side of the trunk. Bits of dried leaves, particles of dirt, and the faint smell of mothballs filled the small area they squeezed into. He draped the blanket around her shoulders. She wouldn't have minded if he kept his arm around her, but instead he took out something from a large paper bag.

"Here's some hot cinnamon spiced tea and New England clam chowder." He handed her two Styrofoam containers.

"Thanks. I'm starving." Touched by his thoughtfulness, she uncovered the tea and took a sip.

"Why is he still here?" He crushed a cracker in his hand and sprinkled it on her chowder.

"I'm assuming she's coming back. Where's your food?"

"I ate at the deli."

She stirred the steaming soup. Between the wonderful aroma and her growling stomach, she couldn't wait until it cooled. "If you take Gina out of the equation, what's the problem? Is he married?" She took a small spoonful, then another bigger one.

"No, widowed."

"Was he a good husband?"

"Yes, very devoted." Aaron handed her a napkin. "You have a little something right here." He pointed to the side of her mouth. "His wife died a horrible death from cancer. He never left her side."

"Yum, this is so good," she said and wiped her mouth. "You don't think it's unreasonable to put a person up on a pedestal all alone and never expect him to falter or fall off when the storm of life rages at them?"

"He's a man of God. He shouldn't falter."

"He's a human being. Her death may have devastated him. He may be lonely and sad. Gina's a manipulator. He may not know anything about her."

"It's too much of a coincidence. He did nothing to stop the few members who were harassing Sofia. In fact, he encouraged it. Now he's sleeping with a woman who is hell bent on destroying Sofia and Armend and anyone else in her way. The writing is on the wall. You're being naïve."

"You're being judgmental," she countered.

"Why are you on his side?"

"I'm not. I think you need to hear him out."

"What if I'm right?"

"Then he needs to be held accountable."

"Are you always so reasonable? Do you never get angry at anyone?"

"Of course I do." Scraping the bottom of the container and licking her spoon clean, she dropped her empty container back in the paper bag.

"Who?"

"You."

"Me?"

"I think we'd be good together. We have a lot in common. We both love the water, sailing, and photography, but you can't see past the scarlet 'W' on my forehead. You know, I don't spend my days hunched over a boiling cauldron casting magic spells. I live a normal life just like you."

"I don't want to talk about this." He tried to inch away from her, but there was nowhere to go.

"I know you like me. Your aura brightens when I'm around. When I get close to you like this." She pressed herself against him and put her arms around his neck. "Your aura pulsates. Small bright lights flash around your whole being."

I–I think we better go," he stuttered.

Startled by the blast of a car horn, they both jumped. Adelina sat up and saw Gina's yellow bug waiting for a family to cross in front of her.

"We're not going anywhere. She's back."

಄಄಄

Gina never understood the concept of giving pedestrians the right of way. How was it more efficient to stop a moving car than to have the people on foot wait a minute until the car passed? It was maddening.

When the man, woman and their little brats were finally gone, she found a spot near the cabin. The closer the better, she had a large box to carry. Damn that bitch Sofia for screwing with her magic. She'd pay dearly for it. If it wasn't for her, with a quick spell and a swipe of her wand, the good pastor could choke on a chicken bone. Nothing suspect there. It happens all the time.

Instead, she paid Mr. Bakos another visit. It was in her best interest to forgive him the honey fiasco. Bakos' Hungarian Bakery was a thriving business in Yonkers, New York. What only a few knew was that Mr. Bakos and his wife were gypsies. In a back room behind the bakery, was a delightful selection of prepared foods and baked goods guaranteed to free you of even the most arduous dilemma.

The weapon of poison was one of her favorites. It was devious and cunning. Its victims never expect it. At the end, when they struggled to understand what was happening, a sense of blissful satisfaction overwhelmed her.

She lifted the box by the two handles on the sides and went to see her unsuspecting lover for the last time.

಄಄಄

Hayward lit the candles on the table. Even though he was angry with her, she returned in a delightful mood with a wonderful dinner. He would miss her, especially in his bed, but she was becoming too dangerous. As exciting as she was, if any-one found out about the two of them, it would be social, politi-cal, and religious suicide for him. No, it was time to move on. He would let her down easy. He was an expert at saying the right thing at the right time.

"Thank you, my dear, for dinner." He pulled a chair out for her. "I see you went home and changed your clothes."

"I thought it best if we talked without any distractions." She sat down.

Her being half-naked was definitely a distraction, albeit a pleasurable one. "Is this quail?"

"Yes, along with a sweet potato and steamed vegetable. I know you're a man of certain tastes. I found a lovely restaurant where they cook gourmet dinners to go. All I had to do was heat it up."

"Where's yours?" He unfolded his napkin and smoothed it on his lap.

"I have to watch what I eat. A grilled chicken salad is fine with me. Eat up."

He cut into his food. The bird was juicy, tender and, cooked to perfection. "I'm sorry I was cross with you earlier.

"No apology necessary. You're right. I think it's time we went our separate ways."

"You do?" The meat melted in his mouth. "Excuse me, but this is delicious."

"I'm glad you like it." She took a bite of salad. "We have *very* different views on things."

It was a shame all women weren't like her. Attractive, sexy, uninhibited in bed, and when it was time for them to go, they accepted it and went on their way. Yes, he would definite-ly miss her. Maybe he could coerce into a farewell roll in the proverbial hay.

"I have enjoyed your company, immensely. I'm glad we were able to share this dinner and end on a friendly note." He wiped his mouth and threw his napkin down on his plate. "That was the most succulent quail I've ever eaten."

"Did you know that quails love hemlock? They're im-mune to its poison, but most farmers don't let them near it."

"If they're immune, why?"

"It's simple, because the people who ingest them, will die a painful death of hemlock poisoning." Her mouth curled in a venomous smile.

"Why are you telling *me* this?" The dead chill of fear pricked at the back of his neck.

"No reason." She threw a necklace on the table in front of him.

"What's this?"

"My pentagram. It's been in my family for years. So has this." She reached down to her side. When she straightened up, she aimed her wand at his head.

"You–you're...a..."

"The word is witch. Yes, I'm one of those pesky conjurers you and your book don't like much. What is the exact quote?" She stood and danced around the table behind him, jabbing the point of her wand into his throat. "Oh yes, 'thou shalt not suffer a witch to live.' Well not only have you let me live, you have done very unsavory things with me." The most grotesque laugh he ever heard left her lips. Her hands landed on his shoulders. She whispered in his ear. "You're surely bound for hell, but don't worry, you won't be alone. Aaron will be right there with you."

He pushed himself away from the table and attempted to stand. His legs gave out and he fell back into the chair.

"Oh you poor dear," she said mockingly. "The first symptoms are muscle weakness. I think you should relax."

A combination of fear, fury, and humiliation clamored in his chest. "Leave Aaron alone. Don't go near him!" he yelled.

"I haven't done a thing to him. His loyalties lie with Sofia, her lover, and her sister, Adelina.

"I don't believe you."

"It doesn't matter what you believe. You'll be dead before you have time to worry about it."

This couldn't be happening to him. He was the pastor of one of the largest evangelical churches in the metro area and a pillar of the community. A devil-loving whore didn't dare walk in and poison him. "Why? I don't understand. I paid you more than you wanted."

"I'm doing what you wanted and ending the relationship."

His throat felt like sand paper. "Water," he gasped. "Please."

"Sorry. No can do."

"You won't get away with this." His voice was hoarse. "Mark my words."

"Don't be so sure." She collected her coat and purse and moved her chair next to him. "Your phone is dead. I checked. I have your charger. No one knows you're here. By the time they do find you, I'll have disappeared." She placed her wand across his thighs.

"What are you doing?" Panic rang in his own voice. He attempted to shove her satanic tool away, but the minute he moved his arm, he winced in pain.

"*Paralizzare*. Just taking an extra precaution to make sure you don't move. Although, muscle pain is setting in, that's symptom number two." She bent over and kissed the top of his head. "I'll be on my way." Her hand reached for his crotch and gave him a brutal squeeze. Her eyes flickered with exhilaration when he grimaced, yet he refused to give her the satisfaction of screaming in pain. "You weren't half bad, but I've had better," she said and walked out the door.

He sat alone, paralyzed by fear, magic, and poison. Tears streamed down his face. He closed his eyes and prayed that God would forgive him.

ฺ/ฺฺ/ฺ

Between her close proximity and ability to perceive his feelings, Aaron knew he was an open book. There was no use denying it. What he was going to do about it eluded him.

Without warning, she scrambled to her knees, cupped her eyes with her fingers, and stared out the tinted window. "Oh no!"

"What's going on?"

"Gina's leaving. Alone. You better get in there and check on Hayward. Her aura is boiling over with negative energy."

His whole body sank down against the spare tire leaning against the seat. He wasn't ready to confront his long time pastor, but he couldn't ignore him if he was hurt. "Come with me."

"I'm sure I am the last person he wants in there."

"He doesn't know who you are." Gina's car sped past kicking up small pieces of gravel in her wake. "Please."

"You go first. I'll be there in a minute."

He waited until the Volkswagen was out of sight before he climbed into the front seat and out the door. He ran toward the cabin and flew up the porch stairs two at a time. He didn't bother to knock and shoved open the front door.

"Hello," he yelled. "Hayward, are you here?"

"Aaron? Is that you?" A weak voice called to him. "Thank God. My prayers have been answered."

He followed the soft words to the side of the table and found him collapsed on the floor. "Hayward, what happened? Let me help you."

"I can't stand. My legs won't hold me up."

He scooped his arms underneath the pastor's armpits and propped him up against the couch for support. "Did you fall?"

"Aaron," he gasped. "It was horrible. She's a witch and she's trying to kill me. Sofia Palmalosi sent her out of revenge for our protests."

His words stung Aaron worse than a hundred jellyfish could have. Shocked the first words he spoke were vicious lies, Aaron backed away from the old man on the floor.

"Don't worry about that now," Adelina said standing in the open doorway. "He's sick. His aura is dim and murky. He needs help."

"Who are you?"

"She's a good friend of mine." Aaron answered not allowing Hayward the opportunity to harass her. "Why aren't you feeling well?"

"Poison."

It didn't come as that big a surprise. He remembered Sofia telling him about the jar of honey. "With what?"

"Hemlock," he wheezed. "By the quail on the table."

Adelina knelt down next to the man. "She told you?"

"Bragged."

"You're going to need your stomach pumped. You ate within the half hour, right?"

He nodded.

"Then we have time. Aaron, call nine-one-one and tell them to hurry, that a man has ingested hemlock. He's probably thirsty. I'll get him some water."

When Aaron pushed the "end call" button and returned inside, Adelina was on the floor next to Hayward, holding a cup to his lips. Where she dug up the resolve to be nice to him, Aaron would never know.

"The hospital isn't far. They should be here in ten minutes. I'm sorry this happened to you and I'm going to do everything I can to make sure you come through this," Aaron said. "But I need to know why that woman was here tonight."

"She called and told me she needed to speak with a pastor about a problem she was having." He gulped down the last bit of water. "She gave this address to me."

"You never met her before this afternoon? Not this morning or any other time?"

"No," he said.

"Enough lies!" Aaron pounded his fist on the table and the plates jumped. "I'm trying to give you the benefit of the doubt."

"I'm not lying. She put an evil spell on my legs to paralyze me."

"No she didn't. She's playing with your head. Her magic isn't working right now." He knelt down and got in the pastor's face. "You know how I know? Because I was with Sofia the night she took Gina's magic away."

Hayward's face twisted in horror. "She was right. You are with *them* now. They have bewitched you."

"No one's done anything to me except you. I know you slept with her. I saw you two this morning. You seemed very well acquainted with each other. I don't think it was your first time." What he was about to do disgusted him, but he did it, anyway. Maybe the way to deal with a liar was to play their game. "I have pictures."

"Aaron!" Adelina said calmly, but he could hear disappointment in her tone. "Don't do this. His heart is weak from the hemlock. This isn't the time."

Unable to look at her, he continued his conversation. "Hayward, tell me the truth. Two strangers don't have dinner by candlelight."

Defeat blanketed Hayward's face. His body slouched to one side. He was a broken man, desperate to hide his secrets, but he had no one to blame but himself.

Aaron listened as he divulged the nature of the business and personal arrangement with Gina. He spoke slowly, huffing and puffing between sentences. He swore he didn't know she was a witch until this evening.

"She gave me the–tainted meal," he panted. "After I found out she hurt the horse—rider and put families in danger—I wanted it to end. That wasn't the deal."

"You would go to these lengths because you lost a bid to buy some property?" Aaron found his motivations incomprehensible.

Beep. Beep. The siren's piercing short signals marked ambulance's arrival. Red and blue lights flashed in the window.

"I'll go." Adelina ran out to direct them to the right cottage.

"Aaron, you—don't understand," he pleaded. "I had plans. A mega church—a television contract."

"You're right. I don't understand. You're nothing more than a greedy bastard."

"Excuse us, sir." Four EMTs rushed in with a gurney. Two immediately began working on Hayward while the other two hoisted him on the stretcher and rushed him out. They no sooner went out the door than the police came in.

Aaron sighed. He and Adelina had a long night ahead of them. One he wasn't looking forward to.

The automatic hospital doors swished open. Aaron stepped outside and zipped up his jacket against the November night air. Hayward was stable and would make a full recovery—physically. Personally was another matter. He'd begged Aaron to keep his indiscretion to himself until he figured out the best way to approach his congregation. Aaron had agreed, for now.

He had no idea what Hayward had told the police. His instincts told him the pastor wouldn't mention the fact that Gina was a witch. It would be devastating enough when the story came out. The addition of witchcraft was a detail best left unspoken.

For close to an hour, just like the other night, he and Adelina spun the truth of what happened into what he trusted was a believable story to the police. Time would tell. He hadn't seen her since she dropped him off at the hospital and wondered how she was. The day had proven to be one of unwanted revelations and she was with him through it all. Hayward had let him down and he had let Adelina down by not admitting his feelings for her. Loneliness smothered him. She was gone and he missed her.

A woman's voice over the loud speaker announcing it was nine o'clock and visiting hours were over startled him from his thoughts. He would have to call a cab to get home.

"Need a ride?"

The streetlight flickered. A gentle glow fell on her like a spotlight. In four large strides, he was upon her, his body against hers. He combed his fingers through her silky curls, tilted her head toward him, and lightly placed his lips on hers. A hint of spice from the tea she had drunk earlier lingered on her lips, enticing him. His mouth came down hard on hers and he kissed her with a passion he had never felt for a woman before.

Adelina slipped her hands in his back pockets and wrapped her right leg around his left calf, securing him tight to her, returning his kiss with a sensual fervor. Her body molded into his, she was his perfect fit. If his pounding heart was any indication, his aura was on fire.

He forced himself to pull away slightly and rested his forehead on hers. She started to speak, but he placed his fingertips on her lips. "It wasn't long ago, I gave someone my heart. She bounced it around like a basketball and gave it back to me, beaten and broken." He put his arms around her waist wanting her even closer to him than was possible.

"I'm sorry you were hurt so badly."

"But you're different from Elizabeth. You are beautiful on the inside as well as the outside." He longed to kiss her again, but if he did, he wouldn't finish what he needed to say. "You're whole and happy. You see life as an unknown journey waiting for exploration. I was glad you were with me today."

"There wasn't any place else I wanted to be," she told him.

"I thought I loved Elizabeth, but now that I've met you, I know it wasn't love. As for Hayward, I don't know how to deal with that." He released her. His arms hanging at his side, he gazed at the ground. "My feelings for you are real. I'm hoping you'll give me a little time to sort some things out."

She cupped his face in her hands. "To be kissed again the way you just kissed me is worth the wait."

His face flushed with warmth. He wasn't used to such compliments from women. Right now, he was the luckiest man in the world. "The dream I was having the other morning was about you."

She flashed him her kind smile. "I know."

"I'm not going to be able to hide anything from you, am I?"

"Probably not." She wrapped her arms around his neck. "Can I have one more of those knee-weakening kisses? Then I'll take you home."

CHAPTER 39

There's just something about letting
a girl have her way with you.
– A.C. Van Cherub

S ofia desperately searched the throng of people gathered in the foyer of the gallery. There was no sign of Armend. According to her parents, he hadn't been in his apartment since Halloween morning after he left her house. Their parting words, said in anger, still rang in her ears. It wasn't her best moment. She wasn't used to a man having this sort of hold on her. She loved his body, soul, and whole being, more than any person should love another. The last four days had been the worst of her life. After combing through the two other rooms open to guests this evening, and having her hopes dashed, she decided to go.

She left through the back door of the gallery into a light rain. Opening her umbrella, she ran to the limo waiting where her father said it would be. She let out a sigh of relief, glad to be away from the suffocating crowd inside.

The driver, it wasn't Patrick, opened the door for her. "Hello," she said and sat on the edge of the seat facing outward. As she closed her umbrella, a hand wrapped around her mouth and pulled her into the darkness of the backseat. The door slammed shut and locked.

မာမာ

"Do you know how hard it's been for me to stay away from you these last four days?" Armend removed his hand, slipped off her damp coat, and threw it on the floor. He ran his fingers down her back. Her body heaved up and down. She was still upset with him, but he knew how to relax her.

"That's the price you pay." She rested her back against him while he kissed her neck. "This charade was your idea."

"It had to be done." He slid his arms around her waist and with skill and determination undid her blouse, one button at a time. "She had to believe I left you."

"It was too damn real. I almost believed it." She shimmied out of her shirt and let it drop on the seat. "I thought you weren't coming tonight."

"*Dashuria ime*, I wouldn't let you go to Sicily without me. It's too far. I couldn't keep my eye on you." He unhooked her bra. It dropped to her lap. "I've been close by."

"Do you have the passports?"

"Yes." He'd missed her more than he thought possible and massaged her shoulders. Her soft, scented skin made him delirious with desire. His heart had certainly grown fonder without her by his side. "For the next week you'll be the lovely Gabriella."

"Gabriella?" With a seductive turn, she faced him. "I like it. It's sexy."

Underneath the twinkling ceiling lights of the limo, her smooth, olive skin glowed. She was a beautiful goddess, her bare breasts mesmerizing. "Very sexy."

She rested her hands on his shoulders. "What will I be calling you?"

"Arsenio."

"Seriously?" She cupped her mouth with her hand to contain her amusement. "I can't call you that with a straight face."

"Why? It means virile."

"Mmm. I'll be the judge of that." She reached behind and unzipped her skirt. "Enough talking. The ride to the airport isn't that long. Take off your clothes."

He loved her feisty side. Actually, he loved *all* of her sides. He yanked his shirt over his head and was undressed in a record breaking instant. She looked breathtaking in nothing but red lace panties. "Come here, baby. I've missed you." He took her hand and drew her into his arms. She felt better than ever.

She gave his beard her usual love tug and reprimanded him. "I won't agree to this again. It's too much to be apart like this."

He tried to answer, to tell her he could never be away from her again, but she caught him with her mouth. He was defenseless and could easily drown in her sea of kisses. She pushed him back on the long seat that lined the side of the limo pinning his arms to the side of his head. Her mouth and tongue were relentless in their pleasure. He closed his eyes and gladly let her do whatever she wanted to him.

CHAPTER 40

Two thousand years ago we lived in a world of Gods and
Goddesses. Today, we live in a world solely of God.
Women in most cultures have been stripped of
their spiritual power. – *Dan Brown, American author*

Sofia shone her flashlight on the entrance to Diana's temple. The soft glow illuminated the two large Hellenistic pillars on each side of the doorway and the long stone across them. Even in ruins, it was the most beautiful building she had ever seen. Her throat clogged.

She was about to meet the Goddess Diana.

The midnight sky was moonless and clear. Only the stars blinked at her. Below, the Mediterranean Sea sang a soft lullaby.

Armend's hand held hers tightly. "This is the only way?"

"Yes," she said.

"I'd feel better if I could come with you."

"Sorry, this is a girl's-only event."

"I'll be right here when you're done."

"I don't know how long it will take. I may not be out until morning."

"I'll be here."

His closeness filled her with strength. Through the ages, the women of her family had stood here, anxious and fearful, but accepting that it was a rite of passage and their duty. She was blessed to have someone who loved her by her side.

"Do you have everything you need?"

"Yes, I checked my bag twice."

He wrapped his arms around her waist and she let his love pour into her.

"I have to go. It must begin at midnight." She tried to pull away, but he squeezed her closer. "Armend, it's okay. I'll be fine."

He released her. "Be careful. I love you."

She tugged his beard. "I love you, too."

പ്ര

Dust, mingled with the smell of decaying blooms, filled the temple's small interior. The ancient altar lay shattered, the benches had crumbled to debris, and weeds sprouted from cracks in the wall. Sofia skirted around the remnants of recent offerings—bouquets, honey jars and fruit—that littered the ground.

Sofia lit white candles and placed them on stones scattered around the dirt floor of the temple. She cleared away the debris and used her athame to draw a circle, large enough for her to lie down in. Positioning herself in the middle, she crossed her legs in a meditative position, and pointed the athame north.

Sofia readied her tools and presented her offerings: dried figs, a cedar stick and covered chalice full of tea.

Balancing the spirit bowl on her lap, she poured a few drops of Liquore Strega inside and struck a match. When the blue flame burned strong and bright, she sat it in front of her.

The last item in her bag was the Diana Dagger. She peeled away the protective silk casing. Its blade gleamed with beauty and danger. She placed it horizontally between her knees.

It was time.

From the terra cotta chalice, she sipped the tea made of Kava root, an herb that would mildly alter her state of consciousness. She dipped the cedar stick into the flickering flame of the spirit bowl and inhaled it's wooden, earthy scent to calm and balance her energy.

Sofia recited the incantation of the Strega given to her ancestor, Messalina, and passed down to the chosen one of her family for millennium.

"From beneath me arises the power of Mother Earth

"From above shines the power of the sun and moon.

"My right side holds the wisdom to control

"and use the power of magic.

"My left side possess the ability of the divine,

"to bless and heal. I am forever grateful

"for these gifts bestowed to me.

A silver mist crept in from the crevices in the stone and wrapped around her. A delightful drowsiness spread through her being and filled her mind with peace and light.

"Sofia," a delicate female voice called to her.

Her throat constricted in awe. "Yes."

"It is I, Messalina, your predecessor and spiritual guide to Diana."

Sofia bowed her head in honor. When she rose up and opened her eyes, there was no one there. "Why can't I see you?"

"It's not necessary. Just know I'm here and always with you, my family. You must state your intention."

"Yes." Sofia placed her left over her heart then her right hand over her left. "I've come to humbly request the gift of knowledge and power of the Diana Dagger."

"Do you come pure of heart?"

"Yes."

"This infinite responsibility stays with you until another is chosen and your soul passes to the next realm."

"I understand."

"Very well. May the blessing of Diana's wisdom be with you as you journey in this life and future lives."

"Blessed Be."

"Farewell, Sofia."

Sofia floated back until her body laid flat on the cool dirt. Her hands remained on her heart and she rested her head to the left. A soft blue hue branched out from a passageway on the far wall.

"Come, Sofia," called a melodious voice.

She tried to follow the hypnotic words, but she couldn't move.

"Not the physical you, but your true self. Release the ties to your body."

Sofia removed her hands from her chest and laid them palms up to receive energy from the being communicating with her. She was buoyant, weightless, and began to glide instead of walk. Behind her, her body remained on the ground, her hands at her heart. As she hovered toward the blue glow, reality, time, and space swirled around her like an old black and white movie. She passed through the opening, the air sultry and warm, into a distant place in time.

The temple was restored to its original majesty. The Goddess Diana, surrounded in a brilliant aura, sat with her bow in one hand and an arrow in the other. An exquisite beauty, her long, dark hair flowed to her lap, her dark eyes kind and welcoming. A red tunic criss-crossed her chest, exposing her breasts, on her feet were gold sandals. Various woodland creatures lay curled at her feet. Sofia felt no fear. Diana enveloped herself in an inviting, serene atmosphere.

"Welcome, Sofia."

Sofia bowed her head. "Thank you."

"You've finally come. You've waited longer than anyone in your family."

"I wasn't sure of my path in this life."

"But now you are?"

"Yes."

"I see you've met the one you're fated to be with?"

"Yes."

"He waits outside. His heart is heavy with worry."

"He loves me."

"So you are pleased with the choice the universe has made for you?"

"Yes. I love him very much."

"Come, closer."

Sofia attempted to take a step, but she didn't need her legs where she was. She floated next to Diana.

"Sit."

Sofia hesitated and then folded her legs, half expecting to crash to the ground. As she lowered herself without falling, she relaxed. One of the young fawns poked her with its cold, damp nose. Sofia massaged the young deer's soft fur and the fawn laid her head on her lap.

Diana put her weapons down and took her hands. Sofia savored the Goddess's energy, potent, resilient, fierce, and brilliant all at once. Self-doubt at her own strength to take on this legacy tugged at her.

"When the fates bring two people together such as you and Armend, there's a reason. A destiny you share. You have a daunting task ahead of you. Tough battles will be fought and hard decisions must be made. You know what the outcome will be or you wouldn't be here."

"I'm afraid."

"Of course you are. You are wise to be. Only fools boast they have no fear."

"I don't know if I can do what needs to be done."

"You are troubled by the darker side of the dagger. I understand, but sometimes a spark of anger at an injustice will lead you to victory over that injustice. Let the dagger guide you. It will be difficult. The right thing isn't always easy."

"I may not be worthy."

"Your family has served me well for millenniums. I chose you because you are kind, but strong and just. You will succeed. Have faith in yourself."

"I will honor you, the dagger, and my family to the best of my ability."

"Our time has ended. Go back to your physical being and rest. Then go to your love, your fate, and fulfill your destiny. I have sanctioned the power of the Dagger to you."

"I'm humbled and thankful."

Diana released her. "Good luck, my dear Sofia."

❧❧❧

Sofia awoke with a start. Flat on her back, she stared straight through a gaping hole in the temple's ceiling into darkness. The candles lit earlier still burned, giving off enough light to get her used to her surroundings. A damp chill embraced her. Sleeping on the cold ground of the temple floor had left her back and neck stiff. She groaned as she sat up.

Rubbing her neck with one hand, she groped through her bag for food with her other. She scooped the crushed almond biscotti from the bottom and stuffed them in her mouth. She filled the empty chalice with Liquore Strega and took a sip. The warmth of the liquor battled her chill.

The Dagger remained on her lap. She no longer saw it as a threat, but a gift, with a clear understanding of what had to be done. To be chosen to employ the power of the Dagger was an honor. Her first duty would be to save Armend's life.

She let the last gulp of Liquore Strega slide down her throat. Collecting the rest of her tools, she swaddled the Dagger in its protective blanket and placed it safely in her bag. The last thing to do was leave an offering. From one of the candles, she lit a small amount of juniper incense and left it burning near the remains of Diana's altar. She lingered, the restorative aroma of the incense recharging her.

She gathered her things and went to find Armend.

He was pacing back and forth. A blanket dangled around his shoulders.

"Good morning," she said. There was a hint of light over the horizon. "I'm just in time to see the sunrise."

Relief swept across his face. "I was getting worried." He swept her up in his arms. "Did you see her? How did it go?"

"It was wonderful!" She jumped in his arms, but winced at her sore back. "Sleeping alone in a cold stone temple isn't that comfortable."

He slipped the blanket off and covered her. "I didn't sleep much, either. I watched the temple all night. It was dark and quiet. From the outside it didn't look like anything happened."

"It was more of a telepathic communication," she said. "I'll tell you all about it later.

"With goddess summoning behind us, can we be normal tourists, now?" he asked with a smile and pulled her close. "Maybe have some fun?"

"Sure." She snuggled into him. "Let's watch the sunrise, go back, and get some rest, then we'll have a picnic. I know the perfect spot."

CHAPTER 41

Next to a battle lost, the greatest misery is a battle won.
— *Duke of Wellington, 1769 – 1852,*
British statesman and solider

Armend marveled at what little remained of Castle Ce-
falu on the north coast of Sicily. The ruins were a
skeleton of the original grandeur of the fortress, dimin-
ished to weather-beaten, crumbling walls. He was sure the
concierge said it was a vibrant tourist attraction, but his Italian
wasn't as good as Sofia's. He must have misunderstood. There
wasn't a soul in sight. It was deserted and eerily quiet.

While he waited for Sofia to finish souvenir shopping, he
spread a blanket on a patch of spongy grass, sat down, and un-
packed his bag: mafalda bread, white canestrato cheese, a
knife, and two glasses. In between the sound of waves crashing
against the rocks below, he heard footsteps on the gravel behind him. Smiling, he uncorked the Il Cantante and poured a
glass for his love.

Wine in hand, Armend turned to find, not Sofia, but Gina
looming over him. Fully clad in black, she stood with her legs
splayed and arms crossed.

"My dear Armend, you've disappointed me once again.
First, you stand me up, not showing at our scheduled meeting.
Now I find out it's because you whisked Sofia off for a roman-
tic holiday, after you promised me you had left her."

"How did you find us?"

"George has been around my family for twenty years.
I've had plenty of time to learn his secrets."

Stunned at her arrival, he was taken by surprise as she
lunged at him.

He hurled the wine glass at her face, snatched up the knife, and bolted to his feet. His body instinctively moved into a defensive boxing stance. He positioned his right hand in front, showing his weapon.

She shook her head and laughed at him. "I won't let you escape your fate." Her armed crept behind her back and flaunted a long, sharp dagger. "One way or another."

A sour taste rose in the back of his throat as he watched the razor-edged blade glimmer in the sunlight. He looked at his small cheese knife and muttered, "Oh, shit."

He crouched, placing his right foot slightly in front of the other, tucked his chin low and put his left fist forward. "Traded in your wand for a dagger?"

"Magic is so impersonal and distant, don't you think? This will be a much more intimate experience for us." She rubbed the knife against her and down between her legs. "I love the feel of the blade as it sinks deep in the flesh." She licked her lips and let out a soft groan.

Was she becoming aroused? He was in more serious trouble than he originally thought. "Maybe, but I think it's because Sofia screwed up your magic and you have no other choice."

"Shut up," she growled. In one clean sweep, her blade ripped through his sleeve, into his skin, and down his arm, knocking the knife from his grip. It fell to the ground. Even his mother, who would kick his ass from here to Albania for hitting a woman, would forgive him as he surprised her with an upper cut. She lurched backwards. He reached down for his modest weapon. She yanked his feet out from underneath him and he hit the earth hard.

Dagger in hand, she was poised to attack. With all his strength, he thrust his feet into her abdomen. She gasped. While she caught her breath, he stood and darted for cover behind a half-standing wall.

He peered around the structure as she marched toward him, the blade firmly clenched in her hand.

"Do you think I have nothing better to do today?" she shouted.

"Do you think this is how I want to spend *my* day?" he yelled back at her. "You're a fucking nut job!"

Armend noticed blood dripping from his arm onto the rubble and dirt. He picked up the cold, blood-splattered stones, took a deep breath, and waited. When she was about sixty feet away, the distance between the pitcher's mound and home plate, he threw his first pitch since high school. He missed. With a determined focus, he tried again and hit his mark. He pelted her with a shower of rocks until she ducked behind a pillar.

With her briefly distracted, Armend leapt up the remnants of an ancient stairway. He clumsily scaled the wall until he made it to the top. Unsteady, he stood on the twelve-inch rim of wall, holding a basketball size rock in his hands. As she got closer, he dropped the rock. His timing off, it grazed the side of her head, and deflected off her shoulder. It left her disoriented with blood dripping down the side of her head. She glanced up at him. "You bastard."

He lost his footing and began to slip. Luckily, he managed to grab onto a protruding ledge and hold on, dangling two stories from the ground. He didn't see her below him and thrashed his feet against the wall trying to find some traction.

Without warning, a searing pain ran through his knuckles as her dagger sliced across all ten of his fingers. She knelt above him, a sadistic smile spread across her face.

Barely hanging on, he watched the blood trickle down his hands. Her body straightened and she placed her foot a top of his head. With a cruel downward thrust on his skull, his body crashed on to the rough terrain below.

She jumped on top of him, clinging to his body tightly. Unable to shake her off, he bore his foot against a rock and pushed, catapulting them down the slope. Entwined, they tumbled toward the sea, bumping and scraping, faster and faster.

His head reeling with dizziness, he was able to make out a small plateau—and the impending cliff below. Pain ripped at Armend as his legs crashed into a boulder. He cursed and released her.

She sat on his chest, her legs straddled to each side, pinning his arms down as she groped for the dagger at her waist. "Your whore is next."

Armend wrestled his arms free from underneath her, put his hands around her throat, and squeezed. "Stay away from Sofia—or I'll kill you."

Gina sunk the dagger deep into his outer thigh. He writhed in pain.

"Really?" She wrenched the blade from his leg.

He screamed.

As she raised the bloodied blade into the air in a last act of vengeance, fury pulsed through his veins. He grabbed her by the waist and flung her over the edge. He heard the brutal splash as her body hit the water.

"Really," he panted.

Armend rolled his throbbing body to one side, trying to slow his labored breath. His clothes soggy with sweat and blood, he closed his eyes and shivered as a cool sea breeze blew over him. He looked down at the merciless sea, silent about the woman it had just swallowed, and tried to accept the fact he had killed another human being.

❧❧❧

Gina tightened her abs, clenched her fists stiff to her side and compressed her rigid body as straight as a pencil, the way Alejandro, her cliff jumping Mexican lover, had taught her years ago. The frothy waves of the moving sea would help break her feet-first fall, if the water was deep enough and no jagged rocks waited for her underneath. She closed her eyes, inhaled a lung full of air, and braced for the impact.

❧❧❧

Sofia stared down at the tousled blanket. A wine bottle had tipped on its side, its contents spilled out like an open umbrella. Shattered glass, dotted with a drop or two of blood lay sprawled at her feet. She drove the foreboding thoughts from her head. He probably cut himself and went to look for help.

Then she saw the larger trail of blood.

"Armend!" She screamed. "Armend, where are you?"

She followed the spots of blood to a wall of the castle, up the stairs, and onto a ledge. The elevated height provided her with the view she needed. She twisted around slowly, keeping her balance, in an almost full circle.

There was Armend, more than halfway down the incline, slumped over, close to the edge of a flat, grassy terrain. She got off the ledge and ran down the stairs as fast as she could. She stopped at the edge of the cliff. Did he fall? Was he pushed?

Sofia struggled to keep a steady foot down the slope of the small mountain. She slipped and faltered as the small rocks underneath her gave way. Finally, with no other option, she slid down the rest of way on her butt.

He lay curled on his side, still as death. She knelt next to him. Blood and dirt caked his hair, face, arms, and hands. "Armend, it's me, Sofia. Can you hear me?" She cradled his head in her arms.

His eyes fluttered open with a vacant stare. "I killed her. Now I'm dead, too."

"Killed who? Baby, tell me what happened." She stroked the strands of his tangled hair.

"She came after me with a knife. After she killed me, she was going after you. I couldn't let that happen, so I threw her off the cliff." His voice was a cold, steady monotone. "Only she knows where her half of the music is and she's at the bottom of the sea."

"Gina? Gina was here?"

He looked past her and didn't answer.

"Did she do this to you?" She peeled back the torn part of his jean at his outer thigh. The wound was deep and bleeding. Thankfully, there was no major artery near where Gina had gouged him. Sofia cupped his face in her hands. "Armend! Look at me. I'll be right back. I think you're in shock. I need to get the blanket from the top." He gave her a faint nod and she gently rested his head back on the ground.

She made the strenuous journey back up, gathered their things, and stumbled back down to him. She elevated his legs and checked his wound. The bleeding had subsided so she swaddled the blanket firm around him for warmth.

She curled next to his body. The air hung heavy with dangerous energy.

She rose to her feet and teetered on the edge of the small cliff. It was about a hundred feet drop and survivable under the right conditions. Even in November, the temperature was in the high sixties and the water remained tepid from the hot, humid summers.

Her Nanta Bag dangled at her side, its strap diagonal across her chest. She dug deep to the bottom and removed her Diana Dagger. With her arms extended, she pointed the golden blade over the water and concentrated.

"On behalf of Diana, Queen of the witches
"I request of the Dagger knowledge steeped in riches
"I ask for wisdom deep
"And a learning I may keep.
"I call for what I need to know
"Allow me to envision the sea below."

Her mind dove deep into a watery abyss. The Mediterranean was dark and empty, possessing nothing it shouldn't.

Sofia turned back to Armend. He was pale and his lips had a faint blue color to them. He needed help, but was in no condition to make it up back up the mountain. They were marooned on a small plateau.

"Armend, can you hear me?" She was back on her knees, her hands on his chest. "You didn't kill her. She's alive."

"Are—are you sure?" His voice cracked.

"Yes. I can feel her, but right now, we have to worry about you. You've lost a lot of blood." She slipped her hand underneath the blanket and clutched his. She closed her eyes and fought back the burning tears, but the battle against her emotions was one she never won. In order to help him, she had to hurt him. "I can heal your stab wound with the Dagger." She wiped away her tears with the back of her palm. "But it's going to burn and hurt like hell. I'm sorry." Would she have the courage to hold the Dagger at his leg when he started to cringe in pain? She wasn't sure.

"I trust you," he said.

She pulled the Nanta bag over her head and handed it to him. "The strap is leather. Bite it, tug at it, or squeeze it, whatever you have to do to get through the pain. It should only last a couple of minutes."

Armend coiled the strap around both hands and yanked it taut. Sofia gently rolled him to his side and removed the blanket. With the blade of the Dagger, she sliced his jeans away from his thigh. Dried blood encrusted the two-inch long gash.

"Ready?"

"Yes."

Between her tears and sniffles, she dipped the point of the blade directly in the center of the hole. "Male energy will work better in this situation. I'm going to call on Aesculapius, the God of health and medicine."

"God Aesculapius
"Hear my humble plea
"Of which I hope you will agree.
"To heal my love of the harm done to him
"Inside to his spirit, outside to his limb.
"Use my gift of the golden blade
"From which your power and wisdom may be conveyed.
"May he become stable and whole
"His body, mind and soul.
"Blessed Be."

The Dagger began to shake uncontrollably. She gripped the hilt with both hands and all her might. Armend's back arched and his body flailed around like a fish out of water.

Sofia whimpered. "I'm so sorry."

His face contorted into a fit of anguish. He pulled and squeezed the strap until his knuckles were white and his fingers red. The noises he made were of a man being tortured. She was no longer crying, but sobbing. She was his tormentor and it was killing her. Resisting the desperate urge to release him from his pain, she held the Dagger with determination. It would be over soon.

The vibration of the knife slowed down. Armend released his grip on the strip of leather. His body gave in to one final jerk and he collapsed.

Guilt and loathing ate at Sofia's gut for what she had done to him. Her only reprieve was that a long brown scab replaced the wound that oozed blood not five minutes ago. She threw the Dagger on the ground as if it were repulsive in her grip, scrambled for her bag, pulled out the one bottle of water, and held the opening to his mouth. He no sooner guzzled it down and started to choke.

"Easy," she sniffed. He took smaller swigs and pushed himself up to a seated position. His pallor was normal and his steel blue eyes clear. "Are you okay? I'm so sorry." The familiar warmth streamed down her cheeks. Damn her unmanageable tears.

"Oh, baby, come here," he said. She buried her head in his chest. His strong scent of sweat, blood, and dirt penetrated through her stuffed nose. Not usually an attractive combination, but to her, he never smelled better. "Please, don't cry. It's over now. I don't understand it, but I feel good, just tired."

She squeezed a handful of his shirt between her fingers. "I hate that I had to do it. I hate that she's here and attacked you. We aren't going to lose. I'll make sure of it."

"I have no doubt that, with you on my side, Gina will go down," he said and stroked her back.

She sat up and reached to her side dragging the bag toward her. "You need food."

"You need a tissue," he said with a small smile. "Why are you so sure she's alive?"

She broke off a piece of the crusty bread. Grabbing the Dagger once more, she sliced a hunk of cheese and handed them to him. "I could feel her wretched energy swirling around, but the Dagger confirmed it." She wiped her eyes and blew her nose into an old napkin that had been living in her jacket pocket for quite some time.

"We have to watch our backs," Armend said between bites. "Every time we encounter Gina, it ends in a draw. Each time she gets more pissed off and dangerous. She made it clear today she wants us both dead."

"She found us here. I won't underestimate her again." Sofia wanted nothing more than to get off this island. She had traveled here many times and loved it, but Gina scarred the beautiful birthplace of her ancestors and their religion. When this was over, she and Armend would return and get her kindred spirit back with her homeland. "Let's go home."

CHAPTER 42

Sometimes to get what you want the most, you have to do what you want the least." – *Jodi Picoult, American author*

Lautner zigzagged himself between Armend's legs and purred. "Sorry, buddy." Armend scooped him up in his arms. "I don't feel like playing today." He and Sofia had been home two weeks and hadn't seen or heard from Gina. It was unsettling, just the way she wanted.

Time was running out. It was the end of November, less than a month until the winter solstice. His biggest fear was that Gina wouldn't contact them and would let the curse run its course. After he was gone, she would then come after Sofia. All she wanted in the end was for him to have a good long nap in the dirt. Sofia wasn't concerned about the lack of communication with the Demoness of Death and tensed up every time Armend tried to talk to her. Ever since her time in the temple with Diana, Sofia's emotions were reserved when it came to the curse.

They strolled to Sofia's small office when Lautner let out a deep growl. "What is it, buddy?" The door was ajar. The cat's black fur bristled. He leapt out of Armend's arms and with two taps from his paws, the door yawned open.

"Happy to see me?" Gina sat legs crossed on the edge of Sofia's desk. Actually, in a sick, twisted way, he was glad she was there. It was better than having her lurk around in the shadows, not knowing what she was planning. "Guess what?" she said with a giggle. "My magic is back." She flashed her wand at a vase of flowers on the desk and it burst. Glass shattered sending water and petals flying through the air. "Get that mangy fur ball out of here or he'll be the next thing to explode."

Armend put his familiar to safety in another room and returned. "Next time I'll throw you off a higher cliff."

"Now, that's not very nice." She hopped off the desk and slinked toward him. "I'm sure you regretted it the moment you realized what you had done. After all, I'm the only one who knows where the music is."

"I guarantee we don't need you alive to find the music."

"That's right. You're in love with the wonderful and powerful Sofia." She spun around in a circle with her arms open. She paused in front of him, took his hand, and stroked the inside of her bare thigh with it. "You loved me once, remember?"

He ripped his hand away. "No. I was drunk and you were *not* memorable."

She was persistent and pressed her body against his. "I really did love you," she purred and played with the buttons on his shirt. He shoved her away.

"But you want him dead?" Sofia leaned in the doorway. "And don't touch my things."

"Don't confuse love and family honor," she said matter-of-factly. "I would have made him happy until his last breath."

"Are you really here for small talk?" asked Sofia.

"No. You're aware of what needs to happen to settle this." The two women stood shoulder to shoulder, facing each other. He didn't like Gina so close to Sofia and took a few protective steps toward them. "I'm not going to hurt her, Armend," Gina said her eyes locked on Sofia. "Not today anyway."

"Yes," Sofia said. "We need to agree on the terms."

"It's obvious what you two want." Gina rolled her eyes. "To live happily ever after. But what do I want?" Gina strode back to the desk and jumped back up on her perch. "I thought long and hard in that vermin infested cave I spent twenty-four hours in after my...swim in the sea. Luckily, three fishermen came to my rescue." She smirked at Armend. "Most men like me."

"Until they get to know you," he snapped. "Are they dead now?"

She shrugged. "Witnesses are never a good thing."

Her casual disregard for human life was repulsive. The thought that he had struggled with temporary grief when he thought he had killed her disgusted him.

"What do you want?" Sofia appeared to be losing her patience.

"*L'ordine di Incantesimo.*" Her voice dripped with smugness.

Sofia lurched back in surprise as if someone had pinched her.

"What's that?" Armend asked.

"The Strega's ancient Book of Incantations. The spells, passed orally from generation to generation, were written in the Strega's Book of Incantations when women learned to read and write. These spells have been in my family for thousands of years."

"No!" Armend pulled Sofia aside. "I won't let you give away a family heirloom. It's dangerous. You don't want her to have your powerful secrets."

"Trust me," she said. "It's a small price to pay to save your life."

He whipped around to Gina. "Your fight is with my family. We must have something you want?"

She tapped her finger on her chin and pretended to think about it. "No, I want the book."

"I agree," Sofia said. "I have a few conditions of my own. First, no one else is hurt. Stay away from Adelina and Aaron and leave Pastor Marshall in peace to recuperate."

"I heard the good pastor survived. His life is ruined. That's a worse sentence than death for him. I can live with that, but I'm *not* happy with the other two for saving him." She let out a defeated sigh. "Fine, I'll leave them alone. No police?"

"No police. And George," Sofia added.

"I'm not going to hurt George. I made a deathbed promise to my aunt that I wouldn't."

"Why should we believe you'll keep a promise?" Armend asked, exasperated.

"I loved my aunt," Gina replied, genuinely offended. "I will keep my promise to her."

He held his head and walked to the side of the room muttering, "You have the most warped way of loving people I've ever seen."

What Sofia said next drew his attention back.

"Weapons."

"One wand each," Gina said.

"I hear you like to fight with a dagger. I, too, own a dagger—"

"Weapons?" Armend interrupted. "What are you talking about?"

"Living on the wild side are we, Sofia?" Gina laughed. "One dagger each then. Agreed."

"Sofia, what's going on?" Armend demanded.

"Armend, dear," Gina said as soothingly as a snake. "Did you honestly think I was just going to hand over the music in exchange for a silly old book?"

He steadied himself against the wall. Was he really that stupid? No. Somewhere deep inside he knew, but wouldn't let himself believe it. He had convinced himself the power of the Dagger would allow her to see where the music was, not fight with it. Each time the deadly truth gnawed at him, he banished it from his mind. Now it was the elephant in the room and he had to deal with it.

Gina rambled on. "Sofia realizes your life is worth fighting for. You're the prize. If I win, you both die. If she wins, you and I both live. She's too nice to kill me."

"This has nothing to do with Sofia. I'll fight for my own life."

"Been there, done that," she sneered. "I want a new opponent to sink my dagger into."

Armend lunged at her. His hands gripped her throat and squeezed. "Sofia," Gina gurgled, "Get him off me—or the deal is off."

"Let go of her!" Sofia yelled and ran to her desk.

"No. She wants to fight. She can fight me now," he growled. Out of the corner of his eye, he saw Sofia open her desk drawer.

"Armend, stop it!" She aimed her wand at him and he flew across the room. He hit the wall and landed on the floor. Sofia wouldn't take her side over him. Gina must be controlling her somehow. He had to get her wand away from her and sprung to his feet. "Stay," she shouted and with a wave of her wand, he stood paralyzed.

"Sofia, let me go right now!" he demanded. She paid him no attention and continued her conversation. Fury pulsed through him. Rage at his helplessness, at Gina, and most of all, at Sofia's betrayal.

"When?"

Gina fumbled through her purse and went to the calendar on her phone. She clicked her tongue and tapped at the phone turning pages. "It looks like I'm not free for a battle until—December twenty-first at three o'clock." She looked at Armend. "Does that work for you?"

He wanted to pounce on Gina, but his so-called *love* had him still as a statue.

Sofia didn't flinch. "It will take place here."

"Home field advantage. Not fair. I want a neutral place."

"Then change the date."

"Sofia, you are full of clever surprises today," Gina said. "I'll be here. Three o'clock on the dot on the winter solstice."

"Swear on the witches' oath?"

"Yes." The two women put the points of their wands together and recited the pledge in unison.

Armend simmered as she agreed to a death vow. "Sofia, don't do this. I'll never forgive you."

She ignored him.

"On my honor I do swear
"This oath to keep and fight fair
"If one of us breaches this pledge
"We agree to succumb to the other blade's edge."

A single white spark spit up from between their wands. "So mote it be."

"It seems his Albanian temper has flared up." Gina stuffed the wand back in her purse. "That's always been his downfall. He can't control it and acts in anger. It's a shame, really."

"He's not your concern. I'll deal with him later," Sofia said. "Now get out."

"You'll *deal* with me?" he said vehemently. "We'll see about that."

"Well, my work here is done. You two love birds have a good evening." Gina slammed the door behind her.

She tapped Armend's shoulder with her wand. "You can move now."

He chose to stay put. "So this is how it's going to be?" he asked. "What happened to 'we're an unbeatable team,' and 'two people who love each other stick together,' huh? You made me promise not to fight her myself and here you are doing that exact thing."

"It was the only way."

"There's always another way. We could have talked about it and had a plan. You blindsided me." She said nothing and her hazel eyes were dull with guilt. "You knew all along, didn't you?"

"When the two parties can't agree on the terms to break a curse, it is always settled with combat between a witch from each side. It's the Strega way. At first, I thought we could do it together, but then things got out of hand. Only I can draw on the power of the Dagger. I'm doing this because I love you."

"This isn't about love. I'll always love you. This is about loyalty, trust, and not turning your back on someone who thought we were a unified front."

"Don't let her do this to us. She's trying to divide and conquer."

"This is one time you can't blame Gina. You've done this to us, no one else." With a bruised ego and his heart in shambles, he turned and walked away.

CHAPTER 43

Men are taught to apologize for their weaknesses,
women for their strengths. – *Lois Wyse,*
1926 – 2007, American author and columnist

Sofia crawled on top of the purple duvet in her old bedroom of her parent's brownstone.

No matter how old you were, there were days you needed to come home, and have your family take care of you. Today was one of those days. She lay on her stomach, face buried in her pillow, when there was a knock at her door.

"Come in."

"Hey, Sis." Adelina always cheered her up.

"Hi, I'm glad you're here." Sofia sat up, expecting Adelina's bright smile and vivacious personality. Instead, her hair was back in a taupt ponytail, her eyes had no sparkle, and her lips pressed tight together. "Man trouble?" she asked. "Join the club." She motioned her sister onto the bed and tossed her a bright orange pillow. They sat cross-legged, their knees touching, hugging their cushions.

"Aaron said he needed time to sort things out. I thought he meant a few days, not a few weeks."

"You haven't heard from him at all?"

"Once. He called and said the first of the year he was leaving for a month of solo sailing on a friend's boat in Florida and that he would call again. He hasn't."

"I'm sorry, sweetie." She leaned in and hugged her sister.

"I scared him away. He's traditional and I was overbearing. He didn't want to follow Gina, but I insisted. He didn't want to climb the damn tree, but I made him. Then there's the whole magic thing. He probably thinks I'm going to control him all the time." She fell backwards on the bed and held the pillow over her head. "I should go to finishing school and learn how to be a proper docile lady."

"Don't you dare!" Sofia ripped the orange blob from her sister's face. "Never apologize for who you are. Your lively personality is what attracted him to you. Anyway, you're too old to learn new tricks." She poked her sister's side. "Unless they're magical."

Adelina stretched out, her elbow bent, head resting on her hand. "Why do I like him so much?"

"Maybe you're supposed to." Sofia lowered her gaze. "Maybe he's your forever one."

"Forever one?"

"Never mind."

"Hey, I'm sorry," she said. "I've been blabbering about my problems. How are things between you and Armend?"

"Strained, to say the least. He left and stayed at his apartment for two nights, but then came back. I guess that means he still loves me."

"Of course, he loves you."

"He's going to visit his parents for a few days…before …you know. He doesn't think I'm going to win, that I'm going to let him down. That's what hurts the most."

"I don't believe that. I'm afraid for you, fighting her. He's probably petrified of what might happen. When men get scared they get super macho." She banged her fists on her chest like a gorilla. "And super stupid."

Sofia laughed at her sister's antics. "He's not ready to fight her alone. It has to be this way."

"When's Mom coming home?" Adelina whined like a little girl.

"Soon, I hope. I want some of her wildly wicked witch tea she used to make us as kids."

"Even on our worst days it always made us giggle."

There was a brief bang on the door before it burst open and Ersilia flew in. "Here's my two beautiful girls." She popped a kiss on each of their heads. "It's time to stop the moaning and groaning. There are two eligible men down stairs to see you." She clapped her hands together. "Adelina, loosen your hair and put on your most wonderful attribute—your smile."

"Who is it?"

"A nice young man named Aaron."

"Mom, what did you do?"

"Nothing."

Adelina cocked her eyebrow at her mother.

"Oh, all right. It was a small matchmaking spell I use all the time. I didn't play with his free will. He was going to call you anyway. Now he realizes things are done better in person. I have no idea what he's going to say to you." She turned to walk out. "Oh, he's a bit confused on how he got here. I'm sure you can smooth that over."

"Why is Armend here?"

"Because I called him. I have something very important to tell the two of you. Now, let's go!"

ɛ⁄ɔɛ⁄ɔ

Adelina peeked into her parent's family room. Aaron was examining the bronze statue of two lovers. He was looking very hot in his black jeans and white crew neck sweater. Her gut tightened like a high school girl and her tongue stuck to the roof her mouth. It was strange how he affected her. She looked down at the box between her sweaty palms. This was the only opportunity to give him his gift. It was now or never.

"Hi, Aaron."

He twisted with a start, his hand falling onto the full backside of the naked bronze woman. "Oh." He quickly removed his hand and stuttered, "Nice, um, statue."

"I'm surprised to see you here."

"It was the weirdest thing. I was going to call you when I remembered your parents owned a gallery. When I got there, you weren't around, so I started walking and bumped into Armend. Imagine that. In a city of millions of people, I see Armend on a street corner. He said he was on his way here so I came with him."

"Life is strange sometimes."

"I met your mother. Is she a…"

"Witch? Yes, the whole family is."

"Oh, okay, just making sure."

He was anxious. She may as well put him out of his misery, and hers. Good-byes are less painful when they're over quick, like ripping off a Band-Aid. "I bought you a winter solstice…err…Christmas present." She awkwardly handed him a box wrapped in Rudolph-the red-nosed-reindeer paper. She found the paper in her parent's storage closet, left over from last year's annual Christmas party the gallery sponsored for Toys for Tots. "For your trip."

"Thanks," he said and sat it on a small table. "That's what I wanted to talk to you about."

"I thought so and I understand. We're too different. I'm sorry to be so forward all the time, but meek and passive isn't in my nature. And I know the hocus pocus thing doesn't help. I hope—"

"Adelina."

"—we can still be friends. If you're ever at Sofia's visiting and I'm in town, maybe we could have lunch." She was talking with her hands, typical Sicilian her friends would joke, and forced them to her sides. "I did want to thank you again for taking the hit for me in the woods—"

"Adelina."

"—that night. I appreciate it."

"Are you done?"

"Since I won't be seeing you again, I'd like you to open your present before you leave." She grabbed the box from the table.

"I want you to come with me," he said.

She paused with her back to him. "What?"

"I want you to come to Florida and sail with me." He was behind her, his hands on her shoulders. "What I needed to work out were other things in my life, not my feelings for you."

She faced him and his arms slipped around her waist as if it were the most natural place for them. "Hayward?"

"Yes, and other things," he said. "Being with me will be difficult on you. I had to decide if it was fair to ask you to put up with my family and friends. I haven't told them yet I'm in love with a witch, but I'm certain of their reaction."

Her stomach knotted again, but this time for a different reason. "Did you say *in love*?" Her heart galloped faster than a racehorse.

"I don't know what else to call it. I've never felt like this before."

"I don't want to cause problems with your family." Most men complained of the trouble being with her would cause them. He was the first to worry about her.

"If there are problems they are the cause, not you. I'm happy when I'm with you and that's the end of it."

Her legs were Jell-O and her body putty in his arms, as his lips pressed down on hers and their tongues swirled around, exploring each other. If his kisses did this to her, what would the rest of him do to her. "I can't wait to get you alone on that boat," she whispered.

"My sweet Adelina, I can't wait for you to get me alone on that boat either," he said with a sly grin. "Until then, though, since I'm an old-fashioned kind of guy and we've never been on a real date, tonight I'm taking you to dinner."

She wanted to jump up and down squealing like a teen-age girl, but kept her composure. His conventional ways melted her heart. "I'd like that. Please open your present."

"I'm sorry. I don't have anything for you."

"That's not the reason to give a gift. Anyway, you gave me the best present by asking me to sail with you."

He sat on the edge of the couch, ripped through the Christmas paper, and let it drop to the floor. "Nice paper." He laughed. When he lifted the top of the box his eyes lit up brighter than Rudolph's nose laying at his feet. "Adelina, where did you get this? I've heard about it, but never seen one. Supposedly, there are only a hundred copies. It's beautiful." Aaron lifted the antique, leather-bound copy of *The Mariner's Bible* and held up it for a closer look.

"There are a small number of shops in New York where you can buy just about anything. You just have to know where to look."

"I love it. Thank you. It means a lot to me." His hand combed through her hair and played with her curls. "I won't need the prayer for calm seas, I'll have you with me," he teased.

"Sofia has permission to ask Mother Nature to change her plans, not me. Although, I may have a trick or two up my sleeve."

"I'm sure you do." He looked down at her bare feet, ripped sweats, and T-shirt. "You might want to change for dinner."

"Sure." She leaned in and kissed him tenderly. "Just so you know. I love you, too."

CHAPTER 44

Some people believe holding on are signs of great strength. However, there are times when it takes much more strength to know when to let go and then do it. – Ann Landers, 1918 – 2002, American advice columnist

Armend hiked up the stairs and down the hall to the room where Ersilia and Silvio kept their altar and Strega tools hidden from the outside world. When he entered, the spirit bowl, already lit, burned in the center of the table. The lights were dim and puffs of smoke rose from the jasmine incense burning in the corner. The altar remained safe in the armoire. He noticed two unfamiliar objects: hand mirrors, both beautifully carved with a pentagram, criss-crossed on top of each other on the table. There were three chairs. He picked the one farthest from the door and waited.

The women's muffled voices approached. They stepped inside and Ersilia closed the door behind them. "Armend, thank you for coming today."

"I couldn't refuse you, Ersilia," he said, but never took his eyes from Sofia. He didn't see her this morning when he got up. Like most mornings, he rose early and left before they had a chance to talk. There was a word for that. He didn't want to admit it, but he was a coward.

Her demeanor was one of sadness, but she still kissed his lips, as she did each night before bed. They exchanged "I love you's," but that was the extent of their intimacy. The division between them was taking its toll. The two nights he spent away from her, he was miserable, and he came back. He would sell his soul right now to take back his words and actions. Hopefully today with Ersilia's help, they could start to heal. Unless she was angry and disappointed with him as well and had called him to this ritual to banish him from Sofia for good.

"Let's begin," Ersilia announced and sat in the middle chair between them. Not a good sign, he decided. "Sofia, did you agree to take on this conflict with Gina alone?"

"Yes and I'm not sorry. I love him and want him alive at all costs. If it causes us to go our separate ways, then so be it." She shifted in her chair. "You know it's the way things are done among us."

"What I know is irrelevant," Ersilia replied. "It's what Armend knew that's important. You were aware of what would happen the moment the Dagger became sanctioned to you. You had no right to keep it from him."

Sofia tried to defend herself, but her mother lifted her hand to her face and stopped her. "No more from you right now." Ersilia faced Armend and folded her hands in front on her on the table. "What do you have to say for yourself? You're not innocent here."

"No," he admitted. He was never one to pour out his heart and instead kept everything buried deep inside. "I've never been so terrified in my life." His head hung so low he whispered his words to the tabletop rather than the two women. "I couldn't live with myself if something happened to Sofia. How could I? She's willing to fight for me and I can't stop her. I'm helpless and it's the worst feeling I have ever had. I am supposed to protect her. How can I justify living if the worst happens to her?"

"Did you tell her what was bothering you or did you get angry and storm out?"

"I'm not proud of it," he mumbled. "But you already know the answer to that."

"Now it's my turn." Ersilia grabbed Armend's right hand and Sofia's left. "Do not interrupt me. I'll let you know when I'm through." She squeezed their hands. "When Sofia was one year old, a wise woman, a seer, paid us a visit as is customary for the family of the chosen Strega. She confirmed Sofia was the choice of Diana, peered deep within the blue flame of the Spirit Bowl, and told of her future.

"She told me that the one my little girl was fated to be with had already been born and was four years old. Even at such a young age, he carried a terrible burden, one he wasn't even aware of yet. The remarkable thing was that he would come to Silvio and me first. We would take him under our wings until the time was right, for Sofia was his destiny and he was hers.

"The most important thing she told us was that the two were a rare and special coupling. One not usually performed by our Goddess Diana, but one that was necessary for each other's continued existence."

Ersilia let go of their hands and spoke to Armend. "Do you know how we knew Sofia was the one to take power of the Dagger?"

"No."

"Show him, dear." Sofia shoved the chair away from the table and bent over, with her head between her legs. With two hands, she pushed the long locks of hair off her neck and parted it with her fingers. Armend stood and moved behind her. At the base of her hairline was a small birthmark, a pink crescent shape facing left like a backwards C.

Armend thought he knew every inch of her wonderful body, but this was the first time he'd seen this particular mark. He stroked it gently with his pointer finger. The softness of her skin reminded him of how badly he ached for her touch. "Oh, baby—"

"Sit down, Armend," Ersilia commanded. "They'll be plenty of time for that later. I'm not done yet."

He took his seat like a reprimanded student. Sofia sat up and her hair fell around her shoulders. He longed to wind his fingers around her two long red streaks, his favorite thing to do at night before they went to sleep.

"Silvio and I assumed you were the one we were foretold about. You appeared at our door, a lost young man, needing a chance. We felt an immediate connection with you and treated you like a son. Now that our daughter's life is at stake, we must make sure."

Ersilia rose from her chair and handed him one of the mirrors. She put her hands on his shoulders and leaned him forward toward the table.

"Mom, what are you doing?" asked Sofia.

"Come here, dear, and hold the other mirror."

With his forehead touching the table, Ersilia fumbled through his hair, pulling, stretching, and parting it. "There! Look." He couldn't see her expression, but Sofia gasped.

"Armend, sit up and position the mirror so you can see the reflection," Ersilia said. "What do you see?"

To situate the mirror in the right place took hand and eye coordination that didn't come easy to him. Sofia wrapped her hand around his and helped him to right spot. It was small, but when he realized what it was, his mouth literally fell open. There in front of him was the same pink birthmark Sofia had. His pointed in the other direction, forming the letter C. If the two marks came together a complete circle would form. A symbol he knew represented they would never be broken. He couldn't believe it. He never knew he had such a spot on him. "I...don't know...what to say? What does it mean?"

Ersilia lowered the mirror and sat down between them. "It means your destines are joined forever. You must let Sofia do this for you. There may come a time when she'll need you to do the same for her."

"Are you saying you know she'll be safe after this fight?"

"No," Ersilia said. "What will happen is a mystery to us all. But she's my daughter and I have every confidence in her."

"I don't understand how you're okay with this."

"A Strega must fulfill her lot in life. It's why they were chosen." Ersilia cupped the side of his face. "Have faith in Sofia and the love between you and everything will be as it should." Ersilia planted a quick kiss on his cheek, then her daughter's. She quietly left the room, the door creaking shut behind her.

"I told you the first night we were together I wouldn't let you die." Sofia broke the thick silence in the room. "I always keep my word."

"I know," he whispered. He wanted to scoop her in his arms, but she might not have appreciated it after his recent behavior.

"I can do it without you and I will, but it would mean so much more if you were with me in my heart and in spirit."

"Oh, Sofia." He took the chance, grabbed her hips, and pulled her into him. "Of course, I'm with you. I always have been and have the mark to prove it. I'm just scared to death for you and that's not going to change." She softened into him and he lifted her chin to face him. "What would I do if something happened to you?"

"Let go of your fear. Fear is negative energy. All I need is your love."

He clutched her tighter and nestled his face in her neck. "It's impossible to let someone you love walk into a dangerous situation alone."

"I won't be alone. You're forgetting how powerful my Dagger is."

"Baby, it's so hard."

"It's a done deal. There is no going back. You have to try to accept it."

Her words stung, but she was right. She had sworn on the oath. If she was going to put her life on the line for him, he should be there for her. "I know," he said giving in. "I'll do whatever you want me to. I'm sorry I've been such a jerk."

Sofia's eyes flickered with love and she gave him an affectionate tug on his beard. At that moment, she had forgiven him. All they needed was each other. It was simple, but he had made it so hard, a mistake he wouldn't make again.

She pressed her body against his, wrapping her arms around his neck. Her lips met his in hungry kiss. He lifted her up, carried her to the leather chaise, and laid her down on her back. He curled in close to her on the narrow piece of furniture. "I've missed you so much," he whispered. "I'll call my parents and tell them I'm not coming."

"No. It's important you see them."

"Come with me."

"I have to prepare. South Carolina isn't that far. You'll be back in two days, plenty of time before the solstice. Tell them I'm looking forward to meeting them."

"Armend," Silvio banged on the door. "The cab is here to take you to the airport."

He rested his forehead on hers and closed his eyes. "I can't leave you now."

"You said you would do whatever I wanted. This is what I want."

"Armend!" Silvio yelled louder this time.

Against his better judgment, he peeled himself away from her. "I'm coming, Silvio." He leaned over and kissed her. "I love you."

He opened the door and walked out, feeling like he was abandoning her once again.

CHAPTER 45

There would be no passion in this world if we
never had to fight for what we love. – *Susie Switzer*

Aaron watched from the doorway as everyone gathered
at a round table. In the middle, the brightest intense
blue flames rose from inside a small, black decorative
bowl. Silvio and Ersilia had been nothing but welcoming to
him. He just met Patrick, the chauffer and his wife, Maureen,
the bookkeeper for the gallery. Adelina was next to Armend,
her hand stroking his back in a soothing motion. He was pale.
His eyes dim, heavy with worry and fear. He was trembling.
Sofia was noticeably missing. Everyone was on edge.

"Today is the winter solstice," Ersilia spoke with a shaky
voice. "This *Treguenda, La Festa dell' Inverno,* is the ob-
servance of the rebirth of the Sun God. Each day becomes
longer and it's a celebration of light, hope and promise.

"Today we will perform our ritual differently than usual.
We'll send our loving energy of light, hope, and promise to
our dear Sofia, who has a hard battle ahead of her today."

Armend let out a rasping groan, Adelina's comfort no use
to him.

Ersilia turned her attention to him. "Aaron, you may join
us if you like. Patrick and Maureen are a different denomina-
tion from you. They follow the Roman Catholic tradition, but
they share your religion."

"You can sit next to me. I'll help you," Maureen said
kindly. "We've been in this circle before and were anxious the
first time, like you. I haven't found that God has minded. We
love Sofia like a daughter."

"There is no judgment here," Ersilia continued. "I know you are very fond of Sofia and want to help her. If you would like to send her your good intentions in your own way, please do so."

Aaron didn't have to think twice, and sat next between Maureen and Silvio. "Thank you. I'd like to do my part to help Sofia." The day Adelina gave him the Mariner's Bible, she had told him she didn't expect him to change. He loved and accepted her exactly as she was and would never ask her to change. This was going to be part of his life now, he may as well get used to it.

"Welcome to our table, Aaron," Silvio patted him on the back. Adelina fixated on him, with an expression filled with such love it almost made his heart stop.

"I'm glad to be here."

"Let us all hold hands and at three o'clock, we will begin," Ersilia said. Maureen grabbed his hand and gave him a reassuring smile. Ersilia took Armend's hand. "Armend, this is very important. During the ritual, you must keep your eye on the flame. When it goes out, Sofia will need you. You must go to her immediately."

ಲನಿ

Sofia stood alone in the clearing. The afternoon daylight was fading. Snow fell from the dark clouds above, covering the hard, frozen ground. The cawing of a solitary crow pierced the otherwise silent surroundings.

She looked up at the black bird, wings spread, soaring through the air. "Solstice, I'm glad you're here. Please stay close."

In a few moments, it would begin. She must defeat Gina and save Armend's life. Sofia's Latin magic was superior to Gina's Italian's verbiage magic. However, stronger magic drained the Strega of energy more quickly. She had a powerful dagger, but Gina was merciless. Would her hand be forced to the darker side of her primordial magic and its consequences?

Dressed in the latest lightweight ski attire, Gina emerged from the woods, her footsteps crunching in the snow. Her stride was strong and confident.

When their eyes locked, her stare was cold and calculating. Sofia's heart pounded, but she didn't flinch.

Gina reached into her pocket and removed an old, ragged piece of paper. She haphazardly tossed the two-hundred fifty year old sheet music into the inches of snow covering the top of a rock. Sofia stared at the beautiful notes drawn on the paper for the first time and choked back her tears. That one, small piece of paper, when joined with Armend's half, would save him.

"I would appreciate you taking better care of that," she said icily. "It will belong to me, shortly." Before the snow and wind could steal the document away from her, Sofia brushed the fluffy snow off the rock and placed her family's ancient book of enchantment, *L'ordine di Incantesimo*, wrapped in plastic, on top it to protect it.

Gina laughed. "I'm not concerned with what you want. The music belongs to my family and always will." She twirled the book around. "Where's the other half?"

"In an envelope safely tucked away in the book. Do you want me to show you?"

"No need. You're too honest to cheat and the oath won't let you." She inspected her rival from head to toe and clicked her tongue as if Sofia were an easy mark. "Can we get this started? I'm not expecting this to take too long."

"Neither am I." Sofia twisted her arm behind her back. Hidden safely in the waist of her ski pants was her Diana Dagger. Eager to strike first, she curled her fingers around the cool, opulent handle of the knife. It might be a long fight. It was necessary to save her strength. The best strategy was to tire her opponent out.

In one quick move, she took aim. Fire streamed from the tip of the Dagger. Gina dropped, rolled, and dodged the attack. She grabbed a knife from her boot. Retaliation. Sofia reacted. Knees bent. Core tightened. A long, vivid streak of sparks flew from Gina's weapon. Sofia leapt to the right. It just missed her.

Gina jumped to her feet and came after her. Sofia spun in a circle with her blade pointed down. *"Magicis circulus!"* The new fallen snow swirled and spiraled into a glistening radiant ring. She turned faster. The twister of snow churned harder and quicker. Soon a whirlwind raged before her. Sofia took a deep breath, placed the Dagger at her chest, and blew with all her might. The cyclone of snow raced at and caught the other witch in its wrath.

Engulfed, the woman fell to the ground fighting against the blowing storm as if a figurine caught in a snow globe. Sofia bolted to the rock and peered over her shoulder. Gina was winning her fight against the waning storm.

Sofia heard the Italian word *fuoco*. Her hand inches from the paper, she screamed and crumpled into the white blanket beneath her. The flame from Gina's dagger sliced through her calves like a razor. Blood oozed down her leg and seeped into the snow.

Sofia raised her weapon. *"Invado Incurro."*

Gina did her best to block the firestorm of sparks but she was weakening. Electric currents sizzled in the air as magic jolted against magic. Sofia gripped her Dagger with two hands and slashed an invisible Roman numeral X in the air. *"Numero Magus Orbis."* Ten small fiery orbs of magic flew from the blade's tip. Gina let out an agonizing scream as the small, inferno-laced balls pelted her entire body. Smoke rose from her sleeves and pants, her arms and legs. Furious, she launched a barrage of electricity. Sofia jerked backwards in pain. Her torso zapped by a potent current.

She continued to fight, nicking Gina once more in the thigh. Her bleeding legs ached. Her shoulder burned. Her arms throbbed. The weight of exhaustion crept in.

With the last bit of strength she could muster, Sofia lunged, her arms straight ahead. *"Magia bianca,"* she shouted sending a white sphere of energy surging in her enemy's direction. Gina twitched and collapsed to the ground, her neck smoldering.

Sofia inhaled the cold air into her lungs, releasing a weary sigh. It wasn't over. Gina was on her belly, fatigued and barely able to drag herself through the snow. She held her Dagger a few inches off the ground, aimed directly at her. Sofia dove behind a big tree trunk, escaping the sting of Gina's firepower.

"*Per affettare*," Gina's hoarse, low-pitched voice commanded. Creaks and cracks echoed above. Sofia's eyes shot upward. The magic from Gina's dagger sliced through the huge, thick branches with the ease of a laser. Sofia darted from underneath the tree, but slid on the snow and lost her balance. One massive limb after another crashed down on her. Her knees buckled. She caved to the ground under the weight. She was trapped, her Dagger knocked from her hand.

Sofia's head twisted in an awkward position to one side, her eyes glaring through the broken tree boughs.

Gina staggered toward her, bruised, beaten, and scarcely able to catch her breath. "I win."

෬෩෬

Armend stared at the blue flame. Its blaze flashed back, mocking him. The incantations had been spoken, offerings made, and prayers said for the safe and victorious return of Sofia. Now he waited for the beacon to go dark.

He closed his eyes and wished he had something of hers he could touch. He might be able to see what was happening.

When he opened his eyes, the bowl was smoldering. He pushed away from the table so fast his chair crashed to the floor. He grabbed the small backpack off the couch and rushed out the door into the blowing snow.

෬෩෬

Gina's face coiled in contempt. "As much as I would love to sink my dagger in that good heart of yours," she panted, "I think it'll be more fun to watch you suffer. In a matter of hours you're precious Armend will die, and you can't stop it. You're a pathetic failure. You didn't break the curse and save his life. He'll die hating you."

Sofia burned with fury. She would not lose Armend at the hands of a psychopath. While Gina ranted, Sofia's fingers, hidden under the branches, clawed to find her weapon. She gritted her teeth in silent pain, as she slid her shoulder over a few inches, feeling the cold metal.

Gina limped to the rock. "Thanks for the lovely reading material," she sneered cradling Sofia's ancient book of enchantments and more important, their piece of the music.

With the icy handle of the Dagger firmly in her hand, Sofia made her decision. She inched her fingers up the blade. Biting her lip against the pain, she slashed her thumb against the sharp edge. Warm blood poured out providing an odd comfort against her frozen hand. She pressed the knife deep into her cut and recited three times, "*Asi Nise Masa. Magia nera di Diana.*" The dark side of Diana's magic pulsed through her veins. Her body began to convulse.

Gina taunted her one last time, dangling the paper that would break the curse, in her face.

In one swift movement, Sofia rolled to one side, effortlessly sending the considerable branches tumbling off. As the spectacle unfolded, her rival's eyes widened and her mouth dropped in disbelief. Sofia was on her feet and within reach of her. Gina dropped the book and document and reached for her dagger.

The power pulsating through Sofia quickened her reflexes and increased not only her strength, but her ruthlessness. She overpowered her enemy, wrapped her arms around the woman's chest, and restricted her movement.

"No, I win," she whispered plunging the Dagger into Gina's abdomen.

Gina kicked and thrashed, trying to break free.

Sofia sank the weapon deeper into the soft flesh of her belly. A small gurgle escaped Gina's lips and she went limp. Sofia released her and she slumped to the ground like a sack of garbage. Sofia hated the brutality that had overtaken her, but she'd had no choice. She knew the risks and did what she had to do.

With a callousness she didn't know she possessed, she kicked the body to its side, pried Gina's dagger from her fingers, and pocketed it.

She scanned the clearing. Blood had spilt and splattered turning the snow a dark magenta color. Small fires choked to stay alive. The sky had cleared. A crescent moon crept up behind the mountains.

The sheet music lay exposed in the snow. A portion of faded ink ran down the corner of the page. Most of the notes were intact, except for the last bar. Would the two halves of music match up if the notes at the end were missing? She didn't go through this hell and take someone's life for it not to.

Sofia steadied herself against a tree and bent down to reclaim her Book of Incantations and the sheets of music. Clutching them close to her heart, she trudged through the snow, stopping to rest every few feet. Her legs were two wet noodles, trembling, as the adrenaline and power from Diana's Dagger left her body. She hadn't gone very far when her body gave in to the exhaustion and dropped to the ground. She laid her head in the snow, the moist coolness refreshing. With her hand, she scooped up a handful of snow and put it to her parched lips.

In the distance, twigs snapped and snow crunched under heavy footsteps. Her stomach tightened. Gina was still alive and coming for her. With her free hand, she fumbled for the security of her Dagger. The footsteps quickened and before she could strike, she was in the air, courtesy of two strong arms.

She gazed up into steel blue eyes. A solitary tear rolled down the side of his cheek, red from the cold. "Hey, baby." He choked out the words and pulled her into his warmth. "Are you hurt?"

"I had to—" This would be the first time she said the words aloud. She thought she might be sick. "—to kill her."

"I'm sorry. I know how hard this is for you."

"It was the only way to stop her and get the music."

"I know, baby. Don't upset yourself." He carried her to a large hemlock tree. "Can you stand?"

She nodded. From his backpack, he took out a silver insulated blanket and spread it out. "Sit down. I have food. Don't think about her right now." He helped her down on the blanket. From a small thermos, he poured a steaming hot cup of herb tea and handed her a piece of cake. "From your mom and sister," he said with a slight smile. "I would have brought beer and pretzels."

Sofia choked out a small laugh even though the weight of what she had done hung heavy in her soul. "I'm so glad you're here." She ate in silence. There was so much to tell him, she didn't know where to begin. "There may be a problem with the music—"

A howl of agony ricocheted through the trees. It sounded human, but it was the worst sound she had ever heard a person make. Armend sprang to his feet. "What was that?"

"Help me back to where Gina is. I think they've come for her," she said with a heart full of dread. "It's not far."

They moved as silently as they could through the snow and took cover behind a boulder thirty feet away. Five people gathered around Gina's body. They had fought the same group the night before Halloween. One man kneeled beside her body. Sofia thought it was the man Gina called on to rescue her. Staying hidden, they watched as they wrapped her body in a ceremonial dressing and, like pallbearers holding a casket, carried her away.

Sofia didn't have the energy to run after them. "Jon," she yelled, remembering what Gina called him.

"Sofia, what are you doing?" Armend pulled her back toward him, but she broke free and walked toward the group.

They paused but kept their backs to her. "I'm sorry. She left me no other choice."

"I loved her," the man said.

Sofia touched his arm in a remorseful gesture. "I'm glad she'll have someone to celebrate her soul's passage."

He jerked away from her. "You have no right to feel anything," he snapped. "You've taken her away from me. Her blood is on your hands. You will never be absolved."

The group continued their trek out of the woods. She shuddered at his disturbing words, but would do it again to save Armend and break the curse.

"Wait." She placed Gina's dagger in his hand. "This belongs to you."

The small procession moved east into the dark woods.

Sofia and Armend went west, both pieces of music tucked safely in their arms.

It was over.

CHAPTER 46

Sexual love is the most stupendous fact of the universe
and the most magical mystery our poor, blind senses know.
– Amy Lowell, 1874 – 1925, American poet

They were naked in front of the fire. Armend held her tight. There was a chance he would be leaving this earth in the next few hours. He was grateful for the short time he had Sofia in his life. She made him come alive even as death closed in.

Red blankets and pillows surrounded them on the floor. Amber incense burned in the four corners of the room, filling the air with its fragrant and earthy scent. They stood inside the ritual circle Sofia had cast, outlined with clear crystals that shimmered with a prism of colors. The two sheets of music lay at the north point of the circle, the Diana Dagger on top of them. A bottle of Liquore Strega, two glasses, dried fruit, and biscotti sat on a tray near the fire. He hoped to be around to partake in the small meal afterward.

He was a condemned man, but in Sofia's arms, he wasn't afraid. They had just taken the most calming and sensual bath in preparation for something she referred to as *The Great Ritual*. He couldn't think of a better way to spend the last hours of his life than making magical love to his beautiful Sofia.

"I'm sorry the music fell victim to the snow and wouldn't join with its other half." Sofia eased herself out of his embrace. "I swore I wouldn't let you die and I won't. With the help of the Dagger, our love will break the curse. Love, and the sexual energy that emerges from it, is the most powerful and sacred tool we have. I hope you trust me."

"I trust you with my life."

"There are a few steps we must take before we begin. First, we have to forgive Gina. Forgiveness is the second most powerful tool we have."

With the tip of his finger, Armend traced the bruises and wounds on Sofia's body from her clash with Gina. He remembered the slashes on the back of her calves that he had caressed in the tub. He thought of the grief his uncle went through. "I can't."

"I have to live with what I did to her, but I forgive her. Her soul passed to the next realm. She has healed and is in her natural state now. When she returns for her next incarnation on earth, let's hope she chooses a healthy body, and not one saddled with the disease of madness." They stood inches apart. She didn't touch him. "You must think of a way to let her actions go."

He closed his eyes and thought of the past months. If it wasn't for the curse and Gina, he wouldn't have been fated to be with Sofia. Through all the horror and darkness the curse caused, she was the one good thing to come from it. "I forgive her."

The instant he spoke the Diana Dagger began to rattle. Through its vibration, the sheets of music crawled closer together. "Once again, your forgiveness has weakened the curse," she said. "We're close now."

eɔeɔ

Sofia handed him a silver goblet. "Drink this. Its tea made from the herb Damiana, a mild aphrodisiac. You may also feel a little high. You'll be happy."

"I'm already happy, here with you."

"It's part of the rite. A couple sips will do."

He took a taste and pursed his lips. "It's sweet," he said, but filled his mouth once more.

She drank the remaining tea from the cup. The clock struck eleven o'clock. They spent too long in the tub, but what a luxurious and intimate bath it was, and they hadn't even made love.

"The next step is a slow, soothing massage, but our time is short. We'll concentrate on the neck area," she said. "In this case, it's gentlemen before ladies. Lay face down." She used a blanket to cover from his cute, tight ass down. It was going to be hard enough to focus on the ritual while caressing his broad, toned back, shoulders, and strong arms. She didn't need any other distractions.

Rubbing warm musk oil between her palms, she kneaded the top of his shoulders and base of his neck in a slow, gentle movement. "This will get our energies flowing." With her thumbs, she moved his hair away from his neck and gazed down at his crescent mark. Everything they had done this evening brought them closer together. While they could touch, there was no kissing until the actual sex began. She raised her fore and middle finger to her mouth then placed them on his mark. "When our bodies and souls unite, the music, too, will come together." She helped him up. "Now it's your turn." She nestled into the warmth of blanket and the blaze beside her, resting her head on her arms.

"I don't want to cover you up. I want to take you all in." Warm oil dripped between her shoulder blades and down her spine. His strong hands were tender and loving. He instinctively knew where and how to touch her. Her body prickled with pleasure. He stretched out next to her. With one hand, he moved her long, dark hair to one side and searched her hairline for the matching spot. He circled it with his finger. "I love you and the bond we share." He laid his head on the small of her back. "I want you to know that, whatever happens-"

"What's going to happen is you're going to live a long life."

୧୬୧

Armend sat crossed legged as she asked him to. She knelt on her knees in front of him. She was radiant. A day didn't go by that he didn't want her, but tonight he didn't think he could get enough of her. Was it the effect of the tea? His body felt like it was floating on a cloud, free of limits, uninhibited.

"I have to state the purpose of our ritual and invoke the incantation," she said. "Afterwards, thing may get emotional. That's the purpose, to show our love exposed, at its most vulnerable." Her breasts heaved with her rapid breathing. She licked her full lips, opened her palms, and raised her head upward, enticing him with her lovely neck.

"I call on the Goddess Diana and the dagger to help our fight
"Pertunda, Goddess of sexual love and pleasure
"Comus, God of feast, drink and pleasures of the night.
"Unlock the secrets of your treasure.
"Our love is true and real
"Deep in our souls we feel.
"Help give us the power to reverse
"This age-old malicious curse
"Blessed Be."

He longed for her skin against his. When she spoke her last word, he held her hands to his face and kissed the inside of her palms. Sofia crawled onto his lap and stroked his hair. "Have I ever told you how much I love your eyes and what they do to me? How they peer deep inside me to a place no one else has seen before?" She kissed the top of his eyelids. "Or how much I love your body?" She ran her tongue over his lips. "Not for its physical attractiveness. When we touch, every fiber in my being lights on fire for you. When you're inside me, you pleasure not only my body, but my soul."

Her lips came down on his and he responded with a driving hunger. He pressed his hands into her back and kissed every part of her neck. She swayed with pleasure in his arms. "*Dashuria ime*, I don't know how to thank you for what you did for me today. I can only say I would gladly do the same for you. I'll love you forever."

"Show me," she purred and shifted her position.

He was as hard as granite and slid easily inside her. She sat on his crossed legs with hers wound tightly around his waist. "Baby, I wish I could put into words how incredible you feel," he muttered between clenched teeth.

Entwined, they rocked back and forth like a cradle. Her skin glistened in the glow of the fire. His hands cupped her breasts, caressing the soft mounds with purpose and affection. He teased her nipples between his thumb and forefinger until they were hard and then sucked them until she cried out in bliss.

Armend lowered her onto the pile of pillows behind her. She eased him onto his back, stroking his chest. Her hand journeyed to his thigh, followed by her warm lips. Just when he couldn't take anymore, she pulled him on top of her gripping him again in her warm, moist tightness.

He moved inside her, slowly at first, but as her body arched beneath him, pleading for more, his pace quickened. She tangled her legs with his and dug her nails into his back. In his state of euphoria, each time he thrust deeper into her, it was as if she were absorbing him into her essence. The experience blew his mind. "Baby," he gasped. "Do you feel it? I want you to feel it."

"Yes, it's wonderful," she said breathlessly. "We're almost one. Please," she panted. "Grab the Dagger."

One hand at a time, he reached above her and took hold of the handle.

"Our love will do the rest." She raised her arms over her head and gripped her hands on top of his with bruising strength. "Don't let go, not matter what!"

The metal warmed against his skin. The Dagger, with a mind of its own, began to tap the sheet music to a measured cadence. His body tightened as a brilliant light illuminated from the blade. When the knife's primal energy combined with their passion, his whole body tingled. Sofia closed her eyes. Her body pulsed under him, her breathing deepening to a low moan. Their bodies came together in a beautiful rhythmic tempo, faster and faster, like a musical crescendo.

"Baby, I love you, but I can't take much more," he pleaded.

She arched her back, her hips rising, pressing against him. "Armend," she gasped. Her body convulsed in spasms of pleasure. "Don't stop." He rode her hard one last time until together they collided into a pinnacle of love and euphoria.

At that moment, the Dagger released itself from their grip, submerging the music into a pool of magical radiance.

*c*ᴐ*c*ᴐ

Sofia raised the glass to his lips. The sight of him, warm and flushed with the glow of their passion, his chest rising up and down with the breath of life, was magnificent. A sheet of music, intact and in its entirety lay on his lap.

He took a sip. "Are you trying to get me drunk so you can have your way with me again?"

"Absolutely." It was well past midnight and the time of his birth. The curse was broken. After everything they had been through, they deserved to drink too much, eat too much, and do whatever else they wanted.

He slid his hand around her neck, his thumb stroking her face. "Baby, you did it. You saved me."

"*We* did it. Together." She lifted the antique paper and held it in the air. Its tattered edges and faded color couldn't take away from its beauty. "This is the most amazing gift we've been given. We have to take good care of it, forever."

"It's all so surreal," he said. "But I do owe my life to that one piece of paper. And you." He shifted onto his side and rolled her over, his chest pressing into her back. He draped his leg over her hip. "How do you ever thank someone for saving their life?"

He slipped his arm across her waist as his lips grazed at her shoulder, causing her body to ache in desire for him. "You're doing a great job right now," she whimpered. "Oh, I almost forgot." She wiggled around in his arms until she faced him. "Let me be the first to wish you a Happy Birthday."

He swept her off the floor and she stretched out long on top of him. Her head rested on his chest. The beat of his pounding heart filled her with joy.

"Sofia, my love, you're the best birthday present I've ever had."

EPILOGUE

Jon turned his back against the frigid January wind that whipped across the Hudson River. Bundled in a winter coat, hat, and scarf, he was unrecognizable. He was just another brave patron who took advantage of the Nature Preserve's free admission on New Year's Day. The glare of the bright sun against the fresh white snow made it almost impossible to see. With one finger, he knocked his sunglasses off the top of his head onto the bridge of his nose.

The six of them huddled together. Sofia and Armend, her sister and her new beau, and last but not least, the proud parents, Silvio and Ersilia. After wishes for a safe trip, hugs, and handshakes, they sent Adelina and Aaron off on their sailing trip.

They each had someone special. He was alone.

He had to go away for a while.

When he returned, each one of the men would lose a love.

THE END

About the Author

Debbie Christiana would sit in her room as a little girl pecking away at an old Smith-Corona typewriter, a gift from her parents. Even back then, the stories that appeared on paper were about ghosts, unexplained events, and things that went bump in the night. She combined her love of the paranormal with her fascination of unusual love stories and decided to write paranormal romance. Besides her two novels published by Black Opal Books, she's had two short stories published: "The Land of the Rising Sun" in *BITES*: *Ten Tales of Vampires* and "The Thirteen Steps" in *BELTANE*: *Ten Tales of Witchcraft*.

Debbie is a member of RWA and the International Thriller Writers, Inc. She is the secretary of her local RWA chapter of Southern Connecticut and Lower New York (CoLoNY). She lives in Connecticut with her husband and three children.